The Royal Descendant

JOHN P FORD

This book is dedicated to the memory of my dear mother Bernie.

It was shortly after her death in 2000, after a long fight against illness, that I finally started to write this story. The idea had been with me for several years, but like many authors who thought they had *'a book in them'* I had never quite managed to put that first word on paper. After completing 30,000 words, I sent a sample to several literary agents to find out if I could actually write and was not simply deluding myself with the kind words of friends and family. Although I had several encouraging replies, no one was willing to invest in the costly exercise of publishing the book. There was no self-publishing in those days.

So I foolishly stopped. Twelve years later my new wife, Jackie, discovered the manuscript and convinced me to finish. She has encouraged me and helped take the raw words and edit and hone them to what you see here. I will always be grateful for her input and sheer hard work. So to all you budding authors, pick up your pen *today* and start writing.

John P Ford

ACKNOWLEDGMENTS

I should like to thank all the staff at the National Archives in Kew for their help in pointing me in the right direction as regards the historical documents on which the early part of this book relies. My wife Jackie for the inspiration to begin writing again after twelve years, my neighbour Annie who published her own book and helped me in the process. And to my daughter Sue and her friend Natalie who edited the manuscript to produce the final version .

Bellstone village, Devon, England, February 2009

Unseen eyes watched as the Reverend Edward Pemberton closed the oak door of St. Peters parish church. A gust of icy wind caught him as he emerged from the shelter of its walls and the slightly built Vicar cursed to himself and then immediately sought forgiveness from the almighty, but it was not a night to be away from home.

The small stone church was, like many, no longer permanently open to its congregation for fear of vandalism and theft. Four hundred years before when its construction had finished, the village was a major thoroughfare for those on their journey to nearby Oakhampton market. But numerous changes to the area through the ages had reduced the importance of the road, finally turning it into a backwater thirty years previously when a by-pass was created for the A30 on its long journey from London to Lands' End, some ninety miles to the south west. It sat, untouched by time but unable to alter its march, at the bottom of a quiet country lane. The village of Bellstone was now largely populated by weekenders from London, and there were precious few God fearing folk amongst them. The old church was, for most, a place to visit only for births, deaths, marriages and if you were unfortunate enough to be around when the vicar called, the summer fete.

But every morning and evening for the past two weeks, the Reverend Pemberton had made the fifteen mile journey from his own parish in Exeter, to open and lock up the church whilst the regular vicar was away. He cursed again as a fresh blast of wind swept the rain down the back of his starched white collar, dug his hands in his coat pockets, and walked, head bowed against the late winter night. Using the graveyard as a shortcut enabled him to park his car in the adjoining lane and save himself the extra job of unlocking the large gate at the bottom of the church path. It also meant he avoided any chance of bumping into old Mrs Wilton who always complained that she could no longer pray for her long departed husband. He felt sorry for her, but what could he do?

He smiled to himself as he placed one hand on the low stone wall and jumped, landing nimbly in the lane; not bad for an old man of sixty. He fumbled for his car keys as he quickly covered the twenty yards to his car, parked in one of the small inlays that were the only places wide enough for two vehicles to pass in the narrow lanes that criss-crossed the county. On either side, the high hedges that masked the green fields beyond swayed wildly as the wind pressed against them like a giant's hand.

As he reached the car, he kicked the flat rear tyre and threw his hands to the sky at the thought of having to change the wheel. He stood for a moment before moving to the rear of the car to retrieve the tools he would need, asking his God what he had done to deserve this punishment. His frustration turned to disbelief as he spun to face the figure that had caused the searing pain in his back. Seeing a flash of silver, he instinctively jolted his head away but felt the same pain in his shoulder.

"What are you doing, what have I done?" he cried out, as he turned to face the figure again, almost tripping over his own legs as he backed down the lane. The rain trickled down his ashen face, mingling with his tears as a wave of terror swept over him. The figure followed him slowly, without reply. He turned and almost blinded by shock and pain, stumbled the five yards back to the low stone wall, his terror driving him on. He threw himself against the wet stone and from somewhere and against all odds he found a foothold and with a superhuman effort hauled himself over the wall, landing in a crumpled heap on the other side. He had taken his assailant by surprise and bought the few seconds he had needed. He pulled himself to his feet and stumbled backwards into the darkness, not daring to take his eyes from the wall. Searching the darkness for his attacker, he backed into a large gravestone and sinking to his knees, crawled behind it, fighting against the pain and panic to suck much needed air into his weakening lungs. He was no doctor but he knew he was bleeding to death. At that moment, as if by divine intervention, the clouds parted to reveal a three quarter moon. Bathed in its soft light, the church door stood only a few yards away. Pemberton patted his side and felt a surge of relief and hope as he felt the sharpness of his keys. Thank God I didn't drop them, he thought.

"I can make it. There's a telephone in the vestry, I can call the police," he whispered to himself. Combing his fingers across his hair and face to wipe away the rain, he watched the clear droplets turn dark as they mingled with the blood running down his arm. He felt the knot in his stomach tighten and gagged on the bile that rushed into his throat. The door was only a few steps away and would take him only seconds to reach, yet his attacker could be lurking anywhere, perhaps behind this very stone. The wave of terror came over him once more and he tasted the salt of his tears. He realised he was losing strength but also knew that he would die unless he did something and soon. He forced his mind to focus on the great oak door as the clouds rolled over, blanketing the scene in darkness once again. But his eyes had become accustomed to the dark and the door remained visible.

Peering cautiously around the edge of the gravestone, he strained his senses for signs of the attacker, but the swirling rain and wind restricted his sight and hearing to just a few yards. He crouched back down, his knees pressing into the soft earth of the grave. 'It's now or never', he thought and pushed himself onto his feet. All at once everything began to swim in front of his eyes and his ears rang. Fighting against the dizziness, he stumbled onto the path that led to the entrance porch, each step seeming like a hundred miles. He called silently to his God for help, not daring to look over his shoulder in case the monster was behind. Reaching the door, he fell against it with a thud of relief and immediately scrambled to retrieve the keys from his pocket. Again the searing pain exploded in his back and he collapsed against the door. Turning around, he slid to the floor and looked up into the eyes of the monster.

"Why?" he mouthed. The question would never be answered as the figure slashed again and again at his throat watching with soulless eyes as the clergyman grasped his neck in a vain attempt to stem the blood flow. For what seemed an eternity the vicar stared up at his attacker, his eyes pleading for mercy as he felt his life slowly ebbing away. The figure stood motionless above him, the weapon clenched in a gloved hand. The Reverend Pemberton's last thought, as the blackness enveloped him, was to ask his God to forgive this poor sinner. The killer turned and calmly walked through the churchyard, climbed over the wall, and disappeared into the night.

Kenilworth Castle, Warwickshire, July 1575

Robert Dudley, Earl of Leicester, smiled to himself as he gazed down on his beloved home from a tree lined hillside overlooking the vast estate. From the back of his tall, black stallion his piercing blues eyes had an uninterrupted view for many miles. At five foot seven he was a tall man for the time, his long black pointed beard clinging to his chin accentuating his angular features. Dressed in a blue and gold striped jacket, topped with a large white neck ruffle, matching baggy briefs, white stockings, and black buckled brogues, his clothing marked him as a nobleman. He removed his feather topped hat as his gaze rested on the castle walls.

The castle, first started in 1125 and added to by successive owners, including several monarchs, dominated the surrounding landscape. Its twenty-five-foot high, ten-foot thick walls stretched for nearly a mile and were capped with the familiar ramparts and towers enabling his men to repel any attack, although none seemed likely on this day. Surrounding the perimeter was a deep, fifty yard wide moat, broken only by the huge oak drawbridge, at present straddling the protective stretch of water.

On this cloudless, sunny day the moat was alive with the sights and sounds of twenty magnificently decorated gondolas, each gold painted hull ten feet long with the head of dolphins and mermaids, on the bow. At the stern an elaborate striped canopy made from the finest Persian cloth, gently billowed in the breeze. A crew of three manned each vessel, one standing at the rear steering with a huge wooden rudder that rose high above the stern. Two more sat in the centre section, each heaving on a gold painted oar. Sheltered from the sun under each canopy two guests lounged eating, drinking and exchanging ribald comments with any boat that came within hailing distance. As the craft made their way lazily around the moat, a much larger vessel manoeuvred constantly to keep in the centre of the flotilla. With a crew of five sailors, ten servants and eight musicians its job was to keep the guests watered, fed and entertained. As a gondola came within a few inches of its hull, one leapt across the divide. He was dressed in a multi coloured outfit of reds, greens and yellows complete with a large pointed soft hat that flopped crazily as he danced and weaved in front of the delighted couple.

On the banks of the moat and from the castle ramparts, crowds of onlookers waved, cheered and cried out to catch the attention of those on the water. From one gondola a handsome young man leapt up and performed an elaborate bow, bringing huge cheers and laughter from a group above as the vessel lurched to one side almost tossing him overboard.

All around the castle, huge coloured tents sat majestically with a group of revellers gathered outside each. A few yards away several fires could be seen, each with an ox, pig or sheep being turned on a spit by a servant boy. One had run away from a hail of blows after being beaten by his master for slacking at his task, before stopping and returning aware that the punishment for deserting his post would be far worse.

Surrounding all this merriment a group of a hundred men heavily armed with spears and swords, patrolled under the command of the mounted captain of the guard.

Dudley was a contented man. He had more wealth than he could spend in a lifetime and his roving musicians, known from Stratford to London were the envy of every man at court. But what gave him the greatest feeling of contentment was the person sitting beside him, also mounted on a sturdy mare.

Queen Elizabeth I, Queen of England, had no eyes for the panorama that lay before her, she only had eyes only for Dudley. A casual observer would have been surprised by the look to be found there as it was not the expression a queen might have for one of her subjects, albeit a well-known favourite. She wore a dress of fine, blue silk that contrasted with her pale complexion and red hair.

"Your Majesty, I think we should return to my guests. It would not be wise for our absence to be noted by those who would seek to benefit from the rumours," said Dudley, turning to look at his queen.

"Yes, my Robin you are indeed correct," she replied, using the nickname she had given him. "Let us hasten. But worry not for your enemies, but think what your allies would say if they saw a weak woman riding ahead of such a noble man of the court. And on such a fine mount."

They both laughed and urging their respective horses forward, raced down the hill. Even at forty two, Elizabeth was a fine horsewoman but her mount was no match for Dudley's stallion and she was unable to stay ahead for long. After half a mile Robert pulled his mount and waited for her to catch up, walking the horses together through the last few hundred yards of forest, happy just to be alone.

"Look, a fine stag," whispered Robert. The rust coloured animal stood motionless a hundred yards away, head bowed as it fed on the lush forest grass. Suddenly it raised its head and looked straight toward the pair. They both knew its three foot antlers marked the magnificent beast as a fully grown male and not to be tackled unless fully armed. The stag watched them walk by, his head raised arrogantly as if knowing they could not harm him until eventually they emerged into the open ground that ringed the moat. Their entrance raised little notice among those on the castle walls and gondolas, they were too busy enjoying themselves. But they both knew that keener eyes would be watching them. Spies who would report anything unusual back to their masters.

As they approached a tent, they were spotted by a servant who quickly summoned several others. One held the rein of a horse whilst another helped each rider to dismount and a small group quickly formed. As Elizabeth walked towards the water's edge every man, woman and child bowed or curtsied as she passed.

"Welcome back, your majesty."

"A fine day, your majesty."

"Did you enjoy your ride, your majesty?"

Elizabeth nodded and smiled to each. She hated this part of her duties the most, but as queen she knew it was important to remain popular, and smiling for a few peasants would give them all a story to tell their children.

For the next twenty minutes, she passed amongst the cheering crowds waving and smiling. At her side were several members of the royal guard, ready to protect the monarch from any overzealous subject, and constantly vigilant for any lurking assassin. But no such attack seemed likely on this day. The sun continued to shine and Elizabeth, like many others who were dressed in heavy clothes, soon began to tire in the heat. After sampling a small piece of roasted pig, offered to her from one of the many open fires, she turned to Dudley.

"I am growing tired, Leicester," she addressed him by his more formal title. "I wish to retire to my chamber."

"Yes, your majesty," he replied and in an instant the human caravan had swung around and began heading for the main castle walls. As they walked across the drawbridge, the new gatehouse came into view. Finished only six months before, it was Dudley's triumph and his contribution to the great castle, which now looked more like a palace. The red brick construction rose five storeys high, its square shape broken only by a small turret at each corner of the roof and the numerous leaded windows.

"A fine building, Leicester," remarked one of the entourage.

"Thank you, Sir," replied Dudley, his chest swelling with pride. "It has taken two years to complete, but I believe it has been worth the labour."

His gaze rested on a magnificent marble fireplace inscribed with the Bear and Ragged staff, which he had commissioned to celebrate his adoption of the symbol of his ancestor Richard Beauchamp, the thirteenth Earl of Warwick, who fought in the Hundred Years War between the houses of York and Lancaster.

The queen's rooms were on the second floor, with unbroken views over the castle walls to the lake and forest beyond. When the group reached the foot of the stairs, Elizabeth stopped and turned to face them.

"I should like to spend some time alone, if you please," she commanded. Each man performed an extravagant bow, one arm swept from ceiling to floor, after having removed its owner's headgear, the other held firmly behind the back. When they looked up, she was already several steps away from them, her ladies in waiting scurrying behind in an effort to keep up.

Arlington, Virginia, July 2009

The headquarters of the Central Intelligence Agency is situated in Arlington, Virginia, eight miles west of downtown Washington DC. The complex comprises two buildings totalling two and a half million square feet and the grounds cover more than two hundred acres. However, a casual driver on highway 260 from Washington hoping to pick up the 25 south to Richmond, would not even notice that it existed.

Andrew Larkin had no such problem as the US navy helicopter began its descent to the landing pad as he could clearly see the entirety of the buildings before him. A familiar face was already visible, standing by the regulation government issue black Ford as the pilot feathered the engine to ensure a soft landing.

At five foot nine, he knew he should have had no problems fitting into the cramped cabin seat. However at thirteen and a half stone, or 189 pounds as our American cousins would say, he was uncomfortably aware that he did. He smiled as the familiar figure grew in size. 'At least I've still got all my hair', he thought. 'When I get back home I swear I'm going to lose some weight'. A picture of an expensive exercise bike, bought the previous summer and used only once, was pushed from his mind.

He was grateful for the soft landing as one wheel gently touched the ground a fraction before its partner. He had a bad head, caused mainly by only managing two hours sleep in the last twenty four, but when the message had come, he had no choice but to leave immediately. He only had to grab the overnighter kept ready for such a call, and as he had had plenty of them during the last five years, he had gotten it down to a fine art.

"Nice to see ya Andy, glad you could make it."

"Did I have a choice, Joe?"

The two walked toward the waiting car, and again Andrew smiled as he placed an open hand on his head in an attempt to stop his dark hair blowing in the downdraft from the rotor blades. That was a problem Joe Chevaski, his CIA liaison officer, did not have to worry about.

"So how is London these days?" asked Joe as the pair settled into the rear of the Ford before it eased across the two hundred yards between the landing pad and the entrance to the building. Larkin ignored the question.

"I can never get over you yanks, Joe. You're so lazy, I swear you wouldn't walk across a room if you could hitch a ride!"

"I like to save my energy for the important things in life," quipped the American, winking at the same time then immediately looking shocked at the realisation he'd said the wrong thing.

"I wouldn't have time for it anyway Joe," lamented Andrew. "I seem to spend all my time on a plane, or worse still, waiting to get on one."

The two emerged into a small, air conditioned reception area, with a glass booth at one end. A marine, Andrew guessed at over six foot six, and with half a millimetre of hair on his head, stood to attention and requested their ID.

"Thank you Sir, this way Sir!" He barked in the way only soldiers can, and they followed him some twenty yards down a narrow corridor ending with a lift.

"Look, I'm sorry to hear about your wife," said Joe in a low voice as the elevator began to rise.

"It's ok, Joe I can talk about it now. It's been over two months and I've been so busy that I don't have time to think about it too much."

The lift stopped and doors opened to reveal a single, windowless conference room. As he settled into one of the two vacant chairs left around the large oval table, Andrew's mind wandered back to the funeral chapel and the site of Nancy looking so peaceful in the casket. It seemed so unfair for her to leave him alone with a five-year-old daughter. He promised himself he would call the head detective covering the hit and run case when he returned to the UK.

"Ok, Mr Larkin, thanks for making it here so quickly. As you know we are not in the habit of dragging you here without good cause." Andrew looked up and into the face of Michael Boschetti, the CIA's head of intelligence for Europe, and Chevaski's boss. "I'll come right to the point." The other dozen or so faces around the table, most of whom Andrew already knew, roused themselves as the lights dimmed and a series of images appeared on the wall.

"These pictures were taken by our new X47B drone at 1400 hours EST two days ago." The pictures showed what appeared to be a group of men unloading crates from a black Range Rover in a desolate desert location.

"I take it these are our Taliban friends?" remarked Larkin. "But what was the X47 doing over there, that's one of your latest birds isn't it?"

Boschetti looked around the darkened room as if searching for something. In response an unseen voice appeared.

"Yes, that's right, we had a problem with the navigational signals, and she ended up straying into Pakistan airspace. That's how we got these shots." Boschetti picked up the lead again.

"As you can imagine it's a little embarrassing for us to admit that we're having problems keeping our latest drone inside Afghanistan, however we felt it would be wrong for us to ignore this important information."

"We can do without this right now," said Larkin. "How much more do you have?"

Joe tossed several large scale photos across the desk.

"About ten miles inside the southern border just west of Spin Boldak," said Boschetti, anticipating Larkin's next question.

Five nights later the contents of a black Range Rover lay on the floor of a warehouse in the corner of Kandahar air base. Andrew looked down at six open wooden packing cases, each revealing ten very impressive replica AK47 assault rifles. They had also found, hidden in the butt of each, a packet containing a white powder. Andrew did not need a chemist to tell him it was heroin, but a nod from one of his team who had placed a small amount on the tip of his tongue, confirmed the obvious. He guessed the street value of the haul at more than $10million.

"The sons of whores got what was coming to them," said one of the assassins, looking down at the two bodies laid out on the floor. "They have betrayed the honour of my family."

Andrew looked up into the face of one of the two tribal militiamen. They, and the SAS team who had provided back up and had now flown back to their base, had done his work, enabling him to wrap up what could have been a messy incident in the quietest way possible.

Looking at the two bodies being removed and seeing the blank look in their eyes, brought back the thought of Nancy's face in his mind. If only he had been around she wouldn't have needed to pick up Charlotte from school that evening.

As he turned and walked towards the waiting car, he knew that he would have many more such thoughts before her face dimmed in his mind. But he didn't want to forget her face. Why couldn't he see her as she was, laughing and joking?

"Straight to the terminal sir?" said the army driver standing by the car. Andrew was jolted back to the present.

"Er, yes, yes the terminal."

"Get me out of these clothes," said Elizabeth, a little irritably when the door to her inner room was finally closed. Her personal lady in waiting began by removing the elaborate neck and cuff ruffles and Elizabeth wound her neck in a circle, happy to be free of their constraint. Next the young maid unfastened the buttons that held her heavy riding britches. They fell to the floor and were hastily removed. Elizabeth waved her hand to dismiss the attendants and they retreated to one side of the room, for it was rare for her to be truly alone. With so many duties and people who wanted her time, almost every waking moment of every day was charted for her by the army of attendants, advisors and ministers that made up her court.

She crossed to the window and gazed out at the distant forest. The sounds of the water pageant drifted across the lake. The only time she was really happy was when she was alone with her beloved Dudley. They had known each other since childhood and had then been imprisoned at the same time in the Tower of London, she by her sister Mary as a protestant threat to the then catholic throne, he by association with his father the Duke of Northumberland who had been executed for plotting to place Lady Jane Grey on the throne. They had rarely seen each other, but had become great friends by whispering during the lonely nights, when the guards had fallen asleep, and stealing glances when either passed during their rare moments in the open. She had learnt later that many of her sister's council had urged her to have the young Elizabeth executed, as they feared she would unite Mary's protestant enemies against her. But somehow they had both survived; she to be eventually crowned queen at the age of twenty five, after her sister Mary's death, he to make his fortune in the army and commerce.

Elizabeth had imprisoned her catholic cousin, Mary Queen of Scots, who was widely thought to be plotting against the new queen, on taking the crown. She had reluctantly taken the decision to deny her the mercy she had received. She had become a woman the day she signed the warrant, but had known that her main advisor, Wallsingham, was right. To unite the country her enemies, both home and abroad, must know she was strong and would not flinch from what had to be done to strengthen her position. Now, seventeen years into her reign, England was no longer the poor, weak island she had inherited, sick from infighting amongst catholics and protestants since the death of her father Henry VIII. But she had paid a price for the stability and growing wealth her subjects now enjoyed. Throughout her reign, the subject of her marriage had been a constant companion. She had considered more than a dozen suitors from England, Scotland and virtually every country in Europe. Each had their political merits, though few the good looks of Dudley, but each a fatal flaw. It was assumed that England would form an alliance with whichever country furnished the chosen groom. England's traditional ties with Spain were growing weaker, due to its opposition to the strengthening power of the Church of England. Elizabeth knew that the country needed to forge close links with France. If it came to a war with Spain, England was still not strong enough on her own, to defeat the strength of the Armada, but a marriage to a 'frog', would only hasten the split with the Spanish. If she married someone from her own island, he would be catholic or protestant. This would be seen as a sign of favour for one group and could lead to the other feeling threatened enough to start a civil war, a disastrous situation that the Spanish were secretly encouraging. Whatever she did it could force England into a conflict that it could ill afford. So for seventeen years she had refused to marry, or name her successor, for that too would sow the seeds of discontent. She and Dudley had remained close friends, a bond existing between them that few understood. It was this friendship that had inevitably grown into the secret love that had kept her strong. When she lay naked in his arms, she felt like a woman. He was the only one who loved her for herself, not as a queen.

She turned away from the window and crossed to the bed, suddenly feeling a little dizzy. She leant on one of the four huge posts that supported the dark, oak structure, and tried to steady herself. She felt the bile rise from her stomach, but could do nothing to prevent it gushing into her throat. She retched violently, doubling up with pain, still grasping the wooden post. In an instant her ladies surrounded her in a flurry as the vomit spilled onto the floor.

"Your majesty, what ails you?" they cried. Elizabeth lowered herself into a sitting position on the floor, her back resting on the bed.

"I am well, stop fussing," she said, unconvincingly. "Bring me some water...., and clear this mess."

"Your majesty, we must call for a physician to attend." The senior maid appeared over the heads of the others.

"We must be sure you are well."

"NO!" cried Elizabeth in a voice that made them all back away. "I am well," she continued in a slow whisper.

"Your Majesty, how many times must you vomit before you will allow the physician to attend you?" said the senior maid, pushing herself forward once again. Elizabeth fixed her eyes on the woman.

"Madam, I am your mistress and your Queen," she said coldly. "I will decide who I see and when." The maid could not hold the Queen's gaze and dropped her eyes to the floor. "I forbid you to speak of this to anyone." She looked around at the three women. "If I discover your tongues have been wagging, I will have them removed. Is that understood?" They nodded as one. "Now prepare my bath." They all turned to go about their duties. "Jane!" The youngest of the three women froze and turned slowly to face her mistress. "Before you do that, summon the Earl of Leicester to attend me at once."

Ten minutes later, Dudley closed the doors of the chamber behind him. There was no one else in the room, which surprised him for it was not wise for Elizabeth and him to be alone. Elizabeth lay on the bed, her head already raised from the pink, silk pillows, on hearing him enter the room.

"Oh Robin," she cried and opened her arms for him. He crossed the room and sitting on the edge of the bed, fell into her embrace. Neither spoke, but Dudley could feel her sobs against his chest.

"What is wrong Lizzie?" he said, softly raising her chin with a single finger to look into her eyes, bloodshot from crying. It took several moments to control the racking sobs, and compose herself enough to speak.

"My darling, I do not know what to do," she began, only to break down again. Dudley could not begin to fathom what had caused her to react in this way.

"Is it that bastard Wallsingham again? I told him you would not marry Alencon," he said, searching his mind for an answer.

"No, it is nothing like that," she replied. "I only wish it were that simple." She appeared to steel herself and wiped away the tears from her cheeks. "No Robert, it is worse" She looked into his eyes and gathered the courage to speak the words she had dreaded for the last two months. "I am with chid."

He looked at her for a moment, disbelief in his eyes, and then promptly slipped off the bed, onto his knees. He sat there for a full minute as she peered at him from the bed above.

"Say something," she eventually blurted out. He rose and started to pace the room, almost walking into the wall.

"Are you sure?" He said finally.

"I have not bled for two months, I know." His broad shoulders hunched over.

"Are you sure it is mine?" He said, not realising the true meaning of his words.

Elizabeth's face immediately twisted in rage. She rose from the bed and walked slowly to where he stood. Dudley could not stop admiring her slim, buxom figure as she approached him. She stopped an inch from his face and looked up.

"I could have you put in the tower for a comment like that," she hissed. Her hand flashed out and he felt a stab of pain on his cheek. "Do you take

13

me for a common whore?" she screamed as she turned and strode across the room. "It is not I who is rumoured by some of murder!" She immediately regretted the reference to Dudley's wife, Amy, who had died from a tragic fall some fifteen years before. Found at the bottom of a flight of stone steps at the castle, many wagging tongues at the court still whispered that Dudley had killed his wife to clear a path for marriage to the queen. She saw his eyes fill with sadness at the slur and rushed over to him. He took her in his arms and they held each other.

"I am sorry my Robin," she sobbed. "But I am so afraid. All the years I have been so strong, and now this." Dudley let the implications of the birth of an illegitimate child to the Queen of England sink in. He knew that many monarchs had sired bastards, that was nothing new. But for a queen who had refused to marry or name her successor for fear of starting a war, at home or abroad, the news would create a tidal wave of mockery and conspiracy. His name would be mentioned immediately, his enemies would see to that. "Robert, if they discover you are the father, they will want your head." She saw the fear in his eyes. "And I don't know how I will prevent it." He began to pace the room once more, deep in thought, then suddenly stopped.

"Who else knows of this?" he asked.

"No-one." He looked at her enquiringly. "My maids have seen me vomit for the last few days, but they don't actually know." Dudley looked into her eyes with a mixture of fear and love.

"It won't take them long to work it out, my love." He rose and began to pace the room again. "I must not stay alone with you for another moment, or it will draw attention," he said, turning to face her, the sun streaming through the window framing him against the strong light.

"But I need you now," she whispered as tears filled her eyes again. Dudley saw the face of a frightened woman, not a strong queen. He knew that she must regain her strength, for both their sakes for there were many who had waited many years for such an opportunity to strike against him. They envied the favour he had with the queen, and would see him in the tower, this time never to emerge.

"My Queen," he began in a formal tone. Elizabeth raised her head to look at him, surprised at his change. "It is vital that no others learn of your condition." She nodded. "You must attend the banquet tonight, and put on your best show for the court." Her shoulders slumped and she sat heavily on the bed. "Listen to me Lizzie," his formal tone replaced by one of exasperation. "I will visit you tonight, and we will talk again, but I must have time to think."

"Yes, very well." He blew her a kiss and departed. She was alone again, and for the first time did not enjoy it. She knew that Dudley was right, she must be strong

Exeter police station, Devon, England, February 2009

"But why the hell would anyone want to murder a vicar?" Detective Inspector Alan Stuart quizzed the group of officers gathered in the operations room of Exeter police station. "Come on, somebody must have some ideas." What Stuart lacked in height, he more than made up for in sheer presence. Fifty three years of age, and with a paunch to prove it, he was feared, yet respected by the men of Devon CID.

"Well," said a junior officer rather sheepishly, "the uniform who was on the scene first said he had a card pinned to him."

"Yes, yes, go on."

"Well guv it, ... well we didn't think to say anything. It just had some coat of arms and a number written on it."

"Just that?" said Stuart, this time in a more thoughtful growl.

"Just that?"

"Where is this card?"

A piece of card, three inches by two quickly appeared.

"No prints, sir," someone volunteered. Stuart took the card and examined it carefully. The number eight was hand written in black felt tip pen in a simple, almost childlike script against a yellow background. On the reverse was the symbol of a bear tethered to a tree by a chain, on this side the background was blue.

"Any suggestions?" queried Stuart and was hit by a wall of silence. "Well has anybody thought to find out the story on the coat of arms?" He sighed in exasperation.

"Yes sir, said a sergeant. I've got a call in to a guy I know who dabbles in this sort of thing. I'm waiting for him to get back."

"OK, let me know as soon as you hear something."

The meeting broke up with the menacing suggestion that as well as the usual house to house, and backgrounds on the victim, the six strong team go back over every step of the vicars movements for the last three weeks.

"Ok guv, but I can tell you now, you could use this guy as a calendar. Same routine week-in week-out. He had done this trip twice a day for ten days straight."

Stuart sat down heavily at the desk in his small office, placed his head in his hands and dug his fingers into his eyes. This was the last thing he needed with the workload he had. The chief constable of the county force had grown up in the village and wanted him to *'Move heaven and earth to find this madman'*. His superior's voice echoed through his head into his hands.

The whole thing made no sense. He scooped up a pile of photographs showing the clergyman's body lying against the church door. There was no sign of the card.

"Bloody uniforms," he cursed. The post mortem results revealed that the body bore the marks of a frenzied attack, but his twenty five years of experience and the facts did not seem to support this. There were two wounds in the back and another in the shoulder in addition to the two cuts to the throat, all struck from different angles by a right handed assailant, and at different depths. Stuart was convinced that the vicar had literally run for his life, from the trail of blood from the car to the door, a distance of fifty yards and a climb over a four foot stone wall. He also guessed that he had probably turned to face his attacker from the pool of blood, forming an arc, found on the road. He therefore had time to do these things, meaning the attacker must have calmly followed him as he fought in vain to elude the blows from what appeared to be a long, heavy knife, a hunting or military model. He made a mental note to ask one of the lads to check all the local stores that could have sold such a knife.

But these things only made him more puzzled. The guy was a bachelor, straight if his colleagues were to be believed. The church was untouched, the keys still in his pocket. Who would have a grudge against a vicar? Probably some religious freak that wet himself in the vestry when he was two! He swivelled on his chair and as he touched the mouse on his computer, the screen sprang to life. For the next twenty minutes he entered the details of the case, using two fingers, into the newly installed national database. But he was tired, had worked a long shift, and there were so many different boxes to fill in.

"Bloody computers. I should have a secretary to do this for me," he moaned to nobody. Then the machine crashed. He restarted it, and completed the basics, but was too tired to enter anything into the *Additional Information* section. So it was that the details of the card never found their way onto the National Criminal Intelligence Service (NCIS) database.

The banquet was a splendid affair. More than 200 guests sat at huge oak tables that lined the gigantic hall. Overhead hung long, colourful banners depicting the Dudley family's crest. At one end of the great hall, Dudley's famous players kept everyone amused with their music, whilst at the other sat the main guests. Twice as many servants scurried to and from the kitchens serving wild boar, beef, venison and chicken. A few of the more travelled ate with knife and forks, newly imported from the continent, but most simply tore at the food with bare hands. Dancers, jesters and magicians moved among the guests, with roars of laughter rising above the steady hum of conversation.

Elizabeth had eaten nothing. Seated alongside Wallsingham, she could think only of how Robert could make things right.

"Your majesty, where is your appetite?" spurted the advisor through a mouthful of what looked like every type of meat on the menu.

"I am a little tired, that is all," said Elizabeth, trying not to look away from the disgusting sight. Dudley sat next to Wallsingham and she caught his eye. She had known him long enough to understand that look and forced herself to smile, picked up a small piece of meat using a silver fork, which she forced into her mouth, forgetting to stop smiling. Dudley could not prevent himself laughing out loud at the sight of Elizabeth, looking like a Cheshire cat with a bird hanging from its mouth. The cat glowered back. Fortunately Wallsingham had his head buried in a large jug of foaming beer, and witnessed neither laugh nor look.

The sound of a distant trumpet greeted the guests the moment dusk settled.

"The fireworks await," bellowed Dudley above the din and at once there was a stampede to the far end of the hall. Servants rushed to pull back several huge doors that opened on to the castle walls and the crowd spilled out, all etiquette forgotten in the excitement. From their vantage point the guests had a wonderful view of the scene below. Along a two hundred yard line, thirty bonfires, sparks flying high into the night sky, lit up the banks of the lake. Alongside each fire a small team manned a wooden platform that acted as a launch pad for the fireworks, whilst a yeoman stood guard over the box containing the powder-filled containers.

On the walls, the crowd parted to allow the main guests, led by the queen and escorted by Dudley, access to the best view. He took a flaming torch from a servant and waved it above his head as a signal for the display to begin.

For ten minutes the sounds of screaming rockets, exploding bombs and crackling gunpowder mixed with the sounds of wonder and excitement. Elizabeth forgot her troubles as she arched her neck into the clear summer sky until a rocket exploded into a shower of reds and greens that slowly floated down on those below. As the display ended and Dudley offered his arm to the queen, he caught site of a familiar face in the crowd.

"William," he called. "It is the playwright, your majesty." A young man emerged from the crowd and bowed theatrically before Elizabeth.

"Your majesty, it is a great honour and privilege to be presented to you on this wonderful midsummer's evening."

"Rise Master Shakespeare," laughed Elizabeth. "I have heard much of your writing sir, although I have yet to see your first play, how is it titled?"

"Romeo and Juliet, your majesty."

"Yes, yes, a tragic story, surely it could never happen in real life?" She shot a glance at Dudley.

"Ah, life is full of joy and sorrow, your majesty," said William. "But tonight is full of joy, yes?" and spun himself around.

"Yes Master Shakespeare, indeed," said Elizabeth with a smile. "What will be your next play, sir?" she asked.

"Madam," he addressed her in a deliberately informal way, "until tonight I was unsure. But on such a grand evening my heart has touched my mind (and I believe God has given me a splendid thought."

"Pray tell us more," asked Dudley.

"Sir I can say little except that it will be about an enchanted people in an enchanted place." He stopped suddenly, looking directly at Dudley and Elizabeth. "And I shall base one of my characters on you, your majesty," he said with a sly smile.

"And what shall you name this masterpiece?" asked Elizabeth.

Shakespeare's brow furrowed and he stroked his chin. He had an audience and was not about to lose the opportunity. After milking the moment for all it was worth he threw both his arms into the air.

"What more fitting a name," he cried. "Your majesty I shall name my new play "A Midsummer's Night's Dream!""

December 1575, Richmond Palace, London

"Your majesty, you must reconsider this proposal very carefully." Sir Francis Wallsingham, the queen's chief advisor, rose from the large oak table. His hands pressed on its dark surface as he leant forward and surveyed the ten others gathered in the great hall of Richmond Palace, the queen's favourite house situated on the Thames ten miles west of the city of London. "Lord Alencon will not wait much longer," he said with as much passion as he could summon.

"That may be so, Wallsingham, but if her majesty does not care for the young man, then that should be that," said the Earl of Leicester, Robert Dudley, seated immediately to the right of Elizabeth. Wallsingham glared across at the man whose advice he knew was not entirely without bias and began to walk around the outside of the group, everyone waiting for him to speak.

"Leicester," he said as he arrived directly behind Dudley, deliberately preventing him from seeing his face, "you are as well acquainted as any man...or lady," he bowed in the direction at Elizabeth at the head of the table, "with the situation this country finds itself in. The Spanish become more hostile to our position each day, and we know they have many supporters among the catholics both here in court and with the Stuarts in Scotland." He glanced across at the Earl of Kent, whom he knew agreed with his view and raised his eyebrows as if in signal.

"Yes, Wallsingham, I agree." Kent picked up the argument adding weight with this new voice.

"The treasury is depleted and we cannot afford to fight the Spanish on our own," he urged, looking around for support. "We must have the French on our side. This marriage will guarantee their support, and buy us the time we need to build up our fleet and armies for the attack of the Spanish that must surely come."

"That is so, Kent, but you ignore the contrary argument." Dudley's ally Essex had seen the expression on his face and took his chance to put forward their case. "If the queen marries the Frenchman, it will send out a signal to the Spanish, and may hasten the conflict that we all wish to delay or prevent."

"And what of the Catholics in this land?" Dudley rose from the table himself, forcing Wallsingham to step back. "They fear Alencon, as he is a protestant. This may give them the reason they seek to gather their forces in Scotland and attempt to place their favourite on the throne."

"STOP" cried Elizabeth, unable to keep her silence any longer. "I have heard these arguments many times before." She glared at Dudley and Wallsingham, who both hastily returned to their seats. "None of you are interested in my feelings for this man, this boy," she corrected herself, remembering that the young French suitor was some ten years younger than she. "I am tired of these endless discussions on if and who I should marry." Her voice began to rise. "I have been your queen for twelve years and it seems this is all we have talked of." She rose from her seat and walked to the large window that overlooked the river.

"Your majesty," began Dudley, but Elizabeth stopped him with a wave of her hand. She spun around, tears in her eyes.

"I will not marry this, or any man," she said, her voice faltering. "I have spent all my life fighting against one form of treachery or another." She stood with her hands on her hips at the head of the table. "We are now stronger and more stable than at any time since my father died and I will not place my people in yet more danger, by pandering to those in France and Spain who seek to manipulate England for their own ends." Her voice rose to a fever pitch and Dudley and two others jumped to her aid as she stumbled against the oak surface and slipped to the floor.

He was the first person she saw as she came round, a few minutes later, quickly realising she was no longer in the hall, but had been moved to her bed chambers. Behind Dudley's concerned face grouped several others including her maids, Wallsingham and those from the meeting.

"Your majesty, what ails you?" Wallsingham spoke first as neither Dudley nor the maids needed to ask why a woman who was five months pregnant might faint when under stress. Elizabeth took a moment to take in the scene, and gather her thoughts before she spoke.

"I thank you for your concern, Wallsingham." She sat up as she spoke, and the group retreated slightly. "I did not eat this morning, and felt a little unwell, but do not concern yourself, I am fine." Wallsingham tried to hide his puzzled reaction for everyone at court had noticed that the queen's figure had filled in the last few weeks. He, like most, had assumed she had succumbed to the pleasures of the kitchen in the same way as her father, so to hear her say she had eaten no breakfast came as a shock.

"Your majesty," said Dudley, "you have been under great stress these last weeks. I believe you need a prolonged rest." Before Elizabeth had a chance to reply, he gently pressed her back onto the bed and gave her a wide eyed look as if to say '*Shut up and follow my lead*'. She did as she was bid, curious to see what he had in mind. "You are due a visit to Scotland, the nobles are becoming restless again," continued Dudley. "You could meet with them

20

after you have had a chance to take a long rest." He looked around the room for any signs of dissent to his plan. Only Wallsingham showed any signs of disagreement. "What say you, physician?" Dudley grasped the moment to take the initiative. The old man pushed through the group and quickly examined the queen.

"Your majesty looks fatigued, that is so," he said studiously and then turned to the group with what Dudley realised was a twinkle in his eye. "But as to why that should be....."

"Thank you that will be all." Dudley cut in. He signalled Kent to usher the man out. All but the wily Wallsingham were too concerned for the queen to notice the slight Dudley had performed.

"Very well," said Wallsingham, slowly, "I will arrange the travel plans immediately. The nobles meet again in four months, that will give your majesty ample time to recuperate." Even he did not see the look of triumph in Dudley's eye as his plan fell perfectly into place. Elizabeth saw it plainly though, and realised that this was the only solution to her problem. She must remain in hiding, in private, until after the birth of the child. The timing of the meeting of the nobles would give her time to recover.

Dudley returned to her chambers after the others had left.

"Robin, my love, you are so clever," she said weakly. "But I will not have the child outside England. How will you find time to be with us?" He did not need to reply, the look on his face told Elizabeth she would be alone when she had their child and the thought made her shiver. Dudley took her in his arms.

"My Lizzie," he said soothingly, "you know I cannot be there, for if the child is discovered Wallsingham will have all the evidence he needs to send me to the block." He looked into her child like eyes. "But I will be with you in spirit, and my spies will keep me well informed." She sank back against the pillows, resigned to the fact that he was right, but filled with a terrible dread, for no one must know of this child.

For the next few minutes they discussed the plan. Dudley repeatedly glanced over his shoulder as if expecting Wallsingham or one of his spies to appear from thin air. Once he leapt from beside the bed and tore back a curtain to reveal a mouse, which scurried under the bed.

"Robin, my love, I will need all my strength. I must know you still love me."

"My Lizzie," he said, "I will always love you. But fate has dictated that I can never be your king." He rose and began to leave, his shoulders heavy with sorrow. "Think of me every day, and when our child is born, hold him to the sun, so I can see him." He left the room before Elizabeth could reply.

She stared into space, not believing he had gone, before burying her head in the pillow to silence her hysterical weeping.

Exeter police station March 2009.

Stuart quickly lifted his feet from the desk as his office door opened. The assistant chief constable, who he knew to be on his way thanks to a tip off from his secretary, would want a full update on the investigation into the murder at the church. But despite all his efforts, and the many hours of overtime claimed by his men, they had drawn a blank. He had known that rounding up the usual bunch of small time thieves and con men would reveal little, but had ordered it anyway. At least it looked as if *something was being done*, a promise the chief constable had given to the local bishop. It fell, of course, to Stuart and his men to turn this into something more substantial.

The crime scene had revealed little, apart from a great deal of blood, all of it from the Reverend Pemberton. The vicar had led an unblemished life and appeared to have no enemies. Discreet, but extensive enquiries in the seedier areas had shown that the he did not share any of the more unfortunate habits of some of his colleagues. The man seemed squeaky clean, so the only explanation was that he was in the wrong place at the wrong time. But this was no opportunistic madman, the crime was planned and professionally executed. The killer knew the car would be parked in the lane, and had lain in ambush. They had discovered a small area in the nearby trees, with freshly broken branches where the killer had probably waited, not surprising given the weather that night. The only clue was the small card as the area revealed no footprints or other evidence.

Stuart's feet hit the floor just as the junior sergeant entered.

"What the bloody hell do *you* want?" he shouted, shocked that it was not the senior man he was expecting. The young detective looked horror struck.

"Blimey guv, I came to fill you in on the card but if you've had a row with the wife, I can come back later." He began to back out.

"Sit down lad, I'm sorry. I'm expecting Tomkins and frankly I don't know what to tell him. Anyway what have you got, something good I hope?"

"Well I just got this stuff from the guy I know who spends his spare time looking up people's family history and all that stuff."

"Genealogy," offered Stuart.

"Yes, but he said he's not really a genealogist, more of a family historian. He looked up the crest and says it belongs to the Warwick family. They go back a long way, I mean hundreds of years." Stuart looked at the sheets. The symbol was the same as that on the card.

"What about the number?" he asked.

"He doesn't think they are connected."

Just then a small tap on the door was followed by the head of the deputy chief constable.

"Hello Alan," he said. "Thought I'd pop in as I was passing." Liar, thought Stuart. They both looked toward the young detective, who made his excuses and left. "The chief is giving me hell over this vicarage murder, Alan." Stuart knew things must be desperate for the deputy to call him by his first name.

"I have a good team working round the clock on it sir. As a matter of fact I've just got some information through on the card found on the body."

"Really?" he said hopefully.

"Well it's not much. It seems the crest belongs to the Warwick family from the same county," said Stuart, reading from the sheets. "They have a long history, going back to the reign of Edward IV with a few C list ancestors along the way. I'll arrange to contact the latest holder of the title and see if we can throw any more light on the subject."

"Do that will you Stuart, and quickly," said the deputy as he rose from the chair.

Two days later, Stuart drove past the Bear and Ragged Staff pub in the village of Norton Lindsey, a few miles outside Warwick. He immediately recognised the sign that hung at right angles to the wall, as identical to that on the card. A few minutes later he swung through the gates of Lindsey Place. As he drove down the long gravel drive, a huge house appeared. He was no historian, but guessed parts of it must have been built at least five hundred years ago. He parked in front of the house and found himself staring up at the battlement topped walls. He was still staring skyward when the butler opened the main door. After waiting several minutes in the large hall, topped with an arched timber roof some forty feet above him, he was led into the study of the present title holder.

"Do sit down, constable," said the man who Stuart put at around eighty, rising from a large mahogany desk and gesturing him toward an ancient looking leather chair. Stuart ignored the instant demotion, thanked his host and sat. "I am happy to help the police in any way I can," the Earl continued, settling himself behind the desk again. Stuart placed the card on the desk and waited whilst the ninth Earl of Warwick examined it.

"Do you recognise the crest, Sir?" he asked.

"I most certainly do, constable," he replied.

"Detective inspector," Stuart corrected him. The earl looked up and studied Stuart as if searching to find a new social position for the visitor, after his sudden promotion.

"Forgive me, detective inspector. This is the crest of my family, where did you find it?" he asked, casually.

"On the blood-stained body of a murdered vicar," announced Stuart, with no attempt at subtlety.

"Good grief," he gasped, dropping the card on the desk.

"Have you any idea why the killer may have done that, Sir?" The earl gingerly retrieved the card and scrutinised it again. Turning it over he read the hand written number then rose and walked to a bookshelf on the far side of the room that stretched from floor to ceiling. He chose a book from a shelf at shoulder height and thumbed through its pages as he returned to the desk. He turned the opened book to face Stuart, and placed it in front of him.

"The bear and the staff have been used in various forms since the middle ages. The two were first merged by Thomas Beauchamp in the late fourteenth century."

"Like the sign outside the village pub?" ventured Stuart.

"The very same, detective inspector," he replied, trying hard to remember Stuart's correct title.

"Have you any ideas on what it might mean, and if the number and colours are significant?" The older man rubbed his fingers along his chin whilst frowning in thought. He returned to the bookcase and pulled another title from a similar position.

"The symbols are used either separately or together in the crests for a number of towns and counties in this area," he continued, pointing out several council crests with bears and trees in various forms. "As for the number eight, there has been an eighth earl in three of four creations of the title."

"Creations?" queried the detective.

"Oh I'm sorry. When the title holder either dies without an heir or has the title rescinded, it lapses. If it's bestowed on someone else at a later date, a new line or creation is established. Few English titles have an unbroken lineage." The earl showed Stuart the details of the individuals, one dating back to 1153. The detective was beginning to wish he had sent someone else to interview the man. "As to the colours," he paused, gathering his thoughts, "blue and yellow were used in the heraldic symbol of the thirteenth century earls." He began to walk around the room, forcing Stuart to swivel his chair. "But they were replaced by red and yellow by the eleventh earl in the mid fourteenth century and there have been numerous changes since." He stood directly in front of Stuart. "So the reference could mean so many things to this person."

"Is there any history of," Stuart paused, choosing his words carefully, "mental illness in your family, sir?" The old man laughed.

"No more than any other, detective inspector. But I can arrange to send you a list of all my current living relatives if you wish."

The earl walked Stuart to his car. "I wish I could be of more help. I do hope you catch this awful man. Do you think he might do it again?"

"Who knows, sir, but it often happens that way." They shook hands and Stuart opened the door of his car. "Do call me if you think of anything else, any point, however small may be of help."

"Rest assured detective inspector."

"By the way," said Stuart winding down his window, "have there been any earls I might have heard of?"

"Why do you ask?" replied the man.

"Just curious," said Stuart.

"It depends on how much you know about history young man. There have been a few traitors, rascals and heroes amongst the forty five holders over the last thousand years or so," he smiled. "My grandfather sold off the family estate to a waxworks company a few years ago. Apart from that you may have heard of John Dudley who was beheaded as a traitor in 1553." Stuart hadn't and started the engine.

"Many thanks."

Alnwick Castle, Northumberland, February 1576

"You must rest, my lady." The chief lady in waiting pulled on Elizabeth's dressing gown to prevent her leaving the bed chambers for the third time that morning. "The baby will come very soon now. It is not safe for you to be seen outside."

Elizabeth sank back onto the bed. She had been confined to the castle for the last two months of her pregnancy, with only the company of her three most trusted servants and the old physician who had correctly guessed her true condition on the day of her fall at Richmond Palace. Each had sworn, on pain of death, to remain silent. The strain of the confinement was driving the queen to distraction. She had not ridden for months and all the people who made her laugh were in London. The old physician had insisted, with the help of Dudley's interventions, that the queen should receive no visitors.

Wallsingham had reached York on two occasions before Elizabeth's personal messenger reached him with strict orders not to make the final leg of his journey to the castle, set on a hill above a remote Northumberland lake. Thank God it takes nearly ten days to make the journey from London, thought Elizabeth. It was the first and only time she was grateful for the distance she had placed between herself and Dudley. She rose and walked to the small window and took in the view along the water to the distant hills, enhanced beautifully by the shimmering reflection of the sun, set low in the winter sky.

"Yes Rose, you are right." Elizabeth turned from the view and walked to her faithful servant." You and the others have looked after me well these last months." She placed her hand on the woman's shoulders in a symbol of friendship. "Has there been any word from my Lord Leicester?" she asked more in hope than expectation.

"No your majesty," said the woman. Elizabeth sighed and sat at the desk in the corner of the room. To her surprise she had a piece of parchment placed in front of her rather than now commonly used paper. After dipping her own Swan quill in the gold inkpot, she began to write.

15th February 1576   *Alnwick Castle*

Dear Robin,

I do not know how much longer I can bear to be apart from you. These last two months have seemed like two years. But soon our bastard will be born. The women have arranged for the baby to be given to a local peasant farmer named Moore. They are childless and have longed for a baby of their own for many years. They tell me our child will be well cared for. I know this is the only way this problem can be solved, for if it were ever known that I have borne an heir then a civil war would surely follow. As queen I must put the nation before myself, but as a woman I do not know what I shall do when my baby is taken. I pray that I will see you again soon and that you will always be there to give me the strength I shall need to carry on. Please get word to me that you are well.

Your loving Lizzie'

She read the letter twice, before signing and folding it. She had written the text in Latin as an extra precaution against prying eyes. Few outside the nobility and clergy could read, less still in the language that until recently all communications had been recorded. She sealed the edge with a candle, pushing her ring into the soft wax as a makeshift seal.

"See that this is delivered at once." The lady-in-waiting took the letter and left the room.

"What have you there?" asked a senior maid as she walked along the corridor, turning the letter over in her hands.

"A letter for Leicester," she answered. They both knew that it would never reach its destination, for Dudley had given strict instructions that he receive nothing that could link him to the queen during her confinement.

"Give it to me."

She reluctantly passed the letter over and scurried back to her tasks. The new courier entered her own bedroom, closed the door, then crossed quickly to a small desk and breaking the seal, read the letter. Its contents confirmed what she already knew, Dudley was the father. She had witnessed enough Court politics to be sure that this letter would see him executed if it fell into the wrong hands. She also knew that it could provide her with an insurance policy, should she ever need it. Carefully folding the letter, she walked to a small, velvet lined trunk that contained her personal possessions. Halfway down one side the cloth had been altered to produce a concealed overlap. She slid the letter inside the gap and worked until she was satisfied it would not be discovered even if the trunk were searched. She locked it, rose and quickly returned to the queen's room.

"It is done," she said as the queen turned from the window.

Three days later Elizabeth went into labour. But it was not easy, for the queen was, at forty two, past the flush of her youth. On many occasions as her ladies wiped her face of the sweat and tears, she cried out for Dudley. The three women and the physician dare not catch the others eye for fear of incriminating themselves. Finally, just as the dawn rose on the second day she cursed like a sailor once more.

"Push, your majesty, push. I can see the baby's head," said the physician urging her to finish the job, sensing the queen did not have much strength left. He had seen many of his patients die in childbirth, for he had no potions to help with the pain without killing the child, nor instruments to remove the stubborn infant from its mother's body. The child would come when it alone was ready. He prayed silently to himself that this bastard would make up its mind soon, or else it would have no mother to suckle. Elizabeth raised her head in an attempt to see her baby enter the world, but she could not hold herself and collapsed back with a cry of pain.

"Remove this thing from me now, you old bastard," she glared at the panic stricken man, "or I'll have you thrown from the castle walls."

"Be still, your majesty," said one of the women. "The child cannot be hurried, or it will be stillborn." She could see the tip of the infant's head, crowned with a dark tuft of hair and gently slid two fingers around the neck, ignoring the cries of the queen. But there was no space for the baby to emerge.

"Give me a blade," she ordered the physician.

"What are you going to do, cut the queen?" He picked up a knife and looked at its glinting edge and then, in horror, at her.

"If we wait, they will both die. Give me the blade." She snatched the small dagger from his hand and pausing to take a deep breath, carefully drew it deep into the queen's flesh, just below the baby's head. Elizabeth screamed in agony, but they held her down. Blood spurted from the wound and covered the baby's head. She dropped the knife, which fell to the floor with a clatter, as the infants head began to appear into the enlarged area. She grasped the top of the skull and managed to dig into the child's head with enough force to fashion a firm grip, pulling with one hand and as the head began to move, pushing with other around the baby's neck. Elizabeth cried out again and then passed out with the pain. But as her muscles relaxed it allowed the woman to gain a better grip and in a few second the shoulders were exposed, followed swiftly by the torso and legs.

"It's a boy," they cried in unison as another cut the umbilical cord with the retrieved knife. The third woman took the child and holding it upside down by the legs, slapped its behind twice before the new-born child took its first deep breath and then cried out in greeting to the world.

"I wonder what will become of you, my boy" she said, cradling the infant in her arms.

"Where is my baby?" said a groggy voice. Elizabeth had come around, as the physician had just finished the final stitch. The women looked at each other, unsure if it was wise to show the baby to its mother, when they knew it would be taken away so soon. The look in Elizabeth's eyes made her mind up and she placed the boy in her arms and the queen looked down at her son. Tears filled her eyes and desperation overcame her as she realised that this was the first and last time she would ever set eyes on her heir. She pulled the bundle toward her. "Be strong, my son," she said softly, gazing into his innocent eyes, "for your life will not be easy. I pray to God that he will look over you and guide you." A hand came out to remove the child, but Elizabeth turned away. "Let me feed my child, once before he leaves, so he may remember a small part of his mother's love." They watched in silent awe as the child suckled to the breast and took its first meal.

Finally, after what seemed just a few seconds to the new mother, gentle but firm hands removed the baby.

"Mistress, it is time," said the physician kindly. "The new parents are waiting." Elizabeth showed no signs of wanting to let the baby go, but they prised the boy from her grasp and quickly left the room. Elizabeth watched until the door closed before wiping away the stream of tears that ran down her cheeks.

"What price to be a queen?" she asked.

The baby was taken quickly to a rear entrance of the castle, where a small cart waited. The lady-in-waiting climbed next to the driver, who gently laid his whip on the horses back. From a window, high in the castle walls a woman, tears running down her cheeks, watched until the cart disappeared over the brow of a hill. An hour later it drew up outside the entrance to a small, thatched cottage, set in the middle of a windswept, ploughed field. In the doorway stood a farmer and his wife. The lady-in-waiting beckoned the woman, and laid the small bundle into her outstretched arms.

"Remember," she said menacingly, "my spies will let me know if you breathe a word to anyone."

"Go on boy," said the driver, and the cart jolted away. The baby's new parents peered nervously at the child and then looked up into each other's eyes and smiled together.

"He's a gift from Jesus, Thomas," said the woman.

"Aye," replied her husband. "We shall name him after my father, Angus... Angus Moore."

Four weeks after the birth of her child, Elizabeth travelled to Edinburgh to meet the nobles of Scotland including the ten-year-old James, eldest son of her cousin Mary who was imprisoned in the Tower of London, suspected of plotting against the queen.

Andrew had plenty of time to think on the military transport plane from Afghanistan. By the time he landed at Brize Norton Air Force base in Oxfordshire, cleared customs and collected his car from the secure pound, he had formed a plan that he was determined to see through. But he had a far more important call to make before setting it in motion. Parking in a lay-by outside the base perimeter, he switched on his cell phone and dialled the number of Nancy's parents who lived in a small Cotswold village less than thirty miles away.

"Hello Mrs Adams, it's Andrew," he said when the line was eventually answered.

"Oh, hello Andrew," said his mother-in-law in that way she always did. Why was it that mother in laws can convey that 'You were never good enough for my daughter' impression in just about everything they said.

"It's so nice to hear from you, how long has it been? Two weeks I believe."

"Yes, Dorothy, I know. I'm sorry but I've been out of the country, business and all that, you know?

"And of course you can't talk about it," she replied dryly. Andrew sighed.

"You know I can't, Mrs Adams, so why..." Andrew stopped himself in mid-sentence. He was tired and had no desire to see this conversation slide in the same direction as most of the others he normally had with the mother of his late wife. "Why don't I come over now and see Charlotte?"

"She's almost ready for bed Andrew. I don't know if it's a good idea. And anyway it will probably only upset her again when you leave and we will be left to pick up the pieces."

"Would you rather I never saw her again, would that make everyone's life easier?" said Andrew, his voice rising in suppressed anger. There was a silence on the line for several seconds.

"How long will you take to get here?" she said in a flat monotone.

"I'm at the air base, so allowing for the traffic about forty minutes."

"Looks like we will expect you in forty minutes then. I'll wait until you've gone before giving Charlotte her bath." The line went dead.

Andrew looked for somewhere to slam the phone in an effort to dissipate his anger. His arm hovered in the air above the dashboard until he realised there was nowhere to aim. He gradually lowered it and stared for a moment at the handset, not knowing what to do, eventually gently pressing the red end call button and tossing the phone onto the empty passenger's seat where it bounced and lodged itself in between the seat and the door. He looked at the phone and without expression leaned across to retrieve it, only to dislodge it and see it disappear. He stared for a moment at the space where it had been only moments before.

Suddenly Nancy's face appeared in his mind and the familiar feeling swept over him. It was as if someone had twisted his stomach into a knot, put his head in a vice and thrown a black hood over his head. He sat, staring out of the window yet unable to focus. It was a physical thing, this grief, and no one had told him it would be like this. His breathing became laboured and he felt nauseous. Why had this thing happened to his family? He had worked so hard, given up so much to make life more comfortable for them and now it all meant nothing. She had been killed instantly in the head on collision, caused when she had swerved to avoid the drunk driver in a white van. He had failed to stop, but the Met had found him and he was now being held in London. The thought brought him back to reality and the road ahead came into focus, the feeling receding. He looked at his watch to find he had been sitting there for ten minutes. Gunning the car into life, he set off towards the house where his daughter now lived, his face set in stone.

In the forty minutes he took to reach the house he made several calls and arranged a visit to Paddington police station. He had needed to call in several favours and twist a few arms for this was way outside his jurisdiction. But he was in.

The car tyres crunched on the gravel as Andrew pulled into the drive of his in-laws house. Set back a hundred yards from the lane, the Cotswold stone, six-bedroomed house looked every bit as impressive as when he had last visited six weeks before. He was just about to ring the bell when he remembered the gift in his briefcase. He hurried back to retrieve the small parcel, and turned to face the bulk of Nancy's mother in the frame where the door had been only moments before. A large, round, grey haired woman of seventy who bore no resemblance to her dead daughter, she turned, not uttering a word or changing the dark expression on her face.

When Andrew entered the living room he was relieved that he would see at least one smiling face that night.

"Hello, George," said Andrew warmly.

"Good to see you, my boy," said his father-in-law. He was a tall, slim man who had managed to retain both his sense of humour and a full head of dark hair into his seventy fifth year. They both looked at Mrs Adams instinctively like a couple of naughty schoolboys. She glared back, and then her eyes and head moved slightly to the right. Following the directions Andrew turned to see his five-year-old daughter standing, half hidden behind a large chair.

"Hello princess," he said, moving toward the little pyjama-clad girl. As he crouched down to her level, she backed away, eyes firmly rooted to the floor, her long blonde hair almost covering her face. "Come on darling," he said, in the most reassuring voice he could muster. "Look, daddy's got a present for you." The girl looked up warily at the gift wrapped parcel perched at the end of Andrew's outstretched arm. After several seconds of indecision she sprang like a cobra, grabbed the parcel and retreated behind the chair. Andrew peered over the top expecting to see her tearing at the paper. Instead she sat cross legged and motionless, the parcel resting on her lap. She looked up at her father and said: "When's mummy coming home? You said mummy would be home soon."

"I know darling, it won't be long."

"Stop," cried his mother-in-law. "I won't have you lying to the child again. For God's sake do you not realise what is happening while you are jetting

31

around the globe? The child is crying herself to sleep every night, wetting the bed and refusing to eat. You simply cannot go on denying the truth to her, Andrew." A hushed silence descended on the room. Andrew looked into the face of his daughter.

"Nana says mummy's gone to heaven, but you said she would be home soon. How long is soon daddy?"

An hour later Andrew walked wearily into the kitchen and gratefully took a large tumbler of whisky from his father-in-law. He swallowed the contents, welcoming the burning in his throat. He was halfway through the second before he spoke.

"That was the worst moment so far," he said lamely.

"Don't worry, son," replied George, "it had to be done sooner or later. Poor thing was so confused. What with the old girl telling her one thing and you another, had to end in tears." Andrew failed to see the pun and glared at the old man.

"Sorry," he stammered. "Bad choice of words."

"Don't worry. Look I'm sorry I've had to leave Charlotte with you like this. It's just that, well I just don't seem to able to face her. She reminds me so much of Nancy, it's almost too much."

"I know, son," said the older man, placing a kindly arm on his son-in-laws shoulder. "Take no notice of Dotty, she's still coming to terms with it herself you know. No parent expects to outlive their child. It's all so depressing." The two chatted for another ten minutes before she joined them again.

"She's asleep now, but I don't know for how long," she sighed. The new, unfamiliar tone caused Andrew to look into her eyes and he saw a reflection of his own sorrow. He wanted to reach out, but there was a barrier between them that would never be bridged.

"Look I do appreciate what you're doing for Charlotte, Dorothy." Andrew said in a low voice. "There's no way my parents could cope with her."

"It's Ok for now Andrew," she said. "But you know it can't last much longer. She needs some stability, and she needs her father. If you leave it too long, you will lose her."

"I know, but I just need a little while longer to sort myself out. I'm owed some leave, I can take a few days off, maybe take her to Disney."

"Just spend time with her, Andrew. She needs your love, not Pluto's," said Dorothy as she turned and left the room, shoulders hunched.

Richmond Palace, London, 24th March 1603

The queen lay silently in her bed, her advisors and physicians gathered around. She had been deteriorating for two weeks and the gloomy shaking of the medical heads told its own story. The seventy year old queen was dying and it seemed nothing could save her.

Sir Christopher Hutton, a long-time advisor, leant over the queen.

"Your majesty," he spoke as loud as he dare in the hushed confines of the room. Elizabeth opened her eyes slowly.

"Mutton," she spoke in a low gasp, "how are you?"

"Well your majesty," he replied. "Your majesty, I must ask you once again. Who would you have succeed you? We need your answer soon." Elizabeth raised her head from the pillow and took in the sea of faces staring back at her.

"My Spirit, Pigmy, Moor," she called out their nicknames, "where is Dudley?" she asked, darting her head to and fro. Hutton looked around the room for help. Dudley had died fifteen years before and the blank faces gave him few ideas.

"The Earl of Leicester is in France, your majesty," he lied, turning his head away from the queen. Elizabeth closed her eyes and lay back, sighing gently. After a few moments a single tear appeared from the corner of one eye. Pausing for a second, it ran slowly down her cheek. Everyone in the room knew the significance, but none dare catch another's eye or utter a word and none of the physicians or attendants moved to wipe the queen's face. After what seemed an eternity she finally spoke, her eyes still closed.

"I will not change my mind, nor will you change it for me," she said in a firm voice. "I will not give you any name to succeed me. I pray my people will remember me as a good and kind queen who made their lives a little better." Her voice trailed off as she spoke. Hutton looked anxiously at the chief physician, who rushed to the queen's side. He held a mirror to her lips, and relaxed as a mist appeared, confirming the queen was still breathing.

The vigil carried on into the night, with no one daring to leave in case they missed the moment they knew would come soon. At around three in the morning Elizabeth called out Dudley's name in anguish. She also called out for her son. The bemused gathering looked at each other.

"She's delirious," said one of the physicians. "It won't be long now, I fear."

Every half-hour the physician placed the mirror against the queen's lips. Finally, just before dawn, he lifted it and showing it to all present, pronounced the queen dead.

Wallsingham, who really had been in France, arrived on his fastest horse an hour later. Bursting into the room, he sensed the smell of death at once. He down looked at Elizabeth's face, fighting to keep his emotions under control. He took a silk handkerchief from inside his sleeve and wiped away the line that still traced her last tear.

"Goodbye my queen," he said quietly, his face set in a stony grimace. He walked to the window that she had looked out of so often. She had been his life. He had protected her and worked endlessly in the early years of her reign, to strengthen her position and thwart several attempts on her life. As he gazed out he could hear her laughter.

"The queen named no successor, my Lord," said Hutton, joining him at the window. He guided them to a spot where they would not be overheard.

"But she did call out for her son. The physicians thought her delirious, what say you?" Wallsingham knew Hutton was laying a trap. The rumours had been whispered within the innermost circle of her advisors for many years. But the only reliable witnesses, the queen's ladies, together with the physician who had attended her had all, save one, died in mysterious circumstances within a month of the queen's confinement. The sole survivor swearing no knowledge of any offspring. With all his effort he set aside the suspicions he too had held and looked the advisor in the eye.

"Given that the queen had no children, I would say the say the physicians are right my learned friend. He paused for effect. "Unless of course you know different." He pushed passed Hutton and returned to the bedside, not daring to look back in his direction.

"Quite so," said Hutton in a whisper.

Wallsingham looked around the packed room. Even in death she has no privacy, he thought.

"This queen will be remembered well in history. Look how strong she leaves her beloved England yet how weak when she was crowned. Let every man, woman and child in this kingdom never forget." He paused in an effort to master his breaking voice. "She gave her life to her country, so that it might become united. Let it be that a Scotsman may now rule this land but better than a Frenchman or Spaniard."

He turned and forced his way through the throng and out into the sunlight. He mounted his horse and rode into the field beyond, stopping only when he reached the brow of a hill and turned the animal to face the palace he would never see again. He had many enemies in Scotland and knew his life would be in danger the moment the Stuarts took the throne.

Three hundred miles away, a twenty-seven-year-old farm labourer toiled in the sticky clay soil of a Northumberland field. He looked up and watched as a dark cloud rolled over the sun, suddenly chilling the air and sending a shiver through his body. He looked around, strangely aware that something was wrong, but there was no one there. He could see the farmhouse in the distance and neither his mother nor father, who he could see moving around the farmyard, seemed in any danger. After a few moments the warmth returned to his limbs and with a shrug, he resumed his work. He was unaware that his mother, the Queen of England had died. Unaware that the throne that could have been his would pass from England to a Scottish Lord. From that moment to the present day, every King or Queen of England would come from a Scottish, Dutch or German family.

Paddington Green police station, London, July 2009

The following morning Andrew rose early. He left promising Charlotte he would return the next day and headed onto the M40 towards central London. Paddington police station is often used to hold the nation's most wanted criminals when first detained, but a more common site greeted Andrew when he peered into the cell.

"That's the suspect, Mr Williams, sir," said the duty sergeant in his most respectful voice. "Not confessed yet, but Detective Cooper says it won't be long sir."

"Is Cooper in yet?" Andrew asked, seemingly with little interest.

"Not yet sir," replied the sergeant. "Is there any particular reason you need to speak to the prisoner, sir. Only we don't often see you special branch types following up on a hit and run driver?"

"Er, yes," replied Andrew a little too quickly. "We think he might have links to a far right group. Can you take him to the interview room, right away?"

"No problem, sir. I'll just check with Detective Inspector Cooper on his mobile, won't take a minute," he said, moving toward a phone mounted on the wall of the corridor. "He gets very touchy if we don't follow rules, does DS Cooper." Andrew could sense his plan coming apart.

"Look sergeant I don't have time for all this." Andrew removed a false special branch badge from his coat pocket and placed it two inches from the man's face. "I don't need Detective Sergeant Cooper or anyone else's permission to speak to this suspect. Get him into the room now!" Andrew glared at the sergeant and could see him making swift mental calculations as to the lesser of two evils. This special branch type or Cooper. Cooper wasn't here, this guy was.

Andrew did not need to stoop to look through the small window of the interview room, nor did he pause there long as he knew his time alone with the man who had killed his wife would be short. A policewoman stood motionless in the corner.

"Pop and gets us some coffee will you love," he said in his best estuary accent." The woman left the room and Andrew closed the door behind him. "Now Mr Richards, do you know who I am?" The man sat perched on a basic metal chair, arms folded across his chest, legs stretched out in front and crossed at his feet. His pose together with the white tee shirt and faded jeans he wore told Andrew everything he needed to know about the man. He did not have the air of guilt or regret that might have been expected.

"Nope, mate," he replied with no trace of interest or fear. "But I'll tell you what I told the uvver geezer. She pulled out in front of me and I 'ad no chance. You can do me for drink drive, but me brief says you'll never make anyfink else stick." He looked up at Andrew and a cruel smile crept onto his lips. Andrew moved around the back of the man, who shifted slightly, not alarmed, but preferring to see where Andrew was. Had he shifted a little more he would have seen Andrew remove a small pistol from his jacket pocket. However the first he knew was when the gun was pressed into the back of his neck.

"Listen you piece of shit," spat Andrew. "We both know that you were pissed and driving like the bastard van driver you are, right?" The man's expression changed miraculously to one of undisguised terror in the blink of an eye.

"Bloody hell mate," he cried trying to turn around to face the unforeseen threat. "I had just had a few with the lads and forgot the time. Nothing personal." Andrew forced the man's head forward and pushed the gun harder into his neck, forcing him off the chair and onto the floor. For all his bravado the man had never had a loaded gun thrust into the back of his neck. He ended up with his head inches from the floor, legs tucked under his thighs.

"It was my wife in that car," said Andrew, his anger beginning to overcome what little restraint remained. At that point the full realisation of what he was confronting came upon the driver and he began to sob and moan. Andrew looked down at the man's head. He had never killed like this, but had seen the results many times on his travels. Nancy's face filled his mind. This thing had taken her away from him and had committed a crime against his family. He was a servant of the state and was charged with protecting it against any enemy. Sweat trickled down his face. So, he reasoned, any enemy of my family must be an enemy of the state and steps must be taken to eliminate that threat. He removed the safety catch with his thumb, whilst continuing to press the man's face into the floor. He was frozen with terror and offered no resistance. Andrew took a long, controlled breath. Remember your training, he thought. He increased the tension on the trigger and tensed himself for what he knew would be a deafening sound in the confines of the small room.

"Sir, please put down the weapon." Andrew did not move, lost in his own world. "Put the weapon down, or I will be forced to fire." The raised tone found its way into Andrew's' thoughts and he raised his head to look down the barrel of a large handgun, joined to two hands and arms that were attached to a police man in a bullet proof vest. The realisation that he might be shot if he did not comply with the order took several seconds to invade his consciousness.

"This man is an enemy of the state and a threat to Her Majesty's Government," said Andrew pompously.

"That may be so, but I must ask you again to raise the weapon and make it safe. I will not repeat that request again."

The room came back into focus and Andrew looked down to see someone holding a gun to a man's head. It was his hands and his gun. He quickly removed the weapon and looked up again to see several other officers straining to enter through the single door. The gun was removed from his grip and he was taken into a separate room. The van driver was taken to the nearest hospital where, amongst other treatment, he was given a new pair of trousers to replace his own, soiled jeans.

Hawaii , June 2009

As far as the young, blond-haired man was concerned, life couldn't get any better. He resided in a lounger on the veranda of his secluded roundel set amongst the palm trees of the exclusive Hawaiian island resort of Lanai. From his vantage point he looked out over the white sandy beach and into the crystal clear waters to the sea beyond. He could see his new wife, emerging from the sea, the sun catching the water as it fell from her body. He sighed and reached out for the brightly decorated cocktail glass that sat on a small table. Placing the straw in his mouth, he savoured the sweet taste of the fruit and rum mixture. The new English premier football season was still seven weeks away and he had been given an extra week off by the manager before reporting back for pre-season training in three weeks' time. He intended to make the most of his honeymoon. It had been a hard year and what with international matches last summer, he managed only two weeks break. This year would be different and he intended to make the most of it, including having a few drinks for a change.

At twenty four, Matthew Black was one of the country's most sought after young players. His team had paid £45million for his signature and the four-year contract would earn him £275,000 per week. More in a month than his father earned in a lifetime. As a young man who had grown up on a council estate in Manchester, he had taken time to become accustomed to the attention of the girls and the press. But the money certainly made things easier. He knew that whatever happened on the field, he was set up for life.

But few of those thoughts entered his head at that moment, all he wanted to do was to get his new wife into bed. He couldn't get enough of her at the moment and as soon as she finished the short walk to their secluded cottage, he would make love to her for the third time that day.

He rose from the chair and walked into the bedroom, sucking the last remnants of the cocktail. Continuing into the bathroom, he left the glass next to his wife's cosmetic bag on the sink, and stepped into the enclosed glass cubicle. Time for a quick shower, he thought. He had just managed to get the temperature right when he was aware of a dark shape enter the room.

"I'm in the shower babe," he called out. "Can you call room service and get me another of those cocktails, I can't remember what it's called." The expected confirmation did not come and he screwed his face up in annoyance. "Julie, did you hear me, love?" Again no reply. Shrugging his shoulders and feeling slightly irritated, he stopped the water flow. He was accustomed to having his every whim satisfied immediately and he was not sure he liked this much. He wrapped a towel around himself as he entered the bedroom. "Julie!" he called out. This was not funny. He spun around, suddenly aware of a scraping sound coming from one of the closets behind him. He crossed warily to the door and mustering his courage, opened the door quickly. Only a row of clothes greeted him. He half turned away when a flash of movement stopped him. He stood motionless, staring at the woman's clothing, thinking it odd that he was able to notice the gold buckle on one of Julie's red dresses which he had bought for her at the airport in London. Suddenly and without warning a figure crashed through the clothes and bundled him backward onto the bed, knocking the breath from his body. "Julie, you bitch" he cried out, realising the figure sitting on top of him was his wife. She burst into an uncontrollable fit of laughter. He rolled over, tumbling her onto the floor where she lay, still giggling like a schoolgirl.

"Serves you right," she managed to squeal in between the screams of laughter. "You thought I would come in the shower and get you, didn't you?" Matthew said nothing, but was taken aback that she could read his thoughts so well. She rose and he noticed for the first time that she was naked. She had stopped laughing, but had a broad grin on her lips and a lusty look in her eyes. Her long, thin body moving like a cat, she crossed to the king-sized four poster bed as Matthew rolled onto his back. Placing one knee on the bed and with the other outstretched, she leant over him, took his long, wet hair in one hand and pulled her lips down to meet his, thrusting her warm tongue deep into his mouth. He felt himself aroused in an instant. She noticed it too and lowered herself onto him. They both groaned softly as she began to rise and fall, gently at first and then faster as the passion increased for them both. He opened his eyes and reached out for her small breasts. His touch caused the nipples to harden and she let out a small moan of excitement as he pushed them between his fingers. They both cried out as they reached their climax together and she collapsed onto him. After a few seconds she suddenly let out a scream of laughter.

"Blimey, I bet they heard that in all five restaurants"

Afterwards, they lay exhausted, watching the fan spin lazily on the ceiling.

"It's going to be great Matt," said Julie dreamily. "We can have anything we want, anytime we want it."

"That's right, doll," he replied happy in the knowledge that whatever she might think, he had the upper hand in the things that really mattered.

He rose and leaving his bride still sleeping soundly, strolled through the shrub and flower-lined paths down to the poolside bar where the waiter served him a soft drink. No use getting pissed up if I'm going scuba diving, he thought.

An hour later, he sat alongside several other guests, hanging onto the rails of a twenty five foot fishing and diving boat, watching the huge trough of white water it carved on its passage through the waves as it headed out to sea. He was aware of the sly stares and elbowing of partners, but he was used it now and felt relaxed, so it didn't bother him. He raised his head toward the sun and closed his eyes, feeling the humming beat of the 500 horsepower engine below his feet.

"What do you do?" asked a young girl, forcing him to open his eyes and look at her.

"I'm something in the city," he replied sullenly. The girl looked slightly bemused as she knew exactly what he did as she had a poster of him on her bedroom wall.

"Melchester City," added Matthew, and burst out laughing. After a few minutes they arrived at the dive site, the boat slowing down and quickly settling into the water. Matthew casually took in the scene. He could actually see the sea bed in places where the ocean floor almost reached to the surface. This was a popular site for divers of mixed ability and he counted another five or six boats within a hundred yards.

"Ok, listen up everyone," called the dive master, a short, stocky native of the islands. "Just remember, an hour in the pool doesn't make you Jacques Cousteau." They all smiled nervously at the joke, suddenly aware of how vulnerable they were in the open ocean. "Now, let's go through the basic signals again." He raised his hand the thumb and second finger forming a circle. "OK." Next he flattened his hand and ran it across his neck. "Out of air." For the next five minutes he took them through the procedures of safe diving. The dive master and his three instructors were all seasoned professionals with hundreds of dives between them. These first timer tourist courses they gave every afternoon were the most boring part of the job, especially as they came to this safe, shallow spot, every time, but it paid better than anything else they did.

"Now," he continued, "we may see several types of creatures today, even though we will be diving to a depth of only twenty five feet. My friend Joshua, here will help you identify the various types with some simple hand signals." The short, muscular Hawaiian stood and slowly waved his open palm through an imaginary sea. "Small fish." He then joined both palms together as if reading a book and flapped them up and down. "Manta ray." The group were captivated by the display and waited in anticipation for the next example. "Small shark," said Joshua, his white teeth beaming through a wide smile as he clapped his hands together whilst keeping his wrists joined. His face suddenly took on a menacing air as he held both arms aloft and then brought them together in a series of loud clapping sweeps far out in front of his head. "BIG SHARK," he cried. Everyone stopped for a moment, taking in the implications of what he had said. Suddenly all the instructors burst out laughing. "Don't worry, good people, we won't be meeting any man-eaters today." They all broke away to prepare the equipment for each guest, leaving their charges to breath a collective sigh of relief.

Each student was briefed to walk off the end of the boat, holding one hand on the mask to prevent it falling off and the other over the mouthpiece. Then they were to surface and check the mask and regulator. When they were happy they should lift the twelve-inch-long tube attached to their inflatable jackets and press the discharge button, expelling any air inside to aid in submerging.

"Most people assume a diver with a lead weighted belt around his waist will sink like a stone as soon as he hits the water," the instructor said. "That won't happen good people, with air trapped in your suit and your natural buoyancy it's easier to stay afloat."

All except one of Matthew's group made it off the boat. One lady had not foreseen the bucking of the boat on the open ocean and weighted down with thirty pounds of compressed air, simply refused to make the final step.

The group had learnt in the pool that, however experienced, you should never dive alone. The buddy system ensures that everyone has a partner and each keeps a watch on the other. Matthew was paired with the young, talkative girl. For him, the most difficult part of reaching the ocean floor, twenty feet below the gentle waves, was standing up and walking to the rear of the boat. The weight of the equipment, almost unnoticeable underwater, was a huge burden on the surface. He nearly tipped backwards as he raised his arm over the mask and put one foot forward. But the dive instructor at his side guided him in the right direction and he hit the water, disappeared, and then found himself bobbing on the surface in an instant. The first thing he noticed was, despite the apparent calmness of the sea, that he was tossed around like a cork. A wave crashed over his head, knocking him to one side. Christ, best get under, he thought. Once he had kicked his way beneath the waves, everything changed in an instant. The noise and commotion of the surface gave way to an incredible calmness, broken only by the rasping sound of his own breathing. As he became accustomed to using the artificial lung, he was able to notice more of his surroundings. The strong sun lanced through the clear blue water in long, silver strands, dancing as the sea broke its lines. Vivid brown rocks covered much of the seabed, some nearly breaking the surface, others just a few inches from the sand covered bottom. A multitude of small fish danced before him and it seemed every colour of the rainbow was represented. He reached out to touch a yellow and blue striped angel fish, but it darted away, only inches from his outstretched fingers. He paused in his descent and looked up to see the bottom of the boat and followed the anchor line from where it broke the surface, down to the seabed where it was lodged tightly against a small group of rocks. He had always wondered what happened to the line when it disappeared overboard.

He now sat on the seabed, his buddy beside him. Through her mask, he could see the slightly nervous look in her eye and reached out to take her hand in his. Her face instantly relaxed and her eyes smiled back at him.

Around them the group circled the dive master. He had waited for everyone to become accustomed to the surroundings. Matthew wished that he had asked the girl her name. She was around eighteen, and reasonably attractive. He had so much female attention that he sometimes forgot to be a normal person. She looked at him with a mixture of pleasure and nervousness, a combination Matthew found hard to understand. He tried to smile, but succeeded only in filling his mouth with sea water, so settled for a thumbs up.

The instructor signalled for the group to follow him, and set off. Matthew placed his hand under the girl's elbow and beckoned for her to go. He pushed his flipper clad feet into the soft sand and together they were soon moving through the clear, warm water. Matthew found that as his lungs filled with air he began to rise toward the surface. Whilst pushing the air from his lungs arrested the climb, but still left him some ten feet above the group. He remembered the instructions given in the pool and adjusted the air in his inflatable jacket by opening the bleed valve and began to sink. Within a few breaths he had learnt to achieve neutral buoyancy, that state where a diver neither rises of sinks, but can float at a particular depth. With a little experience, minor manoeuvring can be made by adjusting the amount of air in the lungs. The girl had seemed to master the art straight away and he found his respect for her grow.

The group swam lazily in a wide circle, the instructors keeping a wary eye at first and ushering those they could see were least able to the front of the group. One took up station a few yards away, a camera capturing the scenes for the video diary that would be on sale to each guest later. Matthew could just make out another group of divers, he assumed from another boat, at the furthest point of his visibility. After a few minutes a large, dark shape emerged from the depths in what was now a clear view of only twenty feet. The dive master was not concerned with the visibility as this often occurred at this time of year. The dark shape turned into a wreck which sat on the edge of a much deeper ravine that disappeared into a black void.

Matthew and the girl had fallen slightly behind the main group, having paused to watch a small boat cut through the surface above their heads, then slow and stop. The dive master looked up, a frown covering his brow. The buoy attached by a line to his suit warned those on the surface that divers were directly below. Aware that a couple of the group were showing signs of tiring, and conscious that novices could often panic and bolt for the surface, he signalled for the pair to follow him. He had placed himself between the main group and the wreck to prevent anyone getting too near the hull, or worse, attempting to swim inside. Many an experienced diver had met an unfortunate end, trapped in the tangle of debris that littered every wreck. But he was content that the famous footballer and his buddy seemed safe and competent, so quickly moved off into the distance. Matthew guessed, from looking at the shape of the half buried wooden hull, and broken masts, that the old sailing ship had been there for at least a hundred years.

As Matthew approached, drawn by the mysterious shape, a gaping hole in the hull appeared. Was that the flicker of a light he could see, deep inside the hull? Intrigued, he moved closer until his hand rested on the slimy wood. He peered into the darkness and the light came on again, this time shining directly into his face. He felt something touch his shoulder and whirled around in panic, to crash into the girl, who had followed him to the hull. The girl looked past Matthew and into the black hole beyond and look on her face told him she would not be going any further. He turned again to peer into the ship and the light was now dancing over his face and body. One of the instructors must have gone in, he thought. He had always wondered what life was like on an old sailing ship. If they can go in, then why can't I, he reasoned as he gingerly entered the interior.

After moving just a few feet he regretted his decision. The sunlight from the hole quickly disappeared and he felt his leg scrape against something solid. But the light beckoned him in like a snake charmer. It seemed to be guiding him, illuminating the area in front of him so he could see and it grew ever larger, whilst on both sides the darkness closed in like a cloak. A sense of unease came upon him as he stared into the darkness. He had no choice but to make for the instructor who would guide him out. He was a bloody fool and should have known better. It was fortunate his manager could not see him. £45million of investment, lost inside a shipwreck, forty feet under the sea. The press would have a field day if this got out. He must remember to have a word with the girl, to stop her getting any ideas of making some easy money. He was shaken out of his daydream by the sight of the instructor, beckoning him with a large flash light. "Must be from another boat." Matthew couldn't remember any of his instructors having long hair, but his relief was overwhelming. The instructor shone the light toward the opening, throwing the immediate area into darkness. As he turned around and started to move away, a slight tightening in his chest was the first sign he had not taken a breath. He sucked on the mouthpiece but nothing happened and he noticed a stream of bubbles erupt out of the corner of his eye and spun around. At that moment he felt a tug on his leg and looking down watched in terror as the instructor looped the end of a length of rope around his ankle. His terror was compounded by seeing the source of the bubbles was the severed end of the pipe leading from his air tank to the mouthpiece. He turned and pushed hard, trying to reach the figure but was pulled up sharply after a few feet by the rope. He thrashed around, trying to remove the tether, but the more he pulled, the tighter it dug into his leg. He began to feel light headed and realised he was drowning. Reaching for the spare regulator which every set carried, he saw that too had been severed, the pipe spewing life giving bubbles into his face.

The urge to breath became overwhelming and as he sucked at the mouthpiece, his lungs filled with seawater. His eyes began to bulge as he fought to somehow find the severed pipe, but it was too short to reach his mouth. Slowly his thrashing stopped and he sank slowly to the floor. The diver, who had retreated into the darkness, waited a few more minutes before approaching the body. Pausing only to slip a small card into the pocket of the soccer star's jacket, before swimming through another hole in the ship's side.

It was half an hour later that the dive master lifted Matthew's body over the side of the boat. He then leant over the stern again to help aboard the grief stricken girl who had first alerted him to the problem. Bloody tourists, always thinking they were immortal. It was then that he noticed the severed airline.

Parliament Square, London, August 2009

Andrew looked up at the statue of Winston Churchill as he drove around Parliament Square. He crossed the Thames on Westminster Bridge and turned right along the southern embankment, as he always liked to see the Houses of Parliament from across the river. After all it was the institutions that this great building represented that he had spent the last ten years protecting. As he crossed back to the northern bank over Lambeth Bridge he could see his destination, Thames House, Headquarters of MI5. Its twin rust-coloured roofs stood atop a seven storey, stone building separated by a large arched entrance, its true purpose dissolved within a dozen other similar government buildings close by. He drove around to the rear of the building in Thorney Street, watched from on high by several discreetly placed security cameras. As he approached the entrance to the underground car park, a camera read his number plate and decided in an instant that this vehicle had a reason for being there. Andrew fed his ID card into a slot and the gate cranked into life.

A few minutes, and three more security checks later, he sat outside the office of his head of section. The smell of the oak panelled walls and furniture reminded Andrew of being in the principal's study at King's College, Oxford. He had been one of very few boys to be accepted from outside the normal private school elite. Smiling, he recalled the first time MI5 had approached him about joining the service. It was all very English, an invitation for tea at the Ritz in London under the guise of a *'job in the city'*. They, of course, had meant the City of Westminster, within whose boundaries he now sat. It was the last thing he could have imagined himself doing and looking back, he probably joined as much because he was flattered to be asked than any great desire to serve his country.

He had spent two years training, which included spells in each of the main branches that make up MI5. Its function, unlike its cousin MI6 that covers overseas intelligence gathering, is security matters relating to attacks on British organisations. Since its inception in 1909 its job had changed somewhat and now included counter terrorism, subversion, organised crime, curbing illegal immigration, benefit fraud and extremists groups ranging from animals rights to Neo Nazis. Andrew had spent six months in each of section A (surveillance, bugging and break-ins), B (personnel), C (protective security- vetting civil servants etc.), F (internal surveillance of radical groups including the IRA) and K (counter terrorism against hostile agents). He had spent the next two years permanently assigned to C section and had been on the point of resigning when, out of the blue, he was offered a vacant position in K2. This involved liaison with friendly powers to obtain information about those believed to be planning actions against the state. For the last six years he had leapfrogged around the globe, usually spending at least six months of each year abroad. He often wondered how he and Nancy had found time to make little Charlotte.

"Mr Neild will see you now." Andrew came back to reality as the door to the inner office was opened by the secretary. This office shared the decor of its neighbour, but seemed lighter due to the windows that lined one wall. Standing, looking out over the Thames was the head of K2, Anthony Neild.

"Sit down Larkin," he said, without turning. Andrew perched himself on the edge of the chair. "Bad show. You've put us under the spotlight you know." Andrew nodded glumly "I've used up every favour I've spent the last year gathering, to get us out from under this."

"I know sir; I don't know what to say. I just couldn't stand the thought of the smug little bastard walking out scot free," said Andrew, beginning to rise. Neild's look caused him to rethink and he sank back into the leather chair.

"That's as maybe, but using a false special branch identity card to trick your way into a police station, lying as to your intentions, and using a gun taken from a batch intercepted en-route to Ireland is really too much." Andrew could see his superior beginning to get into his stride, and he didn't like the way things were going. "I assume you must have called in a few favours yourself to get that lot?" said Neild in a questioning tone that left little doubt he wanted names.

"I'm sorry sir, but I don't think it would be in anyone's interest. If it gets out that K2 informs on its friends then every door will get slammed in our faces."

"My God, man," exploded Neild. Oh dear, thought Andrew and pushed himself further back into the chair. "You have no idea what this department has done for you," continued his superior. "Several very important people wanted you charged with attempted murder, illegal possession of a firearm, impersonating a police officer, and anything else they could throw in. The prime minister himself got to hear about it and spoke with the director. Names!" For the next ten minutes Andrew told the head of K2 what he wanted to know.

"Thank you, Mr Larkin," he said as he finished writing. "Now, as for your future." Andrew went cold. The thought of trying to find a civilian job filled him with dread. Several people he knew who had left had ended up as security advisors to banks and city firms, a fate he had promised himself would never befall him. "I can't see that you can stay here," reasoned Neild as he began to pace the room. "There's sure to be an internal enquiry ordered by the commons security committee once our friends in special branch and MI6 have finished whispering in every ear they can find." He paused, considering what he had just said, then turned on one foot. "Frankly you would act as a magnet and I just can't afford it. With all the budget cuts, it's just the excuse they need upstairs." He finished, looking down at Andrew from what seemed a great height.

"What do you have in mind?" said Andrew, finally plucking up the courage to speak.

"What I have in mind, as you put it, is A3," replied Neild finally sitting down at his desk. He placed a buff folder in front of Andrew and raised his head as a command for him to read it. As Andrew opened the file, Neild swung around on the chair to once again face the river.

A3 was part of the surveillance branch of the service, and specialised in electronic eavesdropping to gather information on suspect individuals and organisations.

"But why Menworth Hall?" asked Andrew.

"It's quiet, out of the way, and a long way from London."

He was to report to the head of A3, Ken Greaves, for a short term posting to Menworth Hall a secret listening post near Harrogate, Yorkshire. This was home to the UK arm of Project 415, the collaboration between

America, Britain and several other of the world's leading democracies, which enabled them, through a world-wide network of electronic listening posts, to monitor and study virtually every piece of information transmitted through cable or airwaves. Andrew had heard that the facility, run by the American National Security Agency, had installed the most powerful computers on the planet to enable them to search the billions of telephone, radio and computer signals for key words that could provide valuable information in the fight against terrorism and international crime.

When he finally looked up from the folder, Neild had risen from his desk to signal the end of the meeting.

"Stay there for a few weeks and let things die down, then you can take up a more permanent post at GCHQ. Your experience in liaising with our American cousins will be invaluable to Ken," he said, his voice far less threatening. "He agrees with me that you should take a few days off before heading on up there." Andrew stood with his hand on the door knob. " Oh, and as you seem so keen to play at being a copper, you'll be happy to know that part of your job will be liaising with special branch and NCIS on any internal matters that arise," said Neild in what passed for a comical tone.

Andrew spent the next week at his parent's house in Dawlish, taking Charlotte with him. The house was on the south Devon coast just outside Exeter and they spent many hours together wandering on the long, sandy beaches. They were lucky and managed to enjoy some rare English summer sunshine which Charlotte made the most of, paddling in the sea and building sand castles hour after hour. But Andrew was happy to see her smile again and he enjoyed the feel of the wind driven spray in his face. Looking out to sea he saw Nancy's face and for the first time she was smiling back at him.

"Terrible thing, don't know what the world's coming to," said Andrew's father Ted. The silver-haired old man was sitting in a rocking chair in the stone floored, pine clad kitchen of their cottage, reading a copy of the local free sheet. *Church Slaying, Police Clueless* barked the headline.

"What's that dad?" said Andrew sleepily as he raised his head from behind the sofa on which he had been laying.

"Didn't you hear about it, son? It's in all the nationals. Local vicar, got himself murdered by some madman outside the church," said his father in disgust. "Blood all over the door. Only just up the road. What next?"

"How long ago was that?" asked Andrew, drawing up a chair to the old pine table.

"Sometime earlier in the year I think, let me see." His father paused as he scanned the article. "Yes here it is," he continued. "February 4th, almost six months and not a sign of them catching the bugger." Andrew took the paper from his father and spreading it flat on the table, read the front page story.

"Terrible," he sighed, folding the newspaper and tossing it onto the table.

"Too many of these people are getting away with murder," said his father, unaware of the dual meaning of his words. Their eyes met and Andrew looked down. When he raised them his father was looking straight at him.

"Fancy a drink?" Andrew laughed

"Sounds like a good idea to me, mum can look after Charlotte."

The six weeks Andrew spent at RAF Menworth Hill passed slowly. He seldom left the sprawling 560 acre site hidden among the mists of the Yorkshire Moors. Despite its name, the air force base was run almost entirely by the American National Security Agency, so he had plenty of time to eat pizza and watch the ice hockey beamed directly via satellite. Through his contacts, Andrew kept himself informed of the efforts of his MI5 superiors to limit the damaging effects of his actions. Only one story, leaked it was assumed by MI6, found its way into the press. Luckily there had been enough other, more popular news items around, which together with a well-placed call to a couple of friendly editors had been enough to push it off the front pages. He twice made the four-hour drive to visit Charlotte, staying on each occasion for two days before retreating from the withering disdain of his daughter's grandmother. Charlotte had started at a local school and appeared to be settling well into her new life. Andrew could also detect a change in his mother-in-law's attitude, having become used to having the little girl around the house. Like many retired people, she had lost her sense of purpose, which looking after her daughter's child had begun to restore. The only good thing that came from his hermit-like-existence was the punishing fitness regime he pursued. The site had a well-equipped gym, sauna and pool and Andrew combined all of these with a five mile run inside the heavily guarded perimeter fence. He was surprised at the size of the many radar 'randoms' that were scattered like giant golf balls on a huge putting green. On one such early evening run he saw several banner waving protestors shouting at him 200 yards beyond the fence. Within minutes they were rounded up and dispatched by the security personnel. Andrew knew that this site was one of the most important outside the US for gathering and analysing data before routing it back to Fort Meade, the NSA headquarters in Virginia and the normal British tolerance for protesters held little weight with the gung-ho Americans. One day, as he was climbing out of the water having completed over fifty lengths of the Olympic-length pool, he noticed a stern looking marine marching purposefully in his direction.

"Are you Andrew Larkin, sir?" said the marine, standing to attention.

"Yes, marine, I am," replied Andrew, smiling to himself as he noticed that a large water drop had landed on the young soldier's mirror like boots.

"Message for you from your commanding officer, sir." Andrew made no attempt to correct the military error. He opened the correspondence whilst standing on a set of scales in the changing rooms, noting that he had lost over sixteen pounds in the last few weeks. It was from Ken Greaves, head of A3 and written in his usual direct style.

Flak died down. Report David Scott, Executive Liaison Group, GCHQ. Contact direct for specifics

GCHQ, Cheltenham, September 2009

Andrew arrived an hour early at the main gate of the government communications headquarters. After spending several minutes waiting in a reception area while his pass was checked, he drove slowly past the rows of huts that ringed the barbed wire topped perimeter fence, to the seven storey main administration block. Spending some time in Cheltenham was going to have its advantages, he thought, as he parked his car and walked toward the entrance. His in-laws were less than an hour away and his own parents house in Dawlish could be reached in ninety minutes, if the traffic on the M5 wasn't too bad.

The ten acre facility was situated on the outskirts of the Gloucestershire spa town, which was around two hours and ninety miles west of London, and fifty miles south of Birmingham. Despite the top secret nature of its work, the site was clearly visible from the ring road that carried commuter traffic to and from the M5 motorway. The quaint town is surrounded on all side by hills, making it a place for asthma sufferers to avoid. Apart from the spa its only claim to fame is the fact that, outside London's Metropolitan force, its police are the most heavily armed in the country. Andrew glanced up at the array of dishes and aerials that seemed to cling to every point on the roof of the building. As he turned the corner and approached the entrance, he could see five huge satellite dishes, each at least thirty feet in diameter.

The receptionist was expecting him; in fact had he taken longer than eight minutes to reach that point, a security alert would have been initiated to locate him. Although the atmosphere at GCHQ, the UK's main intelligence gathering site, appeared typically English, nothing was left to chance. A smiling face greeted him as the lift arrived on the eighth floor and the doors parted.

"This way please, Mr Larkin."

He was lead down a series of corridors and through several swing doors, each opening only after a security code was correctly entered into a keypad.

"We haven't got your clearance through yet sir, so I'll be looking after you until it arrives." What he actually meant, Andrew knew, was that he would be followed everywhere, even to the toilet. This was standard procedure for all high security facilities, so Andrew felt no slight. Finally they arrived at the liaison office that was to be Andrew's home for the foreseeable future.

"This will be your office, Mr Larkin," said the man, opening the door to the small room. Apart from a government-issue desk, chair and filing cabinet, the room was empty. The walls were painted in exactly the same shade of beige as every other facility he had visited. He envied whoever had the contract to supply the paint. Andrew placed his briefcase on the desk and looked out of the window. The office overlooked a row of single storey buildings, and beyond the perimeter fence he could see the stream of commuter cars filing along the main road.

"Andrew Larkin?" asked a voice in a slight West Country accent and Andrew turned to face the new entrant. He was a tall man in his early forties, with a full head of dark, wavy hair. His face had a friendly, down to earth look, and Andrew felt himself warm to him immediately. This was no Oxbridge twit he thought.

"Yes," replied Andrew.

"David Scott, I'm head of this executive liaison group," said the local man, thrusting his hand at Andrew. "Ken Greaves rang me a couple of days ago to bring me up to speed." Andrew detected a brief look of distrust in the GCHQ man's eyes.

"Look David," said Andrew, sitting himself on the edge of the desk. "I'm sure you know all about what happened to me, but whatever you might think, I know how to do a professional job, and that's what I intend to do." Scott moved toward Andrew and placed an arm on his shoulder.

"That sounds fine by me," he said, as if wiping some slate clean in his mind. "Let's introduce you to the others."

A few minutes later Andrew sat round a small conference table, with David Scott standing at its head and three others around him.

"OK, let's begin," said Scott brightly. "As you know, we have delayed this monthly meeting of the executive liaison group to enable our two new members to attend." He glanced at Andrew and a young, fresh faced man who sat opposite him. "I'll start by introducing everyone. My name is David Scott, and I am the section head of echelon group B that covers internal intercepts. My job is to collect the data, decode and translate if necessary, and then pass it on to you chaps to decide what action to take." His accent and cheery disposition seemed at odds with the words he spoke. "On my left is Andrew Larkin from MI5, then Charles Smyth from six, Bill Frost, special branch, and our other new recruit Paul Williams from NCIS. Andrew looked at each in turn and decided he did not like the MI6 man. Aloof looking and obviously Oxbridge, he conveyed an effortless air of superiority. Bill Frost, the world weary special branch man looked OK, at least he had attempted a smile. The young recruit opposite him was, Andrew guessed, younger than himself. He seemed a little nervous and had appreciated the smile Andrew had given him.

A phone ringing brought Andrew back from his daydream. Scott listened for a moment.

"OK, that's great," he said and replaced the receiver. "Andrew, your clearance has come through from London. If you see my secretary after the meeting, she will sort you out with a computer, passwords and all that, OK?"

Andrew nodded and Scott turned his attention back to the group.

"Because we have two new members I think it's worthwhile to take you through the full background to our little home from home." Smyth raised his eyes skywards and sighed.

"Is that really necessary, old chap?" He said in a typically aristocratic tone. "I'm sure these two already know everything they need for the limited scope of their departments." Andrew saw through and ignored the put down, but the young NCIS man was not so reticent.

"Listen *old boy,*" the words came slowly and with emphasis. "The National Criminal Intelligence Service provides a much needed resource to all UK based law enforcement. We don't spend *our* time swanning around the world looking for things to cock up."

"Gentlemen, gentlemen," interrupted Scott, "we're all on the same side. Charles, show a little patience will you, it's a while since we went through this. You never know you might pick up something new."

Scott raised his hand and an aerial image of the site filled one wall of the room. "The Government Communications Headquarters or GCHQ," announced the section head, "is situated in the beautiful town of Cheltenham, Gloucestershire." Charles sank back into his chair and closed his eyes. "It opened in 1972, and now with more than 4,000 staff, we have grown into the hub of the country's intelligence gathering capability. 256 people work directly for intel and therefore report to me." He began to walk around the room as the images showed various parts of the complex. "Here we see one of the many satellite dishes located on site, most are relaying data from sources around the globe. Here is one of the many specialist language units that have more than 200 staff covering various geographical areas such as the former Soviet bloc, South America and so on." He arrived behind Andrew. "Block E6 covers UK and western Europe and I suggest Andrew and Paul pay them a visit." Scott sat down in the vacant seat next to Andrew. "So what do we do with all the taxpayers' hard earned cash?" Smyth opened one eye, seemingly aware that Scott was looking directly at him as he spoke. The special branch man seemed content enough listening to the story again, or perhaps he was asleep with his eyes open, thought Andrew.

"The echelon system was developed in 1985 by our cousins at the NSA in Fort Meade," continued Scott. "It was a natural progression of the UK USA agreement set up in 1948 to enhance the interception capabilities developed during the war, and at first was targeted mainly against the Russians. But as the technology advanced, the cold war ended and new threats appeared in other parts of the globe. The need to expand the scope and efficiency became apparent." The image of a masked terrorist appeared on the screen.

"I know him," said Bill Frost. "He was part of the group that bombed the guardsman in Hyde Park."

"Thank you Bill," said Scott, a slight note of irritation in his voice. "We, together with the American NSA, the Canadian CSE, New Zealand GCSB and Aussie DSD make up the five nations Signals Intelligence Agreement or SIA."

The image changed to a map of the world, highlighting the various facilities.

"Each country has established powerful listening posts that give us the ability to intercept and share the majority of communications traffic generated anywhere on the planet." Scott rose and walked again to the head of the table. "Each nation looks after its own stations, apart that is from the Americans. They effectively run RAF Menworth Hill in Yorkshire, although we do have a few people there." He glanced in Andrew's direction. "These systems intercept literally billions of messages every day. The beauty of echelon is that it enables each country to specify exactly what it needs from the system as a whole. An interception from say the Waihopai station in New Zealand is run through the on-site system and if appropriate is fed, untouched by the Kiwis, to us."

The meeting broke for lunch which Andrew, Paul and Bill Frost took in the staff canteen. Smyth disappeared which was a relief as Paul was still fuming over the slur.

"That Smyth is a real idiot," he said as they queued at the self-service counter.

"Don't let him get to you lad," said the special branch man. "Like most of the MI6 lot, he thinks we're here just to act as servants to them. Since the wall came down they don't know what to do, so they end up trying to muscle in on our patch."

Andrew took a plate and went to help himself to a large helping of lasagne but stopped short. Better stay on the salad, he thought. They paid for their meals and sat together at a corner table.

"How long have you been with MI5?" said Frost.

"Since university. You?"

"Thirty years in the Met, with five in special branch. Only three to go until I get my pension so I'm happy with this cushy number. Nothing much happens here and if it does then I just push it down the line to the boys at Scotland Yard."

Wonderful, thought Andrew, no wonder Neild wanted me here.

"I'm looking forward to working with you two," said Paul. "I've only been with the NCIS for a year. Joined the foreign office from Leicester University but realised I had no chance against the Oxbridge crew, so decided to try my hand at something a bit different."

"But why here?" queried Andrew.

"Well, I want to move onto the centralised computer system we operate. I'd like to think I could help make it the best in the world."

"A noble ideal," interrupted the special branch man. "They'll soon wear you down, my boy."

"Take no notice of that old cynic," said Andrew, smiling at Frost. "We all need to have something to aim for." As the words came out Andrew wondered what he would aim for now.

"Is that the time?" asked Paul. "We should be getting back. We've got a tour of the computer facility and then I want to spend some time with the directory operators."

"Who, or what are they?" asked Andrew as they stood and made their way out of the dining area.

"They interrogate the raw data received from the various echelon stations, and decide what is worth passing on for further investigation."

The computer systems located at GCHQ are amongst the most powerful in the world. The amount of data they are called upon to receive, process and store is greater in a single day than all the UK banks put together in a year. The small group, minus the absent MI6 operative, stared into the climate controlled rooms, at banks of what seemed to Andrew to be large metal cabinets filled with hundreds of blinking lights; he had seen much the same thing at Menworth. Their guide was a senior computer technician.

"Without this massive parallel processing capability, we simply couldn't handle the ten petabytes of data we receive every hour." Most of this went over Andrew's head, all he knew was that it enabled MI5 to receive valuable intelligence in their fight against crime and terrorism. The party spent another ten minutes talking computers, with Paul asking nonstop questions until the technician had to call a halt, as their security clearance was not high enough.

"I'd like to see the op's room where the directory operators call up the screened information," enthused the young man.

The room was more like a crazy amusement arcade. Andrew guessed there were more than a hundred terminals, each with an operator hunched over the screen. In the centre a large, multi-sided bank of screens hung from the ceiling, each displaying information on the types and content of information received. Lights flashed and beepers beeped. As the group entered, a green light above a terminal began blinking and a supervisor immediately joined the young operator as they began an intense conversation.

"They must have found an important message," said Paul. After a few moments, the supervisor broke off and joined them.

"Sorry about that, we've been waiting for that e-mail for the last week."

"Anything interesting?" asked Frost.

"You should know better than to ask that Bill," smiled the man. "Let's just say that a certain group of West Africans will have a little surprise the next time they try to draw social security payments." He moved towards a terminal, followed excitedly by Paul and the rest of the visitors.

"This is where we see the actual messages picked up by the various tracking stations. They are fed directly to us, and processed by the mainframe. Each operator here deals with a specific directory code." Andrew looked puzzled.

"What's that?" he asked. "Forgive me; I'm so used to all this jargon, I sometimes forget not everyone knows what I'm on about." He pointed at a row of four digit codes on the screen.

"Under ECHELON, a particular station's dictionary computer contains not only its parent agency's chosen keywords, but also has lists entered in for other agencies. In New Zealand's satellite interception station at Waihopai, for example, the computer has separate search lists for each of the four other members in addition to its own. Whenever the dictionary encounters a message containing one of the agency's keywords, it automatically picks it and sends it directly to the headquarters of the agency concerned."

"Do they get to see the message?" asked Andrew.

"No one sees the intelligence collected by that station for foreign agencies," replied the supervisor.

"Each of the five station's dictionary computers has a codename to distinguish it from others in the network," he continued. "The Yakima station in the States has the COWBOY dictionary, while the Waihopai station is called FLINTLOCK. These codenames are recorded at the beginning of every intercepted message, before it is transmitted around the network, allowing us to recognise at which station the interception occurred. We are connected via highly encrypted communications that link back to computer databases in the five agency headquarters. This is where all the intercepted messages selected by the dictionaries end up." He keyed a four digit number into the screen. "Each morning we log on and enter the dictionary system. After entering the correct security passwords, we reach a directory that lists the different categories of intercept available in the data bases, each with a four-digit code. For instance, 1911 might be Japanese diplomatic cables from Latin America, handled by the Canadian CSE, 3848 might be political communications from and about Nigeria, like the one we just saw." The group moved closer to the screen.

"We select the appropriate subject category, get a *search result* showing how many messages have been caught in the ECHELON net on that subject, and then the day's work begins. Our people scroll through screen after screen of intercepted faxes, e-mail messages, etcetera and whenever a message worth reporting appears, they select it from the rest to work on. If it is not in English, then it's translated and reworked into the standard format of intelligence reports produced anywhere within the network."

"So we don't get to see our intercepts that relate to, say, Canada?" said Paul.

"That's right," said the man, moving back to his desk, in the centre of the room. "Only the Americans get to see everything."

Andrew's' attention was beginning to wane, he was not a techie by nature. He was only interested in the end result. He looked around at the many faces, young and old, that filled the room. His gaze stopped at a site he had not expected, an attractive woman, standing over a terminal at the far end of the room. Her face had been hidden by her long hair, as she studied the screen over an operator's shoulder. But as Andrew had casually glanced around the room, she seemed to sense his presence, and turned to face him. She smiled, and then slowly returned to her duties.

"OK, Andrew?" said Frost. "I thought you weren't that interested in all this techno stuff?" He took Andrew's arm and gently guided him towards the exit and he followed meekly. Just as they reached the door, he regained his senses.

"You two go on, I'll catch up in a few minutes. "He walked around the room until he could see the girl without her noticing him. Andrew realised that he was drawn to her and the thought made him feel a little guilty. She looked around and their eyes met for a moment. She smiled at him again, this time for a little longer, before turning back. "Damn," Andrew cursed under his breath. He felt himself redden and quickly left the room. He slept fitfully that night, the girl had woken the demons he thought had been beaten and they returned to haunt him with a vengeance.

It was another week before he saw her again, this time queuing for lunch in the canteen. Andrew sat with a group he knew were from the directory.

"Hi," he said in his friendly voice. He was met by silence for a few seconds as the group strained to recall the stranger who had sat at their table interrupting their meal, and the discussion on last night's football match. "Sorry," said Andrew. "I'm from the five liaison group. I noticed some of you when I visited the directory the other day."

"Oh," said one, a slight man in his mid-twenties. The awkward silence returned and Andrew suddenly realised that his presence might cause some anxiety. Any top security establishment is, by its nature, a place of suspicion and mistrust.

"Look, I'm sorry to interrupt your lunch, it's nothing official. I just wanted to know the name of that lady in the queue over there." Andrew nodded his head in the direction of the girl.

"Any particular reason," said the man.

"No, no it's not like that," said Andrew, understanding the question. "It's just that, well, I was just curious, that's all."

"Mary Ward, IT development and support section," said the man, staring down at his food.

"Thanks," said Andrew, rising from his seat.

"But you'll be lucky to get anywhere with her," said another knowingly. "We call her the ice maiden."

Andrew retreated to a table at the opposite side of the canteen where Bill Frost and Paul Williams were in deep conversation, the younger man trying to convince the cynical Frost of the need for even more computers in the intelligence community. They continued their debate as Andrew sat down and watched the girl pay for her meal and sit alone at a table not far from his. After a minute, she lifted her head and looked directly at Andrew. He shifted his gaze, pretending to study the wall behind her head. When he glanced down again, she made a show of looking over her shoulder as if trying to see what had interested him so much. Andrew could not help but laugh. She smiled at him and he felt his stomach turn a quick somersault and his face redden.

"What do *you* think, Andrew?" Paul's voice broke the spell and she quickly averted her eyes.

"What's that Paul?" asked Andrew vaguely.

"That we need all the computer power we can get to help in the fight against organised crime."

"Yes, yes I agree." he answered.

Lower Harpton, Shropshire, September 2009

It had been two days since a customer had bought anything from the antique shop, nestled in the small hamlet of Lower Harpton in rural Shropshire. Since the new centre had opened a few miles away in Kington, business had been slack. It was a different type of shop than the old man was used to, having been in the trade for over sixty years including five as an apprentice French polisher to his father. Rather than buying all the stock, they simply allowed dealers to rent space and take a percentage of the sale price. He wondered how much longer he could carry on like this as he wearily rose from his desk and shuffled towards the rear of the old building. No good just sitting in there staring at the door, he decided. The workshop ended a series of rooms in the single storey area at the rear of the seventeenth century cottage that made up the shop, accommodation being on the first floor. Added on over many years they contained an Aladdin's cave of pieces, now mainly from the house clearances of the elderly from the surrounding area. This rural area on the border between England and Wales was, like many other parts of the principality, undergoing drastic changes. No longer able to hide away from the modern world, its tentacles had begun to reach further away from the coast. There was talk of a new housing estate just a few miles down the road, made possible by the upgrade of the A44 perhaps that would bring in some extra business? Just before he reached the workshop he paused at an alcove. Beneath a pile of chairs and other modern furniture that he really should burn, he spied the old storage trunk. He had looked at it many times over the last few months since it had arrived as part of a clearance from an old lady's house in Kington. It was old by any classification, probably dating back as far as the sixteenth century if it was genuine and certainly worth restoring if he had the time. Well time was something he had plenty of at the moment. It took him the rest of the day to remove the nest of carpet, boxes and other paraphernalia of the house clearance of a 95-year-old widow. Transferring all but a few small pieces to the concrete area at the rear, he lit a fire and left the relics of a life to burn. That was the problem with a house clearance; you had to take the rubbish in the hope of finding a rare jewel. He carefully dragged the trunk into the workshop, clearing a space on the floor amongst the other pieces he was working on and stepped back to assess where to begin. The rectangular shaped trunk measured three foot long by two deep and just under three foot tall. It was made of the oak traditional during the Tudor period which had turned almost black over the centuries, each side having an inlay containing carved figures of the period. The flat lid conformed to the same design and construction as the rest of the box. A large iron clasp was set in the centre enabling the trunk to be fastened to the main body with a padlock, which had long since disappeared. The old man lifted the lid to peer inside. This trunk was clearly the property of someone with money. The entire internal area was covered in what was probably velvet, red in colour, faded and missing in many areas yet it still spoke clearly of its past life. The old man immediately knew this was probably the property of a lady as there were several pockets stitched to the inside walls, no doubt for the storage of small personal items such as brushes, combs and such like. The small carvings on the outside depicted pious religious scenes, unlikely for a man who would have chosen battle and hunting scenes. As if to answer any lingering doubts he saw, attached to the inside of one of the pockets, a hair clasp. It was undoubtedly Tudor and quite possibly the property of the original owner and the sight made him glad he had decided to free the trunk from the pile where it had lain. It had probably sat in the old woman's attic since she was given it by her grandmother or such like. So many of the most important finds have been passed down the generations and lain gathering dust for centuries. He knew just the person who would be interested in a piece of Tudor furniture such as this. He smiled to himself for the first time that day as he switched off the workshop light and left to prepare his evening meal.

The old man rose earlier than he had of late and after a quick breakfast found himself eagerly negotiating the labyrinth of alcoves and rooms strewn with forty years of items collected from every corner of the country, that lead to the workshop. As he gazed at the trunk, sitting in the middle of the floor, he wondered what stories it would tell. There were centuries of Britain's history locked away in the wooden fibres, although he doubted that there would be much of interest in the last hundred years or so, much of that probably spent in one attic or another. He now had to decide how much restoration work to carry out and this would depend on who was likely to purchase it. As a piece of history it would be sacrilege to alter any of the original fittings or renovate the interior coverings. The iron clasp was rusted and pitted, any coating long since worn away. The hinges, three in total, holding the lid to the main body stretched nearly a third of the way across the lid, each having a small fleur-des-lis at either end. They were in a similar state and would require removal and treatment. He was interrupted by the sound of his telephone ringing in the shop and as he hurried back he reminded himself to get an extension fitted in the workshop. How many times had he said that? Whoever had called must have known that it would take the old man several minutes to answer as the handset was still ringing when he finally reached it.

"Hello," he answered, a little out of breath.

"Reginald, are you ok?"

"Yes, just a little out of breath that's all."

"You should get an extension fitted in that workshop you know, save you a lot of time."

"Good idea, but it's about the only exercise I get these days," he resisted any hint of sarcasm in his reply.

"I guess you're calling about the Tudor storage trunk. Are you interested? It's a very fine piece, almost certainly genuine."

"All right Reg, you can drop the sales pitch. Look I'm sure it's as good as you say, but there's not much of a market at the moment for this type of thing. You would probably have more success renovating it and putting it in that new centre. Some young couple might buy it to store the children's toys." The conversation continued for another five minutes in which time the two old acquaintances lamented times past and agreed it would never be the same again. They parted with the promise to get together soon, both knowing it unlikely, especially given the 200 miles that separated them. On the walk back to the workshop the old man reluctantly decided that he would restore the trunk. He needed the money and taking it to the centre might not be such a bad idea. It would present a good chance to see how the process would work and he might even pick up some restoration work too.

Over the next few weeks, Andrew settled into his new role and the Gloucestershire town. He took a six month lease on a small two bedroom terraced house in Leckhampton, a short walk from the town centre. He moved all his belongings from the house in London which he rented as he could not contemplate selling what had been the family home at the moment. He was able to see Charlotte on a more regular basis, being under an hour's drive from his in-laws' house. He suggested that she might like to come and stay with daddy at his new house, but it was obvious that she was still too traumatised to travel. He even began to get along a little better with his mother-in-law, or was that wishful thinking on his part? His role as MI5 liaison was every bit as tedious as he had imagined, but he consoled himself that it would not last forever, or so he fervently hoped.

The weekly review meetings were designed for the various liaison team members to meet and receive a full briefing from Scott. These involved updates of existing investigations and information on any new intercepts, followed by a discussion on how these might affect each of the services represented. The idea for the group was to allow information to be shared across the various departments and for cross co-operation, to ensure the combined resources of the UK security machine was being directed where it was most needed. Despite a common goal, internal politics and simple misunderstandings had led to numerous cases in the past where a snippet of information available to one, had not been shared, sometimes with catastrophic results. Only during the subsequent enquiry had it emerged that the jigsaw piece was vital and would have completed a picture of what was planned. Many analysts believe that the terrible attacks on the Twin Towers could have been avoided if all the scraps of intelligence held by the various US. agencies had been available in a single resource. During the last twenty five years the emphasis had changed from Cold War espionage, through the troubles in Ireland and since the fateful day in New York, the war on terror. The incredible advances in communications technology such as the internet, mobile devices, social networking and others, had increased the amount of electronic traffic tenfold year-on-year, since the turn of the century. In private, officials admitted that they simply could not keep up with the data that was being transmitted and were turning to internet providers and other commercial organisations to help store the vast amounts of information that now existed. GCHQ was also being asked to provide an ever increasing amount of support in the fight against organised criminal activity and the cutting edge world of cybercrime. During this time the criminals and terrorists had also become more sophisticated and better able to disguise their activities from the watching eyes of the security services. In an effort to keep them tied down and as busy as possible, many individuals, organisations and even supposedly friendly nations threw a constant bombardment of cyber and hacking attacks on the state and commercial computer infrastructure in the hope of either destroying vital data, or obtaining information for commercial gain or military advantage. All of these activities were dealt with by different departments within GCHQ and David Scott's job was to squeeze thousands of hours of work into a thirty minute presentation. It was a task which strained even his naturally optimistic nature to the limit on occasions. However, on this particular Tuesday morning he did not have anything to report that was likely to lead any of his audience to feel the rule 'of law or the democratic institutions that made up the UK state were likely to come crashing down around their ears.

"There is currently ongoing monitoring of twelve extremist web sites and 315 individuals who have repeatedly expressed views that are determined to be a potential threat to our national security. These are regarded as low level at present as regards the potential to carry out any physical action. In addition there are sixteen individuals, associated with four separate groups, who have shown that they are planning some form of action. Only one, *The Divine Retribution of Allah*, who we have spoken about in the past, have moved up a notch in their planning."

Scott then led a ten minute conversation in which Andrew and Bob Frost from special branch decided on a short action plan to ensure MI5 and the police fully co-ordinated in any overt operations.

"We have four teams on constant surveillance of the two main players," said Andrew "If we need to move in then my people will contact your anti-terrorist team at SO13 for operational support."

"Ok, that's fine," said Frost, typing an email on his laptop as he spoke.

"Now on to the more mundane stuff, I'm afraid," sighed Scott. "Over the last three months, we have noticed a ten percent rise in the number of concerted attacks on the UK banking system originating from China."

"Nothing new there," chipped in Smyth from MI6.

"Indeed," agreed Scott. "But in the past we have been able to disrupt a far greater number. They are beginning to switch proxy servers at a much faster rate." Scott was describing the widely used method by which an individual or group can use a third party location to disguise the true origin of the computer that is sending a message or attempting to hack into another site, thus making detection and counter measures more difficult.

"We suspect the Chinese have acquired the latest chipset from their industrial espionage targeted at the Americans. It will have enabled them to increase their processing power fivefold and the evidence seems to support that's exactly what's happened," said the MI6 man, finally showing some interest in the proceedings. The meeting ended after an hour and a half and Andrew headed back to the small cloakroom that passed for his office. He spent the next thirty minutes compiling his own weekly report that summarised the overall threat levels in the various segments for which MI5 were responsible, together with changes to any specific projects that were currently active. He typed a paragraph on Scott's update of the Islamic group's activities and pressed the key to send the encrypted message to Ken Greaves, Head of A3 at Thames House. He was just deciding whether to make the effort of going through all the security checks to exit and re-enter the site for a shopping trip during his lunch, when Scott's head appeared in the doorway. He sat down on the corner of the desk and placed a sheet in front of the MI5 man. Andrew looked up a minute later.

"When was this sent?" Scott had stood up in the correct anticipation of Larkin doing the same and as the two walked briskly down the corridor towards the directory department, he filled him in with the details.

"The call originated in Southern Afghanistan at 05:30 GMT and was picked up by the Avios Nikolaos station in Cyprus."

"That's five hours ago," said Andrew, looking at his watch.

"We received the directory file first thing this morning and picked up the keyword that we were expecting as soon as the operator studied the file. I'm sorry Andrew, our workload has increased by fifty percent in the last two years and I have two fewer staff." Scott was reacting to the exasperated look Larkin had given when he realised how long it had been since *The Divine Retribution of Allah's* commander had given the coded signal for the group to begin the final phase of a plot to contaminate the water supply of a large English city. The two hurriedly entered the area through its double doors and almost ran straight into the girl who had captivated Andrew so much on his first visit.

"Sorry Mary," said Scott as they hurried past the startled woman.

"I was just coming to see you," replied the IT specialist, talking to her GCHQ colleague but looking straight at Andrew as the pair turned and returned to where she stood. Mary pointed towards a nearby office and understanding her meaning, the three entered and closed the door. She took three sheets from the brown folder she carried under her arm and passed it to Scott. "I pulled these less than five minutes ago." Scott studied the time the emails had been sent and noted it had been less than ten minutes.

"These are follow-up messages giving detailed instructions for the two separate cells to meet up," he said.

"How did we pick it up so quickly?" said Andrew, taking the sheets from Scott and scanning the content. Mary explained how she had heard about the original intercept and run a special application she had written to search quickly through data from a particular, targeted source. "That's still in test phase and not authorised for live use." Mary looked both embarrassed and irritated at the same time, but ignored the comment

"The app performed a live scan on all data to a range of IP addresses we know that group had been using to connect at this end. I then linked that live stream into the directory and just waited."

Overcoming his bureaucratic instincts, Scott was obviously impressed at what had been achieved.

"That's very impressive Mary. How did you manage to overcome the normal stack limits?"

Andrew listened to the pair converse in a language far removed from anything he had heard before interjecting.

"Ok, guys, I appreciate this is some kind of first and you want to discuss the finer points, but now is not the time." The two apologised for their lapse and Mary excused herself to resume her vigil. Andrew found Bill Frost in the canteen and after a brief discussion the pair headed to his office as it was nearer. Frost terminated the call and lowered the cell phone from his ear.

"Ok, that was Jack Scott, duty commander at SO13. They're mobilising two teams now and aim to be in position at least three hours before the rendezvous time. Can you arrange a team from Birmingham CTU to cover the house in Lincoln and mop up once we have taken them out?"

"Sure," replied Andrew. "What about the other safe house in Manchester?" "I'll arrange for a team from the Manchester CTU to cover that, they have a good firearms squad that can handle it and anyway it's only a precaution in case they leave someone behind. Hopefully SO13 can lasso the whole cell at once." Andrew rushed back to his own office where he was able to contact Ken Greaves on his encrypted cell phone.

"Ok, run the basics past me again." Larkin reminded his superior that the terrorists aim was to enter a major water distribution facility just outside Cambridge that supplies almost a half million people in the east of England. Various intercepts over the previous three months had described how they intended to introduce some chemical contaminate into one of the systems.

"It was unclear until half an hour ago, whether that contaminate was designed to cause disruption or worse," said Andrew. He went on to explain the content and meaning of the delayed phone intercept and how Mary had somehow managed to get an almost live capture of the subsequent e-mails.

"How did she manage to decipher the code?" asked Greaves.

"That had been done before," answered Larkin "It was a simple cross reference to pages, lines and words in the Koran. The clever part came when she realised that there is no chemical terms in that holy book, so programmed the system to look for a range of English terms. That's how we know they intend to kill thousands of people."

"Given your understanding of this Larkin, I think you should get yourself down there to make sure the plods don't mess up. We can't afford to get this wrong or all hell will break lose. We've been predicting this sort of thing for years but the water industry has resisted spending the money to bring their sites up to CNI standard."

Andrew understood his superior's reference to the Critical National Infrastructure project by which transport, food, utilities and other areas, that if targeted could cause severe disruption to the UK's ability to function, were regulated to provide enhanced security measures to important and vulnerable sites.

"I want an hourly update from wherever you are," said Greaves before abruptly terminating the call.

Two days later the trunk had been stripped down to its component parts. The ironwork had been removed and was now sitting in a bath of paraffin oil to remove the worst of the accumulated grime. The lid lay to one side, a slight change of colour in one area evidence of the test that had been carried out to determine how much work would be required to bring the woodwork to an acceptable condition for its new role. Even now the old man was saddened to destroy so much history, but shrugged and turned his attention back to the lining having decided to remove everything and refurbish the box with new material. He did not intend to throw away the original, although he guessed it would end up in a bag somewhere behind him. It took around an hour to carefully detach the material from the wooden case without doing too much damage. He did notice one particular area of cloth had been finished a little differently where extra material had been added to form an overlapping flap. It had clearly been deliberately worked and he would certainly have missed it if he was not as close. As the last piece was finally lifted out he nodded to himself in satisfaction.

"Still got the old touch." He peered at the now exposed inside of the trunk, noting there were vertical supports, each around two inches wide, on the four sides. Apart from a good clean there wasn't much he would need to do here as it would all be covered by the new lining. He made himself a cup of tea and sat down on a small three legged stool to rest, bending over the trunk had caused his back to ache. As he sat thinking of nothing in particular, his eyes came to rest on a tiny discoloured area next to one of the supports. Probably a piece of woodchip blown in and caught in the gap. The more he looked the bigger it grew until eventually he rose, put down the cup, and knelt down to pick off the chip. But as he grew nearer he realised it was no wood chip. Whatever it was seemed to be part of something larger. He found a small bridle from amongst his tools that would enable him to more easily get some purchase as it was securely wedged behind the strut. His curiosity now raised, he decided to remove the obstacle preventing full disclosure of the hidden contents. It would do no more harm than he already inflicted. He then had an idea. Whatever it was could not be that thick, the gap between the wood and the outer skin being small, it must have been slid behind. As he rose his eyes caught the discarded lining and he remembered the little extra flap of material so grabbed the bundle and attempted to reconstruct the basic shape. It was not easy as the cloth was reluctant to co-operate, but he was happy the flap could have been in a similar spot. He carefully slid the flat edge of a set square behind the opposite side of the strut. It appeared on the other side without any additions, but the item had moved, exposing half an inch. Parchment! It was paper. He tried again with the square, but became concerned that he might damage what could be a very old piece. The material was obviously not modern in construction so it was likely to have been placed there some time ago. He decided the paper was worth more than the box, so reached for a small fret saw. He carefully removed a four inch section above and below the parchment, determined to cause minimal damage to the outer skin. Finally the saw broke through on the second cut and the parchment fell to the base of the trunk.

The old man retrieved the now freed article and clearing a space with his free arm, placed it on the bench. He turned on the large overhead lamp and adjusted the spring-loaded arm to flood the area with light, then immediately switched it off, remembering how strong light was harmful to aged manuscripts. He managed to find a weaker twenty watt bulb which he screwed into the lamp. The yellowed parchment had been folded several times, presumably to enable it to be secreted behind the wood. Even in the weak light he could see the shadows of what looked like handwriting on the inner folds. There was a bulge in one corner that he thought might be a seal, although it had been flattened to a fraction of its original bulk. But there were no pieces missing from the edges which suggested, if it was as old as it looked, that it had not been handled extensively. He gingerly took two sides and started to gently prise them apart but suddenly stopped, worried at what damage he might cause in his haste. He spent the next hour on the telephone, seeking advice from a trusted colleague he had known for many years who was an expert in working with old manuscripts and told him what he needed to know about how to safely reveal the contents of the hidden note.

Andrew looked at his watch. He had nine hours before the terrorist cells were due to meet at an address in the outskirts of Cambridge. He awoke his computer and entered the two towns into Google maps. It told him it would take at least three hours to drive depending if he chose the A40, M40 or A14

routes it had calculated. He could call for a helicopter to take him to the nearest airfield, but he calculated by the time he made the necessary calls and fought through the red tape of justifying the expense to some desk jockey at Thames House, he would be half way there. After a quick conversation with Bill Frost, he was able to secure the services of one of the Gloucestershire constabulary's best traffic response team cars to make the journey in record time. As they approached the control headquarters that had been hastily set up in a hanger in at RAF Wynton, some fifteen miles outside Cambridge, Andrew received a call from GCHQ

"Hello Andrew, It's Mary Ward." Larkin felt his chest tighten at the mention of her name. "Are you there?" she queried when she received no reply.

"Yes, sorry," he blurted.

"David Scott suggested I call you myself, I hope you don't mind?"

"What do you have?" Andrew replied, guessing she had some updated information.

"They are just relaying this through to the other units now, but we intercepted a call between the two groups asking for a twenty four hour delay. Seems they are short of one of the ingredients."

"Let's hope they are all as incompetent," said Andrew with a laugh.

"You have a nice laugh mister MI5 liaison officer," she said in a tone that took him by surprise, but before he could answer the line went dead. The car had arrived at the gates of the airbase and he was roused from his daydream by an RAF security policeman tapping on his window for identification. Ten minutes later he was drinking coffee in the officer's mess together with a half a dozen police and security officers when a familiar sounding voice echoed up the hallway, followed by five foot eleven of muscle and bone topped with a shock of ginger hair and freckled covered face.

"I don't like this delay," said Jack Scott, head of the Metropolitan police SO13 anti–terrorist armed response teams.

"There's not a lot we can do about it," replied Andrew, "It's too late to relocate the teams to Lincoln and Manchester, and the sites are both in residential areas."

A decision was taken to billet everyone at the airbase overnight as it was secure, had the facilities to instantly provide food and beds to twenty six men and was away from prying eyes. All Andrew had with him was his laptop bag, although he was expecting to change out of his suit into a more appropriate outfit for the planned mission. He spent the next two hours updating Greaves and discussing the new timetable with Bill Frost who had remained in Cheltenham and sat in on the SO13 briefing. Scott was half way through a set of slides showing the site, when his earpiece sprang into life.

At almost the same moment Larkin's cell phone rang. He could tell by the expression on Scott's face that something significant had happened and so he was not surprised to hear Frost's voice carry an urgent tone.

"Andy, they're on the move."

"What?" Scott was already briefing his team, who were gathering their equipment as he spoke.

"Seems like someone popped down to the local hardware store for the chemicals they were missing and now it's all back on schedule." Andrew ran down the corridor and quickly donned the remainder of the black outfit that would enable him to blend in with rest of the team. He had no intention of going anywhere near enough to get in harm's way, but it helped to prevent any 'green on green' incidents in the commotion that often surrounds such missions. He updated Greaves, followed by the team leader at the house in Lincoln. They had maintained surveillance and informed him that two cell members had left just a few moments before. He left his room just in time to see the last SO13 officer disappear out of the main entrance and had to run as fast as he could to avoid being left behind, his police taxi having long since returned home. During the twenty minute drive to the rendezvous point Andrew could hear, via the communications set he had been given, a constant update on the position of the two vehicles in which the terrorists were travelling towards Cambridge. The journey from Manchester would take around three and a half hours, ninety minutes longer than those from Lincoln who had left some thirty minutes after their more northerly brothers and would therefore arrive around an hour earlier at the present rate. Andrew's vehicle discharged its armed officers and carried on, with the MI5 man still on board, to a pre-arranged holding position some two miles away. The vehicle was equipped as a mobile command centre complete with a bank of TV monitors showing live feeds from personal helmet mounted cameras, hand held units and with the option of linking to a new breed of low cost drones capable of giving a bird's eye view of events from more than 5,000 feet. The drone was at present being prepared for take-off at the base they had left a half hour before and would not be on station for at least a further forty minutes. An unfamiliar voice came over Andrew's earphone.

"Echo one-five, Lincoln vehicle has left the A1 at Stamford, repeat..." Andrew listened intently as the officer in a car trailing the terrorist's vehicle, a blue Ford van, described its directions. This was totally unexpected and had caught everyone by surprise. He heard Scott ordering the vehicle to maintain a safe distance behind and take extra care not to become compromised in the lighter traffic. "Target proceeding through the town..... Turning onto the A6121 heading north." Where on earth were they going? To collect another member or perhaps pick up chemicals from a safe house?

"Echo one-…stand down everyone." There seemed to be an unnatural silence "Targets are just ordering cheeseburger and fries at the drive through." A mixed chatter of relief, laughter and annoyance could be heard over the airwaves.

"I thought they didn't eat meat?" A voice behind Larkin asked.

"Pork, its pork Muslims don't eat." The group ate their meals in the car park of the fast food restaurant and were back on the A1 within twenty minutes.

"That accounts for the early start," Andrew heard Scott say. The immediate panic over, the two teams settled into their final positions.

The site they had chosen was an abandoned factory unit on a rundown industrial estate in Great Stukley, half a mile from the A14, five from the water facility, and almost exactly at the spot where the two routes from Manchester and Lincoln converged. Larkin sat in the back of the command vehicle, the two operators his only company, following the sights and sounds coming from the various SO13 sections. When the two terrorist vehicles were each around ten minutes away, the surveillance drone finally arrived above the site and began relaying live pictures from a height of 3,000 feet. Its advanced propulsion system and small size, coupled with high definition cameras, allowed it to capture a headline on a newspaper in complete darkness. More importantly it allowed those on the ground to ensure, what could be crucial decisions, were made with every piece of information available. The drone was being controlled from the unit's base in Harlow, Essex, some forty miles to the south. Andrew watched as the two cameras, one thermal, scanned the surrounding areas for any, as yet, unseen threats. The team spotted a heat source in some undergrowth two hundred yards from the edge of the estate and dispatched three armed response officers to investigate. This turned out to be two teenagers hiding in some bushes and drinking a bottle of cheap cider.

"Targets converging on yellow zone," came the urgent tone as the operator next to Andrew studied the overall view provided by the drone and signalled that both vehicles were within the one mile radius. Scott came on the line ordering the two pursuit teams to fall back and take up station to provide cover on the two most obvious escape routes should any of the terrorists succeed in evading the net set by the units surrounding the immediate area. The monitors in the control vehicle showed the last minute manoeuvring as individuals took up their final positions. Only he and Scott knew that the final instructions from operational command had just been issued.

"No one to escape," said the commander. "Under any circumstances. You are authorised to use deadly force where necessary, but we need the leader for intel'." There was only one road in and out of the estate, running east to west. Within its confines were around two dozen warehouse and office units, reached by four separate feeder routes that led directly to a small number grouped around a central point. Unit sixteen was at the end of a block of three with one side connected to its neighbour and the other around twenty yards from the chain-linked perimeter fence, beyond which lay open fields. The opposite units were around the same distance and all had a brick frontage and metal clad sloping roof. One half of the facade contained a large roller shutter door which revealed a large area beyond for storage or workshops, the other a single entrance door behind which lay ground and first floor offices, a layout similar to thousands of others across the country. There were over thirty weapons pointed at the building, but not one was visible to anyone approaching. Every other unit was empty and officers were positioned in several of the closest, covering every angle and possible exit route in a vehicle or on foot. They had not attempted to enter the terrorist's destination for fear of disturbing evidence or worse still triggering a booby trap, but knew it was devoid of any accomplices through infra-red mapping carried out earlier using the team's own portable equipment.

"Manchester group have entered red zone, all teams move to full alert," was followed almost immediately by the same confirmation that the second part of the duo had also entered the estate. Andrew had been following the aerial view and could clearly see both vehicles, one a van, the other a family saloon. The car drew to a halt at the end of the access road whilst the van drove past the unit, swung around and continued back to where his partner waited and both vehicles paused for what seemed like an eternity. They were not communicating by cell phone as every channel was being monitored. What they could not monitor was the leader sweeping the area with a pair of infra-red binoculars, seeking out any activity in the darkness, or the military grade communications set scanning for any sign of encrypted signals. Scott had predicted the possible use of both and had ensured every person was shielded by a solid object and all communications had been silenced since the targets had entered the red zone. The next time he spoke all hell would rein down on the five men who waited cautiously not fifty feet from where the commanding officer lay. Eventually the car moved off and stopped outside the unit, dropping off a passenger who warily entered through the single door. He emerged two minutes later, waved for his colleagues to join him and disappeared back inside only to show his face again moments later peering under the rising roller shutter door as its motor pushed it noisily into the ceiling above. The van slowly entered the vacant entrance followed by the car with its two remaining occupants. The moment the second vehicle crossed the threshold Scott gave the order,

"GO GO GO!" He wanted the vehicles trapped in the unit, unable to make a quick escape and everyone inside. The first incline that things were no longer proceeding to the terrorist's plan were several stun grenades simultaneously dropped through the roof skylights and windows on the ground and first floors. The thermal imaging unit on the drone gave five strong signatures all standing in or around the van, but Scott's men were following a well-planned routine to ensure all eventualities were covered. Stun grenades, as their name suggests, are designed to temporarily disorient an enemy's senses by producing a blinding flash and deafening noise. The flash activates all the light sensitive cells in the eye making vision impossible, whilst the blast causes temporary loss of hearing and impaired balance. Seconds after the five men clutched their ears and began stumbling around, five SO13 men crashed through the plastic sections of the roof and abseiled to the floor. The same signal sent another three through the open roller shutter and four hurtling through the front door, two of which quickly climbed the stairs to the offices above. The terrorist leader and one of his accomplices were the first to recover some of their senses and make a dash for the door. One was quickly taken down whilst the other seemed to suddenly gain mystical powers of good fortune. As he stumbled towards the door an officer intercepted him but slipped on a small puddle of oil and fell over the top of him. The man, sensing his chance, clubbed the officer in the face with his fist, driving his protective goggles into his face. He fell back, cried out and instinctively raised his hands to his face. In an instant the Islamist yanked the Heckler and Kosch MP7 machine pistol from the man, snapping the strap that held it around his body. He could make out a sea of shouting bodies through the mist of haze and ringing and lifted the pistol. He knew that his men were among the throng but satisfied himself they would be hailed as martyrs in dying for the cause. The MP7 normally holds twenty rounds, but this version was fitted with an extended magazine holding fifty 4.7mm bullets, each capable of penetrating light body armour. He pulled the trigger and waved the gun in an arc as he indiscriminately fired a short burst. In three seconds twenty projectiles had been discharged, eight of which found a human target. Five of the rounds struck the same man who was standing only three feet away and took the full force of the impact, one skimmed off the side of an officer's helmet, another struck a terrorist in the arm and the last left a neat hole in the forehead of an SO13 man, killing him instantly. The remaining twelve bullets were all fired above head height as the terrorist leader lost his balance and tumbled to the floor. Any thoughts about repeating the feat was abruptly ended by a bullet entering his skull, fired by Scott after he rushed through the open door to witness the carnage. The SO13 commander stood over the body with his gun arm outstretched and abruptly fired again.

"Get those suspects out of here and secure the perimeter." He said, surveying the scene

He was finally ready, his friend having eventually put his mind at rest. In his view, if the parchment had been kept untouched in a dark, moist place there was no reason to worry unduly as it was, after all, animal skin. The first fold was the worst as he was convinced the whole piece would simply disintegrate, but he was determined to read the contents even though it was probably something mundane. It took him five more agonising minutes to fully unfold the document and reveal what appeared to be a letter.

Ego operor ignoro quantus diutius ego can gero futurus seorsum vobis. Illa permaneo duos mensis videor magis amo duos annus. Tamen nunc nostrum bastard ero prognatus. femina fui ordinatus pro infantia ut exsisto donatus ut a locus paganus agricola nomen Moore quod suus uxor. They es infantia minor quod fui optatus a infantia of suus pro plures annus. They dico mihi nostrum parvulus ero puteus tutela pro. Ego teneo is est solus via is forsit exsisto solved , pro si is erant umquam notus ut ego have latus an heir tunc a civilis bellum would nam insisto. Ut Regina ego loco populus pro myself tamen ut a mulier ego operor ignoro quis ego vadum operor ut meus infantia est captus. Ego precor ut ego mos animadverto vos iterum nunc quod ut vos mos usquequaque exsisto illic ut tribuo mihi vires ego vadum postulo proveho.

Commodo adepto vox ut mihi ut vos es puteus.

The date and place were clearly marked on the top in English and the disfigured and flattened seal on the reverse lower edge looked vaguely familiar, but the body of the text was in Latin. He had studied the language as a schoolboy, but although able to understand odd words, the meaning and context eluded him. Had he owned a computer and an internet connection, he could have availed himself of the modern solution but as he had neither he spent the next hour trawling through an old text book and casting his mind back some seventy years to a time of wooden desks and stern masters. The task was made more difficult due to the style of script used and the faded ink. Eventually he sat back and read the contents as a whole. By the time he reached the bottom his hands were shaking. He checked his translation a dozen times before he convinced himself he fully understood its content and meaning. The signature was familiar to any young boy with an interest in history.

Andrew stood in the entrance and tried to take in the enormity of what he saw. The ceiling of the unit was almost completely destroyed with several chords stretching from floor to ceiling. The smell of gunfire still pervaded the scene, mixing with blood and chemicals and a thin veil of smoke still hung in the air like an early morning mist. One officer, still looking both relieved and shocked, was showing a comrade the bullet mark on his helmet. In the thirty minutes since the firing had stopped the two vehicles had been searched and several chemical containers removed by a forensics team that had been waiting a few miles away. There were no firearms found in either, but the van did contain enough plastic explosives to cause a decent sized blast. There was nothing of any interest in the offices and it seemed obvious they had only intended to use the warehouse as a final stopover and kitchen for their deadly concoction. Andrew stepped aside to allow a stretcher, containing the body of the wounded terrorist, to pass on its way to an ambulance. From where he stood, three further bodies could be seen covered in army issue khaki sheets and laying in various positions. Pools of blood were escaping from the side of all three with one having considerably more.

"That's the leader," said Scott, appearing at Andrew's side and pointing at the nearest body. "He fired blindly and didn't care who he hit, friend or foe," he continued, motioning to the second bloodier sheet. "Put at least three or four into one of his own people." He walked further into the warehouse and crouched next to the sheet covering his fallen comrade, gently placing his hand on top for a second. When he rose, Larkin could see the weight of leadership etched on his face.

"Two children under five," he called out continuing his tour of the scene, "and all because of half a cup of oil," the bitterness in his voice evidence of the pain he felt at losing a man. For Andrew, the pain was seeing Nancy's face again, but as before she was smiling and he was quickly able to catch his breath. He turned and walked back to join a group of senior officers who were grouped around a vehicle.

"We'll have an initial de-brief back at the air base in an hour Mr Larkin, if that's acceptable to five?" said one, using the shorthand for the service.

"Fine with me, as long as I can thumb a lift." As he walked towards a waiting police vehicle, his cell phone rang. It was Ken Greaves.

"I've heard the basics, anything to add?" said his superior in his familiar, curt fashion.

"I'm on my way to a de-brief now, but I don't expect anything new to emerge, just the why, not the how." Andrew copied the short, terse tone.

"Just make sure if there's any mud that none of it sticks to us." The line went dead before he had a chance to formulate a reply. The senior officers gathered in the mess room at the base some thirty minutes later. As Andrew had predicted, he learnt nothing new. The plan had worked like clockwork until the ill-timed slip, the weapon literally falling into the leader's arms who fired without thought. Despite the loss of three lives, Scott believed the situation could have been worse as most of the bullets had missed due to the slip on the same oil that had presented the terrorist with the weapon in the first place. The whole area had been immediately sealed and a complete press blackout imposed which, so far, appeared to be holding. The forensics team had not yet tested the containers but if the labels matched then it was clear they were in the process of creating a toxic mixture that would have caused sickness and possible death in hundreds of thousands of consumers across Cambridge and the surrounding areas. The two safe houses in Manchester and Lincoln had been raided, each revealing numerous maps of the area and documentation proving their target and intent. Andrew, who had made several calls since talking to Greaves, reiterated the need for the news blackout and thanked everyone for preventing what could have been a major terrorist incident with a casualty rate larger than anything that had gone before. The meeting broke up at 1.30am and Andrew decided to grab whatever sleep he was likely to get that night, in his room at the base.

Andrew spent the next day at Thames House in a series of meetings. As far as MI5 were concerned the mission had been a total success, their resources having succeeded in identifying the plot and its perpetrators, then neutralising the threat with no public loss of life or harmful publicity leaks. To them, the loss of a police officer was regrettable, but a small price to pay for saving thousands. It had been agreed that the incident would be reported with minimal details and heralding the officer as having died a hero. It was also seen as a success for the executive liaison group at GCHQ.

"Who's the woman who pieced together the full picture from all the intercepts?" asked Anthony Neild, the head of K2 who was seated at the conference table at the head of which stood Andrew, a large monitor behind him showing images of the scene.

"Her name is Mary Ward and she works as an IT development and support specialist."

"Perhaps we should get her transferred to Thames House, we could do with some smart people around here," suggested Neild looking over his glasses at Ken Greaves, head of A3, seated opposite, who made a note and turned to face the screen. The meeting lasted another thirty minutes in which Andrew described the events at GCHQ earlier in the day and later at the industrial unit.

"How did you get from GCHQ so quickly?" asked Greaves suspiciously.

"I poached a lift from a squad car, why?" answered Larkin innocently, knowing that Greaves was trying to catch him commandeering a helicopter." "That must have been an interesting journey," said Neild rising from his seat. "Good job Larkin," he said as he left the room. "Seems like posting you down there was a good move after all. Full report on my desk tomorrow please."

By the time he had finished the meetings and typing the report, it was 5.30pm so he decided to stay over in London and catch a train back to Cheltenham the following morning. He arranged to stay at the Marriot, just across the river at County Hall where the service had a guarantee of a dozen rooms at all times. The hotel was within easy walking distance and it was a pleasant, if brisk, evening as Andrew walked down the front steps of the main entrance. He took the opportunity a gap in the traffic presented to scurry across the zebra crossing and turning left walked across the entrance to Lambeth Bridge. He was then able to stroll through Victoria Tower Gardens with views across the river on his right and the imposing tower of the Palace of Westminster directly in front. He emerged onto the street again almost at the foot of the tower and joined the crowds of commuters and tourists filing between the iron railings of the original walls and the modern vehicle protection barriers, an unfortunate yet necessary mix of old and new. Passing the imposing Lady Chapel of Westminster Abbey on his right, he emerged into Parliament Square, turned sharp right on the corner of Bridge Street and headed for Westminster Bridge. As if on cue Big Ben, the name of the bell in the famous tower, struck the quarter hour. Andrew joined a thousand pairs of eyes in looking up at the giant faces of the clock, some 300 feet above for he, like most Londoners, never tired of seeing and hearing the distinctive sound whenever he passed. A cold wind struck him as he lost the shelter of the building that housed the mother of all parliaments and headed over the river span. He crossed the wide expanse of road most famous for being the original finishing line for the London Marathon and looked up to see the facade of the County Hall. It had once been home to the Greater London Council, but had now been transformed into a site containing two hotels, an aquarium, fast food outlets and the ticket office for the adjacent London Eye. Andrew's room was, thankfully, in the more expensive Marriot as opposed to its budget competitor. He stood on the balcony gazing across the river at the boats leaving

Westminster Pier for the evening dinner cruises. He had decided to dine in the hotel restaurant and after showering and changing into the casual clothes provided by the hotel from a stock especially selected by Thames House, he took the three flights of stairs down to the ground floor and wandered into the bar area.

"Hello, look who's here," said a voice Andrew recognised but could not see through the crowded bar. "Over here Andrew!" A hand rose above the sea of bodies and he headed blindly for the beacon.

"Hello Tim," he recognised his fellow graduate entrant at once and offered no resistance to the giant hand that pumped his. "Long time no see. What brings you back to HQ, I thought you had been banished somewhere awful?"

"Tact was never one of your strong points was it?" said Andrew pushing his way past the six foot six inch Old Etonian to the bar.

"Let me," said the taller man magically gaining the attention of the barman. Andrew chose a lager and was about to suggest they find a seat when Tim turned to ask for the order of two striking young ladies who had been obscured by his larger than life frame. Tim could see the surprise on Andrew's face.

"I'm sorry old chap, let me introduce you to two very good friends of mine. Lucy and Sandra."

"Hi ladies," said Andrew limply, beginning to wish he had chosen room service. The foursome managed to fight their way from the bar and were fortunate to emerge from the crowd just as a couple were vacating a table. The girls almost fell into the chairs and Andrew could sense that both had already consumed several drinks by their lack of balance and unnerving ability to find anything amusing. Tim winked at Andrew as he took his seat between the girls.

"These two lovely ladies have recently started working for us Andrew," he said. The two looked at Andrew and back to Tim for confirmation that the newcomer was one of them. "Don't worry girls; Mr Larkin is with the service, so you can tell him your most intimate secrets."

With that, all three burst out laughing. An hour later Andrew had worked his way through three more lagers and a ghastly concoction called a *Jägerbomb* where a shot glass of the cocktail was dropped into his beer glass and he was forced to drink both in one go, noisily egged on by Tim and the two girls. When Andrew announced his need to relieve himself, Tim offered to accompany him.

"Guess you're staying in a decent room, old chap?" he asked when they were both standing, looking at the wall.

"If you mean did I get a river facing executive, then yesh," replied Andrew swaying slightly.

"With a balcony." Tim's eyes lit up as endless possibilities filled his thoughts. "Excellent, excellent. I'm sure the girls would love to see the beautiful view and share a bottle of champagne." A few minutes later Andrew opened the door to his room and entered unsteadily, followed by Tim and the two girls who by this time could barely walk. He was not certain why he had invited them all to share the view from his balcony and even less convinced he wanted the evening to progress in the same way as his male colleague. The girls seemed very impressed with the room, its view and the contents of the minibar. Andrew had not eaten and drunk far more than he was used to. He was aware that he was drunk and decided to stop drinking, despite protests and jibes from his fellow guests who were having no such inhibitions. It did not take them long to empty the mini-bar and order fresh supplies from room service. By 11.30pm they had given up trying to persuade Andrew to join the party and decided three was not a crowd. At midnight Andrew removed the key card from Tim's pocket and remembering his toothbrush, quietly left the room. His new bedroom was two floors below, somewhat smaller and with a view of the buildings at the rear. But it was quiet and it took Andrew less than thirty seconds to fall into a deep sleep once he had collapsed, fully clothed, on the bed.

He was dragged from his slumber six hours later by a knock on the door and it took several more for him to attain a sufficient level of consciousness to move his body the three steps to the door. When he peered through the crack he was confronted by a face that was all too recognisable.

"Let me in old chap," pleaded Tim urgently. As Andrew opened the door Tim pushed passed him dressed in a white hotel bathrobe.

"Enjoyable evening?" enquired Larkin, looking his friend up and down.

"I have no idea," replied Tim with obvious fear and anger. He paced to the window and turned "The last thing I remember was climbing into the whirlpool bath. When I awoke a few minutes ago I was lying naked in a tub of freezing cold water."

"The girls?" asked Andrew.

"Nowhere to be seen. So I climbed out to discover my soaking wet clothes in a pile in the shower and a note on the bedside table." He handed a sheet of hotel notepaper to Andrew.

Thanks for a great evening.
Sorry we couldn't stay for dessert.

Andrew burst out laughing as he tossed the paper on the bed.

"I think we may have underestimated those two young ladies. Looks like they may have a long career in the service ahead of them," he said closing the door behind him.

Andrew arranged some emergency clothes for his friend, showered and ate a quick breakfast before checking out. He crossed the river to Embankment, took the Bakerloo underground line to Paddington mainline station and caught an Intercity 125 to Cheltenham. His head was aching so he hoped the two hour journey would give him the opportunity to relax and gather his thoughts. He gazed idly out of the window of the first class carriage as the sights of the most English of areas, the Cotswolds, swept by. Green fields bordered by hedgerows and dotted with small hamlets, each with its own church and huddle of buildings, built using the distinctive beige tinted stone for which the area is so famous. Highlights of the previous forty eight hours replayed in his head like a newsreel and he tried to rationalise if anything could have been done to prevent the loss of life. It had come as a surprise that the group had not carried any firearms, but Andrew had suggested they may have considered the risk of being randomly stopped too high. A group of known radical Islamic sympathisers found with half a dozen AK 47s would mean an instant end to their plans and lengthy prison sentences. None of the group feared for their lives, in fact probably welcomed martyrdom, and the successful completion of the mission was their primary goal, not self-preservation. Most thought it likely they had access to a stash of guns and both Manchester and Lincolnshire police forces were already searching the houses for clues as to their whereabouts.

"Would you like a paper sir?" His thoughts were interrupted by a steward handing out complimentary copies of the *Daily Telegraph* which Larkin accepted. The headline *Terror Plot Foiled* jumped off the page as he unfolded the broadsheet on the table. A sub heading *Heroic Officer Killed Preventing Water Poison Horror* neatly summed up the end result of the mission and the one page article that followed, presented the story exactly as had been planned. Andrew wondered if the redtops would show the same level of restraint on their front pages. The operation had saved hundreds, if not thousands of lives and he knew that, however callous it might seem, the conclusions reached at the top of the security services were correct. He felt a pang of guilt when he realised the part played by the executive liaison group had been recognised and its profile raised for all the right reasons. Perhaps it might be the beginning of the end of his banishment from Thames House? He called ahead and arranged for Bill Frost, the special branch member of the liaison group, to collect him from the station and drive to a country pub a few miles outside the town for lunch. Over a glass of mineral water, Andrew recounted the events of that evening including the bizarre circumstances that enabled the terrorist leader to kill one of Frost's people. He was scheduled to attend a hastily convened session of the executive liaison group that afternoon, but wanted to brief Frost in advance. Larkin knew from his own experience the acute sense of loss felt when a comrade falls in the line of duty, and Frost was no different. He had not known the man personally, but that did little to affect the officer's reaction and he almost thumped the table in anger and frustration when Andrew described how the SO13 man had slipped in the oil, almost handing weapon over.

"I just can't believe something as stupid as that can lead to the loss of such a good police officer," said Frost.

"You know the family well don't you Bill," replied Andrew ordering him another scotch. "I'll drive back, don't worry," answered Andrew to the questioning look.

"He was the son of one the guys I worked with at the Met," said Frost "The youngest child is only three. Who is going to tell him his father was killed because one of his mates slipped on a patch of oil?"

Larkin was glad he had made the decision to talk to the special branch man alone. He knew that Frost would have had sight of the interim report, but that did not contain any reference to oil or sliding policeman and nor would those facts ever appear in any official document. Too many awkward questions would be asked and the enemies of the security services, of which there were many in Government, would seize on any opportunity to portray their actions as too little or too much, whichever suited their purpose. They arrived back at GCHQ a little before 2pm and Andrew spent the hour before the liaison briefing updating his report. After what seemed like only a few minutes he glanced at his watch and noticed the meeting started in ten minutes. He closed the lid of his laptop and was startled to find the face of Mary Ward behind it.

"Christ, Mary," Andrew cried, jumping back "When did you come in?"

"Sorry Andrew," she said without the showing the slightest hint that she actually had any regrets.

"I can't talk at the moment as I have a meeting at three," he said, rising from his desk and gathering the laptop. "But I should be free later if you want to pop by."

"It was nothing urgent," she said, following him out of the cramped office. "I gather the powers that be appreciated our hard work?"

"Indeed they did. In fact they asked me to recruit you for five!"

"Not my scene I'm afraid," said Mary thoughtfully "I like my job here but thanks for the offer."

"What exactly is your job?" enquired Andrew, seizing the opportunity to find out more about this intriguing woman.

"Oh a little bit of this and that," she replied evasively. "That's the reason I came to see you, to say goodbye." They had reached the door to the meeting room and Andrew stopped and turned to face her. "I have to visit one of our remote stations to update some software and I'll be gone for a few days."

Andrew caught the eye of David Scott through the glass and nodded. He turned to wish Mary a good journey as he pushed open the door. When he turned to say goodbye she was gone. Strange, he thought. No wonder they call her the ice maiden.

County records office, Lincoln August 2009

"Excuse me sir, but I'm afraid you are going to have leave, Its 6.20pm. We closed twenty minutes ago and my wife will be expecting me for dinner."

Professor Thomas Lambert looked up from the manuscript he had been studying for what he thought was an hour or so.

"Goodness, is that the time?" It had in fact been eight hours since he had begun studying the documents at the Lincolnshire County records office. "Sorry about that," he continued as he hastily gathered his belongings, dropping his notebook on the floor as he vainly tried to juggle several items at once. "I'll be back tomorrow to continue if that's ok?" He had taken a few steps towards the door when the assistant called him back and he turned to see the young man holding his reading glasses, which he had left on the table in his hasty exit. After spending five minutes sorting out his belongings on the steps of the building, he decided to take the long route back to his hotel and grab a pint at *The Green Dragon* on the river. It was a glorious summer evening with clear skies and little prospect of rain, an unusual occurrence in this green and pleasant land. The thought of spending at least part of it in the open air had a strong appeal, particularly given the amount of time he had spent hibernating in one dusty room or another over the last few days. It took him five minutes to reach the pub, perched on the banks of the river Witham. He had visited the hostelry a few times over the years as it was just a short stroll from the records office where he had spent many hours poring over the hundreds of documents stored there, stretching back to medieval times. These included land purchases, taxation and court records all of which gave him a rich source of information not available online or at the National Archives in Kew on the outskirts of London. He balanced his pint of *Bog Trotter* bitter, along with his other belongings, and managed to find a free table on the grassy bank, overlooking the river. As he settled himself and opened his notebook he glanced up to see a group of four rowers glide by and disappear under a small bridge. He walked the dozen or so paces and took up a position on the narrow crossing to watch the coxless fours glide into the slipway of the local rowing club a few hundred yards downstream. Lifting the boat on their shoulders they walked single file into the small hole in the storage shed known locally as the Pumphouse. He had rowed himself during his time at Cambridge, just missing out on selection for the 1987 annual boat race team against rivals Oxford on the Thames in London. At six foot three he had both the height and muscular physique required for that sport. The shock of wavy blonde hair that the ladies used to find so attractive had darkened considerably over the intervening twenty five years or so and he was beginning to notice a few grey hairs appearing here and there. But he still managed to work out enough to ward off any signs of a spreading waistline. He turned his attention back to his notes and took a sip of the dark liquid. Drinking English bitter was an acquired taste which he had perfected, after much practice, during his university days. Poachers was a local microbrewery, one of dozens springing up around the country and heralding a revival in traditional brewing which was much appreciated by fellow members of CAMRA, the Campaign for Real Ale. It marked a small, but important, reversal in the dominance of the multinational drinks conglomerates that now controlled the vast majority of brewing capacity in the UK, leading to many smaller, less well known ales disappearing in the race for the benefits of mass production and brand marketing. As a historian he appreciated how much beer had influenced life through the centuries. For many, including women and children, it would often be drunk in place of water as it was free of the diseases that so commonly afflicted supplies, particularly in large towns and cities. He read through the notes he had made during the day, trying to make sense of the hieroglyphics that passed for his handwriting. He crossed out and rewrote several sections, expanding the text as he began to see the significance of a particular entry. By the time he had finished, he was halfway through his second pint and the light was beginning to fade as the sun dropped behind the buildings on the opposite bank. As he gathered his things and began the walk to his hotel, he slipped on his faithful Barbour jacket to ward off the slight chill that now filled the air. He decided he would eat at the hotel and get an early night as tomorrow was his last day and he wanted to finish his research and catch an early train home.

He had risen, been for a short run, showered, eaten breakfast and checked out of the hotel before 8.30am and was waiting on the steps when the doors to the archives opened promptly at 9sm. Lambert returned to the documents he had been studying the previous day and checked the details once more so he would be in no doubt the assumptions drawn from them were accurate. Spread in front of him was a set of land transactions from the local district of Aisthorpe, dated February, 1693. The particular document he had toiled so hard to locate recorded the purchase of a house in the village of Brattleby by a merchant named Richard Teller. The seller was one Joseph Jackson and the house, with two acres of land, had been sold for the sum of £103. What was important to the researcher was the fact that it proved Richard Teller had a connection to the area. Lambert had spent over three months tracking down proof that the merchant had relocated from London in the late seventeenth century and had helped to set up the fledgling brewing industry.

He had completed his work by 12.30pm and left, thanking the assistant for his help. He consulted the timetable collected from the station on his arrival and noted the next train left in twenty five minutes. Enough time to cover the distance to the station and grab a sandwich for the journey. Lambert did not own a car. In fact he did not have a licence to drive, having never found the time or inclination to learn in his late teens or early twenties. In his thirties he was often abroad on various research assignments and by his early forties had settled into life at the University of Cardiff where he had been appointed a professor at the school of history, archaeology and religion, the youngest to hold such a post. He had everything he needed within walking distance as the Welsh capital covered a relatively small area, and for anything further afield he always used the rail network, finding it efficient and effective in transporting him to his desired location. He did admit to those colleagues and students who derided him for his faith in the often criticised UK system that he seldom travelled during the rush hour and purchased all his tickets online and in advance, thus securing the best possible prices. He would also tell them never to automatically buy a return ticket, two singles often being cheaper for reasons he had long since given up trying to fathom out. He would need to take the 13:40 from Lincoln Central to Beeston, the 14:43 Cross Country to Birmingham New Street before switching to the 16:12 to Bristol Parkway and finally the First Great Western 17:41 which arrived in Cardiff Central at 18:19. He could, of course, have taken the 13:40 with just a single change at Nottingham, but both trains made so many stops along the route that it actually arrived in Cardiff twelve minutes later. Lambert hated stopping as it carried the risk of a noisy group of teenagers or worse still a single, slightly desperate woman boarding the train and disturbing his work. The fact that he could memorise the required routes in his head caused him to pause and consider for a moment if that made him a little nerdy, whatever that meant. He pushed the thought from his mind as the smell from a well-known bakery chain pervaded his senses. He could not resist a good sausage roll and these people certainly made an exceptionally tasty version of the meat and puff pastry snack so loved by the British. One of the benefits of train travel was the ability it gave him to work on the move. Even the most talented would find it impossible to achieve much behind the wheel of a car, whether it was travelling at seventy miles per hour or stationary in a traffic jam. He opened up his laptop and plugged the portable charger into the power socket provided at every table seat on the train. He had been lucky enough to find an empty space at such a seat which afforded him that luxury. The single seats rarely had such a socket which was a constant irritation as it had often forced him to abandon working before the laptop battery expired. He had only possessed one of the portable computers for a couple of years, still preferring paper and pen. He was not a technophile and still shunned carrying out any more of his research online than was strictly necessary. It was only when the college bursar had reminded him that his travel expenses were becoming unduly high, due to his numerous trips to study original documents wherever in the country they may be, that he had reluctantly accepted that much could be achieved via the electronic medium to which so much information had been transferred; both in the form of searchable text and scanned original documents. He had even been approached recently by Glamorgan County Council to oversee the digitalisation of numerous documents found in the basement of an old government building. He started the machine and stared out of the carriage window at the passing countryside whilst it carried out its virtual waking. He had learnt to wait a couple of minutes after the desktop screen appeared before attempting to open any programmes as, after logging repeated calls with the university IT helpdesk, someone had explained the concept of firewalls and virus protection applications. All he knew was that these devils slowed down the machine to the point where he had often been tempted to consign it to a ditch somewhere alongside a train track. He had not checked his emails for a couple of days as he refused to pay the extortionate fees charged by the hotel for internet access, but knew he should catch up on this form of electronic post that everyone now used. Paper was becoming a thing of the past, and as someone who spent their life studying the medium, he still found it went against the grain to communicate in this inelegant way. Logging onto the wireless internet the train provided, he dug into his wallet to find the password details for the annual pass he had purchased on the advice of a student. The wireless was only free to first class passengers and the bursar would quickly be on the war path if he ever made the mistake of indulging himself in that luxury. He had sixty eight unread messages in his inbox, which he accessed after first connecting to the university's network via what was called a VPN. Another user name and password to remember, this one written on the reverse side of the business card that held the magic letters and numbers to access the train Wi-Fi. He felt like a naughty schoolboy tapping the information into the prompt boxes, knowing the IT department would view dimly recording secure information in this way. But he simply could not remember all the various combinations of pin codes, user names and passwords required in the modern world. Recently he had been forced to add a capital letter and a punctuation mark to his work log in, during the routine bi-monthly change of details. This was a rouse he regarded as a deliberate attempt to keep him away from his files as he was always forgetting what element he had changed thus requiring a reset by IT, with yet another change. Scrolling through the list he glanced at the subject lines of each, deleting several inviting him to take up a month's free offer to one research site or another, the price paid for paying a visit sometime in the past. He was more wary than ever of giving his email details, having given up trying to unsubscribe as so many sites seemed to simply ignore the request. Several were invitations to attend or give a lecture at a conference or event, he would handle those later. Hiding amongst the electronic clutter like a letter lost under a pile of papers, was a familiar welcoming message. *London Calling*. He immediately knew it was from his old friend and former colleague John Giddens. They had been on several field trips together whilst postgraduates at Cambridge, he eventually deciding that an academic career would drive him insane. He now worked as the head of manuscripts for a leading London auction house.

Hello Tom

Hope you are well, long time no see. I tried to contact you on your mobile without success. Do you ever turn it on? Call me as soon as you can as I have something that will be of interest.

John

Lambert pulled an antiquated cell phone from his bag, ignoring the contemptuous giggle from the teenager in the seat opposite, and pressed the power button only to discover the battery was dead. He had left the charger at his flat. Another piece of technology he found little use for. He typed out a brief reply, explaining about the flat battery and promising to contact him the following day. He arrived home at 6.30pm after the twenty minute walk from Cardiff Central station. His flat was in the Roath district of the city and only a few minutes stroll to his office in the history faculty in Cathay's. Cardiff University campus is in fact in the city itself as the various departments are housed in buildings new and old scattered in and around the city centre. The surrounding streets are full of tightly packed terraced houses, many rented out to students. He liked living here, even though he was an Englishman through and through. The cosmopolitan capital had transformed itself in recent years into a thriving modern city mixing the culture of the Welsh with a first-class shopping centre and hosting numerous sporting and cultural events, not restricted to the beloved Welsh rugby union, at the magnificent Millennium Stadium sited on the banks of the River Taff. One of the few times he felt an outsider was when the English rugby team and thousands of his fellow countrymen arrived for the bi-annual Six Nations rugby match. Yet even he had to admit an admiration for the emotional way the thousands sang the national anthem *Hen Wlad Fy Nhadau* (Old Land of my Fathers) before the game. He prepared himself a quick meal of pasta and spent the evening updating his research using the information he had unearthed in Lincoln.

Lambert was at his desk in the history department by 8.30am. He had a tutorial session at eleven which would last for around two hours, and a budget meeting after lunch, aside from which his diary was free. He was preparing notes for the tutorial when the telephone on his desk rang and it took him several seconds to locate the handset under a pile of books and papers. He cradled the receiver under his chin and resumed collating the sheets he had just printed.

"Hello, hello," a voice enquired, "Is that you Tom?"

"Who else would it be answering my phone Mr Giddens," Lambert replied, instantly recognising the owner.

"I knew it would be useless waiting for you to call me."

"About what?"

Giddens, sitting in his office at Christie's auction house in King's Street in the heart of London, sighed. His old friend was one of the world's leading experts on historical manuscripts, but he could still be one of most irritating people he knew. Tom Lambert was a smart, good looking and very intelligent man, yet he seemed to find it difficult to exist in the world outside his work. He was single, rarely seeming to even notice the admiring looks he still regularly received from the opposite sex. As far as Giddens knew he had only had two relationships, both of which had ended disastrously as he simply forgot to maintain contact with the unfortunate ladies concerned. But he knew that he was the only person he could turn to with the information he had.

"Tom, I emailed you a couple of days ago, remember?" The professor's silence suggested he had not. "Never mind. Look I've been contacted by an old friend who owns a rundown antiques shop up in Shropshire. He also does a bit of restoration on the side.

"Ah ha," said Lambert showing an interest that surprised Giddens. In fact he was looking for a particular reference book he needed and his eyes, searching the bookshelves that lined the walls had fallen on the required volume. Giddens continued.

"I got a call from him about a week ago about something that could be a real find if it turns out to be genuine." Silence. "Tom, he says he has found a letter from Queen Elizabeth to Robert Dudley concerning the imminent birth of their child."

"It's a fake, John," said Lambert. "If I had a pound for every time someone had unearthed some evidence about the queen having had a secret baby, I could travel first class everywhere."

Lambert was an expert on the medieval period and had written several pieces on the various rumours and theories surrounding the often repeated myth that Queen Elizabeth I had conceived a child. Many named Robert Dudley, the Earl of Leicester, the queen's close confidante and some say lover, as the father. Elizabeth, whose mother was Anne Boleyn, had taken the throne at age twenty five in 1559 after the death of her half-sister Mary, the daughter of Catherine of Aragon. The early years of her reign were a turbulent time in English history with factions from both Catholic and Protestant faiths plotting to either replace her on the throne with her Catholic cousin Mary Queen of Scots, or cement the reformation begun by her father, Henry VIII. The Spanish and French, both staunchly supportive of the supremacy of papal rule from Rome, stood poised to take advantage of any opportunity to fuel the flames of rebellion and reap the rewards of an armed occupation of the rich island that stood alone, divided from the continent by the twenty one miles of the English Channel that had for centuries before, as it would many times again throughout the following five hundred years, provide the only barrier to the invasion of the sceptred isle. Elizabeth and her trusted advisors, most notably Francis Wallsingham and William Cecil, knew that any marriage had to be carefully arranged for fear of giving the appearance of support to Rome or Canterbury. One may give the reason for an invasion, the other a civil war. The queen had therefore spurned numerous suitors that had been presented to her throughout her fifty-year-reign including, most notably the Prince of Anjou. Elizabeth remained single until her death from blood poisoning in 1603, childless and without an heir. Her devotion to her country and the selfless decision to put duty before personal happiness earned her the nickname of the 'Virgin Queen', although no evidence exists to prove that she remained celibate through all of her seventy years. Since her death there had been a constant stream of rumours down the ages that she had produced an heir out of wedlock.

"I can understand how you feel, but the old man is adamant that it's worth getting it authenticated."

"Oh come on John, I can't believe that you would fall for an old trick like that," joked Lambert "If the guy is in the trade, he probably has a production line of relics. Does he have any saintly bones, or perhaps the arrowhead that killed Harold?"

Lambert began to doodle on his tutorial notes in an absent minded fashion. "Tom, I have a feeling about this. Please take a look, as a favour to me," Giddens pleaded. After a pause Lambert relented.

"Ok, get it sent over and I'll give it the once over." There was a silence on the line.

"He won't move the letter, Tom. Says it's too delicate and may get damaged."

"If you think I have the time to travel the length and breadth of the country on a wild goose chase then you..."

"Tom," interrupted the auctioneer. "He lives just outside Ludlow. You can be there and back in a few hours and I'll pay your expenses."

GCHQ, November 2009

A week later the storm kicked up by the terrorist operation had died down. The story given to the press became the official version and as Andrew had suspected, there was no mention of any lubricants in its one hundred and ten pages. Things were fairly quiet around GCHQ and with nothing pressing on the horizon he decided to take a few days holiday and drive Charlotte down to visit his parents in Devon. He collected her early one morning, arriving at Nancy's parents' house shortly before 8am. His daughter was just finishing her breakfast when he entered the kitchen and for the first time he could recall, smiled when she saw him.

"Hello daddy," she said confidently "Grandma says we are going to see Granny and Grandpa Larkin at the seaside."

"Well she's absolutely right sweetheart," replied daddy. "She seems a lot happier recently," said Andrew to his mother-in-law as he closed the car door after strapping Charlotte into her seat.

"Slowly, but yes we have seen an improvement," replied Dorothy." I think starting her at the local school has helped her confidence." Andrew was both relieved and happy to see his daughter settled and beginning to adapt to her new life. He also shared the same emotions for his mother-in-law. Both gave him peace of mind and the chance to concentrate on doing whatever it took to get back to Thames House. The drive to his parent's house in south Devon took him back to Cheltenham where he picked up the M5 motorway, which he followed all the way to Exeter, a distance of some 130 miles. He left the motorway at junction thirty and followed the A347 south, hugging the estuary of the river Exmouth. His parent's house was a mile outside the town of Dawlish and within walking distance of the beach, although to reach it required crossing the famous stretch of railway line where waves regularly crash against passing trains. Charlotte slept through most of the journey which Andrew had to admit was a blessing. He loved his little girl more than life itself but he was not used to the ways of a five year old who could be more demanding than an MI5 head of department and as threatening as any terrorist. They arrived just in time for lunch, which Andrew's father Ted insisted they take at the local gastro pub just a short stroll towards the town. "How are things with you, son?" asked his father as they strolled along the beach after their meal. Charlotte was happily casting stones into the surf with Andrew's mother in close attention, both obviously enjoying the simple pleasure.

"Much better thanks Dad," he replied. "The little one seems to be a lot happier than the last time we saw her."

"It's a real weight off my mind to know she's settled." The little group continued on along the beach and Andrew took his turn playing with his daughter in the sand, building a three storey castle with a bucket and spade bought from a small kiosk.

"How long are you planning to stay?"

"Three days if that's ok. I did ask mum." His father laughed softly.

"I'm the last person your mother tells. The reason I ask is that I have a Rotary dinner tomorrow night in Exeter. It would be nice if you came along and met a few of my cronies, if it wouldn't be too boring for you." His father had caught the uncertainty in Andrew's expression.

"No, I'd love to go. I was just wondering if mum would be ok with Charlotte that's all."

"Don't worry about your mother, she'll be fine."

The following evening they left Dawlish at 7pm for the half hour drive to Exeter. Andrew had made sure the house was well stocked with sweets and soft drinks, something his parents would never normally buy.

"Are you sure you will be ok, mum?" he asked as they climbed into the car. "Of course we will, won't we Charlotte?" she replied as they both waved from the doorstep.

"In bed by seven thirty!" he called as the car pulled off the drive.

Southernhay is one of more than 30,000 Rotary clubs across the world whose million plus members meet on a regular basis to socialise and provide humanitarian services to the needy wherever they may live. Andrew's father had been a member for more than thirty years but was not able to get to as many meetings as he would have liked. This dinner meeting was, like almost every other event, held at the Southgate Hotel in the centre of the city. It was not the largest of the four clubs in the town, but Ted Larkin had enjoyed both the company and the sense of achievement from his long association. There were around fifteen members in the bar when they arrived and Andrew could sense that his father immediately felt at home with his old friends. After the normal round of introductions, Andrew gradually became detached from the conversation which had drifted into a debate about a point of procedure for the forthcoming AGM. He excused himself, walked into the lobby area and called his parents' house to check on Charlotte or his mother, he was confused as to whom he should be more concerned.

"She's fine Andrew. I just read her a bedtime story and she fell asleep within minutes."

"Thanks mum."

"Go off and enjoy yourself and don't let your father get too carried away, his heart isn't as strong as it was."

When he returned to the bar a new face had been added his father's group.

"Ah there you are?" he called as Andrew re-joined the small circle. "Alan, I want you to meet my son Andrew." The man offered his hand which Andrew duly took. "You two should have a lot in common. This is Alan Stuart. Detective Inspector Alan Stuart. He's been a policeman for...?"

"Twenty six years, man and boy."

"Andrew is with the secret squirrel lot," his father said with a mixture of pride and embarrassment.

"Dad, really," cut in Larkin. "I'm with MI5, but nothing very exciting I'm afraid. I've been with them for twelve years now, since I left university."

"Ah," said the local man. Andrew did not sense a feeling of overwhelming approval.

The group quickly fell back into their normal topics of conversation and after a few minutes they were called through for dinner. He was sat at the same table as Stuart and they found themselves drawn into conversation between courses as he either did not know the other guests or perhaps regarded them with the same disdain as the MI5 man. Andrew's father stopped at their table on his way to the bar and leant between the two.

"Alan why don't you tell Andrew about the vicarage murder, he might be able to help?" The two men looked at each other, neither wanting to embarrass the well-meaning old man.

"Do you remember me telling you about it when you were last down Andrew? Terrible crime, and with no apparent motive. You haven't got a clue, have you Alan?" he said, resuming his journey to the bar.

"Sorry about my father, he means well." The Devon man looked dejected rather than angry, a mood he maintained throughout the meal. Andrew did his best to fill in the void by explaining, in terms he knew would not fall foul of the official secrets act, his role at GCHQ.

"Pity the bastard didn't send an email or you lot would have caught him straight away." Stuart's bitterness was evident.

"Listen, I've got DV clearance," said Andrew discreetly showing the inspector his ID card. Stuart looked down at his drink, obviously deciding what he should do.

"Developed vetting you say?" he said finally "What have I got to lose? We are going nowhere fast." For the next thirty minutes Stuart recounted the facts surrounding the brutal murder of the clergyman.

"But why the hell would anyone want to murder a vicar?" asked Andrew. Stuart paused and gave the younger a man a strange look. He fished his wallet from his jacket and produced a folded piece of paper, which he handed to Andrew.

"That's a copy of both sides." he said as Andrew studied the images of a small card. "The bear and tree or ragged staff as it's called, is the symbol of Warwick."

"Warwick?"

"Yes the Earl of Warwick, the town, the county. I paid a visit to the present earl and he showed me all the places it appears."

"And the number?"

"Could be anything," said Stuart leaning forward in his chair to avoid being overheard. "The earl mentioned something about there having been eight earls in four creations and so forth, but it was all so obscure." Before Andrew could ask any further questions Stuart brought the conversation to an end.

"It's been over eight months since the poor man died and I'm no further forward than I was the day after. My lads have questioned everyone in Devon and Cornwall who could have done this. It's not drug related or a grudge killing and all we have is that damned card."

"Have you had any luck running it through the NCIS database?" asked Andrew. "There might be a pattern." Stuart got up to leave.

"Waste of time, lad, waste of time." He quickly said his farewells and excused himself. By the time Andrew had listened to his father repeat verbatim the conversation he had with the chairman on the journey home, he had forgotten his own with the detective inspector.

Two days later Lambert caught the 08:50 Arriva Wales direct service from Cardiff Central to Hereford. There were no power sockets on this service, but since he had not bothered to bring his laptop, this did not cause him any concern. He spent the hour-long journey taking in the views of the countryside and wondering how he managed to let Giddens talk him into wasting a day. An eminent professor he may be, the bursar had said, but the university paid his salary and his position required him to give ten hours of teaching each week. He had missed several classes due to his recent trips, so had needed to muster more enthusiasm than he felt to describe the potential importance of the discovery. On arriving in Hereford he wandered to the bus stop just outside the station entrance. According to the website there was a 10am bus service to Llanrindod departing in just under ten minutes. The Sergeants Brothers coach duly arrived and Lambert climbed on board, collecting his ticket in exchange for the £3.50 single fare. The bus would drop him off in the village of Kington where the old man had agreed to meet him and drive the last couple of miles to his shop.

As the coach pulled into the Mill Street car park in Kington seventy minutes later, Lambert noticed a frail figure standing alongside an ancient looking Land Rover. At first glance he was not sure which was the older, or more importantly, which was likely to give out first.

"Mr Lambert?" The old man had shuffled over to greet him as he emerged down the steps of the coach.

"Yes," replied Lambert in a kindly tone. The man must be eighty if he was a day and his back curved wickedly, making it difficult to raise his head the required amount to look the towering academic in the eye. Lambert accepted the outstretched hand. "Thank you for inviting me to take a look at your document." There was nothing to be gained by shattering the old man's hopes too early and politeness costs nothing his mother had told him as a child.

"I'm no expert like yourself Mr Lambert, and I know better than most that it's probably a forgery." They began to walk towards the vehicle, each step increasing the unease with which Lambert was imagining the journey ahead. "But I have been in this game for over forty years and you learn to get a feel for these things, if you knows what I mean?" The reality of the roadworthiness of the Land Rover was, if anything, worse than Lambert had feared. Luckily the journey was blissfully short, it being only three miles from the village to the hamlet of Lower Harpton the old man called home. The shop owner had explained the circumstances of how the trunk had come into his possession and the sequence of events leading up to the discovery of the parchment. Lambert had heard all of this from Giddens, but nodded and tried hard to pretend he was as excited as his host. Lambert declined the offer of tea as they entered the shop, preferring to get sight of the letter as soon as possible. He had calculated that if he could catch the 12:50 bus, he would make the 14:11 at Hereford and be back in Cardiff by mid-afternoon. He was led, head stooped to avoid hitting it on various overhanging items, down the narrow corridor past what Lambert could only describe as room after room of junk. He was no expert on furniture or object d'art, but he knew junk when he saw it. By the time they emerged into the workshop, he was ready to turn tail and run.

The dark wooden trunk stood where the old man had left it several days before, and this was the first thing that caught Lambert's eye as he straightened to his full height. He had just admitted his lack of expertise to himself, but had to agree that this looked the genuine article at first glance. As he walked past, he could see where the strut had been removed to free the document from its 450-year-old hiding place, or so the story went. He knew of many elaborate scams perpetrated in the antiques and collectables markets and he was not about to put his reputation on the line by falling for the beguiling tale that was being presented to him. The dealer moved silently aside, having removed a dark cloth that covered the find, giving Lambert his first sight of the document. It was laid out on a large leather blotter, the corners weighed down with four different paperweights, no doubt liberated from the vast collection of junk from various corners of the rooms either side of his entry route. At least he seems to know the basics of handling aged parchment, the Professor thought to himself. Keeping the material flat and protected from light were two important points. Lambert removed his jacket and tossed it in the direction of the nearest chair. The base material was definitely a parchment, possibly a calf velum, measuring around eight inches long and six wide. He made no attempt to touch it at this point, preferring to use his other senses to carry out the initial assessment.

The material was in remarkably good condition given its age and the old man had obviously taken great care when retrieving and unfolding the hidden note. He bent down and could smell the distinct animal aroma still lingering in the skin. Parchment was first used as a writing material in ancient times, the first samples being created around 500 BC. In Elizabeth's era, paper had begun to be used widely as the cost and availability of parchment made its use increasingly difficult. Feather quills were the most common form of pen and were usually made from the first three feathers of a turkey or goose, although Elizabeth favoured using Swan. However, there was no way of telling which had been used on the letter. Forensic tests could be carried out to determine the construction of the material and composition of the ink. One part had a raised globule, where a fully loaded quill had first touched the writing surface, enabling a sample to be easily lifted. The wording was informal and unlike most other documents written in her hand. The script, modern in its day, was one known to have been favoured by the queen and the signature looked good, but it's not impossible to copy a signature, even one as elaborate as this.

Lambert lifted himself up and immediately felt his back tighten. He placed both hands on his lower back and stretched, catching sight of an old station clock on the wall opposite.

"Is that the correct time?" The old man nodded. He realised he had been bent over the document for more than three hours without a word being exchanged between them. "Sorry," apologised Lambert. "I seem to get lost in my work and the time just flies."

"No need to apologise," replied the shop owner. "I'm sure you need as long as it takes to make your mind up." Lambert sat down on a three-legged stool and polished his glasses with a handkerchief retrieved from a trouser pocket.

"I'm afraid it's going to take a lot longer than the cursory assessment I am able to make here Mr Carter," said Lambert, answering the implied question. "Congratulations on your translation. Apart from the odd phrase, I couldn't have done better myself, and I see ancient Latin text almost every day." He went on to explain some of the tests that would be required on the parchment, ink and seal to help determine their age and origin. He would also need to consult with colleagues as to the calligraphy, particularly with reference to the signature. "As I'm sure you can understand" Lambert concluded, "the contents of this letter are such that if it turns out to be authentic we shall have to re-write an important part of English history." Lambert rose and allowed his stature to emphasise his point. "Therefore any premature publicity, particularly with my name associated with it, could lead to some rather important conclusions being incorrectly arrived at." He towered above the old man and allowed his words to sink in before he continued in a softer tone. "Mr Carter, I will be honest with you. I only agreed to come along today as a favour to John Giddens, whom I have known for many years. That and the fact that you are only a couple of hours away from Cardiff. Over the years I have seen many documents that lay claim to be everything from the true Magna Carta or Shakespeare's re-written will, through to a sale deed supposedly proving a Mr Brown from

Rotherham was the true owner of the land on which Buckingham Palace is built." The old man looked at Lambert with an impassive expression.

"Did it?"

"Did it what?" Lambert turned to face his host, having started pacing the workshop.

"The land?" Lambert took a second to understand the question.

"No it was a forgery, and a poor one at that." Lambert caught site of the clock and realised he was unlikely to make the 14:50 return coach to Hereford. "Look, I need to get back to Cardiff as soon as possible, I can explain things in more detail on the way." He hesitated "I don't suppose you could take me back to Hereford could you? The bus service..." The old man raised his hand to save the taller man any further embarrassment.

"It would be a pleasure sir. Least I can do you having come all this way as a favour and all."

As soon as they started the journey Lambert began to question the wisdom of his request. The Land Rover seemed more decrepit than on the outward journey from Kington. It was twenty four miles to Hereford and if his back could speak it would have told a tale of forty minutes of misery and pain. Lambert explained in between the crashing of the gears, whining of the engine and bone shaking rattles of the interior, that he would like to be able to carry out the tests on the document at his facility at the university. He had all the necessary equipment and most importantly could store the letter in the ideal environment to ensure it would not be damaged. Having been supposedly secreted in the complete darkness of the trunk since 1576, there was a real danger of rapid deterioration if it were not treated by the most experienced professionals. He had known of many finds that had been lost by the well-meaning attempts of amateurs who thought a ten minute read through an online article made them instant experts. The old dealer hesitantly agreed, on condition that he received an official letter from the university stating that he had ownership of the trunk and therefore the letter. Lambert agreed when the dealer pledged to dig out the receipt he had issued for the house clearance.

"You can help me in the first instance by finding out where the trunk came from, Mr Carter," said Lambert as he staggered from the four wheel drive outside Hereford station. He explained that he would arrange for a team from his department to contact him and collect the letter in a day or so. In the meantime he was to keep it covered and not let anyone know of his find. They parted with a handshake and promises to carry out their agreed tasks. When the old man arrived back at his workshop, he could not resist removing the dark cloth and staring at the letter. He was brought back to reality by the phone ringing in the workshop. I really must sort out an extension, he thought as he negotiated the narrow labyrinth back to his desk.

"Hello Reg, you never guess what? I might have a buyer for that old trunk you called me about the other day." It was the original dealer he had contacted. "A young couple popped in the shop earlier. Just bought a weekend cottage near Tenbury Wells and are looking for something to use for the dirty washing. I don't have anything they fancied, but I remembered your trunk and they said it sounded ideal, being Tudor and all it would blend in nicely with the beams." The old man could not help but laugh. "I thought you would be happy. When can you get it over here?"

"Sorry Peter, I sold it to someone at the new antiques centre. He picked it up today. Taking it to London I think he said."

"Damn!" cursed the dealer, "they would have paid two hundred pounds for that, coming from London and all." The old man smiled.

"Some you win, some you lose. Got to fly, thanks for thinking of me. I will have a root around and see if I can find anything else." After replacing the receiver he sat down in his chair and put his feet on the desk. If the letter was genuine, and he had a feeling in his bones about this one, the trunk would be worth a great deal more than two hundred, not to mention the letter. He had no intention of breaking the agreement he had made with the tall professor from the university. His contact at Christie's had told him that the man, who disliked his old faithful Land Rover so much, was a world expert in this field. His authentication would make the parchment almost priceless, and he was prepared to do it for free. He was content to wait a few days before deciding what to do.

It took him a few days to locate the carbon copy of the receipt he had issued for the house clearance. The old woman had lived in a house in the village of Bulith Wells nineteen miles across the border in Powys. He had been contacted by the solicitor acting for the family in carrying out the probate process. They lived in Manchester and had left most of the work to the local man. This was a common way for house contents to be disposed of, after the family had no doubt cherry picked anything they thought had value. This incredible, but common oversight, kept the engine of the antiques trade fuelled as it was rare for a member of the general public to be able to spot something of real worth, even after watching a few episodes of *Antiques Roadshow* and *Cash in the Attic*. A quick call to the legal representative had secured the name of the lady concerned, one Katherine Grange. Yes, she had been married, to a George Morgan who had died ten years before. He was not sure how much information the professor wanted him to collect and he did not want to arouse any undue curiosity with the solicitor, so he left it at that and thanked the man. He went back to the area where the contents of the house clearance were stored and cursed softly as he remembered he had incinerated almost everything apart from the trunk. It was standard practice to empty the contents of the furniture and leave any paperwork for the executor to decide whether to keep or discard, and this he had duly done. The only way forward was to contact the family or research its history himself, which would be a very time consuming exercise. As he pondered his next move, the phone rang. It was an enquiry about a piece he had advertised in a trade magazine. He needed some cash now, so decided he should concentrate on the here and now and wait to see if the letter would turn out to be his pension.

Andrew stayed an extra day at his parents' as Charlotte enjoyed the sea and sand so much and it gave Andrew the chance to spend some time with his daughter away from his mother-in-law. He would always be grateful for the way Nancy's parents had stepped into the breach after their daughter's death, but he never felt comfortable in their company. Every time Dorothy looked at him she seemed to blame him for the tragic events, although he knew that was unfair on her. On the last evening he found time to walk along the beach alone just as the sun was fading, throwing long shadows across the narrow expanse of sand. He saw his wife's face in the waves and for the first time in many weeks, allowed himself the luxury of grieving. He found a quiet spot and sat with his back against the embankment watching the light disappear and feeling the tears slowly trickle down his cheeks. But his grief was different than it had been in the past. He was beginning to realise, like most who have suffered the pain of such a loss, that it would never leave him completely, but change as time passes. The numbing shock of the first few days is replaced with fear and anger that sweeps like a storm when least expected. The guilt of forgetting her face for an instant after a busy meeting or moment of enjoyment. The unbelievable feeling of love for his daughter, mixed with the pain of seeing Nancy's face in hers. Yet he had proved to himself he was stronger than he had imagined. He had learnt that true strength has little to do with how you handle the good times, but how you face the world during the bad. As he sat on the sand staring out to sea, he sensed that he was making his peace with his wife and she was giving him the blessing he needed to move forward with his life.

"There will never be anyone to compare with you my darling," he whispered through his tears. "But I promise to do everything I can to give our little girl a happy life." Brought back to reality by the harsh clatter of a train on its way to the station a mile up the line, he picked himself up and strode back to his parents in time to read Charlotte a bedtime story.

Two weeks after his trip to Devon, Andrew was preparing for the executive liaison group briefing. He would have nothing of any significance to present to the meeting other than an update on the interrogation of the terrorist gang, captured during the recent operation. They had been unable to learn the details of the Pakistan-based group who seemed to control the cell. Andrew arrived at the meeting room a few minutes early to find David Scott talking with a woman he had not seen at GCHQ before.

"Hello Andrew," said Scott, breaking off from his conversation. "This is Jackie Crowther, she's standing in for Paul Williams as he's on holiday." Andrew remembered the young NCIS representative had been excited about his trip to Hawaii.

"Hello," said the newcomer. "You're from MI5, yes?" Andrew shook her outstretched hand. The introduction was interrupted by the arrival of Charles Smyth and Bill Frost who were deep in conversation as they entered the room.

"And who are *you*?" said Charles, running his eyes up and down her body.

"Very well," she replied. "You must be Bill Frost, from special branch?" Bill shook her hand, leaning across Smyth and making him take a step back. Scott sensed that the MI6 man was about to put his foot in it again and so swiftly called the meeting to order.

"Good afternoon everyone, can you please take your seats as we have a great deal to get through today." Andrew found himself seated next to Crowther and could not help noticing something familiar about her, but he was unable to place what it was. "Ok," started Scott, "today we have the pleasure in welcoming Jackie Crowther from NCIS, who is standing in for Paul. Jackie is part of the team running the central database project."

"And very welcome she is too," said Smyth predictably. Scott went through his normal round up of the individuals and groups they were monitoring.

"Any traffic from our man at *The Divine Retribution*?" enquired Andrew, referring to the emails Mary Ward had intercepted that had led to the Cambridge industrial unit.

"Nothing," said Scott. "Looks like he has completely shut down for now." Each of the members gave a short presentation on their own departments before Scott called on Crowther. She was around five foot eight, slim without being thin, with shoulder length blonde hair. Andrew guessed she was around thirty and not unattractive. He forced himself to concentrate as she loaded her presentation.

"Thank you for inviting me here today," she began formally. "Although I'm taking Paul's place, I was planning to attend this meeting anyway. A picture flashed onto the screen behind her. "We have been working with David and his team for a couple of weeks trying to track down the source of this site." The screen showed a web page with a mauve background. The banner headline 'English Monarchy' was in a Tudor script, below which was a symbol that immediately caught Andrew's eye, although he did not know why.

"What does the bear mean?" he asked.

"It's the sign of the Bear and Ragged Staff," answered Crowther. The site has been live for around a month and is supporting the idea that the monarchy is foreign, has been for hundreds of years, and it's time for a true English head of state."

"There must be thousands of idiots out there with a grudge and the two brain cells needed to put a website together. What's so special about this?" Smyth interrupted. Crowther carried on without acknowledging the remark.

"What makes it different is this."

1	James	Worker of the Land
2	Sarah	Harvester of Milk
3	Joseph	Worker of the Land
4		Tamer of the Mechanical Beast
5	John	
6		Toils on a Water Gate
7		Toils in a cage of brick & steel
8	Edward	
9		
10		Purveyor of Land
11	Henrietta	
12		Musician
13		Seeker of Fame From the Masses
14		A Merchant
15		Man of Many Words but Few Deeds
16		The German Pretender

The screen changed to another page from the same site showing a table containing columns for names and occupation with a number against each. "This is where things get sinister. This is supposedly a list of people who somehow deserve to die for this cause." Andrew remembered where he had seen the bear. He stood and approached the screen so he could read the details. Against the number eight was the Christian name Edward.

"Is there a problem, Andrew?" asked Scott.

"No," said Andrew." It's just that I may be able to throw some light on this."

"Really?" Jackie seemed genuinely amazed.

"I assume you've run a cross check on the names to see if any have died recently?"

"Of course," answered Crowther, slightly irritated at the implied oversight. "As you will see if you take the time to study the boxes in detail," she continued looking directly at Andrew. "You will see that only the first three are completely filled in. We've confirmed that all have died in the last six months in suspicious circumstances."

"What about the numbers?" said Larkin.

"We've only just got this information back from our initial enquiries, but why do you ask Mr Larkin; what do you know?" she said sternly. Larkin relayed his conversation with Stuart to the growing astonishment of the group.

"So I can fill in the blank on number eight," he said finally.

"Excuse me," said Crowther as she left the room. She could be seen through the glass door in an earnest discussion on her cell phone. Five minutes later she re-entered in deep thought. "My people are going back over the data now, but I got them to look up the file on the Devon murder while I waited and there was no mention of a card or the bear and ragged staff."

"I can't answer that question," said Andrew. "But I can assure you that the Devon vicar is number eight."

One of Scott's team knocked on the door and handed him a dozen copies of the table.

"So the first four all worked in agriculture?" said Bill Frost.

"That's right," replied Crowther. "They all died in what were initially thought to be accidents. It was only after we cross referenced the names that a pattern began to emerge."

"My God," said Smyth studying the list. "Number one fell in a slurry tank and the second was a dairy maid drowned in milk."

"The third was a farm engineer cut to pieces in a machine and number four, a poor man crushed under a pile of hay bales," continued Scott.

"It's like something out of a film script," said Andrew shaking his head.

"But how did you find the fourth victim? The occupation sounds more like a crossword clue and there's no name," said Smythe.

"We were lucky that a second murder was committed in Yorkshire and someone made a connection as it was such a bizarre accident," replied Crowther. "He was an engineer named Ian Thorpe who looked after all the local equipment, tractors, combined harvesters and the like."

"Ah I see, very cryptic, so we can fill in that box ourselves," said Smythe.

"And now, by chance, we jump to number eight and discover a brutal stabbing," said Jackie tossing her sheet on the table in frustration. "No attempt to make that look like an accident."

"Let's take a step backwards," said Andrew. "Firstly we're assuming that whoever created the web site either killed the victims or knows who did?" They all nodded. "But it's possible they somehow found out about the deaths and formulated an elaborate hoax."

"And your point?" said Crowther.

"My point is that we're in danger of jumping to conclusions without hard evidence to support it."

"David, have we been able to locate the source of the site?" asked Frost.

"No Bill, Whoever did this really knows their stuff. The proxy servers change very quickly so we have no time to attempt a geographical trace. The only server it stays on for long enough is based somewhere in China."

"The other important point," said Crowther, "is that the first four murders were in sequence. March, April, May and September this year, but the vicar was back in February."

"So there could be other victims that we don't know about?" said Andrew.

"Exactly," replied Crowther.

The group discussed various theories and attempted to decipher the cryptic occupations. There was general consensus the 'Purveyor of Land' was a real estate agent but the others were not so straightforward. After an hour Scott suggested they wrap up and meet again the next day.

"That's if you are planning to stay Jackie?"

"No I must get back to London and oversee the database search. If we can verify that a card was attached to each body it will confirm that they weren't accidents and the work of the English monarchy."

"In the meantime, we have set up a directory search for a number of keywords in case there is any chatter on this," said Scott.

"Is that Mary?" asked Andrew.

"No she's in the field at the moment," answered Scott. Andrew knew better than to seek any further details.

He walked Jackie to her car as it was parked close to his own.

"Are you sure you're ok to drive back?" he asked.

"It should only take a couple of hours if the traffic's not too bad and I really need to be there tomorrow."

"Let me know as soon as anything turns up," he said handing her his card.

The next morning the group met briefly and quickly decided there was little they could do until NCIS came up with further information. It was outside the MI6 brief so Smyth excused himself. Bill Frost had discovered that the deaths were spread literally across the four corners of the country with two in Yorkshire, Norfolk and Durham. Special branch in London were aware of the NCIS interest but did not have any justification for stepping on the toes of the individual forces. It was only of concern to MI5 if national security was threatened or it was decided some organised criminal activity lay behind the scheme. Andrew spoke to Greaves to ensure Thames House were aware of the background.

"Keep an eye on it," was the sum total of his input. He and Frost were having lunch in the canteen and discussing whether to go the cinema that evening, when Andrew's phone vibrated. He immediately recognised the voice.

"It's Crowther," he mouthed at Frost. "Hello Jackie," he replied brightly.

"Get to a computer and call me back," she said and was gone.

The two men were sat in Andrew's cramped office, with a live image of the tabulated web page they had been studying the day before. They had both noticed the changes as soon as it appeared.

"The site was updated at 2.50am this morning." Jackie's voice came over the speaker phone sat on his desk.

"Five and six," said Andrew.

"A miner in June and a lock keeper in July. One fell down a pit shaft, the other drowned," said Crowther. "The significant change is the fact that the lock keeper was found tied to the base of a set of steps at the bottom of the lock and there were signs he attempted to break free."

"Poor man, but the first one to obviously look like a murder," said Frost.

"But why change his MO?" asked Andrew.

"The deaths have occurred over a period of seven months and in every part of the country," she continued. "Making the first few look like accidents would make it less likely that a pattern would be spotted before they were ready."

"But now they want us to know what's being planned," said Andrew.

"Hold on a second can you?" said Crowther. There was a pause on the line. "Look I'll call you back, something's come in at this end." The line went dead.

"Let's have a closer look at this website while we're waiting," said Andrew. They spent the next twenty minutes reading the copy and cross checking the various statements it contained, on the internet.

"So in a nutshell this person or group believes that the monarchy are a bunch of foreigners who should be deported immediately and replaced by the true English successor," said Frost.

"But it doesn't say who that should be," said Andrew.

"I must admit I didn't know that Elizabeth I was the last true English monarch," said Frost.

"Nor me."

"As our friend from MI6 so eloquently put it, there are thousands of people out there with unconventional views," said Frost. "But not many who will take this type of action to see their version of the world become reality."

"Thank goodness. We still have no idea whether any other murders have taken place or any clues to help us prevent them. They are playing a game with us."

"And what about number seven?" said Frost.

"It describes the occupation as 'Toils in a cage of brick & steel', which we think could be an office worker. That narrows it down to about three million," said Andrew dejectedly.

He rose from his chair and would have paced the room if he could. Instead, he looked out of the small window at the traffic passing by on the adjacent road.

"The clue is in the card," he said after a minute. "If one was left on the vicar's body, then it stands to reason the others would have the same clue. It's his calling card. Literally." Andrew's phone began to vibrate. "Larkin."

"Check your emails." It was Crowther. "I got my people to contact each of the forces where the deaths took place and ask them to look again at the information they had."

"You mean with reference to the card?" said Larkin.

"We've just got the last report back. There was a card in all four cases. One was placed on the body, the others found later. One to four in black pen and all with the bear and ragged staff symbol on the reverse."

"And no one thought it was significant?" said Frost shaking his head.

"It's easier for us to spot a pattern, but I agree it is frustrating that the data wasn't recorded," replied Crowther.

"What about the fifth and six murders?" said Andrew.

"I've sent an emergency message to every force to pay special attention for the card and the occupations. I'm still waiting to hear back."

Larkin had found the message Crowther had sent and was studying some photographs of the crime scenes.

"Awful," he said, scrolling down.

"Another problem is that only the lock keeper's death has been treated as a crime scene so we may have lost vital evidence." Frost grimaced at the oversight. Crowther continued.

"I've got a member of my team travelling to every location as we speak to go over the entire thing from scratch, and that includes the vicar in Devon. I'm also applying to the coroner for permission to exhume the two bodies that weren't cremated."

"You've been busy," said Andrew.

"I'm just co-ordinating things centrally Andrew, the ground work is still being carried out by each local force."

"I'll help you with that Jackie," offered Frost.

"Thanks Bill. I'm also hoping we may get something from David Scott's team at GCHQ."

The call drew to a close with promises to keep the liaison group informed of any new developments. Andrew completed a short report which he e-mailed to Ken Greaves. He noted that the organised crime section should familiarise themselves with the details to ensure there were no connections. He closed his laptop at 7.30pm and went home, all thoughts of a trip to the cinema forgotten. But he did remember to call to say goodnight to his little girl.

Andrew was dreaming of collecting honey with his father as a child when he was woken by the buzzing of his cell phone. He was unsure how long it had been sliding around his bedside table, but could see by the clock on the same device it was 2.30am so had no need to switch on a light.

"Larkin," he answered as he sat up and swung his feet out of bed. It was unlikely that a call at this time would allow him the luxury of returning to bed, let alone sleep.

"Sorry to disturb you Andrew." It was Scott from GCHQ

"I'm sure it's important David," he answered almost wishing it was Greaves on the line. At least he could be relied upon to get to the point.

"I'm on my way into the office now. Seems we have picked up some traffic from our monarchist friends."

"Go on," pleaded Andrew.

"I don't have much at this stage except that we've isolated the source of the uploads for the web pages. Obviously they have been bounced all over the planet, but it seems they emanated from the UK."

The executive liaison group, minus Smyth, sat around a conference table an hour later, at its head stood Mary Ward.

"Gentleman," she continued. "We've been tracking this web site since it was brought to our attention two weeks ago. Since then there have been no changes to the content and the files resided on a server in India."

"Any particular reason?" asked Paul Williams of NCIS, who had just returned from his holidays.

"None that we can see," she replied. "The Indians handle a great deal of IT infrastructure outsourcing these days, so it's as likely as anywhere."

"So no one has tried to move or hide the files?" asked Bill Frost.

"That's no surprise," said Ward. "They are of no use to us and have been stripped of any clues as to the origin of the code."

"Do programmers have styles that differentiate them?" queried Andrew who was sitting with his arms folded, the fact that Williams had replaced Jackie had not escaped his attention.

"In some cases individuals have been known to leave signs, but only if they are either arrogant or very confident they are beyond the law."

"And this one?" followed up Andrew.

"Neither. Standard code." Ward flashed a new image on the screen. It showed the updated table with murders five and six completed.

1	James	Worker of the Land
2	Sarah	Harvester of Milk
3	Joseph	Worker of the Land
4	Ian	Tames the Mechanical Beast
5	John	Brings Fire from the Earth
6	Peter	Toils on a Water Gate
7		Toils in a cage of brick & steel
8	Edward	Man of God
9		
10		Purveyor of Land
11	Henrietta	
12		Musician
13		Seeker of Fame From the Masses
14		A Merchant
15		Man of Many Words but Few Deeds
16		The German Pretender

"The site was updated at 2.50am yesterday morning." They all nodded except Paul who had only landed that morning and was suffering from jetlag compounded by being woken only a few minutes after dozing off. Mary looked around the room slightly unsure what to do.

"Don't worry Mary, I'll bring Paul up to speed later," said Scott.

"They've also entered the name of the farm engineer and," said Andrew pausing to check he was reading the table correctly, "the vicar." They all looked at him. "Why complete that box now?"

"Because we know the details of that crime," answered Scott.

"But how do they know that?" Larkin was met by a sea of blank faces. Mary Ward cut into the awkward silence.

"We've been scrutinising the traffic to and from that server for two weeks and were able to pinpoint the exact IP address where the files were uploaded using the methods developed by North-western University in the US. We then simply traced that back to a physical location from the ISP data centre. "There," she said calling up a satellite map.

Cardiff University, Cardiff, September 2009

The document arrived at the history department three days later. Lambert had arranged for it to be collected by the lab technician who would carry out the tests, so restricting the number of people who knew about it at this early stage. He also, by a happy coincidence, owned a car. He was still far from convinced of its authenticity, but had seen enough evidence to justify the tests. He had not yet told the bursar who he feared may be a likely source of any early leak to the press. Any publicity that might raise the university's profile and encourage wealthy donors was too good to miss. Simple matters like authentication were a mere detail that shouldn't be allowed to get in the way. The tests that were to be carried out could not in themselves prove if the letter was genuine. The carbon contained in the parchment could be dated using accepted and well understood methods, whilst the chemical constituents of the ink could easily be established. These would show if the age and chemical makeup were consistent with that used in Tudor England in the second half of the sixteenth century which was a time of great change in writing and printing. As more words found their way onto paper, so the number of people originating those words grew and the language they wished to read was the language they spoke, English. The church opposed the introduction of an English bible as they feared the erosion of the power they enjoyed over the common people. The more the general population could read the scriptures, the less they would need the services of the local priest, who not only translated but would often interpret for the benefit of the church. The first publication of a printed edition of the bible in Latin was in 1456 by the inventor of the printing press, Guttenberg. It was not until 1611 that the general public could study the great book in their native tongue when the King James version rolled from the presses. The use of parchment for some legal and important documents continued until around 1922. Lambert knew the only way of establishing with a reasonable level of certainty, that this letter was indeed in the hand of the last Tudor monarch, was to identify the handwriting style and content. He had seen examples of her signature, most notably on the death warrant with which she had eventually consigned her sister Mary Queen of Scots to the executioner's block in 1587. But a simple internet search would reveal a picture of that very document and so a trained and determined professional forger could well master such a feat. More difficult still would be evaluating the style and content. There were plenty of documents and letters written in her hand but few that contained such intimate information and apparently written under some stress. It would be crucial to get several opinions on these matters and he decided he should contact an old friend at the National Archives in Kew.

Lambert sat at his office desk in the history department studying the short report. The tests revealed the carbon was from a period between four and six hundred years old. It was in fact vellum and made from calves' hide, from which most was produced in Britain at that time. The ink was made using galls, a growth caused by a wasp deposit on oak trees, and iron sulphate, which was consistent with that used in the late sixteenth century. But why parchment and not paper for a personal letter? The note had allegedly been written in secrecy at Alnwick Castle, Northumberland, and it was entirely possible that she did not have access to her own supplies and simply used those at hand. Lambert frowned as he tossed the various elements over in his mind. If this was a forgery then the author was a professional who was either incredibly cunning or very naive. By sourcing original materials but not those immediately associated with letter writing at the time, it created a level of doubt that would serve only to make any expert think hard. If it were too easy then suspicions would be raised for the entirely opposite reasons.

Putting aside his thoughts on the technical aspects and making the massive assumption that Elizabeth had written it herself, a far simpler question nagged at the professor. Why had Dudley hidden it in a storage chest and one that was obviously not his? His sister Mary Sidney had been a close confidante and lady in waiting to the queen for many years. Is it possible that he gave the letter to her? But why? Was it possible that the queen never sent the letter and worried it would fall into the wrong hands, hid it in a trunk? Both these notions seemed implausible to Lambert. Firstly, the box was not fit for a royal. Secondly, if she had not wanted to send the letter and feared its discovery, why not simply burn it? Certainly, if it had come to the attention of any of The Earl of Leicester's enemies, it would have almost certainly have led to his downfall. Adultery with the monarch, even with the protection her favour gave, was a certain route to the tower and would have presented an opportunity the likes of the Earl of Sussex would not have let pass. For the queen herself, the danger of having an illegitimate child was great enough, but with a controversial widower, whom many despised for the influence he had over the lady, would be unimaginable. She knew it would be seized upon by Catholics and Protestants alike as a reason to openly declare their allegiances. Lambert could understand just how much anguish those around the queen would have suffered too, for many knew they would probably be executed for whatever crime could be trumped up. So why put these explosive revelations to paper? If there had indeed been a secret child that had been adopted by a local family who presumably did not know their new baby was of noble birth, why chance the facts becoming more widely known? Lambert reached behind him and slid a white sheet from his laser printer. He wrote down a list of people close to the queen who might have known.

Dudley
Ladies in waiting
Physician who delivered the baby
Wallsingham
Cecil
Whoever took the child to the farmer?

He put a question mark against the last entry. It was possible this person was simply given a bundle to deliver. Children were being born out of wedlock to young girls from both noble and humble stock every day, the local gentry being able to sow their seeds as it took their fancy. The list was growing fast. Lambert could not believe that such a secret could have held if all these people were aware of the facts. Perhaps some had been disposed of after the birth. He would have to investigate who had been around the queen during this time and discover if any had died soon after. His thoughts were disturbed by a knock at his office door.

"You might want to see this Professor."

"So this parchment has been used before?" The technician had led Lambert through to the laboratory that contained the university's facilities for working with the many ancient manuscripts and documents that passed through the department. Around him were a number of test and analytical devices including an electron microscope.

"I first noticed a shadow when I scanned it to a make a copy as you had asked."

Lambert studied the image on the large monitor and could immediately see the tell-tale signs. In several places traces could be seen where the surface of the letter had been scraped, one in particular seemed to bleed over the left hand edge.

"There see?" The technician pointed to a spot on the monitor. "I tried to get a sample of the old ink, but the cleaning has removed everything. I can only be sure as, under the electronic microscope you can see the colour is different." Lambert took the proffered CD from the young man, before returning it.

"Can you generate a 200 per cent paper copy for me and send this to Peter Hughes at Kew by special delivery."

As Lambert walked back to his office he pondered this new information. It was very common at the time for parchment to be re-used. It was an expensive medium and if the original was no longer required there was every incentive to recycle. The process of removing the original ink necessitated scraping the surface. It appeared as if this piece may have been an off cut of a larger document which was consistent with its new use. But this also made the likelihood of it being a forgery greater. Find a piece that was obviously from that period, remove the original text and replace it with something that would be of far greater value. It was past 7pm with the sun fading fast when he finally emerged from his thoughts.

It was not until a week later that Lambert was able to arrange a trip to west London. He passed through the entrance to the National Archives at 11.20am, having caught the 08.25 train for the two-hour journey to Paddington, changing to the London Underground District Line service to Richmond and finally alighting at the penultimate stop of Kew Gardens. From there it was just a short walk to the somewhat unattractive set of concrete buildings that made up this most important of historic sites. As he approached the main entrance, he took a moment to watch two swans that occupied the large man-made pool that, to Lambert, always seemed strangely out of place. The National Archives were created in 2003, combining the Public Records Office and Historical Manuscripts Commission. The majority of records are stored at this new building which opened in 1977, although there is an additional deep storage facility in Winsford Rock Salt Mine in Cheshire. Each year thousands of people visit to research every aspect of the history of the British Isles from as long as man has committed his thoughts and deeds through written communication.

The science of genealogy, once the preserve of a few historians, has turned into a thriving industry, made more accessible with the ability to transfer the original documents onto microfilm, accelerated with the wide scale digitalisation of text, and recently made available to anyone with an internet connection via hundreds of sites worldwide. All this is possible because the source information was recorded, largely by the church. Before 1538 when Henry VIII ordered that all births and deaths be registered, an unregulated method existed where individual clergy kept records on a voluntary basis. Thomas Cromwell introduced a system based on christenings, marriages and burials with each parish ordered to keep a book. In 1597, special registers were introduced and returns sent to the diocese for formal storage. Much of this information has now been made available without the need to search out the original documents, which has also helped to preserve these fragile relics of our ancestors.

Lambert was led into the large maps and documents section where he spotted Dr Peter Hughes immediately, hunched over large ordnance survey map book of Surrey from 1901.

"Hello Tom, good to see you again." The head of research services was a slight, portly man in his mid-fifties, the top of whose balding head was clearly visible to Lambert. He wore a well-worn cardigan and had a set of reading glasses perched on his nose. The glasses dropped as he rose, saved from damage by the neck cord to which they were attached. "Joyce, can you finish this for me please?" said Hughes as he passed a young assistant, Lambert in tow. He removed a pair of cotton gloves as he walked the short distance to his office reached via a door marked *Staff Only*. They talked for a few minutes and shared a coffee from the vending machine located just outside the door. "Ok Tom, let's get down to why you're here." Hughes rose and stood beside a large backlit display board fixed to one wall. He produced an enlarged copy of the letter from a locked draw and fixed it to the centre of the board with transparent tape. Lambert turned his chair through the ninety degrees required to face the man from Kew. "Firstly, only Joyce and I have seen the letter. This was the minimum number I considered necessary to be able to give you a considered opinion."

"That's fine Peter," said Lambert rising to join Hughes at the board. "You can obviously see why I'm keen to keep this quiet for the moment. Any premature announcement or leaks will start a media frenzy that it's unlikely could be controlled. If the letter is a forgery and our names are associated with it, we will be the ones that go down when the truth emerges." Hughes turned to face the copy as if in the hope it would speak before turning, removing his glasses and chewing one end.

"Everyone here is as keen as you to avoid anything that could affect our credibility." They both turned and began inspecting the curved script before them. "This has not been as difficult as you might imagine, Tom," began Hughes. "We have several examples of her signature here and it was a simple matter to take a quick scan and compare the two." Hughes reached into the drawer and produced two clear pieces of film on which the alternate versions of the queen's signature had been printed, and proceeded to tape one to the board. "This is taken from a letter she signed at about the same time, so it should provide a good reference point." He slid the second piece of film over the top. Hughes paused to allow Lambert to assess the similarities.

"Allowing for the obvious variations everyone has in their signature, I'd say that was pretty close," commented the Cardiff professor.

"I agree," said Hughes." But we both know how easy it is to copy a signature, so I spent a lot longer looking at the body of the letter." Hughes explained how he had compared the alleged letter to known originals penned by the queen. He produced various examples which he spread over the adjacent workspace.

"Notice the loops on the t's and open a's."

For the next thirty minutes the two academics studied the various examples of the handwriting before them.

"She was fond of using what was then the newly fashionable italic script style." Finally they both removed their glasses and returned to their respective chairs. Hughes knew what his old friend needed. "If I were a betting man I would say that the odds on this being genuine are about evens. But I have never placed a wager in my life and I don't instead to start now," he said, leaning back and placing his hands on his chest. "There are enough matching characteristics to say that on the balance of probability this was written by Elizabeth I, but given the nature of the contents I can't publicly endorse its authenticity. You can, of course, vouch for the velum and ink yourself." Lambert shifted his weight in the chair. He was not surprised by the findings or conclusions that had been drawn. He too was extremely reticent about allowing a press release on the basis of his own investigations, so agreed with Hughes's assessment.

"Any suggestions?" He knew it was a leading question.

"Well you have some specific information to work with. A date, a location and names. I would have thought it likely that the adoptive family would have to be somewhere fairly close to the castle."

On the journey back to Cardiff, Lambert had ample time to ponder on the outcome of his visit. The velum and ink could be genuine. The fact that it had been cleaned and re-used gave no real clue as plausible reasons could be found to support either argument. Why was velum used at all when paper had become so widely available? He had spent enough time with Hughes over the years to know that he was convinced the calligraphy was authentic. Professional risk aversion was all that was preventing him backing a positive assessment. But he could still not fathom out why such a letter would be written and how it had found its way behind the frame of a trunk. By the time the Intercity 125 had passed over the Bristol Channel, he had made a decision.

Suburban house, Bristol, September 2009

It was 1.30am when Gary Hasting's mother knocked on the door of his bedroom for the third time that night.

"Gary, are you still playing on that computer?" He lifted his gaze from the bank of screens before him and mumbled a curse under his breath whilst placing a hand over the microphone of his headset. "You have college in the morning and I don't want you missing any more classes." He muted the line before turning in his chair.

"Yes mum, just turning it off now. Goodnight."

"And make sure you clean your room before you leave, the place looks like a pig sty."

He could hear her footsteps retreating down the steps from his room, located in the attic of the Victorian house in a quiet suburban area. Gary knew his mother cared for him but thought, like most teenagers, that all she had done in the last four years, since his thirteenth birthday, was keep up a constant barrage of advice and instructions on how to live his life and clean up. He could never understand the reasoning for the latter as the mess just reappeared again the next day. Gary was studying A-levels in English, mathematics and computer science at the local college and was expecting sufficient grades to take up a degree course in computer technology at Nottingham University. He had also been offered a place at his local university and his mother could not understand why he wanted to move so far away when he could have stayed at home by attending that course. But Gary was not sure if he wanted to go any university. His mother was always cajoling him to find a part-time job at the local supermarket, but he had found a far more lucrative way of supplementing the monthly allowance she gave him from the small trust fund left by his late father. Gary was a computer hacker, and a very good one. He had been introduced to the hobby by a friend at college and had quickly surpassed the other boy's knowledge. It turned out he had a real talent for penetrating the defences of various organisations and either removing or adding to their systems. He started, like most of his kind, by hijacking his friends' Facebook and e-mail accounts simply by discovering their passwords. It still amazed him how many people use the simplest combinations and repeat it in almost every account they have. It did not take him long to discover how to link to other people's computers and break into their data. His first sophisticated mission had been shown to him by his friend. This involved creating a small file called a Trojan, named for good reason after the famous horse that enabled its occupants to trick their way into the ancient city of Troy. This file was electronically linked to a picture and sent via email to the unsuspecting victim with an enticing message that would guarantee it would be opened. Once the picture was viewed the Trojan file automatically and secretly installed a programme onto the host computer. Gary's file was called a key stroke logger and was programmed to send him a return file every twelve hours which contained details of every character that had been typed on that computer. He had sent the email to a friend at college and had been surprised at how smoothly the operation had worked. Within two days he could work out many details of the girl's life, including the fact she found Gary attractive. It was she who had provided him with his first sexual conquest as well as his baptism as a hacker. It had not taken him long to move swiftly along the path to ever more sophisticated methods until now he could not only read what others were typing but also create accounts, emails, Twitter entries and almost any other form of electronic communications available. But more importantly he was able to carry out all this without being discovered. By masquerading as another user, he could prevent his real identity and location being uncovered by the various providers. After six months the real breakthrough came when his college friend introduced him to a contact in London who dealt in internet marketing. This company made its money by targeting millions of people with unsolicited offers ranging from Viagra to cosmetic surgery, pornography to cheap loans. They needed bright people with few morals who could keep one-step ahead of the internet providers and large companies who were trying to block and shut down their operations. Gary found the work easy and was quickly earning hundreds of pounds every month. He now used his spare time to indulge in his other hobby, hacking into legitimate web sites and altering the content. He could now bypass many of the sophisticated protection systems to take over a site and upload images or change copy to embarrass its owners. He had recently managed to cause a problem for a major supermarket chain by splashing a banner across their front page advertising thirty-two-inch LED TV sets for £29. He still laughed when he remembered watching the stampede at branches all over the country on the evening news. But Gary was becoming bored with these childish antics and tonight he was talking to his friend about their most ambitious venture yet.

"Have you got rid of your mother Gaz?" asked his friend when he came back on the line. "Are you sure you're allowed up this late?"

"Screw you," replied Gary, giving a one fingered sign to the webcam attached to his monitor.

"Let's not waste any more time man; the firewall won't be weakened for too much longer. The scheduled maintenance is due to finish at 2am our time."

Gary turned to face another monitor which showed an image of the official seal of the Government of Greece. It had taken them more than a week to reach this point, despite repeated attempts and a surprisingly easy start. He had begun by scanning for computer networks in Greece, focusing around the capital and within minutes had obtained lists of IP and postal addresses that surrounded the Central Bank. An internet café, called *The Gladiator*, stood out and he thought it would be funny to impose himself under the username 'Maximus'. Within minutes he had hacked into the café's network, which was easier then he thought. From there he proceeded to scan hundreds of networks in the local area including mobile devices and laptops. It didn't take long to locate a smartphone which was connected to the bank's network and within seconds he had breached the network via the back door and had obtained a low level connection.

Gary had been worried their domain server would be traced and their internet service shut off.

"Don't worry man," his friend had told him. "As long as we follow the rules they'll never be able to trace it back to you. They'll think it's someone in Russia again." Gary thought he could hear his mother talking to someone downstairs, but put the notion out of his head. She must be watching some late night TV, although it was not her usual habit. The clock on his computer status bar informed him it was 2.15am. What on earth could she be watching at this time? There was nothing but porn and bad movies on and he should know. Gary's thoughts were interrupted by a voice in his headphones.

"Christ man, we're in!" At that precise moment the door to his bedroom rattled.

"Go away mum."

The door burst off its hinges and the teenager turned to face three large men covering the ten feet between where the door had been and his desk at an alarming rate.

"Gary Hastings, I am arresting you on suspicion of computer hacking and fraud," said the one pulling his hands behind him. From the floor he could see another holding up what looked like a police ID badge, although he knew such things could be bought on e-Bay for less than £5. Before his headphones were ripped away he could hear a loud commotion at the other end and guessed his friend was also receiving a similar late night visit. As he was lead down the narrow stairs and out of the front door his mother was standing in the hall.

"I said you shouldn't play those over-eighteen video games Gary."

Alnwick Castle, Northumberland, September 2009

Alnwick Castle, pronounced *An-ik,* is situated on the banks of the River Aln in the town of the same name in the county of Northumberland, in Northern England. The first defences were erected on the site at the end of the eleventh century by the Baron of Alnwick, Yves de Vescy, to guard the important river crossing and protect the border area against the marauding Scots who were a constant threat. In 1309 the 1st Baron Percy bought the castle and the Barony of Alnwick and it has been in the Percy family, latterly the Dukes of Northumberland, ever since. The castle changed hands several times during the Wars of the Roses and by 1463 was in Lancastrian hands for the third time. It had then witnessed the surrender to the Duke of Montague in 1464. In Tudor times Alnwick was again the subject of historic events. The seventh Earl of Northumberland, Thomas Percy, was beheaded in York in 1572 for his part in the abortive Rising of the North rebellion against the queen three years earlier. His betrayal is known to have deeply upset her as Percy had been a favourite of Elizabeth, but his Catholic loyalties led him to attempt to liberate her sister Mary Queen of Scots and Elizabeth was forced to act. Today the castle is inhabited by the present duke, having been the setting for numerous television and films, most notably featuring as the imaginary *Hogwarts School* in the first two *Harry Potter* films. It is second only to Windsor as the largest inhabited castle in the UK. At the time the letter was written, the castle was uninhabited after the execution of Percy three years before. Lambert guessed it had still been occupied by servants and kept stocked with food and livestock. It would have been available for the monarchs use at any time and an ideal spot to hide for a few months.

Lambert had been able to arrange a visit to the castle and a meeting with the twelfth duke. He wanted to see for himself the site which he hoped would help him get inside the story and visualise some of the background. He had decided to travel to Alnwick before visiting the county archives, particularly when the duke's housekeeper had managed to reach him on his cell phone insisting that he stay at the castle and join the duke and his wife for dinner. She had even agreed to cancel his booking at the White Swan hotel in the town. On the six hour train journey, punctuated by a single change at Bristol, Lambert had time to study the up-to-date local ordnance survey 5:1 he had purchased, together with some late sixteenth century maps that had been kindly emailed to him by Hughes. Lambert took a small black felt tipped pen and drew a rough circle around the castle. He had to redraw the point where the lines joined after it took a sudden northward deviation towards the Scottish border when the train braked unexpectedly just north of Cheltenham. When corrected he sat back to admire his cartographic skills whilst finishing his cup of coffee bought from a trolley that prowled the aisles. That is if the tasteless, lukewarm, muddy coloured mixture he had just experienced could in any way be said to resemble that rich aromatic blend of roasted beans pictured on the side of the paper cup it had been served in. The circle was actually more like the shape of a three quarter moon as the coast was no more than four miles from Alnwick on its eastern side. Lambert had calculated the probable distance a horse drawn vehicle of the day would have travelled to deliver the baby to an outlying village. Based on an average speed of five miles an hour and a travel time of no more than sixty minutes, he had drawn his outer perimeter to encompass the villages of Newton-by-the-sea to the north, Eglinham, Ingham to the west and the border to what is now the Northumberland National Park, Rothbury, Felton, Amble and Warworth. An area of roughly twenty square miles. Within that area there were more than thirty hamlets and villages, any one of which could have been the destination. To make things harder, the name Moore was common in the north and so he could expect to find numerous references. He could not even rely on the spelling given in the letter as at that time changes were made regularly dependant on who recorded the information, meaning he would need to include More, Moor and Mor. Before he had left Kew, Hughes had carried out a general search of christenings, burials and marriages using the powerful database available, which had produced a list of more than 350 entries for the period 1576-1625 in the Northumberland area. Given the secrecy surrounding the alleged child, there was no guarantee that any christening would have taken place. The letter stated that the couple were childless so the sudden appearance of a baby would have raised comment in the tight-knit community. Lambert could have saved himself the trip to inspect the original records, but he knew of errors in the transposition of data and he had a natural distrust of bits and bytes. If a likely entry was discovered, he wanted to be absolutely sure of its accuracy before making any conclusions that could so easily prove groundless, and professionally embarrassing. But he had agreed to allow Hughes himself to continue carrying out some discrete searches which might provide a clue to point him in the right direction. Any record would be listed under the parish in which the person lived. In the late sixteenth century there were many more parishes than the present day as, over the centuries, churches have closed and communities merged. It was not unusual to face many challenges when researching a family tree, but rare when the person being sought has good reason to have their existence hidden.

The duke had arranged a driver to collect him from the nearest rail station at Alnmouth for the ten minute journey. The castle does not visually dominate the town as it is not set on elevated ground, but its ancient history and recent film fame ensure nearly 200,000 visitors each year. It was not until he was within the castle keep that he was able to appreciate one of the world's most famous exterior castle views. Lambert was shown to his room which overlooked the fusiliers museum and had time to shower and eventually connect his laptop to the wireless network. Hughes had included an excel spreadsheet which listed all the 350 entries with specific references to the original documents stored at Ashington. He had also begun a more general search in other documents held at Kew, which he hoped would shed some light on the whereabouts of the queen at that time. Lambert was shown into the library at 7.30pm in time for pre-dinner drinks. The oak panelled room was lined with rows of bookshelves on every wall, including a balcony reached by a set of ornate steps.

"Nice of you to pay us a visit Professor Lambert." The outstretched hand of the twelfth duke, a tall thin man in his late forties, roused the Cardiff historian from his daydream. After sharing a drink and being shown around the impressive room, the pair were joined by the duke's family and they all enjoyed the typically noisy affair.

"I understand you're researching the links the castle has with Queen Elizabeth I?" The duke's wife eventually bringing the conversation around to the reason for his visit.

"Yes, that's right," he replied gingerly. Only the duke had been told the real reason for Lambert's visit and had been asked to keep the matter confidential. "I'm trying to discover if she ever paid a visit here. Given the influence its occupants had on her life throughout her reign, it seems surprising she never set foot within its walls." After dinner the children and their mother disappeared into the private rooms and left Lambert and the duke alone again.

"Since your call I have been looking through some of the records we have here to see if I could find anything that may help you," the duke said as he led them through a series of stone-lined passages to a small storage room deep inside the heart of the citadel. As they walked, Lambert half-expected a young boy with round glasses and a wand to appear around the next corner. The stone-walled room, which they both had to stoop alarmingly to enter, contained several shelves stacked with both ancient and modern documents and books. They sat down at a table and the duke produced a bottle of single malt whisky and two glasses from a filing cabinet.

"You are welcome to spend as much time as you like looking through these," he said indicating the 700 years of history that was recorded within the small room. Lambert knew that most of the information contained in the files was available at Kew, but what he was looking for may not have been recorded.

"As I explained, sir, my research is of a very delicate nature and I appreciate your discretion." The duke nodded in thanks at the compliment. His wife did not believe for one moment the story he had told her and he was suffering her displeasure at withholding the truth.

"As you know professor, there is no record of her ever visiting Alnwick so I am at a loss as to what to suggest." Lambert allowed himself a moment to appreciate the smooth taste of the malt before replying.

"At that time the castle was officially unoccupied, but I am assuming that it was not abandoned and a number of servants and soldiers would have been present to protect the buildings and keep the place in order?" The duke refilled their glasses before spending the next few minutes shifting through the shelves. He eventually found the volume he sought after seeking Lambert's help to move a dozen or more heavy scrolls and boxes. He placed the leather-bound book on the table between them and carefully opened the front cover.

"These are the household records for that period," he said, turning the pages as he spoke. Lambert joined him on the opposite side of the table and together they quickly scanned the date column. "What month was it again?" asked the duke as he arrived at the first page for 1576. "According to the letter the baby would have been born around February or March." After years of practice, Lambert was quicker than his guest at reading the text and started to turn the pages himself.

"Here we are," they said in unison as a page revealed the date of *January 15th* written in English. The entries listed various items of expenditure including meat and vegetables, wages and services. It appeared the bookkeeper carried out this duty every two weeks in arrears as the next entry was dated February 1st. Lambert could see nothing unusual that would suggest a monarch was staying. No huge amounts of fine foods or wine had been noted although the details varied depending, no doubt, on how much time was devoted to the task. After a few minutes the duke stood up and emptied his glass.

"I'll leave you to it, I have a daughter who wants a bedtime story," the duke interrupted Lambert's thoughts as he opened the small door. "Help yourself to the Scotch."

Lambert removed his jacket, rearranged his glasses and returned to the accounts after having topped up his glass. He retrieved a small notebook and pen and started to make a note of the total amounts of food that had been purchased each period. He went forward as far as May and then back to November the previous year. Not surprisingly the totals varied, with a high in January which would have been invoices entered for the Christmas festivities. Ignoring this anomaly, he drew a rudimentary graph and plotted the amounts against the periods. The points rose and fell by as much as twenty percent with no obvious pattern. He guessed that the number of people staying fluctuated as soldiers and travellers came and went, so the addition of a queen and few attendees would not result in a large rise in the food budget. He spent the next hour going through the entries line by line in the hope of finding a clue. Eventually he closed the book and realised he would gain little from pursuing this line of enquiry. If the queen were staying it would have been impossible to keep it a secret from the staff and the local people. The fact that nothing could be found suggested that was because, quite simply, she had not been present. He replaced the whisky bottle back in the cabinet, noting the line of the liquid was much lower than when the duke had removed it and found his way back to the study with the help of a security man who rescued him from a corridor that looked exactly the same as several others he had explored. After sharing one last malt with the duke, he retired to his room. Whilst preparing for bed, he turned on the small TV and caught up with the main evening news. He shook his head in disbelief as he watched a report on the local northwest news of the discovery of the body of a man found at the bottom of a mineshaft near Durham. The police were working on the theory that it was a tragic suicide. How terrible he thought as the report switched to the amusing story of the evening about a cat rescued from the engine compartment of a car where it had survived a twenty mile journey. He shook his head and turned off the set. As he lay, staring at the ceiling, he wondered if this whole exercise was just a wild goose chase. Was he tricking himself into believing the letter was genuine just because he might prove the long-held rumours that Elizabeth had conceived a child with Dudley were true? Any evidence that did exist pointed to a child being raised secretly near London and turning up as a prisoner of the Spanish after his ship was intercepted en-route to France in 1587. The young man in his twenties had claimed to be Arthur Dudley and said he had been forced to flee for his life from the queen's agents. Much was written about his claims with letters to the queen's councillors from his captors describing his story and bemoaning the cost of keeping him. Historians have argued the merits ever since with many books written and theories put forward for and against. That the man existed is without doubt, but who he was and the true purpose of his journey would never be known. Had Lambert been lying in his own bed he would have abandoned the ridiculous search right there and then, but as he had made the journey north he knew he would have to complete his itinerary.

The next morning Lambert spent a pleasant couple of hours exploring the castle buildings and grounds including the Alnwick gardens which contained a unique section devoted to poisonous plants. As he wondered in and out of various rooms he imagined how it would have felt if the pregnant monarch had been staying. As he gazed out of a bedroom window at the tourists below he tried to imagine how she and Dudley could have disguised the fact that she was pregnant. Unless she had remained behind closed doors for several months this would have been difficult in the extreme. Perhaps she had special loose fitting clothes made? He recalled how it had often been said that Elizabeth had used illness to avoid difficult situations. When he returned to his room to gather his things, his laptop was still open. On a whim he sat down and searched the phrase *Elizabeth illness*. To his surprise the third entry was headed *Elizabeth Feigns Illness*. The unofficial site had several references to occasions when Elizabeth had supposedly feigned illness and taken to her bed to avoid dangerous or awkward situations. A little more investigation revealed several references to comments made by a Spanish ambassador on how Elizabeth looked *dropsical* a term used to describe someone who is swollen or bloated. Could she have weaved a web of deceit and uncertainty around herself to conceal a dangerous truth?

Central Bristol Police Headquarters, September 2009

"The Bristol police are holding them now," said Crowther. "They're college kids, both seventeen." She was standing outside a suite on interview rooms in the Central Bristol Police Headquarters in Portishead talking on her cell phone.

"Initial thoughts?" asked Larkin.

"They've been separated and each given an initial interview."

"And?" said Larkin anxiously.

"Do you think two seventeen-year-old kids are responsible for the slaughter of seven people in four corners of the country?" she said sarcastically.

"No, but they may know who is." shot back the MI5 man. There was a pause on the line.

"I'm sorry Andrew, it's just that I thought we had a real breakthrough when we discovered this was the source of the website."

"I know, me too," said Andrew in a more consolatory tone. "Look, at this time in the morning I can be down there in under an hour. Let's make sure we go over everything together."

"There's really no need, I can handle it perfectly well."

"I know you can, but two heads are better than one, even one as pretty as yours." The last words passed his lips before he even realised they were there. An even longer pause followed, one that was unlikely to be filled by Crowther this time. Andrew was completely lost and so took the cowards way out. "I'll see you in an hour," and promptly disconnected the call.

As he sped along the M5 motorway he ran over the words again and again in his mind. What on earth had made him say that? How would she react? Would she think he was being patronising or sexist? And just when they were beginning to start to build a working relationship. She would almost certainly report him for something, and she could take her pick from quite a few. He had started to wonder where else the service could send him that was more remote than Cheltenham when he was jolted from his thoughts by blue flashing lights in his rear view mirror. He glanced down and realised he was travelling at ninety eight miles an hour.

"Damn!" he cursed as he pulled over onto the emergency lane of the carriageway. He decided to follow the American tradition and stay inside his vehicle as it was cold and the spray would soak him. By the time the traffic officer had invited himself into the passenger seat Andrew had already taken his MI5 identification from his jacket together with his driver's licence.

"Before you get comfortable officer, can I show you this?" Ten minutes later Andrew was on his way with a warning from the indignant young officer who believed he was going to finish his shift with a nice speeding conviction.

Andrew showed his ID to the security camera at the gates of the headquarters of the Avon & Somerset constabulary, a new building in the outskirts of the city. He could see Jackie talking to another plain clothes officer as he walked towards her down a narrow corridor. She looked up and then dropped her eyes when theirs met.

"Where have you been?" she said looking at her watch "It's been an hour and ten minutes." She resumed her conversation and Andrew was left to wait or wander further into a station with no idea where to go. She is doing this deliberately, he thought as he detected her eyes shift minutely to watch his expression. His first reaction was to move away, but then common sense and self-preservation took over and he decided to take his punishment, he would be fortunate if this was as bad as it got. Finally the conversation broke up. Jackie turned to face him and an awkward silence descended on the pair.

"Can I buy you a coffee and perhaps we can discuss recent events?" asked Andrew cryptically.

"Why not." They set off for the canteen, she leading. Andrew was convinced he detected the curl of a smile on her lips as she passed him, head down. They queued in silence and Andrew carried the two cups to a quiet corner. Even at 6.15am the canteen of a police building is a busy place. They sat on opposite sides of a long table, her seat offset to his and concentrated on stirring their coffees. Finally Andrew cracked.

"Look Jackie, I mean Ms Crowther, or is it Mrs?" He glanced down at her left hand to find it devoid of any jewellery and up to see her looking straight at him. "Look, I didn't mean what I said, I mean it just came out. I'm sorry; it was very unprofessional of me." Jackie stared at him for another ten seconds, considering her response.

"So you think I have an ugly face then?" she said with an even angrier look. Andrew realised he was doomed and would have to face Ken Greaves again, this time almost certainly with a termination letter in his hand.

"As it happens, Miss Crowther I did mean what I said. You do have a pretty head and come to think of it the rest of you is pretty good too." He stared back at her and waited.

"Thank you Mr Larkin, I shall take that as a compliment. Now can we get back to the rather urgent matter in hand?" She gave him a smile that made his heart leap and opened her laptop. "Whilst you have been wasting the time of the traffic police," Andrew shot her a glance. "We heard," she continued. "I sat in on the interviews with both suspects. It's clear neither has any idea about the *English Monarchy* or anything remotely connected to it."

"Their computers?" asked Andrew trying not to stare at her.

"A quick scan of both sets of equipment, which is sophisticated but I doubt would be found in Fort Meade, revealed there is plenty to keep the local police busy for a while, but nothing to interest us."

"So they were just a couple of kids hacking into Facebook and e-mails?" said Andrew.

"Not quite," replied Jackie, turning her laptop around to face him. "Look here." She tried to lean over the screen but could not see to point. "Let me come around." Before she realised they were sat next to each other. Andrew kept his eyes glued to the screen whilst Jackie looked at him and slowly turned back to the computer. "They had just broken through the secondary firewall of the Greek Central Bank." Andrew was impressed but didn't know exactly why. "That takes skill and knowledge, so these two are a few grades above posting nasty comments on their friends' Twitter accounts." She clicked on another opened page. "This one was earning hundreds of pounds a month spoofing email accounts to send out millions of untraceable messages across the globe."

"At seventeen?" replied Andrew in awe.

"Once we've frightened the life out of him we'll put him through university and recruit him for NCIS."

"Poacher turned gamekeeper," said Andrew.

"But I'm convinced they had nothing to do with our killer." She closed the computer and turned to face Andrew, waiting for him to reach the same conclusion she had. "Andrew don't you see what this means?" It was too early for the MI5 man and despite the seriousness of the situation he was struggling to pay attention. "Whoever did this knew exactly what they were doing. They made it look as if the web site had been created and uploaded from one of their computers. It's an incredibly sophisticated and difficult thing to achieve without alerting the user." Andrew was beginning to realise the implications of her words.

"So you're saying that whoever is behind this has access to some smart people?"

"Smart? More like genius Andrew," she guffawed. "This is the sort of work I would expect of one of my top people."

"But wait, they didn't achieve it did they? We found them."

"Only because they wanted us to," she replied slowly. "This was a set up Andrew. Whoever did this wanted us to waste time and resources chasing down a couple of kids while they plan the next murder." They both sat in silence contemplating the significance of her words.

"So it could be a foreign government or organised crime?" suggested Andrew.

"Anyone who can afford to employ the best computer brains around."

Lambert was due to catch the train from Alnmouth to Morpeth, a journey of around two and half hours including a change at Newcastle, and a taxi to the Northumberland County Archives at Ashington a few miles away. But the duke would not hear of him taking such a torturous route when his driver could be there in less than thirty minutes, so the professor was treated to the views from the A1 instead of the East Coast Main Line. A former coalmine had been combined with a museum and country park to form the site, which was a first for Lambert. As he walked from the car he noticed the unmistakable steelwork of a large pit wheel towering over the site. He had arranged an appointment with the chief archivist whom he had briefed on the information he sought, but not the reason for his quest. She had pointed out that all the records were available online, but the originals could be made available if he wished as long as he registered online for a Woodman card that allowed him access to the records. He was shown into a room that contained a dozen microfilm readers and invited to sit at one where several boxes containing rolls of film were already in place. He opened his laptop and brought up the file showing the references sent by Hughes, located the correct microfilm roll and loaded it into the reader. It contained a series of images of a hand scribed parish register of christenings for 1576 in the parish of Alnwick. Lambert rotated the handle to step through each page until he settled on the entry for a Thomas Moor who had been christened in January of that year. He quickly dismissed this, knowing the child had still not been born when the letter had been written on February 15th.

Four hours later Lambert was still sat at the reader scrolling through the various pages and studying each one for a clue, but there were no other suitable entries in the parish of Alnwick. Lambert knew there were a further nine adjoining parishes within the area he had drawn on the map. Record keeping at that time was still unreliable and the methods differed so it would be by no means certain that even if a christening had taken place that it had been registered. He knew it was a massive task to find any clues and his head told him he was chasing phantoms, but despite his cynicism something kept whispering in his ear and encouraged him to carry on. He found the archivist and requested the films for the additional parishes.

"Planning to bring a camp bed?" she said with what Lambert thought was a strange smile after reading his request. He had booked a room at the local Premier Inn hotel for the following two nights, knowing from experience the amount of time he would need to check each entry correctly. He left the archives when they closed at 6pm and was given a lift to his hotel by the archivist who seemed in no hurry to leave when he had retrieved his case from the back seat and waved goodbye. But Lambert was too engrossed in his investigations to notice the attentions of a lonely woman. She sighed and drove off back to her single flat and TV dinner whilst he ate in the pub connected to the inexpensive hotel. Most of the tables seemed to be occupied, like his own, with single business people, either reading, punching away at a smartphone or staring into space. He did none, preferring to study his notes and decide on the best place to resume his search the next day. After finishing his meal, he decided he would spend an hour in the lounge area as his room was devoid of any character. He ordered a large malt whisky having remembered how much he had enjoyed the duke's hospitality and excused himself to check his emails using the free thirty minutes of Wi-Fi.

"You can log in anywhere in the building sir," the young barman called after him as he disappeared. Lambert emerged ten minutes later and with the help of the young man, managed to navigate the necessary screens to connect onto his VPN. He had not checked his emails for more than twenty four hours so again had the usual mix of rubbish. Halfway down the list he noted Hughes's name and the subject heading Alnwick Letter. The message was short and to the point.

Turn on your cell phone and call me asap

Peter

Lambert looked at his watch and noted it was, at 9.15pm, too late to catch him now and he made a mental note to call him first thing in the morning.

At 10.30am the next morning Lambert, who had returned to the archives, was interrupted by the same assistant who had been so reluctant to leave him outside the hotel the night before.

"There's a call for you Professor Lambert," she paused. "From the head of the National Archive." She said the last words with the reverence and awe normally reserved for the Pope. Lambert was lead into a nearby office and waited whilst the call was put through to his extension. He was not used to receiving calls from the chief executive and he wondered who he had upset.

"Tom, where on earth have you been?" The voice of Peter Hughes filled his ears. Lambert glanced out of the office at the woman who was doing her best to pretend she was not eavesdropping. She smiled at him and he returned the expression, hiding his irritation at the assumption she had made.

"Sorry, Peter," he said, stretching out to close the door and turning to face the wall "I've been buried in microfilm for the last two days."

"Well I think I may have found something that may make your search a little easier."

Lambert sat down and felt the hairs on his neck rise. Peter Hughes was not someone prone to exaggeration and for him to track him down like this, he must have something worthwhile.

"Go on," was all he could say.

"Normally I wouldn't say too much over the phone Tom, but as you have access to some original documentation up there it seemed foolish to wait until I could see you."

"Go on."

"Actually I have two pieces of information that may help," the NA man continued. "An assistant came to me for help overcoming an issue she had whilst cleaning a scroll as part of the general maintenance we have here." Lambert was beginning to fidget in his chair, but allowed the man to continue at his own pace. "Anyway, I went along to have a look and she pointed to a spot that had faded in response to the treatment. As I looked through the magnifier my eyes were drawn to an unusual place name written just below the offending spot. Tom it was the little village of Shilbottle that's just outside Alnwick. It only caught my eye as it's an unusual name." Lambert sat up straight at the mention, he recognised it immediately as one of the villages within the area he had targeted. "On closer inspection it turned out the scroll was from the exchequer accounts for Richmond & Greenwich Palaces covering the period of interest. The entry was a note that two pennies had been paid for a delivery from Alnwick to Shilbottle in March 1576. It's extremely unusual to have such an entry in the accounts and even more so for another location." Hughes went onto explain how he had discovered that the entry was far from unique and there were several invoices mentioning provisions and services at Alnwick from November 1575 to March 1576.

"But why would such a small sum be mentioned in the first place?" enquired Lambert, now furiously writing in the notebook the young woman had retrieved for him with another smile, this one rather more attractive.

"It's difficult to be precise, but it could be that whoever paid the two pennies did so from their own pocket and was claiming it back. If the bookkeeper had taken the money, however small the amount, from the treasury, he would have recorded it to avoid being accused of theft and to balance the accounts." Lambert nodded his agreement with the theory. "As for the other entries, this also points to sums being paid locally and reclaimed later. Now I have something firmer to work with I'll see what else I can discover."

They ended the call with Lambert arranging to visit Hughes again early the following week. Lambert sat at the table long after he had replaced the receiver. The phone call had changed everything as not only could he narrow his search considerably, but the chances of finding something now appeared to be a realistic possibility. He rose and was about to call out the name of the young archivist when he remembered that he had no idea. He walked out of the office to locate her and straight into the woman, who was waiting outside the door.

"I'm terribly sorry Miss..."

"Cross," she replied looking up, "Jennifer Cross."

"Jennifer," Lambert continued, giving the assistant his best smile, "I need your help."

Lambert explained to the now much more interesting looking Ms Cross about the new information, so far as it affected the search for evidence of a Moore being christened during that year. To someone who spent their working life surrounded by dusty scrolls, books and microfilm and their nights eating microwave meals on a tray in front of the TV, the excitement of the rather attractive and important professor needing her help could only have been surpassed if she had won the lottery.

"If we are limiting the search to the parish of Shilbottle then we should be able to find the young Moore in no time," she said chirpily. "Follow me." Ninety minutes later they were sat snugly together, in front of a microfilm reader examining the last entry in the register of christenings for the parish of Shilbottom, St James for the years 1575-1599. Lambert sat back, aching from being in the same position.

"Could the child have been christened in another parish?"

"It's possible but unlikely," said Cross "The communities were very insular back then and everyone would belong to the same church."

Lambert felt deflated. After the excitement of Hughes's call he had been convinced they would find the entry and take a giant step towards proving the letter genuine. "We can widen the search into other parishes after lunch if you like?" she said smiling. Lambert did not reply as his mind was wandering into despair. He was used to the laborious and often fruitless search for family history, but had truly believed he was on the verge of a historic discovery and one that would give him the book that was long overdue. Academics are judged on their published works and it was five years since his last. When he emerged from his thoughts the young woman had disappeared, bored no doubt with the search. He rose to stretch his legs and saw her coming across the office smiling from ear to ear.

"You look as if you could do with some cheering up," she said, taking his arm. "I've managed to get Marjorie to cover for me this afternoon, so we can go for some lunch at a lovely pub I know."

Lambert was half way across the room before he could think of any objection, but then relaxed and realised that it was a good idea and perhaps just what he needed. The pub was just a few miles away in the small seaside town of Newbiggin. Despite a cold autumnal wind whistling off the North Sea, the food was good and after two glasses of red wine, Lambert had relaxed enough to look at her differently. He guessed she was around thirty five although she looked older, with unkempt shoulder length auburn hair, a slim figure and a pretty if not beautiful oval face. She wore makeup, but he guessed it was not something she regularly used as even his untrained eye could see it had been applied in a rush. At first they talked about their work but as they became more comfortable, the conversation drifted into their private lives, or lack of. They were, like thousands of others, surrounded by people but feeling alone. Lambert could see that she had drunk too much to drive so suggested they take a walk. They passed the links golf course that borders the beach and strolled along the blustery water's edge. At one point she almost lost her balance and clung to Lambert for support. Her touch felt good and she, sensing his mood, linked her arm through his. After half a mile their path was blocked by the waves crashing against a rocky outcrop that jutted into the bay. The pair walked as far as they could until they were sheltered by the rocks and Lambert leaned back against the cold surface. She looked up at him and he instinctively reached down and kissed her gently, not knowing how she would react. He felt her immediately push against his body and her arm reach behind his neck pulling his lips tightly against hers.

They spent that and the following evening in her flat. It had been over six months since Lambert had felt the warm skin of a woman's body and the thought made him realise just how much he had sacrificed for his work. He guessed by the awkward way they first made love that it must have been twice that, or longer for her. The flat, although small, was pleasant and had a wonderful view over the open countryside beyond with a small balcony where they sat, talked and drank wine. He was still finding it difficult to believe that this was the same person who had welcomed him, if that was the right word, to the archives a couple of days before. During the next few days they worked together searching through dozens of reels of microfilm trying to locate some mention of the child or its family, but although there were several references to the surname in its various forms, none matched the age and date range they were seeking. With no definite starting point, they had no way of knowing if any of the marriages, burials and christenings they found was linked to the adopted child. Lambert knew they would normally have abandoned the hunt long before, but the end of the search would mean the end of his visit and neither was willing to accept that. The second night he told her the reason for his trip and showed her a copy of the letter he had brought with him. If she was irritated he had not revealed the truth earlier, she kept it to herself. They shared a curious bond and lay in bed or sat on the balcony discussing theories and ideas surrounding the child in between sessions of love making. He was used to people's eyes glazing over when he discussed his work in detail, but she shared a passion for his work as heated as for each other's bodies.

On the third morning he was brought back to reality by an email from the university. He had been due back the day before and missed two tutorial sessions. The bursar was not pleased and pointed out that the cost of the stand-in tutor would come from his budget as would the additional hotel bill. Lambert was tempted to reply informing him that he had actually saved the university the cost of two night's bed and board, but resisted, knowing the explanation would cause too many raised eyebrows in the faculty. A quick look at the National Rail enquires website revealed a train that left Morpeth at 15:10 that would see him home before midnight.

"Jenny," he looked up from the laptop to see the sadness in her eyes. "I have to get back to the university. I'm already a day overdue and I have a mountain of work to catch up on."

She insisted on driving him to the station and they waited together on the platform until the dark blue East Coast train came to a halt. He held her in his arms until the last possible moment and had to rush to avoid the automatic door closing before he could board. They had not spoken since the train had come into view and now Lambert struggled to find the right words. He pulled down the window and leaned out, despite the stern look from the guard. He knew he was unlikely to see her again and had learned many years before never to make idle promises he could not keep. When he looked in her face she raised a finger to her lips to silence him and then mouthed the words.

"Don't worry," she said, sensing his dilemma.

"I'll let you know how things turn out," he called as the train began to move.

She gave him her best smile and nodded as his window moved off and was tempted to run to keep him in view. But she was a thirty-eight-year-old professional woman and not about to re-enact a scene from an old black and white tearjerker, so she waited until the train had disappeared from view before wiping the tear from her cheek.

Croydon, Surrey, November 2009

"It had nothing to do with me." Ray Higgins sat at his computer screen and read the text again.

"But you're the person responsible for updating the web page Ray, so who else could it be, aliens?"

"Funny guy," replied Higgins. "Someone has been hacking into my computer and uploading this stuff to our site."

"Well remove it will you, it's got nothing to do with us and makes us looks like a bunch of anarchists." The line went dead.

"I already have," said Higgins to the empty airwaves. He replaced the receiver and turned his attention once again to the screen. As the webmaster for the UK Workers Liberation Army, he kept the site up to date with the latest news and views of the organisation. He had been involved with the UKWLA since its creation five years before and had participated in several raids on banks and corporate buildings across the country. As a professional IT support technician with a global banking company, he had been the natural choice to run the group's website and protect the identity of its members by making use of his skills to prevent the authorities locating where their activities were located. He knew that the site had been targeted in an attempt to discover his whereabouts, but had so far been able to evade detection. It had been two days ago that he had seen the new home page when logging in to update the site with details of a raid on a food processing plant in Essex that was exploiting foreign workers. He had no idea what *English Monarchy* was and even less on why someone would choose to hijack his site to plant the notion that the UKWLA were involved in its aims. It had taken him over an hour to remove the references and links on the home page and the three other pages and had he not been keen to keep his identity secret, he would have seriously considered contacting the police given the content. If the information was genuine then people had been murdered and more were in danger from these people. Apparently some office worker had recently been thrown down a lift shaft, not to mention miners and farm workers who had all met untimely ends. The really worrying thing was the fact that whoever was doing this had created a story that linked the UKWLA to this English Monarchy group and gave the impression that they shared a common aim. *Today's monarchy still plot with governments and the global exploiters of labour to deny the people their true rights. Our new ruler will give all subjects a better life.* "Seems like a load of rubbish to me," he said out loud. It had taken less than twelve hours for the site to be hijacked again, this time with the additional details of a vicar. Higgins knew that it was likely that this traffic would be intercepted by the security services which would lead them to his address. The hacker obviously knew what he was doing and had seemed to have deliberately made his IP address visible for just long enough for those with the right resources to track its location. He sat back in his chair wondering how long it would be before the knock on the door.

Lambert arrived home just after midnight. Despite securing a window seat with a power socket, he spent the entire journey lurching between thoughts of Jenny and what he should do with the letter. The old dealer would be disappointed that his find had led to nothing and his parchment worthless. He knew that he would face a dressing down from the bursar and did not even have the carrot of a sensational historic find to deflect his wrath. In his entire career he could not recall an occasion when he felt his work was worthless and thoughts of what other direction his life might take began to creep into mind. He knew this was partly due to how he had spent the last two days, a feeling he had almost forgotten existed and the dark, cold house which greeted him did nothing to raise his spirits. Neither did the sour milk which he poured into the cup containing the last spoonful of coffee. Lambert rang the dealer and Giddens at Christie's the next day to bring them up to date with the details of his trip to Kew and Alnwick. They agreed that the university would keep the letter for a few weeks on the remote chance that something turned up. The meeting with the bursar was as bad as he had feared, tempered only the fact that Lambert's receipts were less than he expected. Thankfully the finance man seemed unconcerned that Lambert had apparently slept rough for two nights, assuming that he had paid the bill himself as an act of contrition.

It was three weeks later that Lambert was forced to retrieve his cell phone from the pocket of his jacket. He was marking some papers without really concentrating and it took several rings for him to realise it was his phone chirping away. A painful memory crossed his mind as he remembered it was Jenny who had changed his ringtone whilst teasing him about the ancient model. As he went to answer the sound stopped. He did not think to check the number, although whether he would have recognised the main switchboard of Kew was doubtful. He tossed the phone on top of a pile of papers and returned to his task. A minute later his desk phone sprang into life.

"Tom, it's Peter, I think I may have found what you're looking for. Check your emails and ring me back, I want you to see it with your own eyes before we talk." He was gone before Lambert had a chance to raise any objection. Luckily he was already connected to the university's network, so it took him very little time to call up his inbox. He noted that Peter's e-mail had an attachment and he sighed with relief after clicking on the message and not getting the dreaded quarantine alert that would have barred him instant access to the scans. Lambert decided to print the three separate pages rather than try to read them from the monitor. He had learned through experience that the printed page gave a better image and did not leave him with a headache through eye strain. Two of the pages were from the Calendar of State Papers Domestic Part 1 (Henry VIII to Elizabeth I, 1509-1603), the third from the taxation records for Northumberland. Lambert recognised both sources, the first a collection of letters, documents and scrolls written by officials and members of the monarch's court which often cast light on important events through gossip and rumour as well as official papers. The second was a record of the collection of local taxes for the Treasury. At that time tax could be collected any time the Crown needed extra cash such as a war or for building grand projects. Lambert concentrated on the latter and scrabbled in a drawer for a magnifying glass he kept for studying annoyingly small documents, an occurrence that seemed to be happening much more frequently. The page was taken from a tax collection book for Northumberland dated August 1588. As he followed the entries down the page he suddenly caught his breath as his eyes rested on the name of a Thomas Moore of the parish of Shilbottle. Mr Moore had been asked to pay the sum of six shillings, based on the assets and land he farmed. But what made Lambert start to shake was the entry underneath. The taxation records often served as a form of census with the names of the whole family listed in addition to the head of the household. Written in neat script, in English was the name of Thomas's only child Angus, aged twelve. Lambert stared at the page for a full minute as if expecting the words to disappear or change. He did not even look at the other two pages before dialling Hughes's number.

"How did you find it!" he gasped as soon as he heard the Kew man pick up his receiver.

"Pure genius old chap." Hughes explained how he had remembered an old trick he had been shown by his mentor over thirty years before, in locating children where no birth or christening record existed. It was not uncommon for priests to simply forget through overwork or drink to make a note of every event, but the taxman was always very thorough as today's child was tomorrow's taxpayer. It had taken him all this time to work his way through the lists. Luckily taxes were not collected at regular intervals as today, but as when money was needed. There were four tax collections after young Moore's birth and this was the first where he had been mentioned. His father must have kept his existence a secret from the others.

"I knew straight away that this was the one you were looking for." Lambert spent a moment digesting what he had been told. There could be no doubt that this proved that a farmer named Moore, living in Shilbottom a village only five miles from Alnwick Castle had a child that was born in 1576. This evidence, together with the entry in the exchequer accounts of a delivery to the same village, made a compelling argument for the authenticity of the letter.

"What did you make of the letters?" Hughes asked.

"What lett.." He quickly picked up the remaining pages and scanned through them.

"I can't think straight Peter, what do they say?"

"They are both letters sent at the time she may have been at Alnwick. One is a reply from Wallsingham to Thomas Wilkes who has been complaining that a decision on some extra defences at Tilbury was being delayed. He says she is indisposed with Oedema."

"That's abdominal swelling or Dropsy, right?" interjected Lambert.

"Yes." Hughes went on to explain the other letter was from Wallsingham to Lord Burghly, both trusted advisors to the queen. "He says he has been prevented from visiting her in her confinement." Lambert looked more carefully at the two pages and noted the dates as December 1575 and January 1576 respectively.

"My God Peter, what have we found?"

"I think we need to be very careful how we handle this Tom, it could still be the work of a very clever forger who's just taken these facts and worked them into the letter." Lambert digested Hughes's words before replying.

"How can we prove this beyond doubt?"

"We would carry out a DNA test, but unless we can find a sample from both that's obviously out of the question," replied Hughes. That was exactly the answer Lambert had expected and he almost leapt from his chair.

"Peter, we do have a sample from the queen, the one I found when we examined her corset!" Lambert had been granted permission to examine a corset that had been worn by the queen shortly before her death which had been left undisturbed inside a glass display cabinet at Westminster Abbey for many years. On close inspection they had discovered a hair which was almost certainly from Elizabeth. A DNA signature could be mapped from this and matched if they could find the grave of Angus Moore.

"The chances of locating a grave of that age are very remote Tom, you would probably have more chance if you traced the lineage a little further."

"I agree, but we can try." They parted with an agreement to keep the information between themselves until Lambert had a chance to begin tracing the Moore family tree. Hughes offered his time and the considerable resources of the archives; Lambert had another person he hoped might be able to help.

Lambert decided there was one individual he would have to inform if he wanted the time and resources to pursue the search. The bursar was both irritated and elated when he realised Tom had been deceiving him about the true motive for his recent trips to Kew and Alnwick. But when Lambert dangled the prospect of an academic paper and bestselling book in front of his eyes, all was forgiven. Armed with his 'pass' he lost no time in calling Jenny and bringing her up to date with the news. Apart from a couple of days when she had visited relatives in Manchester, they had spoken on the phone and swapped emails almost continuously and the thought of seeing her again made him feel like a teenager. He was secretly delighted at how quickly she had picked up on the importance of the find and was already thinking of how and where they could track down the information they would need to discover a grave.

"I have a few things to tidy up here, and a study group I must take before I can leave, so I'll probably travel up in a couple of days."

"That's wonderful," she replied. "What hotel do you want to stay in?" Lambert was a little taken aback at the thought she did not want him to stay at her flat.

"Er, the Premier Inn I guess," he replied sadly. He could hear her stifled laughter and realised he was being teased. "Ha, bloody ha."

GCHQ, Cheltenham, December 2009

As soon as Andrew walked into his office, Paul Williams from NCIS stuck his head around the door.

"David Scott has called a liaison group meeting for ten," he said, almost cheerily.

"Any idea why?"

"Looks like they've picked up some new traffic from our mad monarch," laughed Williams.

Andrew looked at his watch and decided he had enough time to check his e-mails and go over the statements from the two Bristol teenage hackers, before the meeting began. He immediately noticed Jackie's name at the top of his inbox as it had been sent only twenty minutes before and was headed *Workers Liberation Army*. He resisted reading it as he guessed it was linked to the meeting with Scott and instead opened the one sent the day before, also by Crowther, with the subject line *Bristol Teenage Hackers*. The statements of the two boys were attached, together with the NCIS woman's report. He ignored the statements and double clicked on the report. As they had suspected, neither of the two youngsters had been able to provide any useful information on the *English Monarchy* and Jackie's conclusion was that they had been used as guinea pigs by someone with advanced knowledge of internet communications, to create a false trail. She warned that, in her opinion, this significantly raised the risks associated with this group and their ability to carry out their threats. She recommended increasing the protection on prominent politicians and members of the Royal family. Andrew noted the circulation list of the email included the heads of several protection groups including SO1 whose job it was to protect current and former prime ministers and SO14 that covered the Royal family. Andrew sent a copy of the mail on to Ken Greaves and Anthony Neild, the head of K2. He added a paragraph of his own to echo his agreement with the NCIS conclusions as regards precautions, but said he was still not convinced that the group posed a serious threat to the monarch. When he had finished it was 9.55am and he closed down his connection and headed for the conference room.

Scott opened the meeting by explaining why Charles Smythe of MI6 was the only member of the ELG missing and continued with a brief résumé of the information that existed on the *English Monarchy*. Despite intensive activity no additional traffic had been uncovered and it had now been agreed that the site at Bristol had been a deliberate deception.

"So the two youngsters have no idea how or why they were used to host this site?" asked Bill Frost.

"None," said Paul Williams, answering the question that had obviously been asked of Scott. Andrew gave the young NCIS man a quizzical look and turned his attention to the special branch man.

"I wasn't present at any of the interrogations Bill, but I'm sure you have seen Jackie Crowther's report. I agree with her conclusion that it was an experienced professional who was behind this." The group spent the next ten minutes discussing the various options, with Williams adamant that the Bristol pair should be questioned further.

"I think we've accepted their explanations too readily," he argued.

A knock on the door halted the conversation and Scott waved Mary Ward into the room. "I think the information Mary has will make our conversation somewhat redundant," he said as she connected her laptop to the overhead projector.

"Good morning gentlemen," she said, greeting the group. "I'm sorry I'm a little late but I wanted to present you with the latest data we've received." A web page of the *UK Workers Liberation Army* appeared on the screen.

"This group has been on our radar for a while," said Frost. "They were responsible for a lot of the incitement on Facebook during the London riots the other year."

"That's right," said Ward. "But over the past forty eight hours they seem to have branched out into a new project." A new homepage filled the screen and Larkin immediately noticed the bear and ragged staff image in one corner of the page. Ward quickly stepped through three further pages.

"As you can see these pages contain similar statements and content to the *English Monarchy* site."

"With one notable exception," broke in Scott. "Thank you Mary, I'll take it from here." Ward nodded at her superior and made to close her laptop. "Leave that for now." Scott waited until she had vacated the room before continuing. "I want the discussions and actions we agree next to be confined to those with the minimum of an enhanced DV clearance."

"I agree," said Williams.

"Currently the *UKWLA* website contains the details of two murders not on the *Monarchy* site," said Scott flashing live feeds from both sites on a split screen. "We now know the details of murders seven and eight."

"That's the vicar?" said Williams. Andrew sat upright and studied the screen. The murders were described in a chilling detail absent from the business like table of the *Monarchy* site.

"Have the *UKWLA* been associated with this level of violence before?"

"Good question, Andrew," said Scott. "We looked back at the types of threats they have issued in the past and they have been careful to limit themselves to inciting others to carry out any action, although we know they have an active unit that's carried out raids on some soft corporate targets."

"So this looks like an escalation?" said Frost.

"Yes, but this is a trend we've seen before with these types of groups," said Scott. "They have some success hitting an easy target and suddenly start believing they can overthrow the government."

"But why would they target ordinary people if they're supposed to support the working classes?" argued Andrew.

"Collateral damage, if past excuses are anything to go on," suggested Frost.

"The question is," said Andrew, "given the time we've spent chasing shadows in Bristol, how much credence do we give this?"

"We can't afford to ignore it," said Scott "and in all honesty it's the only line of enquiry we have." Andrew's cell phone interrupted the meeting. He was about to reject the call when Bill Frost's phone joined in the chorus, closely followed by Scott's and Williams.

"Must be important," said Andrew and all four headed for a corner of the room to answer their respective calls. Andrew listened for thirty seconds before speaking "Where's he being held?"

Northumberland Archives, Ashington, December 2009

By the time he arrived in Ashington the hunt for Angus Moore had unearthed more results. Jenny had discovered an entry for a burial in the same parish in 1637, making him sixty one at his death. She had contacted the vicar at St James and discovered the present church was built in 1885 to replace the earlier building. He had checked and there was no trace of a grave, but was not surprised as it was probable the plot had been reused at least once. She had also found a reference to his father Thomas, who had suffered the loss of his right to farm the land under common law, commonly known as enclosure in 1590. Angus became a tenant farmer and took over from his father. They sat together studying the original documents Jenny had retrieved from the archives storage facility.

"Without locating a grave and retrieving some bone fragments, we'll never be able to prove a conclusive link between Angus and the queen." Lambert stood up and began to pace the room.

"We'll just have to trace the male line until we find a grave," said Jenny gathering up the documents.

"But that could take ages and there's no guarantee we would get permission to exhume the body," sighed Lambert.

"Not unless you revealed the truth."

Over the next few days they worked together to begin piecing together, through birth, death and marriage entries, the life of the Moore family at the beginning of the seventeenth century. Angus had married and his wife Mary had produced two children, Richard and Rose. Richard was christened in 1600 and his sister four years later. Rose had died at the age of ten, but Richard had gone on to produce an heir, James before dying at the great age of seventy two in 1672. James had maintained the family tradition of farming and had remained in Shilbottle like his relatives. This was not unusual as with transport slow and opportunities to relocate rare, most families stayed within a few miles of where they were born for their entire lives. None of these descendants had graves that could be traced. James had died in 1683 having a son Thomas to pass on the family line, born in 1645. At this point the trail went cold as no record of Thomas having married or passed away could be found.

"He must have moved out of the parish," said Lambert, cleaning his glasses with his handkerchief.

Paddington Green police station, December 2009

It took Andrew just over two and a half hours to reach Paddington Green police station in central London. During the journey he made and received several calls including one from Jackie, who arranged to meet him there. On arriving at the seventies built concrete building he entered through the same main entrance as on his previous visit. However, on this occasion he immediately headed for the single door in one corner of the reception area. This lead down a flight of stairs to a corridor ending with a heavy grey steel door. He pressed the intercom button and waited.

"Secure custody suite." The distorted voice coming from the speaker gave no indication as to what lay beyond. Andrew looked into a camera mounted over the door and held up his MI5 ID badge.

"Larkin, MI5. I'm expected." A loud buzzing noise together with the door opening confirmed his request had been granted.

The secure custody suite below Paddington Green police station was refurbished in 2009 at a cost of £0.5million. It comprises sixteen cells, each around nine square yards in size and is designed to hold terrorist suspects for questioning for periods of up to twenty eight days. It also contains interview rooms and an audio-visual system to allow inmates to enjoy some stimulation during their confinement. In its thirty year existence it has housed both members of the IRA and British nationals released from detention at Guantanamo Bay. Each cell is self-contained and its occupant constantly monitored by CCTV. Andrew was shown into a small conference room where several others had already gathered including members of special branch, the Met and Jackie Crowther from NCIS.

"Has anyone here spoken to him yet?" asked Andrew as he hung his coat on a chair. On the wall a large flat screen monitor showed a thin set man sat with his elbows resting on his knees perched on the bed of one of the cells.

"Not since he arrived here," answered a uniformed officer who had appeared in the doorway behind Andrew. "I'm Adam Tozier, duty officer for the suite."

"Thanks Adam, I'll take over from here." The duty officer nodded and took a seat next to Andrew. "My name is Detective Superintendent Mike Ferguson from the Met," continued the plain clothes officer. "I'm based here at Paddington and have been put in charge of the case at least until we can sort out where he fits."

"Can you run through the facts again DS Ferguson for the benefit of those who may have missed some of the communications?" said Crowther.

"Of course ma'am," he replied. "The suspect presented himself at Croydon Police Station at seven thirty this morning and asked to speak to someone." Ferguson paused to consult his notes "*Someone who knows about the English Monarchy murders* were his exact words." Everyone automatically looked at the frail figure on the screen.

"He was placed in an interview room for thirty minutes until the duty sergeant could find someone to interview him. Once the detective constable understood the full story he immediately contacted special branch who arranged for him to be transferred here."

"What I can't understand is why he just walked into a police atation and confessed after spending so long evading all attempts to track him down for work with the UKWLA," said Andrew.

"It all seems too easy," agreed Crowther.

"Well that's what we're here to find out," said Bill Frost.

"Adam, can you transfer the prisoner into an interview room," said Ferguson "I'll conduct the interview and you can monitor proceedings from here," he said pointing at the screen. As he left the room the group watched an officer appear in the cell and remove the suspect. The image of the empty cell remained on the screen for two minutes before switching to an empty interview room. Andrew took the opportunity to catch Jackie's attention and give her his best smile, which didn't go unnoticed by Frost who was sitting next to her. Crowther did her best to ignore Andrew and maintained a stony expression, but he was sure her eyes betrayed something different. The man could be seen entering the field of the camera and sitting at a table. Ferguson's voice broke the awkward silence

"I'll leave him in the room for a few minutes to make him sweat a bit."

"I could do with a coffee," said Andrew walking into the corridor. He immediately found a small kitchen containing the compulsory machine and was waiting for his cup to fill when Jackie appeared at his shoulder.

"What was that all about?" she said in a loud whisper. He retrieved his drink and turned to face her.

"Cappuccino?" She took the cup and walked to the end of the small room. Larkin pushed the same combination of buttons and studied the machine as it clunked its way through the cycle. "I'm sorry, was it that obvious?" he eventually said.

"Was what obvious Andrew?" she asked with a mixture of irritation and teasing. He carefully examined his coffee for several seconds, not knowing how to respond.

"I thought," he started.

"Thought what?" she interrupted him.

"I thought." He was searching for the right words and she was not making it easy. "I thought you might like to go for dinner one night," he blurted out in a defiant tone. She looked at him with a serious expression and Andrew's heart sank, then suddenly brushed passed him to peer around the corner of the room, before turning to face him.

"You can't make it look so obvious Andrew. It'll make life difficult for both of us." He realised that she was right and that it would be impossible for them to work together and see each other. He looked up sadly into her eyes and was amazed to see a completely different woman. "I thought you'd never ask," she said with a devious smile and disappeared out of the door only to reappear a few seconds later. "But for goodness sake keep that smile to yourself."

"Thanks," said Frost as Andrew placed a coffee on the table in front of him. "I think we'll be starting in a minute or two." The image had not changed except for a drink on the suspect's table.

"Whilst we're together, let me bring you both up to date with the results of the tests carried out on the two exhumed bodies," said Jackie.

"Sorry Jackie, we both got copied in on those a couple of days ago," said Frost by way of an answer.

"And the cards found for the miner and lockkeeper?" she continued.

"In the miner's locker and the lock-keeper's lunchbox," replied Andrew. The sound of a door opening distracted the group and signalled Ferguson's entrance whilst the rear of the detective's head sitting at the vacant chair confirmed his presence.

"Interview in room two of Paddington Green custody suite timed at 3.18pm, Wednesday December 10th. Present Detective Superintendent Michael Ferguson and Sergeant Adam Tozier." The suspect looked up for the first time and glanced behind Ferguson at the figure of the custody officer who was out of camera shot. "Ok sir can you start by stating your full name and address."

"Raymond Anthony Higgins of 23 Sampson Close, Carshalton," said the man, the first words the group had heard him utter.

"Ok Mr Higgins," continued Ferguson in a less formal tone, "can you tell us why you presented yourself at Croydon police station and what exactly you want to confess?" everyone in the room already knew the answer to the question, but Ferguson needed the story recorded in the man's own words.

"Well," he began hesitantly, "as soon as I saw that stuff on my website, I knew you lot would be on to me."

"Can you explain what you mean in more detail," interrupted the policeman.

"I work in IT, that's how I've been able to keep the website source secret for so long. I knew MI5 or whoever would be trying to find out where I lived so they could shut us down."

"So you thought it would be a good idea to walk into a police station and give us your address?" said Frost. They all looked at the special branch man.

"Whoever put that *English Monarchy* stuff on the site knew what they were doing. I took it off twice and it just reappeared a few hours later. I could see that they'd hacked into my system and had complete control over everything and I knew they were deliberately allowing my IP to be traced, so I decided I would hand myself in before I got a knock on the door at four in the morning."

"Have you any idea who it was that did this Ray?" asked Ferguson.

"Do you think I would be sitting here if I did?" he replied. "The bastards have stitched me up and if I ever find out who they are they'll be the ones who are murdered." Ferguson then moved on to questioning the man on the activities of the UKWLA and Andrew and the others, apart from Frost, began to lose interest. He and Jackie wandered back to the kitchen.

"I don't expect this was part of the plan," said Jackie.

"How do you mean?" said Andrew.

"Well if this guy is telling the truth, and I suspect he is, then this is another red herring designed to waste our time and resources chasing the *English Monarchy* into a dead end."

"But why spend all this time and effort deceiving us like this, why not just carry out the murders?"

"Because," said Crowther passing a coffee to Andrew, "they need to tell the world what they're doing, it's all part of the theatre."

"You keep on saying they, Jackie. What makes you so convinced it's more than one person?" Jackie took a sip from her own cup before replying.

"I can't see how one person can carry out several brutal murders all over the country and have the time to concentrate on this level of computer espionage." Andrew looked at her and smiled.

"Are you sure you just don't want to admit that someone who is obviously so intelligent and skilful could be capable of such brutality?" Crowther shot him the irritated glance he was already getting to know.

"I look at the facts Andrew and I don't cloud them with any preconceptions."

"What do we know about the seventh murder?" he asked, changing the subject.

"It didn't take long to locate the incident," she replied. "Thankfully not too many people fall down lift shafts. Apparently a man was working late in his office on the twenty fifth floor of a high rise block in central Bristol in October. His wife raised the alarm around 11.30pm when she couldn't get in touch with him."

"How terrible for her," said Andrew, feeling his demons rising again.

"He was found at the bottom of the lift shaft. His body was in a pretty bad state, twenty five floors is a long way to fall."

"Did they find a card?" said Andrew.

"There was nothing on the report I saw but, as we now know, that means nothing. The local police are going over the scene again now. I expect they'll find it in a drawer or something." As if on cue Crowther's phone rang and she moved down the corridor to take the call. Andrew sat at a small table and stared at the bottom of his cup thinking of the dead man's wife and how she would have to go through the same pain. Jackie's appearance brought him back to the present.

"His wife found it in his jacket pocket. She didn't think to contact the police assuming it was connected with his business."

"My God," said Andrew, "whoever is doing this is playing games with us."

"I know," said Jackie. "So far the only card placed so it would be found immediately was on the vicar's body, so we must assume that the killer's timetable has changed."

"Not necessarily changed Andrew, this could all be panning out exactly as planned."

"But what the hell are we supposed to do?" Andrew rose from the seat and paced the corridor feeling angry and helpless. "There's not much more we can do here," he said glancing at his watch. "It's4.30pm, if I leave now I'll hit the worst of the traffic and it will take me at least three hours to get back to Cheltenham." He left his words hanging for a few seconds before eventually continuing. "Or I could book myself into the Marriot at County Hall?" Jackie was watching the monitor showing the Workers Liberation Army man giving Ferguson every detail of its operation and jotting down a note. "Or I could book myself..."

"I heard you the first time Andrew," she said, holding the note over her shoulder. "Pick me up at eight, I know a nice quiet restaurant just a few minutes' walk from my place." Andrew took the note, which contained an address in Notting Hill. He turned and walked toward the thick metal doors without a word, but with a grin as wide as the Thames.

Portsmouth, December, 2009

The old town of Portsmouth has seen a thousand ships pass between the Round Tower and Fort Blockhouse on their way to and from the Royal Naval Dockyard just a few hundred yards beyond. At its narrowest point, the gap between Portsmouth and Gosport is just over 700 feet but it has witnessed the passing of the largest ships of the line throughout history. The dockyard first opened in 1495 with the building of what is the world's oldest dry dock for Henry VII. It is also home to Nelson's famous flagship *Victory* in which he led the British to the glorious defeat of the French and Spanish fleets off the Spanish coast at Cape Trafalgar in October 1805, which confirmed the small island's global naval supremacy. As the headquarters and main point of embarkation, many of the 7,000 ships and other floating craft which delivered 50,000 tonnes of equipment and more than 156,000 fighting men onto the beaches of Normandy on a June morning in 1944, passed through that same 700 feet. In 1980, millions witnessed the homecoming of the South Atlantic Task Force after its recapture of the Falkland Islands from the short-lived Argentinean occupation. Over the last twenty years the number of ships available to the Royal Navy had fallen to seventy eight, many having been sold, mothballed or scrapped. Its last significant act had seen the departure of the aircraft carrier Ark Royal on her way to the breakers yard a few years before. During all of the five hundred years since the first Jack Tar had boarded the early fighting ships of Britain's premier service, the good townsfolk of this proud naval town have done their best to look after their guests. Whether brought to town by the press gangs or as a volunteer every one of those sailors had two needs in common, women and beer. By 1900 there were around 800 pubs within two miles of the waterfront and the matlows regularly filled the coffers of every one. It was from one such hostelry that the Chief Petty Officer emerged. Actually he had been thrown out by the burly landlord for whom the last straw had been the sailor's insistence that his wife really didn't mind giving one of Her Majesty's fighting seaman a passionate kiss. It was not the first time he had been ejected from a bar; indeed it had happened in just about every port across the globe. After twenty five years' service, the navy was his life and when in port he always felt out of place, except when he had hold of a pretty lady in one hand and a pint of good bitter in the other. But tonight both had disappeared when the money some kindly stranger had placed behind the bar had run out and he had finally exhausted his own funds, which seemed to happen more often than he liked. He looked up and through the glaze recognised he was in the old town. He started to sway down Penny Street towards what he knew was the sea, drawn by deeply buried memories and his nostrils. The combination of drink and years at sea made him immune to the biting cold sea wind that funnelled down the narrow road. As he drifted along he tried to think how and where he could get another drink. He had no cash and did not have a clue where the nearest ATM machine could be. If he could find another pub they might have one of those portable ones in the corner. That had saved him a few times before when he found himself potless. He dug into his back pocket and after a struggle, in which his trousers almost emerged victorious, held his wallet in his outstretched arm. By this time he had reached Battery Row and could see the raised walkway that overlooked the entrance to the harbour directly in front of him. Wrestling his bank card free from his wallet, he tried to focus on the slim plastic card which was the route to his next drink. He had needed every part of the limited concentration available to successfully put one foot in front of the other with any degree of consistency and the additional co-ordination required to remove and study the thin card proved too much for his addled senses. Something had to give and his brain, somewhat unfairly decided it would cease communicating with his legs. The seaman slowly toppled to one side, still keeping a close eye on the card, and crashed into a raised flower bed beneath the ramp that led to the walkway beyond. On a freezing cold Wednesday night in December, there was little chance of anybody being around to rescue the matlow as he wallowed in the dirt, but his luck was in. As if by magic a helping hand appeared to pull him into a sitting position. Another, it could have been from the same person, produced a bottle with what looked very much like his next drink. Things aren't so bad after all he thought, gulping down the fiery liquid. Two more, these in gloves, helped him up and guided him up some steps and onto a grassy bank behind the wall. It was cosy here, out of the wind and hidden from the glare of the streetlights. Another gulp and another until the bottle was empty. Damn. Another appeared magically in front of him, those hands again. Bless you, he thought, they were even helping him to make sure he didn't spill any of the precious liquid.

"Thanks mate," he slurred, trying to focus on the face beyond without success. After finishing the bottle with some help from his new friend, he decided that even he had drunk enough for one night. He tried to gain some grip on the ground to begin the perilous task of standing, but this was proving impossible, partly due to the fact that those hands were pushing him back. He felt the smooth edge of another bottle being pressed between his lips. As he raised one arm from the ground to push it away, he fell back, thumping his head on the ground. The hands now began to force the bottle into his mouth and for the first time the taste was proving unpleasant. He tried to grab the bottle but the hand easily brushed his aside. Was it the strength of the hand or his weakness that made that so easy? Oh well, no point in refusing a free drink, he thought, as he slipped into oblivion. The figure tossed the empty bottle aside and reached into a rucksack for another. Straddling the prone sailor the content was emptied down his unresisting throat. Then another, and another, five in total. The pure Polish vodka was eighty percent proof, nearly double the strength of normal spirits and not even a hardened sailor's drink-sodden system could cope with that much alcohol. The hands replaced the plastic bank card into its allotted space in the wallet and added a small business card with a handwritten number on one side.

Notting Hill, London, December 2009

Andrew pulled up outside the small three storey town house in the fashionable west London suburb at exactly 8pm and checked his features in the rear view mirror. Having thrown a few items in a bag before he left Cheltenham, he felt he looked respectable. He had made sure he left the hotel as swiftly as possible to avoid any chance of running into his impromptu drinking partner Tim Stevens again and covered the three miles in just under twenty minutes, which was good for central London. There were no parking spaces outside the house and it took him ten minutes of crawling around the adjacent streets before a car pulled away just as he turned a corner. By the time he jogged back to the house he was fifteen minutes late. As his finger hovered over the bell the door opened.

"Fashionably late?" Andrew hardly recognised the woman that stood in the doorway. Her shoulder length hair, normally tied back now framed her oval face. Her makeup and lipstick was more pronounced than he had seen before, but still applied with a delicate and skilful touch, and she wore a calf-length blue dress that matched her eyes. Andrew felt himself blush, not out of embarrassment at his late arrival but out of guilt for his feelings.

"Sorry, I couldn't find a parking space," he mumbled as she closed the door and led him by the arm down the street.

"Our table is booked for eight thirty and they'll let it go if we are more than five minutes late." Andrew had taken several steps before he fully understood her words.

"You're joking," he said "Just where are we going?"

"You'll see," she said linking her arm through his.

"Two stars!" They stood outside the brown painted building looking at the menu.

"Come on, we're late, you can look when we get inside." She pulled him through the door at exactly 8.36pm and they were immediately shown to their table. Andrew felt relaxed and happier than he had since returning from Menworth and ordered champagne which, at £16 a glass, was just as well. He ordered flame grilled mackerel with avocado followed by saddle of fallow deer with beetroot. Jackie started with a salad of green beans, hazelnuts and peaches with a main course of roast turbot with grilled leeks. They decided on white wine and settled on a 2005 Pouilly Fume. They chatted easily throughout the meal, Jackie explaining how she had joined the Metropolitan police straight from University at twenty one and spent three years pounding the streets of the capital before being accepted into a newly formed unit targeting computer crime. Her degree in computer analytics and statistics readily equipped her for the task.

"I was headhunted by the NCIS when they set up the central database project three years ago," she said. "It was a wrench leaving the Met, but I was assured I could go back at any time."

"That's good," said Andrew. He explained how he had come to join MI5 and the events that had lead him to his present post at GCHQ.

"I'm so sorry Andrew," she said, instinctively placing her hand over his, "it must be awful and for your little girl too?"

"She's settled with Nancy's parents for now and is bearing up really well considering," said Andrew aware that she had made no attempt to move her hand. "So what about your love life?" Jackie gently withdrew her hand and a sadness came over her face. "I'm sorry." She smiled at him.

"You have a habit of apologising don't you?"

"Sorry." They both laughed.

"I was married for four years to a fellow police officer," she explained. "He wanted children, I wanted a career, there's not much more to say really. I see him now and again and he's happy with his wife and two children." Andrew leant over and took her hand in his and smiled. "Thank goodness," she said with a sparkle in her eyes. "If you'd smiled like you did earlier I probably would have run out of the door screaming!"

They walked arm in arm back to her house and he felt her lean into his body as a blast of late autumn wind whipped down the street. She reminded him of Nancy, not because of her looks, but because of the way he felt when she was close. They eventually arrived at the front door and they both sensed that a moment had arrived for which neither was sure they were ready.

"Look Andrew, I've had a really lovely evening," she began awkwardly. Andrew placed a finger gently over her lips.

"Please don't worry," he said. "So have I and I wouldn't want anything to spoil it." He let his finger slide under her chin and bent forward, kissing her softly on the lips for a fleeting moment. She looked up and smiled. Andrew turned to leave feeling happier than he had since that fateful day, when he felt a tug on his hand. He felt her hand pulling him back into her embrace and she pulled his lips onto hers and felt her tongue. When they broke his sight was filled with a key. Jackie had a very different expression on her face and Andrew was surprised and instantly aroused.

"Are you sure?" he asked.

"Shut up and take me to bed."

Andrew awoke at 5.30am feeling strange to wake up next to another person for the first time in months. Jackie lay with her back to him, her deep breathing signalling she was still sleeping peacefully. There was enough light from the bedside clock for him to see and he studied the shapely curve of her body beneath the bed covers. Her shoulders and upper back were visible in the soft light and he was tempted to caress her skin it looked so inviting. Half her blonde hair lay on the pillow behind her head and Andrew could not resist running it through his fingers. He felt a reaction beneath his own covers and at the same time Jackie must have sensed his presence for she slowly stirred and half turned towards him. Andrew pressed against her back and felt himself ease between her legs. She moaned softly as he entered her and reached over to pull his head towards hers, searching for his mouth. Jackie's cell phone lit up throwing a beam of light on the ceiling and began to vibrate, demanding attention. Andrew pulled away as she leant over, but she pushed herself against him and shook her head.

"Don't you dare stop," she said as she picked up the phone. Andrew could hear the sounds of a voice but not the words, which made things easier for him. She listened for thirty seconds before speaking.

"Give me an hour." She disconnected the call, tossed the instrument across the room and turned to Andrew. "Well are you going to finish what you started?"

Twenty minutes later Jackie leapt out of bed and straight into the shower.

"Who was that?" asked Andrew sliding the door behind him and taking the soap from her hand.

"No time for that now Mr Larkin," she said pushing him out of the door. "We have another murder on our hands." Despite the shock at hearing the news he could not stop himself admiring her body through the glass. "Stop staring at me and get ready, there's a spare toothbrush in the cupboard," she said opening the door and flicking soapy water at him. Jackie was able to get herself dressed and ready for action in less time than it took many men Andrew knew. He made coffee and they sat briefly in the kitchen eating toast.

"Happened last night," she said between mouthfuls, a habit Andrew knew he would have to wean her off. "Seems a sailor was found in Portsmouth with a record amount of alcohol in his system. Whether anyone would have made a connection with the *English Monarchy* is doubtful, but our friend kindly left his calling card in the dead man's wallet."

"So we were right in assuming that the stakes have been raised," said Andrew. "I think we should get down to the scene straight away."

"I have to get to the office Andrew, you go. It's not really part of my brief anyway and it would look odd if we turned up together."

"You're right," he said, quickly washing the cups and side plates they had used.

"Glad to see you're domesticated," said Jackie putting on her coat. "Call me when you get there and have talked to the guys on the ground." They parted at her front door and Andrew was left to walk alone to his car. He waited until he was heading back towards the hotel before calling Ken Greaves.

"I see," he said in his usual manner. "What do you suggest we do?"

"This sailor is murder number nine, the queen is sixteen, we have a long way to go before things get really serious but we know the intended victims become more prominent so it won't be long before someone in the public eye gets hit."

"We don't want it to reach that stage," said Greaves. "Surely with all the resources available we can find these people?"

"They've been very clever up to now and seem to have enjoyed some good fortune, but it's only a matter of time before they slip up and when they do we'll be there."

"I do hope so," said Greaves. "I've not bothered anyone senior with this so far and I sincerely hope it will prove unnecessary."

"You mean there's been no increase in protection for her majesty?" said Andrew in a surprised tone.

"A discreet word in the right ear, but as you said, we have three or four potential victims before anyone important is in danger." Andrew could barely suppress his distaste for the man and he seemed to sense his displeasure. "It's not your job to catch every criminal Larkin, we leave that to the uniforms. Concentrate on your brief."

The line went dead. Andrew collected his things from the hotel and checked out. He rang Bill Frost from the room and arranged to meet him at the scene, then sent Jackie a text explaining what he knew before checking on the best route to the naval port. After spending forty five minutes covering the nine miles to Kingston Vale, the remaining sixty four took just seventy five, most of it on the A3 dual carriageway and A3M motorway that cut directly through the Surrey and Hampshire countryside. The journey was made quicker by the recently opened Hindhead tunnel which bypassed the village of the same name that had become notorious for its traffic jams. Frost called him just as he reached the end of the M275 motorway where the city began.

"You need to head for the Old Town," said the special branch man by way of direction. It took him twenty minutes to find the spot where the murder had taken place after weaving his way through the back streets of the old naval town.

Andrew parked his car on a cobbled street just ahead of the police cordon and had his ID ready before the local uniformed officer had covered half the short distance from his post. He caught sight of Frost as he bent under the tape spread across the narrow street and he broke away from a group gathered around the renovated statue of Admiral Lord Nelson staring across the harbour.

"The body has been removed, but I can show you the scene," said Frost, taking Andrew by the elbow and leading him away from the statue. Larkin sensed that Frost was keeping him from the others.

"Any problem with me being here Bill?" he asked.

"You know what it's like Andrew; they resent what they see as outside interference in a local matter." Andrew stopped and looked straight at the special branch man. "Remember they're not aware of the bigger picture and even I met with some resistance when I arrived."

"Where's the card?" said Andrew shaking his head in exasperation.

"Taken away for forensics, but from the way it was described I've no doubt we're dealing with the same killer." They walked up a small grassy bank to a sheltered spot beneath the shadow of the tall brick wall. A uniformed officer stood in front of a taped-off area in which two white suited forensic technicians were on their hands and knees minutely inspecting the ground for even the smallest fibre or other clue that might ultimately lead to the apprehension of the culprit. Several others were combing the wider area with the same hope.

"They removed four empty bottles of Polish spirit from around the body," said Frost. Andrew tried to imagine what had happened. The murdered sailor was a seasoned serviceman and so it must have taken a powerful or skilful assailant to overpower him. He turned to take in the wider view.

"This is a public place," he said. "Why take the risk of being discovered?" Frost moved away from the spot and Andrew followed him to a quieter area out of earshot of the others.

"The man was thrown out of a pub just a few minutes' walk from here," said Frost. "He was already very drunk and hardly able to walk so the killer must have followed him here and offered him another drink."

"Something he was unlikely to reject," said Andrew. "But this place is so open, how could the killer be certain that would happen?"

"I spoke to the landlord myself and he told me that a taxi driver had brought in an envelope containing two hundred pounds with a message asking him to keep all the servicemen in drinks as thank you for being heroes."

"Has the driver been traced yet?" said Andrew.

"I was discussing that when you arrived," replied Frost. "Seems he was reading a paper when a gloved hand thrust two envelopes through his open window. He couldn't see the face and whoever it was didn't speak. One contained the drinks money and the other a fifty pound note with instructions on the what to do written on it."

"Why didn't he just take both and disappear?"

"Simple really," replied Frost. "He said he wouldn't steal from a serviceman. That and the promise of another fifty when he returned." Andrew opened his mouth to speak. "It was left in an envelope, taped to the inside of a bin," Frost answered his next question as to how the extra money was given.

"So the odds were in the killer's favour that an inebriated serviceman would emerge from that pub," said Andrew.

"The killer could have picked him up at any time after he left," said Frost. "The local force are carrying out a door-to-door of the area in the hope someone saw something."

It was a cold but sunny day and Andrew readily agreed when Frost suggested they take a stroll and take in the sea air.

"We can attend the conference that's being held later at the main city station." They walked up a ramp onto the old battlements that formed a sea wall next to Battery Row.

"So it looks like we have another confirmed kill by the *English Monarchy*?" said Andrew watching a small yacht leaving the protection of the harbour and entering the wider channel.

"The card was left in his wallet so there's no doubt it was meant to be found immediately," said Frost.

"When you look at this as a whole Bill, it's almost comical."

"What do you mean?" asked Frost, stopping to sit on a bench.

"There's been a different method for every murder," Andrew sat next to his colleague. "Each is somehow associated with the victim's profession." Frost frowned. "The first few all worked the land and were victims of slurry, hay, and milk and farm machinery."

"Right," said Frost beginning to understand.

"The miner fell down a pit shaft, the lockkeeper drowned."

"In a lock," Frost interrupted.

"And the vicar was killed in a church."

"Isn't poisoning a sailor stretching the theory a little too far?" suggested Frost.

"Sailors are known to drink," answered Larkin, "and perhaps after two drownings he wanted a change." There was a small tower at the end of the walk. They descended a set of circular concrete steps inside the structure, emerging in Tower Street, and walked down a narrow mews barely wide enough for a small car, until the buildings opened into Bath Square, a quayside area that overlooked the harbour on three sides. They could see the Isle of Wight ferry docked across the narrow expanse of water, loading its cargo of cars, goods vehicles and passengers for the forty minute crossing to Fishguard.

"Fancy a drink?" asked Frost. Andrew nodded. They had a choice of two adjacent pubs, *The Spice Island Inn* and *The Still & West Country House* and chose the former simply because its outdoor seating area gave an uninterrupted view of the impressive 560 foot Spinnaker Tower on the Portsmouth side and across to Gosport on the opposite bank of the harbour entrance. Frost disappeared inside to fetch the drinks and Andrew found a spare table and gazed out at the hypnotic sight of dozens of small bobbing craft moored across the stretch of water in Gosport Marina. Even at this distance he could hear their guy ropes clanging against the tall metal masts. Feeling the chill of the sea wind cut across the exposed quay, he pulled his coat tightly around him, thinking that perhaps they should have sat inside. His mind wandered to the events of the previous evening and Jackie's face filled his mind's eye. Should he feel guilty for what had happened? Was it all too fast? He forced himself to take a rational view of the events; two adults had been out to dinner and ended up in bed for a night of fun, although it was more than that for him as he was not a person who was comfortable with one night stands. But that did not mean that she would want to see *him* again, especially as she had been so worried about how any relationship could affect their work. The face in the water melted into that of his wife and he realised that he was incapable of making any decisions on his private life. He needed to think about Charlotte and how he would bring her fully back into his life as she could not stay with Nancy's parents indefinitely. He let out a long sigh just as Frost emerged with two pints of the local *Pompey Royal* bitter.

"I hope you like a drop of old English ale Andrew?" he said, carefully placing the frothy beer in front of them. He noticed Andrew's melancholy expression and sat down opposite him on the bench concentrating on his drink.

"Oh, sorry Bill," said Andrew suddenly returning to the present.

"No problem Andrew, you must have a great deal on your mind?"

"No more than most people," he replied. The special branch man was the last person in whom he could confide his recent thoughts.

"So where do we go from here?"

"Unless we come up with something from the crime scene here, we're no closer to identifying the killer," said Andrew.

"Or killers," added Frost.

"Indeed," said Andrew sipping his beer. "Our best hope seems to be tracking down the source of the website."

"I'm starting to come under pressure from the top brass," said Frost. "Seems some people in high places are starting to get nervous."

"Understandable," said Larkin staring down at his glass to hide his thoughts. Either Greaves was shielding him from this pressure or his attempt to keep a lid on things was proving unsuccessful. He couldn't understand the workings of his superior's mind and his hope was that he would not have to spend his whole career trying to fathom him out. "Until now the killer or killers have been lucky. The victims have been anonymous and the police believed they were accidents, so the investigations have all been carried out in isolation and on that assumption." Frost nodded in agreement. Andrew pointed at his top lip which was covered in the white frothy head from his beer.

"Eh? Oh sorry," he said wiping it away with his hand. "We may get a lead from one of those but I wouldn't count on it."

"So what are you up to at the weekend?" They chatted for twenty minutes, both grateful for the break from the depressing reality that they had no clues. Andrew decided that he would give the police conference a miss and head back to Cheltenham, Frost could fill him in with anything of interest. As he drove out of the city he dialled Jackie's number on his hands free, but her line was busy and switched to her message.

"Hi this is Jackie Crowther, I can't take your call right now so please leave a short message." It felt good to hear her voice and helped to lighten his mood.

"Hi Jackie, it's Andrew, nothing much to report. I'm heading back home and will try and catch you later." He realised that sooner or later, the full implications of the *Monarchy's* threats would appear on the radar of those at the very top of the government. They would want answers and at the moment they had very little to offer. Just a series of bloody murders committed by someone with a grudge and the skills, or access to them, to run rings around some of the most talented computer people in the country. Perhaps he should suggest they contact the Americans for some assistance. He turned on the radio to distract himself and give his mind a rest and pressed the pre-set button for BBC Radio Four. The station was airing a programme on family ancestry and how popular it had become in recent years. The presenter was interviewing someone from the National Archives at Kew in London.

"Have you seen a fall in visitors now that much of the information you hold is available on the internet?" she asked.

"Quite the opposite," replied the man *"Easier access has increased the awareness of the general public to what information has been recorded and we have a generation of retired people with the spare time to carry out research."*

Andrew listened for the next twenty five minutes as the programme contrasted the different way research was carried out on the web as opposed to locating the actual documents.

"Most people have little difficulty tracing their family back to 1813, the date of the first census, but then things can get a lot trickier," commented the man from Kew. *"All records relating to births, deaths and marriages were created and kept by the church. Many have been transferred to the internet but the accuracy can be inconsistent. The real challenges start if you want to go back further than 1538."*

"Why is that?" asked the presenter.

"When Henry VIII created the Church of England he decreed that a record be kept of every christening and burial. This was the beginning of the system we have today, before then it was entirely at the discretion of the local parish priest."

The programme concluded by explaining how those genealogists tracing pre-sixteenth century families used a variety of documents including land and tax records to piece together a picture of their background and history. However, many of these related only to the wealthy including the nobility who could afford to own land and pay tax. The five o'clock news followed and Andrew noted the killing in Portsmouth was the fifth item on the headline and it was clear from the two line introduction that the media had no knowledge of the card or a link to the other deaths. He had no desire to be depressed any further so opted for the sound of the road and his thoughts for company. His thoughts had returned to the programme on family ancestry which had piqued his interest and reminded him of his conversation with Stuart, the local detective in charge of the church murder.

Stuart's investigation into the Warwick family had turned out to be a dead end and no link had been established as to why the killer was using the bear symbol. He was struck with the need to read the content of the *English Monarchy* website again and so pulled into a roadside restaurant on the A34 near Winchester. Over a barely edible meal and coffee he studied the pages from the site he had saved on his laptop. Was it true that no true English king or queen had ruled since Elizabeth I? He asked for the password for the free Wi-Fi and began looking at sites on the monarchs of England. When Elizabeth had died the throne had passed to James I, a Scot and the first of the Stuarts. This line was broken when William of Orange, a Dutchman, was placed on the throne in 1689 to prevent a Catholic son of James II from succeeding. From 1714, when George I was crowned, every monarch up to and including the present queen, had descended from German stock. He was beginning to understand the thread of the murderer's argument, if not the means of attracting attention to the cause and could vaguely remember from his schooldays how the choice of the sovereign was often decided by murder, politics and war, rather than birth. The present queen had only been crowned because her uncle, Edward VII had abdicated for the love of an American divorcee, Wallace Simpson in 1936, passing the throne to her father George V. So there would be numerous occasions when people were denied what they and their supporters believed a rightful claim. Surfing the internet, he stumbled on the story of a descendant of Richard III whose body was believed to be buried under a supermarket car park in Leicester, England. The man, a Canadian in his fifties, was interviewed in a video clip. He had travelled to the site and seemed unconcerned that he was not the present King of England. Andrew realised there must be dozens of people around the world who could trace such a link. Could it be that the killer was one of these? But what would make their claim any more legitimate than the others? He realised that he needed to speak to an expert to provide the detail he lacked? What was the name of the man on the radio programme, from the archives?

"Kew!" He exclaimed out loud, causing everyone in the restaurant to look in his direction. "Sorry," he said sheepishly. Why had they not thought to contact these people before? All their energy had been spent following the path laid down by the killer and obviously deliberately designed to keep them from the source. It was time to set their own agenda. He packed up his laptop, paid for his food and resumed his journey, resolving to contact the BBC the following morning. He arrived back in Cheltenham at 8.30pm and after dropping both the executive liaison group and Jackie an email outlining his thoughts, spent the evening watching television with a bottle of Merlot for company.

Andrew arrived at his desk at GCHQ at 8am following morning. The first thing he did after hanging his coat on the back of the office door was to call Charlotte and wish her a happy day at school. She had settled in so well at the local school that even her grandmother could find nothing negative to say when they spoke.

"She seems to be quite happy," he ventured.

"Yes, she is Andrew," replied his mother-in-law. Andrew signed off with a promise to take Charlotte for the weekend which turned out to be the high spot of his day. He had assumed that a simple phone call to the BBC switchboard would put him through to the correct department who would be happy to furnish him with name of the expert from Kew who had featured on the programme the previous evening.

"It is not the policy of the BBC to give out the details of corporation staff," said the first person he spoke to.

"But I don't want the name of a staff member. I want the name of someone featured on a show."

"If the person's name was not given on air then we cannot divulge that information."

"But it was given on air, I just don't remember it." After retreating and licking his wounds, his second attempt got him over the first hurdle and into the Radio Four system. He was then confronted by the Data Protection Act which in his experience was often an excuse given by those who were too lazy to actually do anything to help. He was tempted to take a more official route and declare he was from MI5, but guessed that would cause even more problems and not achieve the goal of accelerating the process. He broke for a coffee at around 9.30am and was waiting for the cup to emerge from the inner workings of the machine when Mary Ward turned the corner.

"Hello Mary," said Andrew, "I haven't seen you for a while." The IT specialist was obviously deep in thought and almost collided with Larkin.

"Sorry," she said, retreating.

"No problem," he said. "Deep in thought?"

"Yes, I've been running a set of new diagnostics to try and trace the source of the *Monarchy* uploads."

"Any luck?"

"It's very frustrating," she said pointing at Andrew to remove his cup from the machine. "Whoever is doing this is very, very good. I have tried locating the actual postal address where the computer was located through the ISP provider that hosted the proxy server. That's how we managed to track the teenager in Bristol. But as we know that was clearly a red herring. But it's changing constantly so whoever is doing this must have a backdoor into the servers. "Andrew looked blankly at Ward who was speaking a foreign language.

"Seems difficult to imagine someone that clever could murder nine people," said Andrew.

"I've seen them all here," she replied. Andrew explained his theory and frustration at trying to locate the expert through the BBC. "Why don't you try calling Kew and asking them? They can't have too many people appearing on the radio on a daily basis." No wonder she was a specialist thought Andrew as he watched her disappear with his coffee.

"That would be Dr Peter Hughes," said the receptionist at Kew as soon as Andrew asked the same question he had of the BBC switchboard operator.

"Would it be possible for me to speak to Mr Hughes?"

"I'll see if he is free. What was your name and company again?"

"Andrew Larkin and I'm ringing from the Ministry of Defence."

"Oh." The line went silent for a moment.

"Hello this is Peter Hughes, Head of Research Services, can I help you?" Andrew explained how he had heard his comments on the radio programme and believed that he may be able to help with a matter of some sensitivity relating to national security.

"Are you covered by the Official Secrets Act Mr Hughes?"

"Yes, I am Mr Larkin. May I ask if I should be concerned by this matter?"

"No, no not at all," said Andrew reassuring him. "I don't really want to say too much over an unsecure line. Is it possible we could meet?"

"Of course," said Hughes opening his Outlook calendar. "How about next Thursday?"

"How about tomorrow morning?" replied Andrew.

"I see. If it's important I can rearrange my diary."

"That would be good," said Larkin. They agreed that it was better for him to visit Kew.

"Are you able to give me any idea of the subject matter?" asked Hughes. "It may give me a chance to carry out some initial research." Andrew hesitated, weighing up how much he should reveal over the telephone.

"I'm afraid I can't say any more, but I look forward to seeing you in the morning Mr Hughes."

As soon as he put the office phone down, Jackie rang on his cell.

"I looked up this bear and ragged staff symbol on the web last night," were the first words they had exchanged since they had parted the previous morning.

"Good morning to you too," replied Andrew slightly hurt.

"Oh I'm sorry Andrew; it's just that there are so many different links to the symbol." Andrew explained the calls he had made that morning.

"So I've arranged a meeting with the guy from Kew tomorrow."

"If you're coming up to London again, why don't you come over to my place in the evening?" said Crowther.

"I'd love to Jackie, but I promised my in-laws I would take Charlotte for the weekend so I'll probably get her on the way back to Cheltenham." He hesitated before continuing. "Look I don't know if you're free on Saturday, but we could get together. I have someone I'd love you to meet." Andrew cringed as he said the words knowing he was taking a chance introducing his daughter at this early stage.

"Er, I've arranged to visit my mother in Luton."

"No it's ok, it was just a thought," he said, thinking he had misjudged her.

"But I would love to meet Charlotte. Why don't we meet somewhere for lunch on Sunday that's a good place for her?"

"That would be great!" he said, a little too enthusiastically. Jackie laughed.

"I'll leave it to you to find somewhere. In the meantime let me know what happens at Kew."

"Anything new at your end?" asked Andrew, changing the subject.

"No. We've ruled out any involvement by the UK Workers Liberation Army, although the killer has unwittingly enabled us to take them out. Higgins gave Ferguson all the names and details of the future operations they were planning."

"Jackie let's not assume anything that has been done isn't in some way part of an agenda. The killer could have picked any site to hijack, so why this one? Perhaps we should look deeper into why the kids from Bristol and the UKWLA were chosen?"

"I'm already working with Paul Williams to make sure we gather and analyse everything we and GCHQ have on both of them."

Andrew called together the members of the ELG after lunch so he and Frost could bring them up to date with the events of the past few days. Williams was not available, but Charles Smyth and David Scott did attend.

"So I've arranged to meet Mr Hughes at Kew tomorrow." Andrew concluded his outline.

"Bill?" said Scott.

"The initial forensic tests on the Portsmouth site and card have proved negative," said Frost. "But I'm coming under pressure to release the details of the card to the media. They think someone out there might know something."

"I'm not sure," said Andrew.

"We could get dozens of people giving us false leads." Frost continued. "The problem is that the killer is getting closer to some important people, if the website is to be believed, and at the moment we don't have any concrete lines of enquiry." Andrew turned to Scott.

"Are we any closer to tracing the true source of the *Monarchy* site or who hijacked the other two?"

"Whoever did this is as adept at covering their tracks as they were in the original deception," said Scott. "Since we discovered that the probability of a senior politician or member of the Royal family being targeted had increased beyond fifty percent, we've been working with Fort Meade."

"Have they come with anything new?" asked Smythe.

"If I'm honest Charles, I'm not sure how much processor time they've actually given us so far."

"Let me have a chat with one or two chaps I know. Anything new from NCIS?" Andrew stayed deliberately quiet and let Scott speak.

"Paul has been working with his people in London in trying to establish if there are any links between the murders, but I know they're also beginning to push for the information on the card to be made public."

"For all we know there may be other murders that we don't know about," said Frost.

"Seems like I'm in a club that's losing all its members." remarked Andrew. He made a mental note to ask Jackie how she felt, next time they spoke. "Can I suggest we wait until after the weekend before issuing a final recommendation from the group?" Everyone nodded and the meeting finished with an agreement to meet in four days. Frost signalled for Andrew to remain in the room after the others had left. He waited until he was sure the others would not return before guiding him to the far corner.

"What on earth is the matter Bill?" said Andrew, slightly bemused.

"Firstly, despite the agreement to wait until after the weekend, the top brass want the card released. I can hold off until Monday but make no mistake the decision has been made." Andrew sighed.

"Ok, now will you tell me why you held me back?" Andrew knew Frost would not have acted so dramatically just to tell him about the card. Frost seemed to hesitate and shuffle, which worried Andrew. He waited for the special branch man to find the right words and was convinced he had discovered his relationship with Jackie. Only his training kept him from pre-empting Frost.

"We think there may be a problem with Williams," he said finally.

"What?" Blurted Larkin, almost in relief.

"You know that we are all subject to routine checking by MI5, even you."

"Especially me if Ken Greaves has any input," said Andrew.

"David Scott came to me a few days ago and said he was a little concerned about the amount of time Paul had been away from GCHQ over the last few weeks." Andrew frowned.

"But we've all been away more than normal, there's a serial killer on the loose."

"Yes, but he's got an uneasy feeling about him."

"Has anybody spoken to his colleagues at NCIS?" Andrew could see a slight change in Frost's expression as he listened to the question. So he did know something about Jackie.

"No," he replied. "I suggest we keep this close until we can find out a little more about what young Williams may be up to." Andrew nodded.

When Andrew arrived back at his desk it was 3.30pm. He decided he would drive up to London that afternoon rather than chance the M4 in the early morning rush. He rang the Thames House central travel booking service and arranged a local west London hotel for the night before paying a visit to David Scott on his way out.

"It's difficult to put a finger on it Andrew," he said shifting a little uncomfortably in his chair. "But I have a very specific duty to report anything, however trivial it may appear."

"I fully understand David, so why don't you share it with me?" Scott opened a drawer and withdrew an A5 notebook.

"I find it best to keep a note of my thoughts as things happen."

"Of course," agreed Andrew, realising that working for years in such a toxic atmosphere created a type of paranoia.

"He's been asking questions about the working patterns of two or three of my people."

"You mean what duties they perform?" said Andrew.

"Yes, and also their shift patterns." Andrew considered the response.

"Anyone and anything in particular?" he asked?

"I know what you're looking for Andrew, but I think he's being careful not to talk too much about any individual. He was certainly keen to know who has access to the directory set-up files." Andrew looked puzzled. "They're the files that set the keywords and phrases we search for," said Scott.

"And why does his interest arouse your suspicions?"

"Apart from the fact it's information above his clearance level," he replied. "It was the casual manner he dropped the question into the conversation." Andrew understood from his own experience that unearthing something like this in the security community was as much an art as a science. He had helped expose a young secretary at the counter terrorism unit in Manchester who had been compromised by an Eastern European and was passing information on communications protocols. One of her friends had posted a comment on Facebook about a new boyfriend, teasing her about not coming out with them. It is standard procedure for anyone with a high security clearance to have their private life monitored and the new social media provides a useful window into people's lives. The anomaly came to light when a colleague noticed a picture of her with her friends on her phone. When innocently asked when it was taken, she had claimed it was the previous night. Unfortunately for her, the colleague was also the CTU vetting officer and was aware of the new boyfriend. Andrew was asked to investigate the officers feeling that *'something was wrong'*, and after having the boyfriend followed and his communications intercepted, it emerged he was working for a criminal gang who were planning to import vast quantities of illegal vodka. They hoped to gain access to police and security communications networks to gather information and disrupt any attempts to intercept the containers. Andrew refocused on the present dilemma.

"Ok David, I've spoken to Bill Frost and we'll take it from here."

"I've also made my feelings known to the internal security officer here at GCHQ as is standard procedure."

"Of course," said Andrew.

Andrew drove home and collected the bag he always kept handy for a quick night away and set off for London. He called Thames House and spoke to an old colleague and asked him to pick up William's case from Bill Frost. The officer agreed to give Andrew a discrete call as soon as they had established Williams's movements and contacts. He kept to a steady seventy miles per hour, not wanting a repeat of his last brush with the local traffic police. He needed to speak to Jackie, but was unsure if he should mention the situation with Williams. Normally that would have been an easy question to answer, in fact it would probably never had arisen, but he hoped she might be able throw some light on Williams and help establish if there was any substance in Scott's concerns. But before he made that call, he dialled his in-laws to arrange a collection time for the following day.

"Hello Andrew," said his father-in-law. "Do you want to speak to Charlotte, she's just arrived home from school?" Before he could answer his daughter's voice filled the car.

"Hello daddy, I made a pot at school today."

"That's wonderful darling."

"And I painted it blue 'cause it's mummy's favourite colour." The reference to Nancy caught Andrew by surprise, tugging him into the past with a guilty jolt.

"Well that's very thoughtful of you," he said feeling his eyes misting. "I'll look forward to seeing it tomorrow."

"Yes, yes, yes," she squealed and promptly dropped the phone as she danced away.

"What time do you want to collect her Andrew?" his mother-in-law had picked up the receiver. "About four thirty if that's ok," he replied.

"So that could be anytime up 'till midnight then," she said with a laugh which might have been sarcastic or playful, he could not decide. When Andrew finally dialled Jackie's number it was diverted to her voicemail.

"Hi, it's me. I'm on my way down to Kew now. Thought I would avoid the morning dash and catch up on some emails at the hotel. If you can spare five I'd like to talk over something. If you can spare an hour after eight, I'm staying at the Petersham Hotel in Richmond." Well if you don't ask you don't get, he thought.

Andrew arrived at the hotel at 7pm after an uneventful journey on the M4 and M25. After checking in he took a quick shower and changed, deciding where to eat. He knew a good Italian called Grouchos on the river in the town but could not muster up the energy for the ten minute walk, so elected to stay in the hotel, not admitting to himself that he might miss Jackie if he left. He ate a well prepared steak washed down with a half a bottle of Chilean Merlot, hoping he would have company to share the wine with. At 9.30pm he wandered into the lounge and decided to have a brandy and warm himself by the open fire. He reached over from a comfortable old winged backed leather chair he had settled into and picked up a well read copy of *The Times*. He was engrossed in an article by the columnist Matthew Parris when his drink arrived.

"Would you like your brandy warmed sir?" asked the waitress. That's unusual these days thought Andrew as he fought between his manners and his interest in the article. "Well do you or not?" The change in tone caught him by surprise, bringing him out of his trance.

"I'm sorry," he said lowering the paper. Jackie was sat in the chair opposite with an expression poised between irritation and playfulness.

"Hello," they both said at the same time.

"Do you always treat waiting staff so rudely?" she said.

"Do you always serve brandy in such a surly fashion?" he replied. A silence ensued, broken when Andrew rose and guided her onto the settee that kept the two chairs apart.

"It's nice to see you Ms Crowther," he said and kissed her gently on the lips.

"How do you know I'm not here on official business, in which case you have just assaulted a member of Her Majesty's Constabulary?" Andrew stood and held out his wrists.

"Well if I'm going to be arrested, I might as well get my money's worth."

An hour later they lay in each other's arms enjoying the lovers' experience of silence and contentment. Andrew felt her drifting into a light sleep as the rigours of the day fell away. He could feel her body moving against his as she breathed and felt himself slowly relax. He was not sure how long he had slept but sensed she had gone before he opened his eyes. He felt a shudder of concern until he heard the shower running and wandered into the bathroom to watch her through the steaming glass until she noticed him and called out over the sound of the streaming water.

"Pervert!"

"Oh yes, when it comes to you."

"Good," came the reply as the shower door slid back. "Let's keep it that way." He held out a robe and wrapped her in its folds before playfully pushing her out of the door. "I've got to get home tonight darling," she said apologetically.

"I understand" he said, taking her in his arms and giving her a long lingering kiss. They chatted about nothing whilst she dressed and Andrew was aware it was becoming more difficult to see her simply as a colleague, but knew it was vital not only for the success of the investigation, but also their careers. It was only after she left that he realised he had not raised the subject of Paul Williams and he slept fitfully that night switching between thoughts of Jackie, Williams and what he might discover at Kew.

He arrived at the National Archives at 9.10am having taken much longer than he had envisaged fighting his way out of Richmond and along Kew Bridge Road. He was becoming accustomed to the lighter traffic in the shires. Peter Hughes was waiting for him in the reception area and moved to introduce himself as soon as he heard Andrew ask for him by name.

"Mr Larkin?" Andrew turned toward the sound and immediately recognised the man as an academic by his unkempt appearance and obvious lack of any fashion sense.

"Professor Hughes?" Andrew addressed him by his full title.

"Will it be ok for us to talk in my office, or.." He left the question unfinished. Andrew was a little surprised at his reaction and realised he was apprehensive as to why someone from MI5 would want to speak to him.

"Professor, let me put your mind at rest straight away. I'm here to seek your professional judgement in a matter wholly related to your work here at the archives." Hughes's whole demeanour changed and he could not prevent himself from smiling.

"Well Mr Larkin, I'm delighted that you believe I can do something to help your people. Coffee?" They had reached his department and after choosing what the most drinkable muddy brew on offer appeared, sat down in Hughes's small office. Andrew looked around at the shelves stacked with books, ancient and modern. A large backlit panel filled half of one wall with a table underneath on which various manuscripts and a scroll were spread. Hughes watched the man with a mixture of fear and curiosity. He had appreciated his attempt to sooth his nerves, which had certainly allowed him to put any thoughts of immediate arrest to the back of his mind. Despite his warning, Hughes had spoken to the director who had made a call to a contact somewhere in Whitehall. Discreet enquiries had revealed he was a genuine civil servant who worked at MI5, but nothing more could be uncovered as to what position he held. The director had advised him to hear what Larkin had to say and if he felt threatened or compromised in any way that he should refuse to answer any further questions and refer the man to him. Andrew could sense from the professor's nervousness that he had suspected the worst when he had been contacted. He knew that someone from the Ministry of Agriculture had searched for his details on the government intranet directory as all such requests are logged and flagged to security services personnel and had received an e-mail at 7.30pm the previous evening. Andrew pondered whether he should tell the professor he knew that he had ignored his request to keep their meeting confidential, but decided it might cause the man even more angst, besides breaking with his own protocols regarding secrecy.

"Professor," Larkin began. "You are no doubt wondering why I have asked to meet with you in person and at such short notice." Always start with a question to which you know the answer smiled Andrew to himself. Hughes forced a thin smile and nodded.

"What can you tell me about this?" said Andrew, placing the card on the desk. Hughes picked it up and studied it for a few moments.

"It's known as the bear and ragged staff," he began, "and is the symbol associated with Warwick if my memory serves me correctly." So far so good thought Andrew, although he would have been disappointed had the man not known this most basic piece of information. He decided to dispense with any preamble as he already knew as much as he needed about the symbol and its immediate background from the Devon detective's visit to the Earl of Warwick.

"Professor Hughes, the original of the card you have in your hand was recovered from the body of a murdered vicar at a church in Devon a few months ago." Hughes raised one eyebrow but showed no signs of shock.

"And you want me to tell you of its potential significance?" he said with obvious relief.

"Yes," replied Andrew. "But it's more complicated than that."

Larkin explained the background including the murders and the *English Monarchy* website. Hughes examined the site on his computer and Andrew sat in silence as the academic absorbed the full meaning of the text. He eventually leaned back in his chair, hands clasped as if in prayer.

"Where to begin Mr Larkin," he said slowly. He rose from his chair and stood in front of a whiteboard. "First let's deal with the historical facts.

Elizabeth I could be described as the last true English monarch by a certain definition." He began to draw a rough family tree on the board. "James I, who succeeded the queen in 1603 was a Scot by birth and part of the Stuart lineage. Elizabeth's death marked the end of the Tudors." He carried on scribbling the names of the kings and queens of England as he spoke, grouping some with a country of origin. "So you see, by that definition every king or queen has been from Scottish, Dutch or German descent. Many were born in England but were not from English stock. The present queen comes from a German family although I must say it's difficult to imagine anyone more English."

"Yes," agreed Andrew. "Do you think it's possible that the killer believes that he's the rightful heir to the throne?"

"Of course it's possible," said Hughes. "But if you think that will narrow your search then I fear you will be sadly mistaken."

"I did some quick research on the internet, so I can appreciate what you mean. I came across the story of the Canadian man who's descended from Richard III," said Andrew. Hughes had completed his two minute timeline of the monarchs of England since the mid-sixteenth century and returned to his chair.

"How many victims are on the website?" he asked, leaning over to pull a sheet of paper from his printer.

"Sixteen in total including the present queen," replied Andrew. Hughes began scribbling on the sheet.

"Let's assume that the gap between each generation was an average of twenty five years." Andrew could see that he had written a column of numbers from sixteen down to one. Against the top number he had written the dates 2009-1987, the next 1987-1962 and he was busy completing the maths as Andrew watched.

"I'm assuming that your killer has not chosen the number of victims at random Mr Larkin," he said as he wrote. "My guess is that by working back we can arrive at an approximate time when the sixteenth descendant was born." Andrew understood the calculation and immediately saw a quicker way of arriving at an answer and so took out his phone and began tapping the screen. The two sat engrossed in their respective tasks until he set down his pen and turned the page for Andrew to read the date at the bottom of the page. 1612. Andrew showed the professor the same number on his phone app.

"Of course, it's only an approximation," he said. "But it does confirm my suspicions." He paused seemingly undecided on something.

"Which are?" Andrew prompted the man.

"Well it's only a theory," he said.

"At the moment the investigation has precious few of those professor, so please continue."

"As I said it's logical to assume the number of victims chosen is not random. By calculating the approximate dates for the births and deaths of sixteen generations we can speculate that an event, significant to the killer, may have occurred around that time." Andrew's respect for the academic rose dramatically as he realised he may have discovered the reason for the number of victims.

"What event happened at that time?" he asked. Hughes smiled.

"Mr Larkin, there could be a hundred reasons and we *are* trying to work out the thoughts of a mass murderer."

"Ok, I understand but let's speculate a little shall we?"

Hughes sat back and again assumed the prayer position, his thinking pose thought Andrew. His phone rang, breaking the silence in the small room and causing them both to jump slightly. It was Jackie, but Andrew rejected the call as he could think of nothing more important at this moment than hearing the professor's next words.

"James I was on the throne at that time," he said. "He was the first of the monarchs of non-English descent mentioned on the site, but his succession was unchallenged as Elizabeth had no children. His problems came from the likes of Sir Walter Raleigh and a certain Mr Guy Fawkes who as you know…" Hughes stopped speaking in mid-sentence and was staring into space. Andrew waited a few seconds, assuming he was going pick up where he had left off, but the silence continued.

"Are you ok, professor?" The words seemed to break the trance and he looked at Andrew directly.

"Mr Larkin, would you mind if we resumed this conversation a little later as I need to make an urgent phone call?"

"Professor, I'm sorry to impose on you but I need to have your undivided attention until I can be certain that this line on enquiry is exhausted." Hughes rose from his chair and began to usher Andrew towards the door.

"Forgive me, but the call is related to our conversation. I need to consult with a colleague."

"I'm happy to stay whilst you speak to him or her," said Andrew resisting Hughes's guidance. "It's a matter of some delicacy Mr Larkin and although I appreciate you are literally dealing with a life and death situation, I would appreciate the courtesy of making this call in private." Andrew's first reaction was to refuse the request and the academic must have sensed his mood.

"Once I have spoken to my colleague I will be happy to share my thoughts with you. Why don't I get one of my staff to take you on a short tour of the facility?"

"I would rather have the use of an office where I can make a call of my own professor. My call won't take long and I'm sure yours won't either," said Andrew deliberately setting out the terms of the arrangement.

Andrew was shown into a similar office. The small symbol on his phone told him Jackie had left a voicemail but he ignored this and called her number. She answered with a cheery voice.

"Hi, how did you get on at Kew?"

"I'm still here and I might have stumbled on something."

"What do you mean, might?"

"The professor I am seeing suddenly became all coy and said he needed to speak to someone. It's my guess he is checking his facts." Andrew explained his conversation. "So there must be something around that date that he remembered," he concluded. "Anyway I'm glad you called as I wanted to talk to you about something a little delicate."

"Go on," said Jackie cautiously.

"How long have you known Paul Williams?" he asked.

"Ok, I think I know where this is going," she said slowly. "About two years, since he joined us from university. I don't know him that well; I've never really spent much time with him. I do know he is very able when it comes to computer networking."

"Ok, thanks," said Andrew.

"Oh come on, that's not fair, what's happened?"

Andrew hesitated, sorry that he had brought the subject up.

"I shouldn't be talking to you about any of this, but I hoped you might have been able to throw some light on it."

"It being?" she said.

Andrew explained Scott's worries.

"I do know he's been burning the midnight oil for the last couple of weeks as I get a report on the times all staff are logged on to our VPN, but that's hardly surprising given the circumstances."

"We've put him under low level surveillance and I'll let you know if anything turns up. It's probably paranoia on Scott's part."

Andrew noticed that Professor Hughes was peering through the small glass area of the door and so must have finished his call. "I've got to go, the professor's calling me back," he said, acknowledging Hughes.

"Ok, let's catch up later."

"Sure. I'll let you know when I'm on my way to collect Charlotte. You sure you are still ok for tomorrow?"

"Of course. I'm looking forward to meeting her. Must go, got another call coming in, bye." And she was gone.

Hughes dialled Lambert's cell phone as soon as the man from MI5 left his office. The thought had struck him like a thunderbolt as he sat staring at the list of dates he had written, but he had dared not mention anything before speaking to Lambert. The whole subject of the letter was a closely guarded secret and it was not his place to decide who should know of its existence. Besides which it was still far from certain that it was genuine and the last thing he wanted was to open up a can of worms only to have their reputations torn apart and waste the authority's resources in the hunt to find this maniac. The phone rang for the fifth time and Hughes realised that it was a waste of time calling him on this number as he rarely carried his phone and even then the battery was invariably low and the conversation short. He terminated the call and dialled his direct line at the university, but this immediately diverted to his voicemail. Hughes left a short message

"Tom, it's Peter. I need to speak to you urgently, can you call me at Kew as soon as you get this."

He had known Lambert for many years and liked and respected the man immensely, but he drove both friends and colleagues to despair with his attitude to modern forms of communications. He turned to his computer and sent a short e-mail in the forlorn hope he may be online somewhere. He sat staring at the screen wondering what to do next when his office phone rang.

"Peter Hughes," he said, absent-mindedly lifting the receiver.

"Hello Peter, your name came up on my phone as a missed call, did you want to speak to me?" The voice of his old friend filled his head and he smiled in relief.

"I'm amazed you have the thing turned on, let alone programmed with my name," he replied.

"Ah," said Lambert, "I can't take any credit I'm afraid, I have Jenny to thank for that. She's determined to drag me into the twenty first century."

"How is she?" said Hughes.

"You can ask her yourself if you like, we're in Newcastle still trying to locate where John Moore went after he left Shilbottom."

"Tom," Hughes cut across his friend. "I need to speak with you urgently, I have someone in another office waiting for me to speak with you."

"About what?" asked Lambert, becoming serious.

"Tom, this person is from the security services and has been telling me a rather disturbing story about a serial killer who seems to have a grudge against every king and queen since Elizabeth I."

"That sounds terrible Peter, but what can I do to help?"

"Tom, this MI5 agent seems to think that the killer may believe they have a claim to the throne."

"Along with a thousand others," replied Lambert disdainfully. Hughes ignored the comment.

"I worked the dates back for sixteen generations, one for each of the murders that have either been committed or are predicted on a website called *English Monarchy*.

"So this madman is giving notice of his victims?" said Lambert in astonishment.

"But listen Tom the letter, it suddenly struck me."

"The letter?" said Lambert.

"Yes, what if the letter is genuine and there is a descendant of Elizabeth and Dudley out there? The date I calculated corresponds to the time the baby was born."

"Assuming what you say is correct, the descendant probably wouldn't even know who they were," said Lambert.

"Yes, yes, but what if they did know and what if they had arranged for the letter to be found as part of a plan?"

"I think you could be running away with yourself Peter. I must admit that I'm beginning to think the letter may be genuine, or at least the main fact about the baby is accurate. But it's a huge leap to link any of this with a murderer 450 years later."

"Of course you're probably right, but I think that these people should be told about your search and decide if it's something that should be investigated further."

There was silence on the line and Hughes knew he had taken Lambert by surprise, having agreed to keep knowledge of the existence of the letter confined to a very small group until and if, they had irrevocable proof of its accuracy.

"Tom, I know how you feel but I'm sure they'll be willing to keep everything confidential," said Hughes trying to convince his old friend.

"Once they get their hands on it they'll do whatever they want in the name of national security," replied Lambert coldly.

There was another pause as Lambert pondered his options. Hughes allowed him time to think without interruption. Eventually he spoke.

"Set up a meeting for some time next week and I'll arrange to come down to London."

"Tom, I don't think they'll wait that long,"

"Well what do they expect me to do, drop everything and catch a plane?" said Lambert irritably

"Probably," replied Hughes. "Keep your phone switched on and I will call you after I have spoken with him."

"And where is Professor Lambert at this moment?" Larkin was again sat opposite the professor in his office, behind him the large backlit board showed an oversized copy of the letter. He had listened to Hughes explain his phone call, the events regarding the discovery of the letter and Lambert's ongoing investigations.

"Newcastle. He's trying to discover the whereabouts of a descendant who probably moved out of the Alnwick area around 1665."

"How many people know of the letter's existence?"

Hughes took another piece of blank paper from his printer and wrote down the names of everyone he could recall Lambert had mentioned were aware. He passed it across the desk and Larkin counted six names including Hughes and Lambert.

"The others are my assistant, the old man who found it, a dealer at Christie's whom he knows and a lab technician at the university."

Larkin folded the paper and slid it into his jacket pocket.

"Oh I forgot," said Hughes

"Tom, Professor Lambert, is working with a young archivist from Ashington where the records are kept for that area. She's with him in Newcastle right now." Andrew looked at Hughes with the sternest face he could muster.

"Are there any other names you've forgotten professor?"

"None I can think of but I don't know if Professor Lambert has informed anybody else. I have carried out all the research here myself."

"Can I have Professor Lambert's number please?" said Andrew, passing the folded sheet of paper back across the desk. Hughes recovered the number from his own phone and wrote it on the sheet.

"Hello Professor Lambert," said Andrew when the line was answered "My name is Andrew Larkin and I am with Her Majesty's Security Services."

"Hello Mr Larkin," replied Lambert solemnly "How can I help MI5?" The reference to his department did not go unnoticed by Larkin.

"Well you could begin by collecting me from Newcastle airport when I arrive there later today."

Manchester, December 2009

"I promise we can still make it love, honest!"

The young man sped along, one hand on the steering wheel of the Mini Cooper, the other cradling his smart phone under his chin. "It's a viewing of that two-bedroom in Sale that's been on the market for ages. They sound really interested and I can't afford to miss the opportunity as I need the sale to hit my target for this month. Terry has been on my back again."

She was not happy as this was the third time this week he had been asked to carry out a late evening viewing by the branch manager of the upmarket property agents. His figures were down and he knew it was a punishment to show him who was in control. He sped along the Chester Road, crossing the M60 at junction seven and after 500 yards, a left turn took him into Dargle Road which led directly to his destination. He was five minutes late and offered a silent prayer that the client wasn't one of those irritating 'know it alls' who would disappear if you arrived a minute late. As he screeched to a halt outside the house he looked for any sign of someone peering through the windows or leaning against a parked car. He could see neither. Relief or despair? He could not tell. He jumped from the car and swung the door closed behind him before having to return to gather the keys and his folder. As he frantically pushed open the door to the house, he was faced with a large pile of mail and free newspapers, much of which became trapped underneath as he strained to clear a wide enough opening to squeeze past. It took him a precious minute to wrench the jammed paperwork free and he expected to look up at any moment to see the client standing over him. He stuffed the papers into a cupboard under the kitchen sink in the hope that it would be the last place someone would inspect on a first visit, although stranger things had happened. The house had been unoccupied for several weeks and this was only the second viewing in that time. The husband of the couple selling was moving with his job, so they could afford to move into their new home down south somewhere and leave the house unsold. He quickly scanned each room, vaulting the stairs two at a time, to check everything was tidy. He returned to the living room and drew a deep breath, checking his watch. It was now ten minutes past the agreed time. Bloody clients, he cursed to himself. For the next five minutes he paced the room, every two minutes straining at the window to scan the road on either side for signs of an approaching car. Charlene is going to kill me, he thought. "Fucking clients." he said out loud. He decided he would wait another five minutes and if the bastard had not arrived by then, he would go. He cursed again, this time as he realised the opportunity for a sale was ebbing away with each passing minute.

Unknown to the visitor to the house, the client had already viewed the property the previous night. During the visit a quick search through the property had revealed that the gas supply entered the house via a feed pipe that passed through the kitchen wall. The supply then split, with one pipe leading to a gas cooker and the other a wall mounted boiler which supplied the house with water and heat. It had been a simple job to isolate the supply and install a small device in between the inlet pipe and the safety cut-off valve. After a quick check, the supply was restored and the visitor left by the back door. The visitor now stood some fifty yards from the front door looking at the mini parked outside the house. As soon as the eager salesman had appeared, a button on the cell phone was pressed, triggering the free flow of the flammable gas into the surrounding space. A simple calculation had given the answer of eleven minutes as the time it would take to permeate throughout the house before the scent that had been added to the naturally odourless gas, would become powerful enough to raise concern. It had now been ten minutes since the salesman had disappeared through the door.

The agent had stood for the last three minutes watching the second hand on his watch sweep through three hundred and sixty degrees and telling himself each time when it reached the top he was leaving.

"OK, that's it, I've had enough."

Peering out of the window, he had one last look up and down the street and gave a loud curse before leaving the lounge to turn off the lights in the house. As soon as he entered the hall he was immediately struck by the smell as he stirred the air around him. He stopped, frowned and sniffed the air. He looked at his watch and thought of his girlfriend's face when he got home. He rushed upstairs and turned off all the lights, hoping that on his return to the ground floor he would have been mistaken and would not have to call out a plumber and wait around for hours until he arrived and rectified the problem. His panic at the fate that would await him on his return home blinded him to the danger he faced. He walked gingerly into the kitchen, clearly the source of the smell. The boiler sat staring at him from the wall and he approached, sniffing the air like a bloodhound. He could hear a faint hissing sound and lowered his head in an effort to catch a glimpse of the inner workings of the box, not that he had the slightest idea what he expected to find. He never got the opportunity to expand his knowledge of domestic appliances as, after a couple of clicks, he saw the pilot lighter spark into life. Two hundred yards away the visitor decided enough time had passed since the upstairs lights had been extinguished and pushed another button on the mobile. Pieces of the windows were found embedded in trees more than 500 yards away as they were the earliest missiles to be launched from the house. A ball of flame and smoke erupted from every window and door as the force of the explosion ripped through glass and wood. The front door took off like a missile and smashed through the upstairs window of the house opposite, embedding itself in the rear wall. Debris was thrown into the air, landing in the waterway behind and properties all around the site. The agent's Mini Cooper was lifted and deposited in the opposite front garden, the igniting petrol tank adding to the fireworks. The fire crews that arrived some six minutes later were met with a scene of complete and utter devastation, the interior of the house simply a shell with four walls. The ground and first floor ceilings had disappeared allowing an uninterrupted view of the roof above. Several holes were apparent and the fire chief was surprised the whole roof had not been deposited further down the street as had large parts of the chimney. At that point it was impossible to know if anyone was in the house. But had there been, they would almost certainly have been evaporated by the force of the blast.

The visitor had continued walking immediately after triggering the catastrophe. Five minutes later a train, heading away from the city centre, pulled into the Metro line station at Brookland's and twenty minutes after that, arrived at the terminus of Altringham. The station is ideally placed for those wishing to travel easily in and out of the city and it took only a few minutes to join the M56 and then the M6. Thirty five minutes after the blast, just as the fireman had started to get the blaze under control; a small car gathered speed as it drove down the southbound motorway ramp and joined the flow of evening traffic heading towards Birmingham.

Amongst the post delivered two days later at the Salford branch of Sextants estate agents was a card. The branch manager Terry, opened the envelope, removed the card and read the words on the front. *In Sorrow.* He felt something inside the card flutter down to the floor and stooped to retrieve it.

Strange, he thought, as he looked quizzically at the small business card with a bear logo. They included this, but forgot to write anything inside. He replaced both in the envelope and dropped it on his desk. He was sad about the death of his colleague, but head office had already been in touch asking when he was going to recruit a replacement. He would get the office junior to forward the card to the girlfriend. On the reverse of the business card the sender had remembered to add the number ten in black felt tip.

Newcastle, December 2009

Andrew emerged from the arrivals hall at Newcastle's International Airport just before 6pm that evening having caught the 16.30 British Airways service from Heathrow. The flight time was just under an hour but he barely had time to open his laptop after the seat belt signs went out, before the announcement of their impending decent. He realised that including the time it had taken him to get to the airport, park and arrange a ticket on the first available flight, it would have been quicker to leave his car at Kew and travelled by train via King's Cross Station in central London, with the added advantage of working on his computer the whole way. He had telephoned his mother-in-law at the airport to explain why he would not be collecting Charlotte as planned. He told her a little more than he should so she would fully understand why he had to disappoint his daughter, and himself. He also called both Bill Frost and Jackie to explain the latest developments

"Bill, given what's happened we must keep the information about the card out of the media, at least until we can establish how important this line of enquiry might be."

Jackie was in a meeting discussing Paul Williams as the investigation into his erratic behaviour had become known to her officially. She returned his call just as his flight was being called.

"Sorry, can you say that again Andrew, I didn't catch what you said." He briefly explained the call with the genealogist and his travel plans.

"I'm not sure when I'll be back, so I let Charlotte's grandmother know I can't pick her up tonight."

"That's sad, but you have to follow this through. Let me know when you've spoken to this professor and…" Her voice disappeared as the last call for his flight filled the air.

"I'll call you when I know what's happening," he replied, hoping he had answered the right question.

"Ok," she said.

"Got to go, being called back into the meeting."

Andrew searched the arrivals hall trying to catch a sight of someone who looked like a professor at the same time as Lambert scanned the exit for someone who resembled a spy. It took them a full minute to identify each other as Larkin looked nothing like Daniel Craig and Lambert, at six foot three with a full head of hair, bore little resemblance to the balding bespectacled academic in Andrew's imagination. They finally made the connection just before they almost collided.

"Mr Larkin?" asked Lambert.

"Professor Lambert?" said Andrew.

They both nodded and Lambert, some six inches shorter, looked up at the genealogist.

"This is my colleague Jenny Cross."

Jenny shook hands with the man from MI5 and she beckoned him to follow them.

"My car is in the short stay car park just across the road." After a few steps Lambert stopped. "Where would you like us to take you Mr Larkin?"

"You can call me Andrew. Where are you staying?" he replied.

"We're on our way back to Ashington where Jenny, Miss Cross lives." A quick glance at his companion told Andrew that she was more than a work colleague to the professor.

"It's about half an hour depending on the traffic, say forty five minutes on a Friday night," said Cross.

"Sorry, I assumed you would be staying at a hotel in the city. I am booked in at the..," he slid a piece of paper from his jacket, "The Jury's Inn."

"I know where that is," said Jenny. "Why don't we take you there and we can tell you what we know about the letter on the way. We could have some dinner if you haven't eaten?"

She glanced at Lambert who nodded his agreement.

"That would be good," said Andrew. In the thirty minutes it took to cover the eight miles to the hotel, situated on South Shore Road in Gateshead on the banks of the River Tyne, Lambert had given a brief outline of events since he had been made aware of the letter.

"So what has convinced you that the letter *is* genuine?" asked Andrew as they drew up outside the hotel entrance.

"I'm not, Mr Larkin," replied Lambert. "But the investigation has shown that the facts contained within it, namely that Elizabeth bore a child at Alnwick Castle in 1575, do stand up to scrutiny."

"We'll find somewhere to park whilst you check-in and meet you in the lobby?" suggested Cross, turning around from the driver's seat.

Andrew dropped his bag in his room and immediately returned to the ground floor. As the elevator doors opened, he spotted them sitting close together on a settee at the far corner of the lobby. The girl saw him immediately and they were both standing by the time Andrew reached them.

"There's a nice restaurant just a few minutes' walk from here with a view of the river and the bridges," said Cross as the full force of a north east December evening hit them as they emerged from the hotel. Andrew only had his suit jacket and shivered involuntarily.

"It takes a while to get used to the climate, Andrew," she said smiling, but not immune to his discomfort. "The restaurant really is close so hopefully you will survive."

They walked past the Baltic Centre and immediately emerged onto a smart new walkway with views of the city's famous bridges. The modern Millennium Bridge is made up of two thin metallic arcs spanning the river like the giant jaws of a beast, one vertical, the other almost at right angles and filled with people crossing to the north bank to enjoy its nightlife. Both spans were brightly lit, one white, the vertical a shimmering purple, its reflections dancing in the waters below. In the distance, the famous Old Tyne railway bridge that symbolises the city for many, its single arch resembling Sydney Harbour bridge. The chrome and glass of the fashionable *Six* restaurant sat in the shadow of the Contemporary Arts Centre with an uninterrupted view of the bridges. They were fortunate to be seated in a quiet corner by the large windows and Andrew could enjoy the lights of the city across the Tyne. After a few minutes of small talk, they ordered their food and Andrew resumed the earlier conversation.

"So professor, what have your investigations in Newcastle uncovered so far?" Lambert waited whilst a waitress served their wine before answering in a low tone.

"We have traced four generations of descendants including Angus, who we believe was the illegitimate son of the queen. His heirs were Richard, James and Thomas. Thomas had a son and daughter and although the girl was older, the rights to any property or titles would pass to the eldest son. We could find no trace of John in the Shilbottle area so assumed he must have left."

"Any idea why?"

"At that time the main industry in the north east, apart from farming, was coal mining," said Jenny. "This area was probably the first in Britain to excavate coal, there's evidence of the Romans burning it locally."

"The seams were close to the surface and near to the river and sea so easy to remove and transport to London and the rest of the country," continued Lambert.

"Coals from Newcastle." said Andrew.

"Indeed," said Lambert. "We took a chance and went to the Durham Mining Museum in Spennymore a few miles south of here. They've brought together much of the surviving documentation on the industry including details of those working for the mining companies." Jenny produced a photocopy from her bag and passed it to Andrew.

"This is a list of wages paid to the employees who looked after the horses at Ravensworth pit, near what is now Sunderland. The fifth name is John Moore." She pointed across the table as she spoke.

"But how can you be sure it's the correct John Moore?" said Andrew.

"That was just the starting point," said Lambert. "From there we were able to trace his address from other records kept by the company. We knew he rented a cottage in Ryhope, as we found a ledger showing his wife and two children as tenants. He was killed in an accident in 1718 and his death certificate records his date and place of birth."

"Impressive," said Andrew.

"It's what we do Mr Larkin."

"So where next?" said Andrew and passed the paper back to Jenny.

"The family would have had to leave the rented cottage as they were only for workers," said Jenny.

"But the man died whilst at work," said Andrew.

"Very different times," said Lambert.

"We know this happened as another family are recorded as holding the tenancy just three months later," said Jenny. "We have the name of his wife and the two children, William and George. There is a chance she may have moved back to her family after the accident. On Monday we intend to uncover some evidence of where she may have gone."

"Such as a forwarding address or such like," said Lambert.

Andrew pulled two folded sheets from his jacket and passed them to Lambert.

"That is a list taken from a website," he said.

"*English Monarchy?*" said Lambert.

"Yes," said Andrew.

"To date, the killer has disposed of numbers one to nine. We have very few clues or evidence on who the killer or killers might be and the motive is unclear."

"We took the opportunity to study the site this afternoon after you called," said Lambert. "I must say that I agree with the hypothesise that this person believes he or she has a claim to the throne."

"I'm glad you agree on that point," said Andrew, "as that makes your continued involvement all the more important."

"Continued involvement?"

"Professor, we have a maniac on the loose who has published a target list of sixteen people, nine of whom have already been murdered." Lambert could not help but study the list. "If we have interpreted it correctly, the higher numbers include some very important people and number sixteen needs no introduction." Lambert folded the list and looked directly at Andrew.

"I understand the importance of what you are saying, but I don't think you understand the enormity and uncertainty of the task we face."

"What I understand professor, is that lives are at stake, important lives." Jenny had taken the list from Lambert and was studying it as the two men spoke.

"Mr Larkin, I'm sure we both want to do everything we can to help your investigation. I don't wish to speak for the professor, but he has worked hard to keep the existence of the letter confidential. If it turns out to be a forgery it would cause severe embarrassment to a number of people." Chiefly the professor, thought Andrew. Jenny reached into her handbag and retrieved a list of her own. Andrew continued.

"Professor, I can assure you that it is not the intention of Her Majesty's Government to leak or publish any information. We are as keen as you to keep this whole thing under wraps." Lambert looked across at Jenny for her opinion but she was preoccupied with her paperwork.

"Mr Larkin?" she said looking up.

"Andrew, please."

"It appears there may be a pattern here." Both men looked at her expectantly. She cleared a space on the table and laid out the two sheets. "Each victim's occupation is in the killer's list."

"Yes," said both men simultaneously.

"The first four are all farmers or farm workers and the fifth a miner." Both nodded. "Angus Moore was a farmer and so were his children, grandchildren and great grandchildren; three generations."

"And the fourth worked in the coal industry," said Lambert, scooping the pages from the table. "If this is true it gives us a trail to follow," he said, running his finger down Andrew's list.

"How do you mean?" said Andrew, trying to keep up.

"It says the next victim is a lockkeeper, so that would mean William worked on the canals," reasoned Lambert.

"That's a little early for canals," said Jenny reaching into her bag again, this time retrieving her smartphone. Lambert and Larkin fell into an awkward silence as Jenny tapped away on the device. "There," she exclaimed, offering the phone to Lambert.

"What?" he replied, studying the screen. Puzzled, Jenny took the phone and shook her head in exasperation.

"You put your thumb on the screen and deleted the page."

"Not guilty," he replied, defensively. She passed the phone to Larkin who accepted it carefully and studied the page.

"The Bridgewater Canal was built between 1759 and 1761 to transport coal to Manchester." Larkin passed the phone to Lambert and the two acted out an elaborate dance to ensure the chosen web page survived the transfer.

"Suppose William left the north east in search of work?" said Jenny.

"But he would have been nearly sixty," said Lambert.

"We don't know what he might have done," she replied. "He could have been an engineer or had some other skill they needed. Remember this was one of the first canals ever built so a mining engineer would have been a useful man to have around when you're excavating a lot of earth."

"It certainly seems worth investigating," said Andrew.

"We can head over to Manchester on Monday," said Jenny, looking at Lambert.

"Fine by me," he replied. "I'll head back to London first thing in the morning and catch up with you Monday afternoon."

They finished the meal and walked back to the hotel. Andrew could easily see that it was a strain for them to appear unattached, the professor unable to stop himself from glancing in her direction every few seconds. That's what I must look like when I'm with Jackie, he thought. Andrew realised that despite the terrible events surrounding them, he had enjoyed the evening and the conversation of his dinner companions.

"Where is the letter now professor?" said Andrew as they reached the hotel entrance.

"Safe at the university," replied Lambert. Larkin suddenly recalled an important question he wanted to ask the professor

"Do have any idea how the bear and ragged staff symbol could be connected?"

"Didn't Peter Hughes at Kew mention it?"

"I know it's connected with the Warwick family but I'm not aware of any connection with Elizabeth I." Lambert raised his eyebrows.

"You're only looking at one side of this equation, Mr Larkin," he said. "Robert Dudley, Earl of Leicester and the alleged child's father, had a link to the Warwicks through his paternal grandmother. He was fascinated by Richard Beauchamp, the thirteenth earl who fought in the Hundred Years War, and eventually adopted the symbol, together with his brother."

Andrew was taken aback at the simplicity of the reference.

"Are you sure?" Lambert laughed.

"Have a look on the internet when you get to your room Mr Larkin. There are plenty of pictures of the splendid fireplace Dudley had built in the gatehouse at Kenilworth Castle. Study the surround."

"Well I'll let you two be on your way. Please let me know the minute you find anything more, however trivial it might seem."

"Don't worry Andrew," said Jenny, "he will." She took the genealogists arm and led him towards the car park.

"Goodnight," said Andrew with as a smile, as the couple turned their heads around; Lambert with a terrified look and Jenny with a knowing smile. Before he retired Andrew found the picture the professor had mentioned. On each side of the enormous marble fireplace sat a crest flanked by the letters R & L, for Robert Leicester, with the bear and ragged staff symbol expertly carved within a shield.

Andrew fumbled in the dark, not knowing where he was or the time. The only light coming from his vibrating cell phone. It seemed to be brighter than a spotlight and he struggled to focus as his eyes adjusted to the sudden brightness. It was Jackie.

"Hello," he croaked into the handset, "what time is it?"

"Five thirty, sleepy head." Andrew could tell that she was moving from the rushing background noise.

"It's nice to hear from you, but did you have to call so early? Where are you anyway?"

"On the M1 motorway just north of Milton Keynes, I think." Andrew found the switch for the bedside lamp and pulled himself into an upright position.

"Nice. Are you going to tell me why?"

"When you're awake." Andrew rose from the bed and pulled back the curtains to reveal the lights of the still slumbering city.

"Ok, I'm alive," he said, turning on the small kettle that passed for room service.

"I'm on my way to Manchester and should arrive around eight. I assume you're still in Newcastle?"

"Yes. Look what's going on, have you found Paul Williams?"

"Did you hear about the gas explosion at a house in Manchester a few days ago?"

"Er, yes I think so."

"It turns out a young estate agent was in the house when the explosion occurred." Andrew pulled the list from his jacket pocket as he listened and scanned down, finding the tenth victim's occupation immediately.

"As soon as I received the report from the local police I got them to search for a card."

"And?" urged Andrew, pouring hot water into a cup and watching the tea bag string disappear into the liquid.

"Nothing on the body or in the area. But that's not surprising as it resembles a war zone." Andrew did not have to imagine the scene; he had seen it on the TV news. "So I contacted the officer in charge and asked him to speak to everyone the victim knew. It only took him a few hours to confirm what I had feared."

"Go on," said Andrew, struggling with the lid of a small plastic pot of UHT milk.

"Our killer sent a condolence card to the guy's boss with a card attached. The manager had not thought to inform anyone. The card had the number ten handwritten on it." Andrew glanced at his watch.

"I'm not sure of the quickest way for me to get to Manchester, but I'll get across as soon as I can. Text me the address details." Andrew said his goodbyes, immediately dialled the hotel reception and asked the quickest way he could hire a car.

"I'm sorry pet," said the receptionist, "I doubt anywhere in the city will be open before nine on a Saturday morning. You could try the airport."

"When is the first flight to Manchester?" said Andrew, deciding that he may as well take the quickest route.

"There's no direct flight to Manchester from Newcastle."

"Well I need to get there as soon as possible, how on earth do I do that?"

"Catch the train, pet."

Andrew stood looking at the departure board at Newcastle Central Station. It was 6.30am and he had a choice to make. Catch the 06.45 and change at York, or wait for the next direct train at 07.43. He had not travelled on a train for as long as he could remember and so instinctively wanted to get on the train here and alight at his destination. But that half hour wait would mean he would not reach Manchester until 10:19, an hour later. He made his decision and bought his ticket from one of the automatic ticket machines, before grabbing a coffee and Danish from a platform kiosk. He then realised he had no idea where platform ten was or how to get there. He glanced at his watch and realised he was in danger of missing the departure. Desperately he looked around for a station employee to help him, but could find none. He then spotted a sign for platforms six to ten. He would have to negotiate a flight of steps and cross a bridge. He bounded up the steps spilling his coffee over his hand and dropped the cup as he yelped in pain. As he crossed the bridge he could see the platform. It was 06.44. He danced down the steps and approached the nearest train door.

"Sorry sir, I'm afraid you're too late," came a voice from behind. Andrew span around to see a station guard. "For safety reasons the doors are locked a minute before departure," he said, with a hint of a smile on his lips. Andrew had decided to get this train and so he reluctantly put down his bags and pulled his MI5 identity card from his wallet.

"I'm sorry too. But you see I'm afraid I am going to have to insist this train doesn't leave without me, it's a matter of national security."

"I've seen every trick in the book sonny, that's not going to fool me." He waved the small baton in his hand and Andrew watched as the train began to move. "Don't worry, there's another in ten minutes from platform six." Andrew turned a walked towards the stairs. "And I wouldn't try using that fake ID again. It's one of the worst I've ever seen."

Andrew arrived at Manchester's Piccadilly station at 09:49. After speaking to the guard on the second leg from York, he decided to take the city's

Metro to the nearest station at Sale which was the quickest way to travel. As he sat on the bright yellow train, he called Jackie and arranged to be collected at the station.

"That's handy," she said. "Seems like our killer may have used the Metro to make his escape." The street was still cordoned off at both ends and Andrew was struck by the carnage as he and Jackie approached what was left of the house.

"They've found pieces of his watch and fragments of a briefcase," said Jackie as they surveyed the scene. "Phone records place him here as he called his girlfriend just before he arrived."

"Was he driving a Mini?" said Andrew, looking at the sight of the small car with the obvious markings of a real estate agents, perched up against the front door of the house opposite. Crowther ignored the question and guided Andrew away from the others.

"The police have interviewed a number of people who were in the vicinity."

"I don't suppose anyone saw anything?" said Andrew.

"It seems an old lady was looking out of her window a few minutes before the explosion. She saw a suspicious looking man opposite her house trying to hide in between the houses."

"Thank goodness for nosey neighbours," said Andrew.

"She was able to give a fairly good description of the man."

"Great," said Andrew. "Have they got an artist to put together a photofit yet?"

"No need," said Crowther, "her description matches Paul Williams perfectly."

"I can't believe it," said Jackie as they joined the motorway. Andrew sat opposite her in the rear of the unmarked car. They had both paid a visit to the neighbour and heard her describe the slightly built man in a raincoat.

"He caught my eye as he obviously didn't want to be seen," said the old lady. "He kept creeping out from between those two houses and looking up the road." She pulled aside the curtains and pointed across the street.

"How soon before the explosion did you first notice him?" said Andrew. The woman returned to her seat before answering.

"Terrible noise you know, frightened the living daylights out of me. I was lucky that van was parked out front or my windows would have gone too." Larkin had noticed the shell of the vehicle as they walked towards the house. Andrew and Jackie exchanged glances and realised there was little to gain from questioning the woman further. They thanked her for the tea she had made and left the house. As they reached the end of the path they turned to see her standing in the doorway. "He was there at least half an hour before that poor man was killed."

Andrew turned in his seat to face Jackie.

"How much do we know about Williams' background?"

"He was born and raised in Cardiff in what seems to be a typical family environment," replied Jackie. "He had a flair for maths and managed to win a place at Oxford, which is where we found him."

"Do we have any information on his ancestry?" said Andrew.

"I doubt it," said Jackie, "not beyond the normal SC vetting checks and they wouldn't go back more than a generation or two at his security level."

"I've been in touch with Bill Frost and we've put out a national alert for him," said Andrew. At that moment his phone rang. He could see it was Ken Greaves, head of A3 and so dispensed with the normal pleasantries.

"When were you planning to let me know that the most prolific serial killer since the Ripper works in national security?"

Hello to you too, thought Andrew. "We have a nationwide search underway for him, sir. And we have no direct evidence he is the killer."

"Find him and quick," said Greaves "I've had Downing Street on the phone sensing that this will not play out well in media. *Security Services Fail to Find Mass Murderer in Their Own Backyard* was the headline someone suggested to me."

"We're pulling out all the stops, sir," said Andrew.

"I assume that means you will stop wasting your time chasing some irrelevant professor to the furthest reaches of civilisation?" said Greaves in an icy tone.

"Sir, whoever committed these crimes almost certainly has a link with an ancestor of Queen Elizabeth I," said Andrew.

"I don't care who his relations were. Find him and stop him or I'll find someone who can."

The line went dead leaving Andrew drawing breath to answer the threat.

"Not good I gather?" said Jackie looking sympathetically in his direction.

"Too many people at the top more worried about headlines than facts."

"You're not convinced that Williams is the killer?" said Jackie, gently putting her arm through his. His expression changed instantly at her touch and he had to concentrate hard to stay focused.

"We certainly need to locate him quickly and find out if he was definitely at the scene," he replied. "But there are too many unanswered questions and too many unsubstantiated facts to stop all other lines of enquiry."

"I agree, but until we do find him, I doubt we'll be able to call on a great deal of resource for anything else."

They sat in silence for most of the three and a half hour journey back to London apart from taking calls from various agencies co-ordinating the search for the missing NCIS fugitive.

"Do you think you'll get any spare time tomorrow?" Andrew asked as they approached the outskirts of the capital.

"Perhaps a few hours, but it's hard to tell."

"Only I wondered if you wanted to spend some time with Charlotte? I'm hoping to travel down there early in the morning."

"That sounds nice, let's see what happens this afternoon."

Andrew collected his car from Heathrow and after arranging to speak to Jackie later, headed straight down the M4. He arrived at GCHQ at 5.45am and immediately joined the meeting he had arranged en-route. David Scott was joined by Bill Frost, Charles Smythe and to his slight surprise, Mary Ward. Scott must have sensed his thoughts.

"I invited Mary as she spent some time with Williams and initially alerted me to his strange behaviour."

"Fine," said Andrew. The MI5 man gave the assembled gathering a brief overview of the events of the last twenty four hours.

"Were the CCTV images not able to identify him?" asked Ward.

"Unfortunately the recording equipment at Altrincham malfunctioned and there are no cameras in the station car park anyway," said Andrew.

"I don't understand how this genealogy fellow fits in old boy," said Smythe.

"We know from the website that the killer has an issue with the monarchy," replied Andrew. "This letter, points to Queen Elizabeth having an illegitimate son who was raised by a peasant family."

"Very interesting I'm sure, but what connection has this with Williams?" Andrew explained how they had discovered the link between the descendants of the child and the victims.

"That could be just a coincidence," said Scott.

"Yes, it could. The professor and his assistant are going to the North of England Institute of Mining & Mechanical Engineers on Monday to see if they can find any references to William Moore. If it turns out he worked on the canal then I think we can safely assume there is a direct link."

"And what about Williams' family, do they have a claim to the throne?" said Frost.

"It's too early to tell. I'm trying to keep this side of the investigation under the radar until I have some concrete evidence that there is a direct link." They all nodded in understanding. "All my section head is interested in at the moment is finding Williams. He doesn't care who he's related to, he just wants him off the streets." There was a murmur of consent around the table at the rationale.

"So are you convinced that he's the killer?" said Ward. Andrew paused before he answered the question, aware that his comments would probably find their way back to Ken Greaves.

"I agree that we need to find Williams for a number of reasons, not least that he has access to sensitive material and a detailed knowledge of this investigation."

"Had," said Scott. "All his access and admin rights have been removed."

"That's good," said Andrew. "But we don't know what he may have copied before he went AWOL."

"We've alerted every force in the country and both Interpol and the FBI," said Frost.

"And I've set up a directory on the system to intercept any mention of him in any medium," said Ward rising from her chair in response to a buzz from her phone. "If you'll excuse me I'm wanted elsewhere." Scott nodded his approval and she left the room.

"If he surfaces anywhere we will locate him," said Scott. "We know he's got the knowledge to conceal most of his digital footprint, but we are treating this as a priority one. We even have the Americans giving us some satellite time so we can carry out visual surveillance of any area in the UK within an hour."

Andrew was impressed at the resources GCHQ had brought together, it would help to keep Greaves off his back too. The meeting broke up at 6.30am and Andrew walked to his car with Frost.

"Bill, I didn't want to say too much in there, but I'm not as convinced as everyone else that Williams is our man."

"Why is that?"

"It's just too convenient."

"I know it's hard to imagine someone from inside the security community being capable of doing this, but we know our man has extensive and highly developed computer skills." Andrew suddenly stopped and turned to face his colleague.

"Perhaps we can use that to our advantage," he said.

"How?" said Frost.

Andrew's mind was a blur as he tried to fathom out how to turn the thought that had suddenly struck him, into a workable idea.

"We need to tempt him out into the open."

"Obviously that would be a good idea," said Frost with a shrug of his shoulders.

"No I mean in a way that would allow us to verify some of the things we don't know for certain."

"Great plan, but how?" asked Frost in growing exasperation.

"I'm sorry Bill," he replied. "I have an idea but I'm struggling to think how best to make it work."

They had started walking again and reached Andrew's car.

"Let me know if that mind of yours manages to sort something out," said Frost as he continued walking.

Andrew was home inside fifteen minutes and immediately arranged to collect Charlotte the following morning. He then called Jackie in the hope that she could join them.

"Crowther," she answered formally.

He knew she would have seen his number on her phone so guessed she was in company. "Hello Ms Crowther it's Mr Larkin. I assume you can't talk?"

"That's correct."

"But can you meet me tomorrow as we discussed?" A pause.

"I think that would be fine."

"Great, I will e-mail you the address later, together with a few kisses."

"Thank you, I'll have a look at that as soon as it comes through."

The line went dead. A hundred miles away Jackie terminated the call and looked up from her desk at her director of operation, Colin Jackson, and a man she had heard of but had never met until twenty minutes before.

"So Ms Crowther," said Ken Greaves, Andrew's section head at MI5, "you're happy that the liaison with my department is working efficiently?"

Jackie glanced at her superior but found no support or guidance in his eyes. Is this a setup, she thought? Of course it is, Greaves knows about our relationship.

"I've had all the support necessary to carry out my duties from the departments involved in the executive liaison group," she said, looking Greaves in the eye. "As regards Andrew Larkin, we've been working closely together to ensure no stone is left unturned."

"I'm sure," said Greaves rising from his chair. "Everyone here knows that Williams must be apprehended at all costs and as an utmost priority."

"Of course," said Jackson. Greaves turned as he left the room.

"I'm told you're very good at what you do Ms Crowther. I do hope you're equally adept at prioritising your work life balance."

Bastard, he does know, thought Jackie. Two minutes later Jackson appeared in the doorway.

"What the hell was that all about?"

"I have no idea."

"He really gave me a hard time and wanted to know everything about you."

"It's just the political flak from this case."

"Well make sure you do everything to find Williams. It's a real embarrassment and just when the funding review is due."

"He must be under enormous pressure," said Andrew.

He and Jackie were standing either side of a children's slide watching Charlotte gingerly climb the slippery steps. It was a cold December afternoon but the little girl had insisted on a visit to a park to show her daddy how clever she was. Andrew had collected Charlotte on his own as he did not want the added complication of explaining Jackie to his mother-in-law. She had reacted very well to the fact that he had cancelled the planned weekend late on Friday and made no comment. Andrew decided he would follow her example and kept the conversation as light as he could.

"When do you think you will catch this fellow, Andrew?" asked his father-in-law, bringing him back to reality.

"Soon, I hope," replied Andrew. "But please remember there is a news blackout on all of this."

"Don't worry, I will make sure he keeps quiet when he goes to the golf club." said Dorothy smiling at her husband.

"I'll feed and water her before I get back tonight," Andrew said as he strapped his daughter into the car seat.

"Not too late, please, she has school in the morning remember."

"We're going to meet a friend of mine darling," said Andrew, as the two chatted as they drove.

"I made an angel at school daddy. Grandma put it on top of the Christmas tree."

"That's wonderful, you must show me when we get back later."

"Will you be there when Father Christmas brings my presents daddy?"

Andrew had not given the approaching festive season much thought and Charlotte's question shocked him into the realisation the holiday was only a week or so away.

"Of course I will. We can leave the milk and cookies out for him together."

"Don't be silly daddy, it's a pint of beer and a carrot for Rudolph. Grandpa told me."

A pang of guilt shot through Andrew as he realised that his absence had meant that his own childhood traditions had been replaced by those of his in-laws.

"Of course, silly daddy."

They arrived at the small village of Lechlade just after midday and drove into the riverside car park as arranged. Jackie was already there, parked in the centre of the bustling courtyard. Andrew could not see her face as it was hidden behind a copy of the Sunday Times. He parked next to her and gave a quick tap on his car horn. The paper shot up in the air and Jackie's shocked face appeared. She was just about to berate the idiot who had aged her ten years when she noticed the little girl staring at her from the rear seat. A quick glance to one side revealed Andrew's face, half laughing, half worried. She wound down the window and the anger instantly disappeared.

"Sorry, I didn't mean to startle you."

Jackie waited whilst Andrew removed Charlotte from the car before attempting to make any contact with the child.

"We're going to have a walk along the river and feed the ducks," said Andrew as he fussed around his daughter, putting on a pair of gloves and placing a hat over her bright blonde curls. Charlotte spent the entire time staring at Jackie and she started to feel a little uncomfortable as she was not used to children.

"Hello," she said finally, not able to hold the child's gaze. Andrew looked up at Jackie and smiled.

"Darling, this is the friend I told you about. Her name is Jackie and she's going to spend the day with us."

Charlotte disappeared behind her father's legs.

"Come on Charlotte, say hello to Jackie," said Andrew trying to unravel the child from his legs. But she stubbornly refused, wrapping her arms tightly around his knees causing Andrew to lose his balance and topple against the car door. Jackie squatted down to the child's level and spoke in a gentle tone.

"I need someone to help me feed the ducks on the river. Could you help me?" There was no movement.

"Ok, I guess the little baby ducks will have to go hungry."

Andrew tried again to wrestle her arms from his legs but she had a vice like grip. "Oh well, I will just have to feed them myself."

She rose and retrieved her scarf and the half a loaf of bread she had picked up on her way out of the house, locked her car and walked across the car park to the riverbank. She had a splendid view of the small Cotswold stone bridge that crossed the Thames. People were peering over the edge at a canal boat that chugged its way sedately along the water. As she approached the bank, two swans from a larger group glided towards her in the hope that she would be carrying some food. Once they saw her begin to unwrap the bread and break it into small pieces, others began to approach. Just as she was about to toss a second handful she felt a tap on her shoulder and turned to see Andrew with Charlotte, still hidden. Jackie turned and tossed the bread and was surprised to see the little girl suddenly appear next to her.

"That one is the mummy swan," she said in a confident tone.

Jackie offered her a slice of bread which she took and simply tossed into the water in one piece, prompting a scramble amongst the dozen or so birds of various types that had been attracted by the food.

"It might be better to break it into smaller pieces Charlotte. Is that your name?"

Charlotte nodded and took another slice of bread.

"Well my name is Jackie. Would you like me to help you tear up the bread?"

"No thank you Jackie, I can do that by myself."

Jackie looked at Andrew who was grinning from ear to ear.

"She likes you," he whispered.

Within twenty minutes neither of the adults could squeeze a word in between the five-year-old's chatter as they walked along the river bank.

"She looks just like you," said Jackie during a small gap in the one way conversation.

"Do you think so? All I can see is Nancy."

They returned to the car park and enjoyed a traditional Sunday lunch in *The Riverside* pub. Charlotte insisted on sitting in between the couple sensing that the newcomer had some of her father's attention. Andrew fussed over his daughter and Jackie saw a side to his character she had not seen before. After lunch the little girl insisted on showing them how fast she could career down a slide and so they drove to a nearby play park.

"That's not really the point is it?" replied Andrew steadying his daughter's descent down the wet slide. "Turning up at your office unannounced was very unprofessional and intimidating. It's typical of the man."

Jackie helped Charlotte from the base of the slide and watched her run around to the steps for another go.

"It's certainly unusual, but it just reinforces my point about resource. Until we find Williams, we'll struggle to divert anyone to help your genealogy friends." Andrew nodded.

"Let's hope that they're as good as I think they are."

They walked back to his car and Andrew strapped Charlotte in her safety seat.

"Goodbye Charlotte," said Jackie peering into the car.

The child pulled her head towards her and planted a wet kiss on her cheek.

"Will you be there to watch me open my presents on Christmas day?" she asked.

Jackie could feel herself blush as she turned to look at Andrew who was also taken aback by the unforeseen question.

"We'll have to ask Grandma about that," he said.

"I will speak to her," said Charlotte in a tone that eerily mimicked Andrew's mother-in-law. There was an awkward silence between the two adults that Jackie eventually broke by pulling him towards her and kissing him passionately.

"Nothing would make me happier than spending Christmas day with you," she said feeling Charlotte watching them through the window. "But I completely understand if it's not what you want or it's too difficult."

Andrew took her head gently in his hands and looked into her face.

"It is what I want."

He hesitated and she tried to give him an opportunity to say no.

"It's ok, I understand how difficult it might be for Nancy's parents."

"Let me talk to Dorothy and take the temperature," he said in reply.

They broke away and Andrew watched her climb into her car and lower the window.

"Let's talk later," he said kissing her through the opening.

"Oh, I forgot," he suddenly lifted his head and cracked it against the window frame. Jackie could not help but laugh at the sight of the MI5 man hopping about in pain. "I have an idea how we can flush Williams out," he said, massaging the painful spot "It totally slipped my mind."

"I'm not sure this is the best place to discuss this?"

Andrew put his head back inside the window and kissed her again.

"We need to set up a website and play him at his own game. If he takes the bait we verify his involvement and possibly trace his whereabouts."

"Sounds a good idea. Let me give it some thought on the way back and we can talk later."

Andrew watched her pull away before he returned to his own car.

Liverpool, December 2009

Lambert and Jenny set off early Monday morning for the 180 mile journey to the National Waterways Museum in Ellesmere Port near Liverpool, where they hoped to find evidence that William Moore had been employed on a canal project. Lambert had wanted to travel by train but Jenny overruled him, winning the argument by sitting in her car until he joined her.

"By the time we would get into Newcastle, we'll be half way there," she reasoned.

The professor was quickly learning that winning a discussion with her was an impossible folly, even when she was wrong she was right.

"The museum opens at ten, but someone should be there from nine," she said as they sped south on the A1.

"I'll call the main switchboard and hopefully be able to speak to the director," replied Lambert. "He should be able to make a start before we arrive," said Jenny more in hope than expectation. "Larkin said to call him if we have any problems, although I dread to think what he might have in mind for the poor fellow if he doesn't co-operate, the tower I shouldn't wonder."

Lambert finally spoke to the director at 9.30am after leaving several messages on an answerphone.

"This is a little unusual; we are carrying out some alterations as this is a quiet time of year for us," said the man "Is it not possible to visit in the New Year?"

"I'm afraid not Mr Ennis," said Lambert getting slightly exasperated with the man's attitude "As I explained, we have been asked by the authorities to carry out some research that's connected with an ongoing investigation."

"What time will you arrive?" said Ennis reluctantly.

"About ten thirty," mouthed Jenny, able to hear what the man was saying.

The museum was an impressive six-storey brick building located on a tributary to the southern bank of the river Mersey and Ennis was waiting in the small reception area when they arrived. "I'm afraid all of the records relating to that period have been placed in storage boxes for the alterations," was the first thing he said as they approached.

"Good morning Mr Ennis," said Jenny, preventing any chance of Lambert repeating his opinion of the man as expressed in the car. "Just show us where they are and we'll work our way through."

They were led through to a small room filled with boxes and the paraphernalia of exhibits. They cleared a space on a table and with the help of Ennis, found the appropriate boxes.

"This is everything we have on the Bridgewater canal," he said, placing a dozen ledgers of varying sizes on the table. "We do have a number of the original engineering drawings, but I assume they will be of little use if I understood your requirements?"

He left the two visitors to their own devices and they began to sift through the books, identifying the contents.

"Most of this is about the project itself," said Jenny after ten minutes.

"Same here," replied Lambert. "A treasure trove of information if we were researching the engineering and financial background to the project."

They spent the next two hours painstakingly sifting through each of the ledgers and books, searching for any mention of William Moore. They learnt how the idea for a canal had originated from letters from the third Duke Francis Egerton to his principal engineer James Brindley, and the strong arm tactics used to remove tenant farmers from their land and homes to clear the swathe of land needed for the thirty nine mile route from Worsley to Manchester. Amongst the many letters and documents, one name was conspicuous by its absence.

"There doesn't seem to be much information about the people who designed and built the canal," said Jenny placing another journal back in a box.

"It looks like most of this information has come from the duke's records, probably donated by his family," said Lambert.

Eventually the museum receptionist, a middle-aged woman, brought them coffee and stayed to talk.

"Yes, that's right, the documents we have were given to us by the duke's family when the museum was set up forty years ago," said the woman picking through boxes. "What exactly are you looking for?"

Jenny briefly explained the background to their search without mentioning the ultimate reason. "I don't think we have anything from the construction phase of the project."

"No employee records of any kind?" asked Lambert.

"I'm afraid not. It was one of the earliest canals built so we were grateful to receive anything we could exhibit."

It took the two another three hours, punctuated by a brief break for a sandwich, to sift through all of the information.

"We'll just have to revert back to the parish records to find him," said Jenny stretching her arms in an attempt to bring some life back into her limbs.

"But where?" replied Lambert, "here or back in the North East?"

"Given the seriousness of the situation, I suggest both," said Jenny. "If Larkin wants us to carry out this research in such a short time, then we'll need extra people to help, it's as simple as that."

"I'll call him from the car and explain the situation."

They had just decided to leave when the receptionist came into the room juggling two cups of tea with a bundle of papers under her arm.

"Here are a few of the drawings, you haven't seen these yet have you?"

"No," said Jenny appreciating the helpfulness of the woman.

The assistant returned with an armful of additional drawings a few minutes later. The two researchers glanced wearily at each other and began to spread the large sheets on the table.

"These are plans of the canal route and other engineering drawings," said Lambert. "We're not going to find any information on William Moore here."

He continued idly searching for the date of the document before him.

"This one was drafted in November 1760 by a George Arnold," he said quietly.

They both stopped and looked up at the same instant.

"It's too much of a long shot, surely?"

William's name was hand-written as the originator of the tenth drawing they spread out on the table. Dated November 1759, it showed detailed plans for strengthening the sides of the canal with timber frames during construction to prevent collapse, with a recommendation to purchase a Newcomen steam engine to pump excess water.

"Exactly the skills a mining engineer could transfer to a canal project," said Lambert.

"So you're sure that William Moore worked on the canal?" said Andrew.

"I think the coincidence is too strong to ignore," answered Lambert. "We also spoke to the Mining Museum in Spennymoor and confirmed that William was employed as an engineer in a Durham pit."

"I see," said Andrew. "So what next?"

"If we're going to trace the next generation we need to find out where he lived and more importantly, details of his family," said Lambert. "It's a huge task, Andrew, if you want this done quickly we're going to need more people."

"I'm afraid that's not going to be possible Tom," replied Andrew. "We need to keep this away from the media and we just don't have the resource."

Lambert paused before replying.

"Perhaps I have misunderstood the importance of this work, or are you keeping me in the dark about something?"

"No," replied Andrew, a little too quickly.

A silence descended on the line which was eventually broken by Larkin.

"Look, my people have placed finding Paul Williams as the most crucial element in the investigation and I can't pull anyone away from that."

"So they don't think the letter is genuine?" said Lambert.

"At this time they see it as irrelevant Tom. If Williams is the killer then it doesn't matter who his ancestor was."

"But what if he's not the killer?" said Lambert.

"Good question, which is why I need you to continue your hunt. I'm not convinced and if I'm right then your work could prove crucial."

"I could ask Peter Hughes at Kew to work on the Williams' tree. He knows about what we're doing and it won't take him long to trace his family and once we get beyond 1801 we should be able to trace things considerably faster," said Lambert.

"Why is that?" asked Larkin.

"That was the year of the first complete census of Great Britain," replied Lambert. "Since then, with the exception of 1941 during the war, the entire population has been counted and analysed with every detail recorded and published. It made the job of following a family's history a great deal easier as we can see much more information from these entries."

"So why 1801 and not before?" said Andrew.

Lambert explained how a government official named John Rickman had championed the need for a census of the general population, initially to ascertain how many men of fighting age were available for the Napoleonic wars. He had laid out twelve reasons for a bill to be passed in Parliament, including defence and industrial manpower resources, the need to know how much food was required and maintained that it would stimulate the life insurance industry. The first four undertaken, up until 1841, were mainly concerned with headcount, but each added additional questions as the wider social and economic benefits of having detailed information on the population became apparent.

"A little known additional Act was passed in 1812 that required the ages and occupations of those mentioned in births, deaths and marriages to be taken and recorded in special register books. It also required a uniquely numbered certificate to be issued for every entry."

"So that was the beginning of birth certificates?" said Andrew.

"Deaths and marriages as well," said Lambert.

"Ok, speak to Hughes, but remember to make sure he does everything himself."

A quick look at the online church register list for Cheshire revealed that a number of records were available. Lambert watched whilst Jenny went through repeated searches on her laptop to locate any reference to a William Moore in the Cheshire or Lancashire areas. He knew it was the right thing to do in the circumstances, but his instincts made it difficult. Perhaps he resented the ease with which records could now be located, which seemed to take away the mystery that had first drawn him to the work, yet knew he needed to embrace the new methods or become a dinosaur.

"Nothing yet," said Jenny, looking up from the screen.

They were sitting in a service station where the M56 and M6 motorways intersect, nursing a coffee which gave them access to the free Wi-Fi service they were using.

"The problem is we have no idea what he did when the canal was finished, so it's really a shot in the dark," she continued.

They sat for another few minutes chatting about the situation.

"Looks like the Bridgewater canal was the start of what was a real boom time for canal construction," she said idly skimming a canal history site.

"There's no reason to suppose William would not have moved onto another similar project when the Bridgewater finished," said Lambert. "At that time his skills and experience would have been in short supply in this part of the country."

Jenny immediately picked up the professor's train of thought. She looked back at some previous information she had read on the Bridgewater project.

"Even before the canal was finished, the duke was planning to extend it to the Mersey," she read out loud.

"So he could easily have been kept on," said Lambert.

Jenny selected the internet tab she already had opened to search through the available church records.

"Typical," she sighed, "they extended the route both ways at the same time, towards Manchester and Liverpool."

"Different record offices?" enquired Lambert.

"Obviously," replied Jenny slightly irritated at the question. "But it also makes it a more difficult job online as the information is spread over more than one site."

Lambert suppressed a smile at the thought the internet still did not have all the answers at the touch of a key.

"We know he was born in 1700 in the North East, so let's try something a little different," said Jenny.

She selected a criteria that included the year of birth even though she was searching for a record of a burial. She knew that sometimes additional information was recorded by local clergyman.

"Bingo!" She cried out, causing a dozen or more heads to stare in her direction.

Lambert, who was returning from a trip to purchase a newspaper, came scurrying over at the sound of her voice. She spun the laptop around as he sat down.

"St Michael's Church, Flixton," she exclaimed.

"January 1775," said Lambert.

She entered the details in Google maps.

"It's eleven miles towards Manchester, we can be there in half an hour."

The small church was set back from the main road that ran through the small village. Coincidently, the last few miles had taken them to within a few hundred yards of the route of the Manchester Ship Canal, built more than

100 years after William's death. They parked in a small tree lined road that ran adjacent to the church wall. As they climbed out of the car they could see the unusually large graveyard stretching into the distance. The church notice board confirmed that the church was not open every day, but a call to the church warden whose cottage was adjacent to the grounds enabled them to arrange a meeting after lunch. They decided to try the Church Inn for no better reason than the entrance to the establishment was only twenty feet from the gates to the churchyard. At precisely 2pm a smartly dressed man in his seventies marched into the bar and without hesitating headed in their direction.

"Professor Lambert, I presume?" he said thrusting his hand into Lambert's with a grip that confirmed his suspicions of a military background.

"Yes, and this is my assistant Jenny Cross."

"Brigadier Watson," he replied.

"Would you like a drink Brigadier?" asked Lambert offering a chair to the man.

"Love one, but mustn't touch the stuff before six, doctors' orders you see."

The warden listened intently as Lambert explained the reason for their visit.

"1775 you say. I'm not sure if we still have the records here for those years. So much is now on the computers or has been taken off to the County Records Office, but let's see what we can find."

The trio left the pub and covered the short distance to the church in less than a minute.

"I spoke to the vicar a few minutes after you called and he confirmed he's happy for me to help," he said opening a small side door.

They descended a small flight of stairs and made their way along a stone lined corridor to a small room which was lined with wooden shelves containing row upon row of large dusty volumes.

"Just as I suspected, I'm afraid the registers have been removed elsewhere," the warden said after checking the shelves.

"We just wanted to confirm that he lived in the area before making more extensive enquiries," said Jenny "I noticed the church has a large graveyard, do you have a map of the grave locations?"

"Why of course my dear," he replied, reaching for what looked the smallest book in the room. "What was the chap's name again?"

It took the warden less than two minutes to locate the name.

"Here we are," he said. "The churchyard is divided into sections A to G and then into rows. Your man was in the old section B, but I doubt the grave is still intact, most likely the headstone has been moved to make way for new arrivals. Would you like to visit the plot anyway?"

The gravestone was found against one of the walls of the site covered in moss and the wording almost impossible to make out. But fortunately the records contained details of the inscription

William John Moore
Loving Husband and Father
1700-1775

"It was paid for by his son Robert and there was also a donation from the then Duke of Bridgewater, Francis Edgerton. Your man must have been very important?"

Lambert and Jenny smiled at each other.

"Yes, very important," they said in unison.

A visit to the County Records office in Manchester the next day revealed William's burial details, which included confirmation of his birthplace in the North East.

"So assuming Robert was his heir, he would be descendant number seven," said Lambert looking at the list of victims from the website.

"They think the clue relates to an office worker," said Jenny.

"Today possibly, but not in the late eighteenth century," he replied.

"Toils in a cage of brick and steel," Jenny read the words out loud. "Sounds like someone is describing a prison, not an office."

"We could take weeks to locate him, but if we can use this information, it could make things easier," said Lambert.

"Or lead us down a blind alley," cautioned Jenny.

Just as she spoke an archivist walked past the desk where they sat.

"Excuse me," said Jenny.

The woman turned and approached them.

"Can I help?" she said pleasantly.

"We're looking at a likely profession for a man who lived in the Flixton area and was of working age around 1760."

The woman shrugged her shoulders.

"That was a time of huge changes to the area," she said. "Canals, agriculture, and the beginning of the industrial revolution."

Jenny showed her the killer's description without explaining its source.

"Sounds like a prison or the like, very dark," was her first response. She thought for a moment. "1760 you say?"

"Or there abouts," said Lambert.

"Dark satanic mill," said Jenny.

"Well yes, it could mean that," said the archivist. "With the steam engine allowing the mechanisation of the process, there were a number springing up at that time."

"Where would have been the most likely place for a man to find work in that industry?" said Lambert.

"You can take your pick from a dozen or more," replied the woman, "Blackburn, Bolton, Burnley, Bury, and that's just the Bs."

GCHQ, December 2009

The next morning Andrew was at his desk at GCHQ before 8am. He had decided against asking anyone at Cheltenham to build the website he had decided to create to hopefully flush Paul Williams into the open, as he wanted to restrict to a minimum the number of people who knew its true origin. He logged in to his computer and connected to the *English Monarchy* site to check for any changes. The list had not been updated with the latest murder, so the perpetrator still thought that was undetected, or they had no access to a computer. Andrew walked to David Scott's office and talked him through his idea.

"It's important we keep this on a strictly need to know basis," said Andrew. "I want to be sure we keep complete control."

"I agree, I will ask one of the directory supervisors to put something together today," said Scott. Andrew shifted in his chair.

"Is this something you could do yourself David? As I said I really want to keep this to the absolute minimum number of people."

"Well, yes I can create a website easily enough I suppose, but if you want to track the source I will have to work with others to set things up."

Andrew thought before answering.

"Let's see if we get a response first before we worry about tracing the source. Chances are, with what we have seen so far, our killer will be too clever to give us anything like that anyway."

"Ok, if that's what you want. What shall we call it?"

"How about *The True Monarchy*?" said Andrew. "Mimic the look and feel of the *English Monarchy* site so there will be no doubt there is a link."

"I'm a bit rusty on web optimisation Andrew, so it might take a little longer for the site to appear on the search engines."

"Don't worry about that," said Andrew. "The one other person who I want involved in this is Jackie Crowther and she can help on that side of things."

They parted with Scott agreeing to have a draft prepared in time for the Christmas break.

"If we can get it live over the holiday then it will give us something positive to start the New Year." said Andrew.

Andrew spent Christmas with his in-laws and saw Charlotte open her presents. Despite saying that she wanted to share it with them, Jackie eventually spent Christmas Day with her mother in Luton.

"She'll be on her own, Andrew," she had said. "I can come over for Boxing Day if the invite still stands?"

Nancy's parents welcomed Jackie despite Dorothy's initial reluctance when he raised the subject on Christmas Eve.

"Do you really think its right to bring your girlfriend to your in-laws?" she had said.

"Don't be such an old stick in the mud Dotty." His father-in-law George had come to his defence. "The lad's got to move on and Charlotte can't stay here forever."

Andrew had noticed the look of pain in her eyes at the mention of Charlotte leaving. It was obvious that it had given her a new lease of life; she certainly seemed fitter for chasing the youngster around.

"I don't think Jackie is expecting me to propose just yet, George," said Andrew with a smile.

Jackie arrived mid-morning and after spending some time opening presents and having lunch, the small party walked around the village on what was a bright and crisp winter's afternoon. They stopped at the local play park and after pushing her on the swing and around the roundabout, Jackie helped Charlotte up the steps of the frost covered slide. Andrew could sense his mother-in-law scrutinising every move and calling out warnings at every opportunity despite Jackie's close attention.

"Be careful on those steps Charlotte."

Andrew caught his father-in-law's eye and saw seventy five years of experience behind the look. They both understood that she was unused to another woman usurping her role. Andrew nodded his understanding to George and looked at the woman who had taken his daughter under her roof in the most traumatic of circumstances. Without her, he could not have survived those first few months and he realised he owed them both a debt he could never repay. He walked over to her side and together they watched the little girl squeal in delight as she careered down the slide.

"Thank you Dorothy," he said.

"Well I couldn't very well turn the woman away could I," she said in her stern tone.

"No, I mean thank you for everything. I've never properly thanked you for what you and George have done for me and for Charlotte."

"For you?" she turned to look into his face. "What have I done for you?"

"I couldn't have taken care of Charlotte after Nancy died, I could barely take care of myself. To lose a child of your own and then have your life turned upside down by a baby must have been almost too much to bear."

Andrew looked into her face and saw her expression change from the stern woman he knew all too well to the kindly face she always gave Charlotte, the face of a mother.

"Andrew, it's good of you to say these kind words and I appreciate the fact that you are aware of our pain, but I didn't consider doing anything else, not for a second." She took his hand and they both turned back to watch Charlotte. "My Nancy lives on through that child Andrew," she said, her voice faltering. "Losing a child is a parent's worst nightmare whether they are five or fifty five."

"I can appreciate that," said Andrew.

"It's me who should thank you," she said turning to face him again. "Without Charlotte to care for I think I would have given in to the grief."

Andrew hugged his mother-in-law tightly and kissed her lightly on the cheek.

"Daddy, why are you hugging granny?" Bellowed Charlotte, running towards them both.

He scooped her up so the little girl was sandwiched between them.

"Because I wanted granny to know how much we all love her," said Andrew.

Charlotte flung her arms around the old woman's neck and held her grandmother tightly.

As they walked home with the sun setting fast and the temperature falling faster, Andrew and Jackie found themselves a few paces behind as Dorothy and George had walked ahead to prepare supper. Charlotte swung between them as they walked.

"It was good of Dorothy and George to allow me to spend the day with you all," said Jackie trying to place her arm through Andrew's. However, Charlotte was not going to allow anyone to divert her father's attention, least of all another woman.

"Swing me, swing me," she insisted.

So they walked a yard apart through the dusky light and back to the cottage. After supper, Jackie mentioned that she needed to leave by 7pm to return home. However Dorothy insisted she stay the night.

"I have made up the spare room," she said "It has a very comfortable *single* bed," she continued, looking at Andrew as she spoke.

The young couple burst into laughter the moment Dorothy had left the room after Jackie had accepted the invitation. After supper they had played a board game before Jackie and Andrew read Charlotte a bedtime story. The elderly couple excused themselves at 10pm leaving the pair alone for the first time that day. Expecting his mother-in-law to appear with a bucket of cold water at any moment, Andrew restricted himself to a brief hug and kiss before settling into George's chair.

"It's been a lovely day, I hope you enjoyed it?" he said.

"Every moment."

"I feel so much better now I know Charlotte is so settled here," said Andrew with a smile.

"But I assume you will want to take her at some point?" said Jackie.

"I'd love to see her more often," he replied. "But I would need to employ a full-time nanny and with me living such an unpredictable life, she is much better off here."

Andrew rose from the chair and joined Jackie on the settee having decided the chances of a soaking had receded sufficiently to take the gamble.

"So tell me about this website," she said.

Andrew explained his thoughts and the conversation with David Scott at GCHQ. He booted his laptop and showed Jackie the draft files Scott had prepared and emailed to Andrew on Christmas Eve.

"We were hoping you could help with the optimisation," he said.

"Sure," she replied, "although we don't want this appearing at the top of the search engines, do we?"

"We just need to find a way to ensure our killer finds the site as soon as possible."

Jackie took the laptop from Andrew and began checking the source code which Scott had used to create the three separate pages that formed the site.

"I see he copied some of this from the original site," she said.

"Oh, is that bad?" asked Andrew.

"No, quite the opposite," replied Jackie "It's more likely to provide the type of link the search engines might pick up on to put the two sites under a similar search result."

She began amending the code and Andrew watched in admiration. His knowledge of computer programming could be written on the back of a postage stamp, with room to spare. "We'll place a link to the original site on every page," said Jackie, looking up from her work. "That's a sure fire way of leading anyone who is following that site to ours."

For the next hour they worked on the site, adding the text that Andrew wanted to use as the bait to attract the killer.

"By including some references to Queen Elizabeth's child Angus Moore, hopefully we can flush him out into the open," said Andrew.

"What domain name shall we use?" asked Jackie.

"Is that the www dot something?"

Jackie laughed.

"Don't blind me with science. Let's see what's available."

She typed in a website address of a domain registration company into the computer.

"Any ideas?" she asked.

"How about Truemonarchy.co.uk?"

Jackie typed the address into the search field and laughed out loud.

"Would you believe, it's taken!"

"Try *TheTrueMonarchy*," said Andrew.

"Yes, that's free and only £25 for two years," she exclaimed after typing in the new name.

"Well I guess we need to do our part in saving the taxpayers money in these austere times." Ten minutes later Jackie looked up from the laptop.

"There, all done."

"Wow, that was quick," said Andrew.

"I set up an account using one of our bogus companies," she said. "I uploaded the files to a hosting service run by the same company who register the domain so it will be virtually impossible for anyone to locate where the files were uploaded. It will be live in the next hour or so."

"Find out who has the *True Monarchy* site," said Andrew.

They both laughed when it turned out to be a rapping artist based in the west of London. They decided to wait until the morning before attempting to access the site through a search engine, although Andrew sent an e-mail to David Scott bringing him up to date.

Ashington, December 2009

Lambert spent Christmas with Jenny at her small flat. Neither of them had much enthusiasm for the festive period, having been alone for most of their lives and without children to fuss over and get excited. They spent most of Christmas Day in bed, only rousing to prepare a microwave dinner and grab another bottle of champagne from the fridge. On Boxing Day they returned to the pub in Newbiggin where they had enjoyed their first lunch together and again, walked along the beach. Lambert tried to remember if the North Sea wind was as cold and biting on that day as it was now. It seemed to reach inside his body and he pulled his coat around him in a vain effort to keep warm.

"Don't be such a southern softie," joked Jenny, breaking free from his embrace and running down to the water's edge like a child.

Lambert watched her and smiled. It was good to see her relaxed and able to enjoy such a simple pleasure. She beckoned him to join her and they walked for a while along the water's edge, dodging the incoming waves and tossing pebbles into the foaming sea.

"I've got to go back to the university for a few days," he said as they drove along the narrow country lane for the short journey back to Ashington.

"How long do you think you'll be gone?"

Lambert was not sure if he would be returning at all. He had received a curt e-mail from the vice principal of the university a few days before pointing out the amount of time he had been away from the campus and the cost of providing tutors to stand in for his absence. He knew he would almost certainly have to call upon the intervention of Andrew Larkin if he were to remain on the investigation, but that would also bring about its own problems as regards maintaining the confidentiality of the investigation. He decided he would call Larkin the next day and ask for his help. Perhaps someone at MI5 was an old school friend of the vice principal and the old boys' network could be put to good use.

"I'll get the train back tomorrow, the sooner I put in an appearance the quicker I can hopefully get the situation sorted and we can get back to work."

Since the discovery of William Moore's grave a week before at Flixton, the pair had been researching the history of the early Industrial Revolution in the North West. The woman at the museum had been right as every major town in the area had experienced an explosion in the growth of factories, particularly in the production of textiles. The creation of the canals had led, within ten years, to the halving in the price of coal and a tenfold increase in the amount shipped. This rapid expansion fuelled the new automated processes created by machines, such as Richard Arkwright's Spinning Jenny and Carding Machine that powered these new factories, turning the area into the world's supplier of cotton. Although fascinating to Lambert and Cross, it presented what appeared to be an insurmountable problem in tracing William's son Robert through an association with the industry. By 1760 when Robert would have been twenty five, there were factories springing up all over the area. It would be logical for them to begin any search close to the Flixton area, but the era when families remained in the same location for generations was swiftly coming to a close and there was a distinct possibility that young Robert had moved away from the area. They had no evidence of his profession, just the cryptic clue from the killer's website which they may have interpreted incorrectly.

Lambert woke early the next morning and leaving Jenny still sleeping, crept into the kitchen to make himself a coffee and check his e-mails for the first time since Christmas. After deleting the deluge of offers for January sales and discounted membership for the half dozen genealogy websites that they had visited, he was left with three. One from the vice principal, confirming that he would meet with him the next day in Cardiff, the second from Peter Hughes from Kew requesting a call to discuss his research on Paul Williams and a third from Andrew Larkin, also requesting a call. Lambert checked his watch. He doubted Hughes would be at his desk at 6.30am, but guessed Larkin would be up and about. The phone was answered on the fifth ring by which time he was beginning to doubt the wisdom of calling at this hour.

"Hello Mr Lambert," said a bleary sounding voice.

"I'm sorry Mr Larkin, have I woken you?"

Andrew leaned over on his elbow and looked at his watch.

"No, it's OK, I just had a late night."

"Not too much of a hangover I hope?" Joked Lambert.

"I wish," replied Andrew "Working on the case as it happens. What can I do for you?"

"You asked me to call *you* Mr Larkin."

"Oh yes, sorry."

Andrew sat up and rubbed his hand over his face in an attempt to massage some life into his brain.

"I just wanted to catch up as soon as possible. See how you were getting on and your immediate plans."

"Well, Mr Larkin," Lambert shifted uneasily in his small kitchen chair before replying. He never liked confrontation and he guessed that the MI5 man would not be happy that he was returning to Cardiff, probably for good. Andrew sensed his hesitation.

"Not good then?" The question jolted him out of his thoughts.

"No, quite the opposite. It's just that I've been summoned back to the university in Cardiff. The vice principal is unhappy about the amount of time I have been away."

"I see."

Andrew's first instinct had been to tell the professor to stay exactly where he was and contact the vice principle himself to explain the importance of the work. But if the university objected it could find its way to Greaves through the network and he would see it as a direct contradiction of the instructions he had given Andrew only a few days before. He struggled to decide on the best course of action. He needed more time and more resource, but the killer was not working to their agenda.

"Hello, are you still there?" asked Lambert.

"I think it's best if you return to Cardiff and meet with your people. Let me know how that goes and we can take it from there."

"OK, and what about Ms Cross, she is expected back at her job next week."

"She should return as normal for now. I would hope that you can both carry on the research when you get a spare moment," said Andrew.

Lambert brought Larkin up to date on their discoveries regarding William and Robert.

"So you see, there's not much we can do outside the Manchester area."

"I understand," said Andrew nursing a coffee his mother–in–law had brought him on hearing his voice through the adjacent bedroom wall. "I appreciate your efforts so far. Just do what you can."

Lambert caught the 11.21 train from Morpeth. He would have liked to remain a little longer but the later trains required two changes including one at Newcastle. Jenny offered to drive the extra fifteen miles as she had to drop him at Morpeth anyway, but Lambert wanted to get back to Cardiff as soon as he could to allow him time to review the work he had left and prepare for his meeting with the VP. Jenny stood on the platform and watched the train until it disappeared from view. But this time it was a smile on her face as she knew she would be seeing him again. Lambert called Peter Hughes as soon as he had settled into his table seat. Purchasing his ticket at the station, he had not had an opportunity to book a seat but was lucky to secure a table seat complete with socket. The train did not enjoy on-board Wi-Fi, but he had managed to download a number of documents before departing.

"Happy New Year, Tom." Hughes answered the call.

"You too Peter," replied Lambert above the rush of the train.

"As you can probably hear, I'm on a train on my way back to Cardiff so I might lose you. What have you managed to find out about Paul Williams?"

Hughes had anticipated his friend's question and pulled a small folder from a drawer.

"In all honesty Tom, I haven't had a great deal of time to spend on it. December is a busy time for us with year-end etcetera."

"I understand Peter."

"I obtained the birth certificate easily enough. He was born in Cardiff in 1982 so is twenty eight. It only took me a couple of hours to trace the family back three generations to Paul's great grandfather Gavyn who was born in 1895 in Aberbargoed, about twenty miles north of Cardiff."

"And his father?"

"He was also born there in 1952 so it suggests the family moved down to Cardiff at some point, possibly after the coal mine closed in 1977," continued Hughes.

"So nothing to suggest any links with the letter or the *English Monarchy*?" said Lambert.

"Nothing, but things could change once I get a chance to trace the family further back."

They agreed to keep each other up to date with any developments with Lambert providing the link to MI5.

Lambert arrived home shortly before 6.30pm that evening after stopping at the local store on his way from the station to collect a few essentials. He dreaded to think how the inside of his fridge would look after nearly two weeks, but was pleasantly surprised. Apart from a small carton of milk that he placed in the plastic bag he had ready, without troubling to remove the lid, the other assorted contents seemed to have survived remarkably well. After a moment's reflection, he was not convinced it was such a positive sign. Goodness knows what how much preservative they've added to this food he thought, and promptly transferred the entire contents to the bag. He spent the evening going over a pile of unmarked papers that he should have completed by the middle of December. He knew that he was not devoting enough time and attention to each to give the student the critique it deserved, so marked everyone a grade higher than the work merited. Looking around the spacious flat that had been his home since arriving in Cardiff, he felt alone for the first time and realised he was missing Jenny and no longer yearned for solitude. It was good to share your life with another person and in the last few weeks he had been happier than he could ever remember. He decided on an early night so he could rise early to prepare for his encounter with the vice principal. In his present mood, he was likely to tell the man exactly what he thought which would not be a good career move.

Next morning, he called into his department before the meeting to check over his desk. It was almost deserted for the holidays, apart from the lab technician.

"Hello professor," he said, making Lambert jump out of his chair.

"Sorry, did I startle you?"

"I didn't expect anyone to be here that's all," he replied.

"Just catching up on some work whilst it's quiet."

"Anything exciting happened?" asked Lambert.

"Not really," he replied.

"OK, I have a meeting with the vice principal in an hour and just wanted to catch up on anything outstanding around here."

The man smiled and went back to his work.

"Oh," he called when several steps away. His face appeared again.

"That antique dealer called a couple of times asking what's happening with the letter. He said his friend from Christie's wants verification so he can decide whether it's worth selling."

Lambert had last spoken to the man a few weeks ago and had completely forgotten to bring him up to date. The thought caused him to contemplate directly for the first time in weeks whether he considered the letter was, in fact, genuine. It was clear that a farmer named Thomas Moore had lived close to Alnwick and had a son named Angus whose descendants he had traced through six generations. But that did not prove the boy was Elizabeth's child which was the most vital piece of evidence missing, without which he had spent the last few months chasing the family history of an obscure farmer. This was exactly what the vice principal thought and he still had nothing concrete with which to argue another conclusion. Whether the letter was genuine and written in her hand would become irrelevant if Angus's Royal parentage were proven and until then academics would delight in disagreeing about its authenticity which could never be established beyond doubt. You can't prove a negative, he thought. He quickly penned an e-mail to John Giddens at Christie's and explained that he had yet to find any evidence of the link to a child and so could not possibly authenticate the document at this point. He asked if John could inform the antiques dealer and promised to keep them both up to date, adding that he needed to keep the letter for further tests. He did not like acting dishonestly but knew he could not risk informing him of the entire story for fear of the information leaking. This would cause problems with MI5 and the possibility of the antiques dealer seeking to reclaim the letter. Lambert knew the only way to show beyond reasonable doubt that the letter was genuine, at least in content, was to gather a DNA sample from one of Angus's descendants and match it with the hair he had found on Elizabeth's corset at Westminster Abbey. To do this they needed to find a grave and then get permission to exhume the body. He would leave the latter problem to Larkin if and when the time arose.

Lambert spent an hour with the vice principal in which the man took full advantage of the upper hand he believed he enjoyed.

"All our professors carry out field trips, but everyone except you seems to be able to combine this with their responsibilities to the university and their students."

The meeting ended with Lambert agreeing to remain in Cardiff until the Easter break and ensure his students were equipped to get the grades they were predicted.

"Our grades reflect directly on the university's funding and ability to attract foreign students professor."

Lambert called Jenny after the meeting and they decided she would travel to Cardiff for the New Year so they could spend it together.

"I'll drive," she said.

"But it will take you hours."

Lambert was horrified at the prospect having hated every moment of the drive to Ellesmere which was only half the distance.

"No longer than on the train, she replied. "It's fortunate that it falls on a Friday so I can stay an extra couple of days before coming home for work."

They spent midnight on the ice rink outside the city's Civic Hall and watched the spectacular firework display from London on a giant screen. Two days later they parted and Jenny drove the 350 miles home to Ashington. They both knew that it would prove difficult to maintain a relationship at this distance but for the time being both ignored the fact and enjoyed the feelings it had brought.

"I'll see what I can find out from the earl's estate at Worsley," said Jenny as she climbed in her car.

"OK," replied Lambert closing the door and leaning through her window.

"At this point and with limited time, I agree it's our best chance of moving things forward."

"If your friend Peter Hughes at Kew discovers that this Paul Williams is related to Robert then that will save us a great deal of work."

"You're right, but I very much doubt that will happen. But I could be wrong."

He kissed her and waited until she had turned into the stream of traffic at the top of his road, feeling like a teenager when he looked up and waved before disappearing behind a building.

Riverview Tower, South Embankment, London, January 2010,

The view was magnificent and she knew she would never grew tired of it. Tonight the city looked beautiful with a thousand twinkling lights of every colour dancing on the water below. From her vantage point high above the north bank she had an uninterrupted view along the river as far as the eye could see, in either direction. To her left beyond Lambeth Bridge, were the Houses of Parliament with the tower of Big Ben illuminated like a beacon, contrasting with the giant wheel of the London Eye slowly rotating, giving the occupants of its thirty two glass pods a view that rivalled even hers. The river then took a sharp right turn and disappeared, but in the far distance the dome of St Paul's and the blinking light atop Canary Wharf were painted against the backdrop of the red tinged sky. Turning to her right the ornate balustrade of Vauxhall Bridge and beyond Battersea Power Station and Chelsea Embankment. In front the South Bank was filled with expensive riverside properties like hers, filled with equally successful people. Her kind of people.

This was only her second night in the penthouse apartment she had purchased outright with her latest bonus. A new year and a new home. At £3million it was worth every penny, and her accountant had assured her, could be used as a tax concession if purchased by her company.

"I don't have a company," had been her reply.

"You do now madam."

So it was that Pussycat Enterprises and not Henrietta Douglas owned the apartment. She was just a rent-paying tenant. She allowed herself a smile as she emptied the last of the Armand de Brignac champagne from the cut crystal glass before tossing it in the ice bucket. The stem broke off, but she had turned away so did not notice. As the only female senior trader in the derivatives section of the city investment bank, she had to be better than the male colleagues around her in every way. Smarter, quicker, harder working and more successful. She had also needed to sleep with one or two strategically placed managers to ensure they did not fail to notice her undoubted skills. Last year she had made the bank more than £1billion profit so a measly £4million on top of her £100,000 basic was a great return for them. She hated every one of the bastards, but knew she would only need another five years to be able to walk away with enough money to spend the rest of her life on a beach.

Her peace was interrupted by the intercom from the concierge in reception. She skipped across the lounge area to stop the yapping tone. She would have that changed tomorrow without fail.

"Yes," she said in an irritated tone as she punched the reply button on the flat screen panel set into the marble lined walls of the kitchen. There was a pause at the other end of the line. "Well, are you there or what dumb-wit."

"Sorry madam," the flustered voice finally replied. "It's just that the reporter you said would be here at seven thirty hasn't arrived yet. I leave at eight you see and need to handover to night security."

"Well fucking handover then."

She walked into her bedroom, not bothering to prolong the pointless conversation a second longer. She spent every day talking to complete idiots, and was damned if she would do it in her own time. If that reporter failed to turn up she would get the bastard fired. This was her chance to finally get noticed outside the confines of the dealing room and she was not going to miss it. *Dealer of the Year.* It sounded good. She was not sure how the magazine had found her private number, but was secretly flattered that they wanted to do a piece on the new rising female start of the city, and in her new apartment too. It would look great and raise her stock with her superiors immeasurably. Her thoughts were interrupted by the buzz of the door.

"I'll throw that little turd down the rubbish chute," she said as she strode to the door. She flung it open and was just about to launch a tirade of abuse at the concierge.

"Hello Henrietta," said the reporter who was then forced to take a step backwards to avoid the advancing banker.

"Sorry I'm a little late, traffic."

Henrietta pushed past the startled figure and stared in either direction down the lobby.

"How did you get in?" she said, puzzled. "I thought everyone had to be sent up by the guys at reception?"

"Nobody there," said the reporter, "so I just came on up as I was running late."

"OK, I suppose you better come in."

Henrietta closed the door with her back as the newcomer looked around the apartment.

"Nice, very nice. This will make a great double page spread."

Henrietta's head emptied of any negative thoughts and was replaced by that image. They both sat down on the white leather sofa and talked for a few minutes.

"I don't suppose I could have some of that champagne?"

"Of course," squeaked Henrietta to her new-found friend. She opened a new bottle and they toasted her success.

"Do you have a picture of yourself as a child?"

She bounded into her bedroom and spent a few minutes hunting through a box of old photos. When she returned, they continued the interview for the next ten minutes.

"Could we have a look at the view from the balcony so I can work out some picture ideas?"

"Sure," said the banker jumping up and sliding open one of the glass doors that ran across the entire width of the room.

"Wow!"

They both strolled onto the balcony and took in the view.

"More champagne?"

"Mmmm please."

She ran inside, grabbed the bottle from the ice bucket and went flying onto the sofa.

"Whoops too much bubbly," she giggled to herself as she returned a little unsteadily. When she became aware of her surroundings she noticed the balcony was empty and the outside lights off.

"Hello...."

She suddenly remembered she did not know the reporter's name and walked to the far end of the darkened deck which was empty. She was a little annoyed. Was someone prying in her bedroom? As she moved to go inside the view began to swim in front of her eyes. She was vaguely aware of a figure emerging from the shadows at the other end of the area. The reporter seemed somehow different with gloved hands closing the sliding door to the living area. Henrietta's mood changed in an instant from anger to fear as her instincts told her something was wrong and she fought to compose herself. Five years working in a bank had made her someone who could handle intimidation and drink.

"What the hell do you think you are doing?"

The figure made no attempt to answer the question but simply stood against the glass door. The banker found herself on her knees and staring up at the increasingly blurry image.

"Whash the fluck are you nup to?" Were the last words she spoke as her vision shrank to darkness.

The figure slid open the glass door, re-entered the room and erased all traces of the presence of a visitor. On returning to the balcony, the banker was slumped totally unconscious on the decking, the drug placed in the stupid, arrogant girl's drink having worked exactly as planned. The remaining contents of the champagne were forced down her throat, with copious amounts spilling on her dress. Nice touch. The girl was lifted under her arms into a sitting position, and then hauled up so she was standing with her back to the four-foot-high balcony wall. She was turned around so her arms flopped over the edge from where it was a simple job to grab her ankles and with a heave, tip her over the edge. The comatose figure disappeared into the void of a 110 foot drop. A card was placed on the coffee table, just before the door closed behind the reporter. Five minutes later the figure emerged from the underground car park, having used the same private elevator as earlier.

"The killer must have been in the flat."

Andrew stood in the doorway of the luxury penthouse watching the forensic team in their distinctive white bio-suits. Someone handed him a bag containing such a suit and signalled for him to change before entering.

"I can't see any other explanation," said Bill Frost as he and Andrew clambered into the ungainly suits, complete with slip on shoes.

"What do we know so far?" said Andrew, who was interrupted by his phone. "Hello Ken," said Andrew.

"I want you back at Thames House as soon as you have finished there. The PM has called a COBRA meeting at two this afternoon and I want you to give a briefing." The line went dead.

"What's up?" said Frost.

"Looks like certain people are starting to believe our killer could actually get to the queen." Andrew spent twenty minutes looking over the crime scene and speaking with Frost and the CID officer in charge. They stood on the balcony, the icy mid-January wind particularly acute at a hundred feet.

"We need to ensure that everything that could contain a fingerprint or DNA evidence is examined." The head of the forensic team joined them and nodded.

"This is the first time we have an enclosed, uncontaminated crime scene and if a clue has been left we have to find it."

Frost walked with Andrew to the lobby, where the MI5 man removed his suit.

"What have we got from the in-house security people?"

"Not a great deal. Seems she was expecting a guest at seven thirty who was late. They didn't see anyone come in but the access control system shows several people entering the underground car park between seven and nine."

"CCTV?" asked Andrew.

"Plenty including the lobby and lifts. We're sifting through it now to eliminate all known residents."

"If you can stay and oversee this operation Bill, I can assure COBRA that any clue will be found."

"Don't worry, Andrew," said Frost as Larkin stood facing him in the open lift, "every killer makes a mistake and this could be our chance, we won't let it slip through our fingers."

University of Cardiff, January 2010

January was a busy month for the university as the students had exams and the professor was required to examine and mark the papers before sending them for external verification. He and Jenny kept in touch by e-mail and phone, she even persuaded him to activate his laptop webcam - the existence of which he was unaware of, and set up a video link for their chats. She needed to catch up on a number of projects that been put on hold during her sabbatical and had also been warned to avoid any trips in the near future. Jenny had contacted the Earl of Bridgewater's estate at Worsley, near Manchester, and the site of the mines from which the canal's coal was transported to the city. They initially proved unwilling to provide any meaningful help and told her that all the information relating to the canal had been donated to the museum. Only with persistence did she discover that the rest of the families' archives were located at the main family seat at Ashridge in Hertfordshire. By the middle of the month she had discovered that Robert had been born in Flixton in 1735, although she could find no record of his marriage or death in the same parish. This was frustrating but added weight to the view that he had moved away from the area.

"The next step is to get down to Ashridge, but I certainly can't get the time away from the archives."

"Nor I," said Lambert. "I'll have a word with Andrew Larkin and explain the situation. There's not much else we can do unless they declare a State of Emergency."

Cabinet Office, London, January 2010

The Cabinet Office Briefing Room A, or COBRA, is an emergency council that meets to discuss high-priority issues that cross departmental borders and are deemed to require a high-level co-ordinated response. The office used to host the meetings is no longer in 70 Whitehall, the home of briefing room A, but on the first floor somewhere in the cabinet buildings. There are no permanent members of the committee, the makeup depending on the nature of the issue. The group facing Andrew as he entered consisted of the heads of the three commands that make up the specialist operations directorate of the Metropolitan Police, namely protection, counter terrorism and security command. Each branch specialised in different elements including diplomatic and royal protection, anti-terrorism and specific sites such as airports and the Palace of Westminster. Also in attendance were the director general of MI5, his ultimate superior, the home secretary and the prime minister. Other officials, including Ken Greaves and Anthony Neild, his superiors at MI5, filled the room making it immediately seem overcrowded and stuffy. The meeting had started twenty minutes before and Andrew had been asked to wait in an adjacent room until called.

"This is Andrew Larkin, Prime Minister," said Neild as Andrew placed his papers on the large wooden desk that filled the centre of the room. "He is the MI5 member of the executive liaison group based at GCHQ and has been part of the team investigating this group for the last few months."

Andrew noticed that the presentation he and Greaves had put together that morning was already displayed on the monitor wall that filled one end of the room. Anthony Neild continued.

"We have already briefed the group on the background and briefly discussed the *English Monarchy* website," he said. "We need you to go over the investigation to date and outline the steps that are being taken to neutralise the threat this poses."

Nothing too much then thought Andrew. He could see that he was being used as a shield by Neild and the others to deflect any criticism away from them and sensed the hand of Ken Greaves behind the decision to throw him to the lions instead of another member of the ELG. He looked around the room at the expectant faces and made a decision.

"Ladies and gentlemen I believe we're looking at a clear and present threat to senior business, and political, figures in this country and also to the queen." The look on the faces of the PM, the home secretary and one or two others told him what he had suspected.

"That's a very alarming statement Mr Larkin," said the prime minister looking at the DG, "and a very different view than that expressed by your colleagues."

Andrew knew his career and even his liberty was now at threat.

"Prime Minister, I think Mr Larkin has perhaps become too embroiled in the investigation and become confused by the blizzard of conflicting information being generated." Greaves had been forced to make a contribution under the fierce gaze of the DG and Neild. The PM raised his hand to stop any further comment.

"Go on Mr Larkin, but I hope you have some sound evidence to back up your theory."

"To date eleven people have been murdered since February of last year. Each victim had a card left with the body, depicting a symbol associated with the Warwick family." Andrew clicked through the slides until he found the image. "The early murders were treated as accidents by the forces concerned which meant that we didn't discover the pattern until the killer published a list on the website pointing us in the right direction." Andrew showed a slide with the latest version of the table showing the banker. "This was taken from the site an hour ago and as you can see, shows the addition of the banker found yesterday."

"We know all this Larkin." Greaves interrupted.

"If you do that again before Mr Larkin has finished, I'll have you removed from the room," replied the PM.

Andrew felt the steely stare of his superior across the fifteen feet that separated them.

"The supposed motive behind the killings is that the monarchy is foreign and should be replaced. There are many in this room who think this is a red herring being used as part of a smokescreen to confuse us."

"But you don't?" said the home secretary.

"No ma'am, I do not." Andrew showed a slide of the letter from Dudley. "This is a letter found a few months ago hidden in a trunk."

He spent the next ten minutes explaining the story of the letter and the discoveries Lambert had made.

"This is incredible," said the PM. "Can it possibly be true?" he asked looking around the room, but his question was answered with total silence. Andrew was completely on his own.

"Sir, Professor Lambert is currently working on tracing the family history of Angus Moore to the present day."

"And what have his team found so far?" said the PM.

"It's a rather small team, sir so he's taking a little longer than would be hoped."

"How small?"

"Two."

A nod from the PM sent one of his officials scurrying from the room.

"And presumably this is Williams, the NCIS man?"

"No sir, I don't believe he is implicated and I have an archivist at Kew confidentially tracing his family to prove it."

"Go on Mr Larkin."

"So far we've traced the family line to a Robert Moore who was born in 1735 near Manchester. He's the seventh descendant." Andrew selected a slide showing the family tree e-mailed to him by Jenny that morning.

"What makes the theory compelling is the professor's belief that the letter is genuine and the fact that the occupations of each of the seven match those of the victims," said Andrew. A buzz went around the room.

"So let me make sure I understand what you are saying," said the PM. "You believe that an individual, who is a descendant of the illegitimate child of Elizabeth I, has murdered eleven people for no other reason than they shared a profession with one of their ancestors?"

"If you put it that way, sir," replied Andrew.

"And what way would you put it?"

"If we don't find this person quickly, they are smart and resourceful enough to kill both you and the queen."

Thames House, London, January 2010

"The PM has taken your theory very seriously."

The director general of MI5 looked across the table at Andrew who was seated in a meeting room in Thames House together with twenty or so others including all the members of the GCHQ ELG and Jackie Crowther. "So what resources do you need to carry out your personal agenda?" he added, the words not lost on Larkin or the other members of the ELG.

"May I say something?" asked Jackie.

"If you must," replied the DG.

"I think it's fair to say that everyone on the ELG, including Andrew, agree it's a priority to find Paul Williams."

"I'm glad *we* can get at least one thing right," the DG replied in an icy tone.

"But I've been working on this descendant theory and agree that it's a line of enquiry we shouldn't ignore."

Jackie's phone buzzed on the desk alerting her to an incoming e-mail. Everyone looked at the small box as it vibrated.

"Something more important than the life of the monarch?" said the DG.

"If it's what I am expecting then it will have a direct bearing on the case."

The DG waved a hand and Jackie read the mail.

"As I thought sir."

"Well do enlighten us Ms Crowther," he said.

"Since we became aware that the murder of the vicar had occurred sometime before the information was released on the site, I have been carrying out a search on the deaths of anyone who falls into the victim's occupations."

"And?" said Neild impatiently.

"Murder number thirteen is obviously someone famous although the clue is very obscure." Andrew could tell she was losing the group and so stepped in.

"So Ms Crowther, I assume this e-mail relates to this line of investigation?"

She picked up the inference to omit the preamble immediately.

"In June of last year Matthew Black, a prominent football player, drowned in a diving accident in Hawaii. I've just had confirmation that a card with the number thirteen written on it was found on his body."

The DG looked across the table at Neild as Jackie read the e-mail.

"It says the lines from his air tank had been cut and his feet tethered so he couldn't swim to the surface."

"I was involved in checking that case," said Charles Smythe from MI6. "It was closed as accidental death."

"The authorities wanted the matter wound-up quickly," said Crowther. "Bad for tourism if your high-profile guests get murdered."

The DG made a short note to speak to his opposite number at MI6.

"Sir, I know I shouldn't have been so dramatic in the COBRA meeting, but." Andrew glanced at Greaves and Neild before continuing. "But I've been prevented from pursuing this line by a lack of resources and putting it bluntly, I felt as if I was being offered up as a sacrifice to pacify COBRA."

If the atmosphere in the room had been tense when the meeting began, it could now be cut with a knife. The DG gave an imperceptible nod to Neild before speaking.

"That's all very well Larkin, but we don't have time for internal politics now." He rose and stood in front of a large monitor displaying a live feed showing the table of victims on the *English Monarchy* web page. "We need to find whoever is carrying out these murders. It's a miracle we've been able to keep it out of the media but that can't last much longer, even if we put a suppression order on the information."

Andrew noticed that Jackie was staring strangely at the DG and was becoming worried it would be noticed.

"If the story breaks then things will really heat up," he stressed.

Jackie stood without warning and walked toward the DG.

"Yes, Ms Crowther?"

Jackie walked straight past him and studied the screen.

"There." she pointed at the name next to murder thirteen. "Black's name has just been added to the site."

A few at the table looked at each other slightly bemused, but Andrew realised the significance immediately.

"We've just discovered the identity of this victim and a few moments later it appears on the site."

Jackie walked to the laptop and leaning over the person seated at the table, switched the view to the home page. The occupant gave way and she sat down. Within a few seconds she had located a new link which connected to

TheTrueMonarchy.co.uk. However the front page was not as had originally been uploaded. A picture of the queen had been placed in the centre of the page with text underneath.

Too easy, you must do better. You finally found the fame seeker, but who will be next? The pretender can put an end to the bloodshed by abdicating and acknowledging the true heir.

Andrew had dialled David Scott's cell phone as soon as he saw the altered page.

"David, can you see the *True Monarchy* site?" he said walking to a corner of the room.

"I got an alarm on my system the moment the files were uploaded," he replied "I'm running a scan now to see if we can pinpoint the address. I'll call you back as soon as I get anything." Andrew relayed the conversation to the group.

"This is a website that I set up a week ago. Only three people know who created the site, Scott, myself and Ms Crowther."

"We should put a squad on standby in case we get lucky," said Frost.

"It's clear you people have work to do," said the DG gathering his papers. "Use whatever resources you need to find these people," he continued looking at Neild and paused at the door. "And I want Williams' details released to the media tonight. Needed to help police with their enquiries, the usual."

Andrew's phone vibrated.

"We got a trace from an internet cafe in Birmingham," said Scott.

"Send the details to Bill," Andrew replied. "I'll get a team from Birmingham CTU there within fifteen minutes."

A hundred miles and twenty minutes later, two unmarked cars and a black van stopped outside the *NetWorld* internet cafe in the suburb of Aston. The shop front was plastered with posters advertising cheap calls to every part of the globe and made it impossible to see inside the premises. Five heavily armed officers in full protective outfits quickly jumped from the van followed by several more lightly armed men from the cars.

"I want every house within a half mile radius searched within the next hour," said the commanding officer. "Get the local uniformed in to help."

"They're on their way sir."

"Five bodies showing inside," said the officer viewing a thermal imaging device.

"Ok let's go."

The door to the shop was opened with one swift kick followed by a small flash grenade which exploded almost immediately sending smoke pouring from the doorway. Three officers rushed in a few seconds later shouting.

"Police, don't move."

The commanding officer waited outside, giving a commentary to the live video stream from the hand-held camera operated by one of his team. Andrew sat in a command suite at Thames House watching the events unfold with the other members of the ELG. Five minutes later they received confirmation that the site was secure and four men and a woman of various ethnic backgrounds had been detained.

"How long ago was the site changed?" asked Andrew.

"Under an hour," replied Scott at the other end of the line.

"It's too obvious," said Andrew. "My guess is that this is another deliberate attempt to make us look like fools."

"Well it certainly seemed to have worked. Can you imagine the headlines when the press get hold of this," said Greaves. "There were dozens of people who saw what happened and it will not play well given the area and the innocent people we have just treated to a close encounter with a stun grenade."

"Make sure we get the place repaired as soon as possible and issue a statement giving the usual line about preventing a terrorist plot," said Neild. "Larkin, can I have a word?"

Andrew followed the head of K section into an adjacent room and closed door behind him. Neild was in his favoured position looking out of the window; however this one did not enjoy a view of the river, but the wall of the building opposite. He turned to face the newcomer. "Larkin, you have placed us all in a very awkward situation with your outburst. What on earth did you think you were doing?"

"I told you why in the meeting with the DG," replied Andrew. "Ken Greaves has been trying to undermine everything I've done on this case. He has failed to take the whole thing seriously and pass on my concerns."

He knew he was way out on a limb now in openly criticising his superior.

"Look, I just want the resources to follow up on all the enquiries we have and to make everyone aware of what could happen. These people have killed eleven innocents and are playing games with us."

Neild went back to the window as if seeking some divine power from the light. "You will report directly to me from now on," he said finally. "This is too important to have petty vendettas get in the way which could bring us all down if we're not careful."

"I understand" said Andrew, secretly smiling inside.

"I want a report on my desk first thing tomorrow with full details of your plan. Make sure you get everyone on the ELG signed up to what you are doing. Once I have seen it, I'll distribute it to COBRA; that way we can dilute the blame if it all goes pear-shaped," said Neild walking to the door. "And for God's sake stop chasing shadows and think twice before sending out armed response units to terrorize innocent civilians every time you get a sniff of something."

Andrew stayed in the room for a minute collecting his thoughts. As he left he almost walked straight into Ken Greaves leaving the command room. Their eyes met for the briefest of moments, but long enough for Andrew to see the hatred burning within. He would need to be very careful from now on as he knew Greaves would plot to bring him down, given the opportunity.

Larkin walked back into the control centre and called everyone from the ELG into an adjacent meeting room. They called David Scott at Cheltenham and included him on a conference line.

"I assume that by now everyone knows that my meeting at COBRA this afternoon together with the follow up here a few minutes ago has resulted in us being given all the resources we need to track down not only Paul Williams but also provide Professor Lambert with all help he needs to trace the descendants of Angus Moore."

"About time old boy," said Smythe."

"Charles, how much satellite time can you get us?"

"For what?"

"I want to cover the site of every murder in case the killer returns. If we simply set up surveillance teams they may be spotted or compromised, plus it will take a great deal of manpower which will be better deployed elsewhere."

"I'll speak with our boys and my contacts in Washington," said Smythe.

"David, have you picked up anything over the last day or so? Any chatter or internet traffic?"

"Nothing that we haven't been able to isolate and discount," he said. "A few people who have randomly found the *Monarchy* and even a couple who want to join the crusade."

"We picked them up quietly a couple of days ago," said Frost shaking his head to indicate nothing of interest had been discovered.

"That makes a welcome change," said Jackie.

"David if you need any additional resource just let me know and I can make sure there are no delays."

"Ok Andrew but in all honesty we have all the necessary Echelon directories set up and we've even persuaded the Americans to run the master data going into Fort Meade through them so we don't miss any traffic wherever it's generated on the planet. If he communicates we'll pinpoint him."

Andrew wished he could be as confident as the GCHQ man that all the billions of pounds of technology could find the killer. So far it had emerged second-best, seemingly outthought and outmanoeuvred.

"Paul Williams' face will be on every television and front page tomorrow so we are bound to receive a deluge of sightings and leads to follow up."

"Bill and I have taken over one of the Silver Suites at Scotland Yard which will be manned by Met and NCIS staff," said Jackie.

"The official line is that he has had health problems and depression and needs treatment," added Frost. "So if he starts announcing he is the rightful king everyone will assume he is unwell."

"That's good. I'll handle the professor. If I need any help it will be some decent researchers so if you can think about who may be suitable."

The meeting broke up with everyone knowing their tasks. Andrew called Neild and brought him up to date before placing a call to Tom Lambert.

University of Cardiff, January 2010

Lambert answered on the second ring and Andrew smiled at the change in the academic since they had first met. It's amazing what a woman can do, he thought.

"Hello professor, how are things in Cardiff?"

"I can imagine how Indiana Jones must have felt after one of his adventures Mr Larkin." Andrew laughed at the comment.

"I'm glad to hear you're able to laugh. Look I'm ringing for a very important reason that's going to mean us spending some more time together."

Lambert sat upright in his chair.

"So I'm happy for you to call me Andrew."

"Well Andrew, it sounds fascinating but I must tell you that I'm under a strict curfew from my vice principal."

"Don't worry about that," said Andrew. He explained the background to COBRA and MI5 to the academic, sparing the more graphic details of the two meetings.

"So this is now being treated as a matter of the highest national security."

"Wow," said Lambert, "so the prime minister himself knows about me?"

"He knows about your work and the letter, so I don't think your VP is going to present too much of an issue."

Lambert described the situation and Jenny's limited efforts since the New Year.

"Ok, can you send me an e-mail right away with all the details and I will arrange everything," said Andrew.

"Ashridge is a National Trust property Andrew and they don't normally allow people to research their archives without special permission, which can take weeks to arrange."

Andrew smiled.

"How long will it take you to pack a bag Tom?"

Ashridge Estate, Hertfordshire, January 2010

Lambert arrived at the Ashridge estate at 11am the following morning after a three hour drive from Cardiff in an unmarked car full of very frightening individuals. The vice principal had been there to see him off and even managed a weak smile as the two cars sped away. He was sure some of the men had guns. Lambert had printed out a few notes on the estate which he read on the journey to the site some forty miles north west of London. Thomas Egerton, a relative of the 'Canal Duke', as he is known on the estate, was a chancellor to Elizabeth I and the grounds were a popular hunting spot for her father Henry VIII. As the cars drove towards the main house through the woods, he could make out the distinctive pinnacle of the nineteenth century Bridgewater Monument, dedicated to Egerton. They pulled up outside a group of buildings set aside from the main house and Lambert was met by another frightening looking man who looked as if he'd come straight of the set of an American secret service movie. He tried to retrieve his bag from the car.

"Someone will bring your things professor, please follow me."

As he disappeared inside he heard the sound of a helicopter and turned to see the whirling blades glide just a few feet above his head. He was led down a corridor with a series of doors either side. His escort stopped at one and waved him inside.

"This will be your room professor," said the frightening man. "You have a briefing in the conference room just down the hall in half an hour."

His bags arrived soon after and he was left to settle in to what was obviously going to be his home for the next few days at least.

Thirty minutes later Lambert gingerly opened his door and was immediately confronted by another of the men who was obviously guarding his room.

"This way sir."

The man walked swiftly down the corridor, across a reception area filled with people being handed room numbers, and into a large auditorium complete with a small stage. Lambert recognised Andrew Larkin immediately and walked between the rows of chairs. Larkin turned and jumped down to greet him with a handshake.

"Good morning Tom, I hope you had a good journey and have settled in?"

Lambert was still bewildered by the events of the last twelve hours and finding it difficult to adjust to the sheer number of unfamiliar people he had seen since his arrival. Andrew broke the spell by guiding Lambert onto the stage.

"May I introduce you to the director of the National Trust and his colleague who has direct responsibility for the archives here at Ashridge?"

Lambert shook hands with the two men and began to understand what was happening. In typical government fashion, the situation had gone from one extreme to the other. From famine to feast, or in this case gluttony by his initial assessment.

"Tom, we'll begin by gathering all the team in here for a briefing in about half an hour. But I wanted us to have a chat beforehand so the gentlemen here know exactly what we're looking for."

Lambert took Andrew by the arm and led him to the corner of the stage.

"Were those an army of researchers checking-in out there?"

Andrew nodded.

"We've gathered a number of highly qualified people to help you find the information quickly."

Lambert threw his arms in the air. "But it doesn't work like that Mr Larkin, Andrew. It's like a jigsaw puzzle and throwing more people at it doesn't necessarily help solve it any faster. People can get in each other's way."

"Would you excuse us for a moment," said Andrew leading the professor out of the building into a courtyard beyond. "Professor I'm not sure you quite understand what's happening here. The prime minister has declared that everything possible must be done to apprehend the perpetrators of the *English Monarchy* killings." Lambert listened to the MI5 man in silence. "Eleven people are dead and this person or group or whoever is behind this has proven they have the capacity, resourcefulness, technical ability and brutality to carry out the remaining five."

"Yes I understand" replied the professor.

"Do you professor?" Larkin almost shouted the last words. "To be brutally honest professor, the people I work for don't really concern themselves too much when a farmer or a vicar gets murdered. But when eleven of them die and the next in line are people like themselves or even the monarch, that's when they become interested. And that's when things start to happen. Things like this." He waved his arm around him.

"What do you want from me?" said Lambert.

When they returned to the auditorium Jenny was talking to the two men from the National Trust.

"She landed about forty minutes ago," said Andrew anticipating his question.

The two archivists greeted each formally but with a glint in their eyes which did not go unnoticed by Andrew and the small group then discussed the background to the Egerton family's involvement. Over the next twenty minutes the room gradually filled until there was an audience of around twenty people seated in front of them. Andrew invited one more person to join them on the stage who was introduced as the team leader who would co-ordinate the researchers as directed. When everyone was present, Andrew approached the small lectern and the murmur of conversation evaporated. He began by reminding everyone present of the confidential nature of the project and then introduced the five members of the panel. As he spoke a group of the security men entered the room each carrying a number of boxes of varying sizes and composition. By the time he had finished there were more than a hundred lined up on several lines of tables. A dusty haze drifted over the end of the room.

"I will now pass you over to Professor Lambert from Cardiff University, who will give you the detailed information you will need when sifting through the documents behind you."

Lambert explained the link between the third duke and the Moore family and described how he and Jenny had unearthed William Moore's journey from a coal mine in Newcastle to a gravestone near Manchester. As instructed, he gave no indication to his audience as to Williams' relations, past or present.

"Our hope is that the duke mentioned Robert in a letter or document. The aim is to locate where Robert lived and died."

The audience was split into small groups and each team began the slow process of examining everything. After two hours Andrew and Lambert walked behind the tables digesting the sheer volume of volumes and papers.

"Most of this should be after 1600, but it's difficult to guarantee as it's never been catalogued." The National Trust lead conservationist for Ashridge was a step behind them.

Jenny was engrossed; helping to sort out the various items into an order which would allow a systematic approach and avoid the nightmare scenario of missing what was essentially a needle in a large haystack. The first reference to the third duke was found in a copy of The Times dated 1759 describing the parliamentary debate on the bill allowing the Bridgewater Canal to be constructed. However it was a false hope as the newspaper lay on top of a collection of estate accounts dating back no further than 1953.

"This is really going to be huge task Tom,." said Jenny.

They sat at a table in the small canteen that had been commandeered for their use, surrounded by their fellow needle hunters.

"I know, but we have to carry on no matter how small the chance."

"If we have unlimited resources at our disposal why don't we send someone to each of the records offices in industrial towns around Manchester." said Jenny.

Lambert nodded in agreement.

"After seeing the task we have here we may as well take a similar scatter gun approach in finding Robert's marriage or death records."

Larkin entered the canteen and Lambert beckoned him over.

"How many people would you need?"

Lambert turned to Jenny who was busy jotting down place names on a napkin.

"There were factories all around the Manchester area which covers a number of different counties and other districts."

Andrew waited patiently for his answer.

"Much of the information is now available online," she continued. "But I've already tried a few of those sources without luck."

"Meaning?" asked Andrew.

"It's not uncommon for records to be lost, incorrectly transposed from the original or a number of other reasons why they don't respond to a computer search," interrupted Lambert. "I would be out of job if it were that easy."

"The further back in time the more likely a manual search will be the only way to be sure." said Jenny.

"More likely than finding something here?" said Andrew

"Difficult to say," answered Jenny.

"Would half a dozen be enough?"

Andrew turned and called for the team leader to join them.

"I think one of you should lead the team," Andrew said.

"I'll go," said Jenny. "It's my line of work and you will be of more use here in case they stumble across something."

Lambert knew she was right but was sad that she was leaving just a few hours after they had been reunited. He watched as the helicopter lifted off from the gardens behind the house and returned the wave she gave through the small window as the aircraft rose and banked throwing a torrent of air in his direction.

Had any of them realised the enormity of the task at Ashridge it would not have delayed or curtailed its implementation. Andrew knew he had a small window of opportunity to find the heirs to Angus Moore, whether they were connected with the murder or not. Greaves, Neild and probably the DG would all be waiting like vultures perched on the top of the MI5 building for the chance to bring him down. Robert proved to be an elusive man. After three weeks not a single mention of the Moore family had been uncovered in the hundreds of letters, accounts, books and diaries amongst the mountain of paper stored at the stately home. Jenny had fared little better in her quest amongst the record offices of north west England. Every online database had been scoured without a trace of the man. She had a team of three experienced researchers and had managed to persuade her employers to release a colleague to help for a week, all with no result. She had decided to begin at the largest offices in Manchester and Liverpool as they contained the greatest number of records. It was unusual for someone to request to see so many records at the same time as most research was carried out remotely and this caused innumerable delays whilst Andrew overcame the petty bureaucracy that always seemed to make it easier to say no. She was determined to remember this experience when she returned to her normal routine, a thought that she pushed to the back of her mind. She spent many hours trying to understand the reasons why a man born in the mid-eighteenth century could fail to register in the records of the time. She had several conversations with Peter Hughes at Kew who explained the erratic nature of record gathering, documentation and storage before civil registration became compulsory in 1837 and certificates were issued for births, deaths and marriages. They knew that once they passed into the next generation, Robert's children, those magic dates of the beginning of the national census and registration should make their job much easier and above all, faster. Robert and the third duke were almost the same age having been born only a year apart, but their lives must have been very different. One born into a life of luxury, the other uncertainty. Jenny pondered if the fact that the earl had contributed to William's grave stone might have meant that he would also help his son Robert. The obvious answer would have been to employ him in one of his companies, but without access to any records, finding any evidence of this was difficult. She spent one evening on her laptop searching through the British Newspaper Archives for any mention of the duke. She found numerous entries, mostly concerned with the canal, and a few social entries in the London Times but no mention of a Moore, William or Robert.

Lambert worked with the teams at Ashridge sifting through the acres of papers. One of the unintended consequences of utilising trained researchers was the fact that they were naturally curious. Lambert lost count of the number of times someone commented on an interesting find and had obviously spent several minutes reading the particular document, lost in the story it told.

"Please concentrate on the mission in hand ladies and gentlemen," called the team leader on what seemed like an hourly basis. After three weeks of continuous work the contents of the boxes had been sorted into some kind of order. It was decided to scan some of the more likely documents to capture the copy for analysis. A team of three worked on the array of equipment delivered one morning and began the painstaking task. Lambert wondered if the effort was worthwhile, but it did produce a reference to the Bridgewater Canal project, if none to the Moore family. He reflected that it was only the name on a single engineering drawing that had given them the confirmation they had needed, so they must continue the hunt.

Andrew left the professor and his team after a day and headed back to Cheltenham. He wanted to be close to the place he felt was most likely to yield a breakthrough in the hunt for Paul Williams. Charles Smyth had managed to collect a number of favours from the CIA which gave them a twice daily sweep of each of the murder sites when combined with their own more limited satellite capabilities. It was, he knew, a long shot but many killers return to the scene of their crimes and Andrew had little else to work with. Several people, including Frost and Jackie, had argued for using drones to monitor the sites, but Andrew knew that Williams would be expecting just such a deployment and they had no way of knowing if he possessed the ability to gain access to the various networks managing the technology. The *English Monarchy* site was unchanged and the files remained on a server in India. Scott's team monitored literally billions of e-mails, text messages and phone conversations across the entire Echelon network for the clue that would spark the investigation back into life. As the days turned into weeks, Andrew began to wonder if something had happened. The pattern of murders had begun in February with the vicar's death in Devon and continued with further deaths in every month except August and November. During December and January the rate had accelerated and he assumed that the next victim would be targeted much sooner. The website had given only the broadest of clues, *Musician,* which he guessed was deliberately vague. There were more than 30,000 professional musicians registered with the Musicians' Union, and that ignored the many millions who played for recreational reasons. He and Jackie, who regularly came to Cheltenham on the excuse of meeting the ELG and conveniently stayed in Andrew's flat, had spent many hours trying to second-guess where the killer would strike next.

"It's impossible for us to offer even the most basic protection to even a fraction of those 30,000." said Andrew.

"That's assuming the target will be a professional," sighed Jackie.

"But I think we should assume that this victim will be famous or important in some way."

"Why?" asked Jackie.

"Matthew Black was the first victim to be publicly known and the last is too," said Andrew pacing the living room of his flat. "So I think it's safe to assume that each of the last few victims will all be in the public eye."

"A reasonable observation but I wouldn't like to base our whole strategy on it," Jackie poured them both a glass of wine.

"Agreed, but perhaps we should issue a discrete warning through the normal channels that we have non-specific information about a threat to a leading figure in the music industry?"

"Ok, I think that's a sensible idea," said Jackie.

"It's been over three weeks since the last murder and we're no further forward with locating Paul Williams or Robert Moore."

Jackie walked over to the window where he stood, removed the glass from his hand and kissed him warmly.

"Why don't we forget about the case for the rest of the evening," she whispered and led him into the bedroom.

The publication of Paul Williams' details had, as expected, led to a deluge of sightings and information to come flooding into the incident room set up in Scotland Yard. After filtering out the insane and the ludicrous, they were left with around a dozen lines of enquiries that Frost and Cross considered credible enough to pursue. Three additional people had come forward to say they had seen a character fitting his description either on the Manchester Metro train or at Altrincham Station. One lady, that Jenny drove to Manchester to interview personally, was convinced she had seen him drive out of the station in a small dark coloured car. By calculating the time of the various sightings, Jackie was able to work out a number of possible routes a car may have taken on leaving the station, the most obvious being that heading towards the nearby M56. Unfortunately the station was the same distance from three of its junctions and there was no way of knowing the shortest route to the killer's destination. It wasn't much further to junction seven of the M60, Manchester's orbital motorway, so the number of possible sightings was immense. This station had not been chosen by chance, she thought. Undaunted, she obtained the CCTV footage from every camera in the vicinity and with the help of the MOD surveillance team, analysed the footage using the latest video analytics software. This enabled the characteristics of an object to be programmed into the software letting the computer trawl through the hundreds of hours of images from over fifty cameras that covered a five-mile-wide radius from the station. The lighting conditions were erratic as some of the images were captured at night, but the new software was able to select a particular vehicle model. In addition she was able to obtain the data from a small number of automatic number plate recognition cameras that were located within her perimeter. These specialist cameras were able to capture and cross reference a vehicle's number plate against a database. The data from numerous units could be interrogated to provide evidence that a vehicle had taken a particular route and had been at a specific point at a specific time. However this data was useless to Jackie unless she had a licence plate. She also obtained some older footage from the cameras covering the station car park so she could eliminate those vehicles that parked at the station on a regular basis. After a week of searching the team came up with three potential vehicles, the owners of which were visited by their local police. After reading the reports Jackie had to accept that it was unlikely any of the owners was their killer.

Hyde Park, London, April 2010,

Twenty five thousand fans roared in unison as the drum beat began thumping out across the open space. After a few seconds the bass guitar joined in, the low notes adding the basis of a tune to the repetitive thud. Then the keyboards kicked in, repeating the familiar melody that every one of the crowd knew by heart and had listened to a thousand times. This carried on for a full minute before the lead guitarist and rock legend Bryan Stewart emerged onto the stage, his long blond hair flowing behind his wiry frame, sending the crowd wild as he struck his first chord in unison with the white hot blaze of a hundred spotlights exploding onto the stage.

Hyde Park in the heart of London was not a place normally associated with rock concerts. But the purpose-built open air arena, complete with many creature comforts including a champagne bar, had proved a great success. A series of concerts, featuring many of the world's top performers, was being opened by what many regarded as the greatest guitar player alive.

The British-born rock star was certainly one of the wealthiest and was playing here more for pleasure than money as his last open air performance in New York's Central Park had been attended by more than 100,000 fans. Stewart's promoters had taken the unusual decision to hold an open air concert early in the year, but the gamble had paid off and all five nights were sold out and the capital was avoiding the typical April showers and basking in a mini heat wave.

The crowd rose to their feet clapping and swaying in time to the beat, and as Stewart began to sing he was almost overshadowed by the voices that accompanied every word. He drifted into one of his famous guitar solos and as the notes screamed over the thousand watt sound system, he ran first to one side of the stage, and then the other, skidding to a halt each time on his knees. As the song approached its finale he ran to the rear of the stage and as he had done in every previous live concert, leapt onto one of the large Weston amplifiers and stood, legs wide apart, extending the final note by raising the guitar. The band watched and waited for the signal that would end the song. Finally the guitar came down and the drummer crashed symbols and snare together in the final note.

The crowd erupted again as Stewart strutted the stage like a monarch. Two roadies rushed from the wings to wipe his sweating face and replace his electric guitar with a twelve string acoustic. A hush descended as the crowd attempted to guess the next song. A few distant voices drifted onto the stage, calling names of well-known past hits. Stewart walked to the front of the stage and looked around at the vast sea of faces before him. This was what it was all about.

"Good evening, London," he called out.

"Good evening," came the reply.

"Hey come on you guys, you can do better than that. Good evening, London."

"Good evening," only ten times louder.

"That's great. I'd like to play you one of my favourite songs, right now." His voice dropped. "I hope you enjoy it. It's called Love Me Always."

The crowd cried out as he began the slow, love song on the acoustic. It seemed that every person had raised their arms and were swaying from side to side in a rhythmic pattern.

But deep in the crowd, one set of arms remained firmly at the sides of their owner. They swayed to and fro with the rest of the crowd, only because to resist would have been virtually impossible and liable to draw attention to their owner. However, a closer inspection would have revealed a clever disguise. This, together with dark make-up, gave the appearance of a dark, Mediterranean character. One arm felt inside the pocket of the coat and was reassured to feel the edges of the cell phone.

The band played for an hour and a quarter, before Stewart raised one arm in the air and cried out.

"Goodnight everyone, it's been great. We'll see you all again soon, I hope."

He then ran from the stage, handing his guitar to an assistant as he bounded off. The drummer emerged from behind his kit with a handful of drumsticks, which he proceeded to launch into the crowd, each one plucked from the air before it could disappear amongst the sea of heads. The crowd, knowing that this was not the end, began chanting and clapping the ritual.

"We want more. More...more"

The owner of the cell phone wondered what the artist would do if everyone started to leave, instead of pandering to his gigantic ego. After a minute or so, the drummer reappeared, followed by his fellow band members. The familiar beat was set up for Stewart to appear to another huge cheer, guitar in hand. This scene was repeated twice more before Stewart decided he had enough.

"OK, boys, last number. I'm exhausted."

Every band member knew the last song was an all-time classic, and the one that always finished his gigs. A face in the crowd tensed as the first chords burst out of the huge bank of speakers that lined each side of the stage.

The song was particularly energetic and Stewart began to tire as he bounded from side to side and then the rear of the stage. He decided that he would end the song a little sooner tonight. The punters have had their money's worth, he thought to himself. As the song approached its climax he bounded up the stairs that flanked the drummer and stood above and behind him. He glanced down at his amplifier, the top of which was just a foot below his feet, but he didn't want to take any chances when he 'leapt' onto it in a few seconds time. He played out the solo and theatrically jumped on top of the box and the crowd, sensing the song was about to end, raised their voices even higher. Stewart signalled to the band with a nod of his head that he wanted the song wrapped up and each, knowing his part, prepared for the finale. The face in the crowd had been watching, waiting for that nod and a finger hovered over a button on the phone. Stewart raised the guitar as he entered the last few seconds of the song and the crowd leapt into the air. Stewart reached the final notes and began beating the air with the guitar like a hammer in unison with the drummer crashing the symbols. Both slowed and then, as the guitar was raised for the last time, the drummer's arms disappeared in a blur of motion. He looked up and waited for Stewart's signal. When it came, he crashed down in one, final effort. At the same instant a hundred powerful spotlights sent a blast of blinding light into the crowd. Stewart, crouching down, was suddenly engulfed in a spectacular explosion of sparks that erupted several feet on all sides. He jerked both arms in the air and stood motionless for several seconds before slowly falling forwards into the drum kit below. On cue the stage was thrown into darkness for the performer's exit. The crowd were still cheering and clapping, enthralled at the great new stunt performed by their hero. After a minute or so, it became clear that the concert was finally over and the crowds began to drift toward the exits. One person among the crowd was aware that this was no stunt. The hand was still wrapped around the cell phone as the owner slipped through the throng and out into the park, pausing only to drop a small card into a waste paper bin, before leaving the park adjacent to the Piccadilly underpass and crossing into Berkeley Square.

The scene on the darkened stage was somewhat different. As soon as Stewart hit the drums, sending pieces flying in all directions, everyone on and back stage realised something was wrong. This was not part of the act, not even Bryan Stewart would throw himself seven feet into the forest of sharp edges that made up the maze of drums, symbols and metal stands. He lay motionless, half-covered by the large bass drum. The drummer still sat, wide eyed, on his stool, smoke coming from his hair. The first roadie to reach them stopped in his tracks and stared at the sight with open mouth. Plotting a route through the tangle, he reached out to touch Stewart. Immediately a huge crack rang out followed by a flash, which sent him flying six foot across the stage, ending up in a bundle. Several people in the crowd turned instinctively to see what had happened.

"Someone turn on some lights for Christ's sake," shouted the stage manager.

Several thousand fans could still see the stage as the grizzly scene emerged under the powerful lights. Nobody could fail to see that Bryan Stewart was seriously hurt, his drummer more so.

"Hey look," said one, "something's wrong."

Faces turned and began to move toward the stage.

"He's lying in the middle of the drums," called another.

The rumour spread quickly through the crowd and the surge changed its direction until more were returning to the arena than leaving. Sensing the disarray a few jumped onto the stage, leaping and charging around, mimicking their idol, burly security guards chasing and detaining them without ceremony.

The stage manager tried to take in the enormity of what lay before him. Stewart was still twitching, smoke drifting gently from several parts of his body. As he looked closer he noticed the singer's hands resembled black, smouldering stumps, the arms seemingly worse than the surrounding areas. The drummer was frozen to his stool, his eyes almost bursting from the sockets, hair and beard smoking, hands rigid by his sides, still holding the drumsticks that had crashed out the final note signalling their deaths. He turned to look where the roadie had been thrown, and suddenly realised that a massive electrical fault had occurred.

"The bloody guitar," gasped the man in a whisper. "The bloody guitar's electrocuted him" This time in a loud cry.

As well as every crew member in the stage area, several fans also heard the stage manager's cry. Within seconds the message had flown to the thousands outside and a tidal surge began to push back, desperate to confirm for themselves the substance of the rumour. For the few police and security guards manning the exits, this was the last thing they expected, and they were powerless to prevent the rush. A panic set in as the strong and unruly began to grow impatient at not moving quickly enough. Women and children were brushed aside, some falling and screaming out, further raising the feeling of panic among those caught in the midst of the crowd and they too began to push and shove. The arena was designed to funnel the crowds towards the two main exits, with six-foot-high metal barriers on either side. With so many attempting to re-enter at one time a bottleneck was inevitable. A few people managed to clamber up the barriers, some attempting to drag others from behind with one arm hanging, ape like, the other grasping the metal mesh. Above them, onlookers from the hospitality area looked down with a mixture of horror and disgust. One guest, realising what was happening, opened a window and stretched down, trying to reach a woman who was standing on top of the barrier. She looked up at the outstretched hand and in doing so, lost her balance. Her arms began to windmill in the air in a comic book attempt to regain her balance. Failing, she fell, screaming into the throng below, disappearing without trace. With each new horror, the panic rose, the atmosphere quickly turning ugly, arguments broke out and fists flew. A large family formed a ring of bodies around several women and small children and forced their way, like some Roman legion, towards safety. The area in front of the stage was now awash with those who had pushed their way through. They were the strongest and most unruly element who saw no reason to let the small barrier of the stage prevent them from discovering the truth, and having some fun at the same time. A dozen rushed the now alert security guards and quickly overcame them. Others followed, clambering over each other and on to the platform. The stage manager and his crew tried to block their passage, running towards the growing mass, arms waving frantically.

"Stop, you bloody fools, it's alive."

His warning was ignored as twenty or more ran to the death scene. They all stopped at once. One eager fan reached out in the hope of claiming Stewart's famous guitar for himself.

"Wouldn't touch him if I were you, sport," said an Australian standing next to the souvenir hunter. "Lot of spark left in old Bryan yet, mate. Take you with him to heaven..."

He turned to look at the man.

"Or hell."

An eerie silence fell on the onlookers. Their gruesome message quickly reached the crowd and despite the panic, the rampage seemed to end as rapidly as it had begun. Soon the cries of the trampled were joined by those of the mourning. People wandered around in a daze, some searching for those lost in the crush, others trying to take in the events around them. Within minutes fires appeared, dotted around the arena, fuelled by rows of wooden seats.

When the police and emergency services finally arrived in force, they expected to find a battle, instead they were confronted with all the horrors usually found in its aftermath. In the sixty yards between the main exits and the arena, more than a hundred people, mostly women and children, lay motionless. Around most were frantic friends and relatives, some attempting with varying levels of success, to administer first aid, others crying out for help. With only two paramedic crews in initial attendance, most of those who died did so for lack of swift attention, despite the heroic actions of those who rushed from group to group, trying in an instant, to decide who needed attention first. For those who were beyond help, the medics had to endure the looks of grief and horror on the faces of those tugging at them to remain.

Miraculously, only twelve members of the audience lost their lives, plus Bryan Stewart, his drummer Alan Blaines, and stage assistant Roger Davis.

Cheltenham, April 2010

Andrew and Jackie were together at his flat in Cheltenham for the first time in more than three weeks. Their various duties had kept them apart for many days at a time and the lack of any movement in the case was beginning to cause rumblings at the top. Andrew had been called in to see Neild, the head of K at MI5, just a few days before to explain why the investigation seemed to have ground to a halt.

"The killer hasn't made contact or changed the website," said Andrew. "There's been no traffic picked up at GCHQ regarding anything to do with the case and Paul Williams seems to have disappeared from the face of the earth."

"That's impossible," said Neild, turning from the window. "He has to eat so he must have visited a shop or a bank machine, people don't just disappear."

"We've been monitoring his bank accounts and credit cards but there's been no transactions so he either has other accounts in a false name or has enough cash to last."

"I have a COBRA meeting in a few days and the PM is becoming increasingly frustrated at the lack of progress. I need something to give him Larkin."

Andrew travelled down to Ashridge where Lambert and his team were nearing the end of their marathon hunt through the estate papers.

"There's not a single reference to anyone called Moore," said Lambert as the two stood in the auditorium watching the team sifting through the last few boxes. Andrew relayed the outline of the meeting with his superior and the frustration with a lack of anything tangible.

"No-one is more frustrated than me I can assure you Andrew," said Lambert. "Jenny hasn't found anything either which is very surprising given how she has access to the original material."

"Has Peter Hughes at Kew had any luck with Paul Williams? In its own way it's just as important as finding the Moore family as it would allow us to definitely rule him out."

"I spoke to him only yesterday and he's still stuck at Thomas who was born in 1846 and lived in the valleys around Merthyr Tydfil and worked in the iron industry."

"That was a few weeks ago," said Andrew.

"Yes, I know, but he's drawn a blank after that. Thomas's father is listed as David but there was no other information on the birth certificate." He went on to explain that certificates only came about in 1837, all records before that being kept at parish church level. "Despite sending a small team to the area they've been unable to locate any trace."

"I'm not sure how much longer I can keep you and Jenny working on this full-time unless we get a breakthrough."

"I know, she's had the records office in Ashington chasing her for a date for her return and I've received one or two searching emails from the vice principal."

"Is there nothing else we can do Tom?" Andrew pleaded.

"Some people just don't want to be found," he said walking Andrew to his car. "If it's any consolation, if we can get to the early nineteenth century then the amount and type of information will dramatically increase and we should be able to trace the Angus family and join up the Williams' link."

Andrew had watched the professor turn and walk back towards his papers in his rear view mirror.

"Do you want to watch the ten o'clock news?" said Jackie wrapping a dressing gown around her as she walked out of the bedroom.

"OK, turn on the TV," said Andrew, shaken from his thoughts.

Andrew watched her walk down the hallway before climbing out of the bed they had shared since shortly after her arrival three hours before. As he walked into the lounge she came out of the kitchen and handed him a coffee before hunting for the remote and switching on the screen. She wrapped herself around Andrew and they both watched with only passing interest. After twenty five minutes Jackie grew restless and began kissing Andrew's ear. Within two minutes the news became a background hum as they tore at each other's clothes.

"*We are getting reports of an electrical explosion at an open-air concert in Hyde Park,*" the newscaster reported. The screen changed to a still shot of the stage with a voiceover by a reporter on the spot. "*Hello, yes I am outside the perimeter of the outdoor venue set up to host concerts throughout the spring and summer.*" The voices somehow managed to penetrate through to Andrew's consciousness and he froze.

"What's up?" she asked, thinking she had done something to make him stop. He rolled off of her and sat on the edge of the settee.

"*Details are just beginning to emerge of a tragic accident in which people may have lost their lives.*" Andrew disappeared into the bedroom and emerged almost immediately with his cell phone to his ear.

"Bill, what do you know about this Hyde Park thing?"

"I got a call about five minutes ago," replied the special branch man. "Seems like some sort of electrical fault, that's all I know. They can't get any medical teams inside at the moment as there are thousands blocking the entrances."

"Call me as soon as you know more."

"Ok."

"Bill, we need to make sure we're on top of this as soon as possible. Anything to do with music makes me very uncomfortable."

The couple sat for the next two hours watching the full horror of the tragedy unfold live on the screen.

"I'm standing outside the concert venue with some of the survivors." The networks had scrambled their outside broadcast teams to the site and the reporter was surrounded by a dozen dazed looking people under the harsh TV lights.

"I was standing about half way back," said a man. *"The band was just finishing its last number when there was a tremendous flash and noise. Everyone thought it was fireworks."*

"And then what happened?" said the reporter.

"We were all leaving when someone said that Stewart was still lying on the stage."

"Everyone started turning back to see what was happening," a woman broke in. *"Then people started pushing and shoving."* The woman stopped and stared into space for a moment before breaking down. *"People got crushed man, I saw a woman get trampled and she never got up."*

"I think we should get back to London as soon as we can Andrew." Jackie stood at the bedroom door watching the scene unfold.

"Yes, you're right. Nothing is going to become clear until daylight and we should be on hand."

They left the flat thirty minutes later in Andrew's car and arrived at Jackie's house shortly before 3.30am. Jackie took a call from Bill Frost as they drove which confirmed there had been some fatalities but it was too early to know the full picture as the casualties had been taken to several London hospitals. Both of them spoke to their respective superiors and arranged their plans for the morning. With only one car they agreed that Andrew would drop her off at the nearest underground station before heading to Thames House for a 7.30am briefing.

"Jackie, can you keep in touch with David Scott this morning and ask him to carefully monitor the *Monarchy* site for any changes."

"OK."

She kissed him and disappeared down the steps of Queensbury station.

Andrew's meeting at Thames House was interrupted by a call from Bill Frost.

"I'm on site now Andrew. It seems there was some form of electrical fault that caused an explosion as the group was finishing their act."

"Bill, I'm putting you on the speaker phone so everyone in the room can hear."

The meeting room contained most of those who had been present at the post-COBRA meeting earlier in the year.

"As I said it was an electrical explosion."

"Who is confirmed as dead?" asked Neild who was sitting across from Andrew.

"Well we know for certain that the singer Bryan Stewart and two of his people definitely died. As for the crowd, I am hearing conflicting numbers but at this stage we have four confirmed and another hundred or so seriously hurt," said Frost.

"Any sign of a calling card?" said Andrew.

"Nothing on the bodies, but they're very badly burnt so it's been difficult to carry out a proper search as yet."

Andrew brought the call to an end promising to join him within the hour and reminding him to ensure the site was quarantined until a minute search could be carried out.

"Well Larkin, what are your thoughts?" Neild rose and walked to his favourite spot.

"It's too much of a coincidence," replied Andrew. "The clue may be vague but Stewart is one of the most famous rock stars around and it fits with my theory that the targets will now all be public figures."

"That will reassure the PM," said Neild.

Andrew ducked under the yellow tape that surrounded the cordon and showed his ID to the young constable on duty. The site was surrounded by a ten-foot-high green wooden fence. As he neared the entrance he spotted Frost walking towards him, having sent him a text message alerting him to his imminent arrival. Andrew donned the bio suit offered to him and the two entered the enclosure. The initial scene was exactly as anyone would have predicted in the aftermath of an open air event attended by thousands. The ground was littered with hundreds of plastic bottles and litter of every description. Frost pointed towards the stage and the pair ascended a set of steps and surveyed the carnage that greeted them. An area of the stage around twenty feet in diameter had been turned charcoal black and an acrid smell still filled the air. The remains of several items of equipment littered the area with the shattered drum kit in its centre. Guarding the area were three uniformed police officers. Frost handed Larkin a small handheld tablet that contained a series of grizzly photographs of the bodies, taken before their removal. They walked around and behind the stage itself to see the effects of the explosion. Frost caught the eye of a fellow officer and beckoned him over.

"Andrew, this is Peter Arnold, he's an electrical engineer and part of the Met's special operations group."

The pair shook hands.

"Well Bill, from my initial survey and discussions with the onsite engineering team, I would say that this was not caused by any equipment failure."

"How can you be so sure?" Andrew asked.

"An explosion like this would only normally occur at a transformer or somewhere that uses many thousands of volts. The systems used on stage use normal mains voltages, all the heavy stuff is back stage."

"So what could have caused this?"

The trio walked out to the centre of the stage and Arnold picked his way through the debris, pausing at the carcass of the large amplifier on which Stewart had been standing. He beckoned the two to join him and when all three were in position he pointed towards a collection of twisted metal in the centre and gave the three young officers leave to take a short break.

"I didn't want to say too much over there where we could be heard," he said looking tentatively around. "This is a mini high-voltage transformer. It would normally be found in use on an industrial site such as a power station or on the rail network."

"So it has no place here?"

Arnold shook his head.

"If someone connected this up correctly and short-circuited the 450 volt three phase mains, it would certainly have caused the type of explosion described." As he spoke a voice called Frost's name and they all turned towards the figure of a plain-clothed detective ascending the stairs, carrying something in his gloved hands. When he reached them he produced a small card inside a plastic envelope.

"We found this in a bin just outside the east exit sir."

"No doubt it was him then?"

Andrew stood on the stage talking on his cell phone to Jackie.

"Seems that way," he replied.

"David Scott said the site was updated at around 9am this morning." Larkin took Frost's tablet and examined the table from the *Monarchy* website complete with details of Stewart's death.

The vain maker of music now meets his maker, struck down by manmade lightning. I call again on the German pretender to stand aside of her own free will. The time fast approaches when the rightful hand will strike her aside.

"He's been trying all morning to trace the source, but again it's been bounced around so many servers that it's impossible to pinpoint a location."

"I can't believe it's impossible with all that equipment they have there," said Andrew in frustration.

"It's not the amount of equipment Andrew; it's just the facts of how the internet works," said Jackie. "All the internet service providers allocate temporary IP addresses on a random basis, it's the only way to ensure everyone can gain access when they need to. There simply wouldn't be enough to go around otherwise."

Andrew paced the stage in an agitated fashion listening to the unpalatable facts with growing anguish.

"Trying to locate the computer that uploaded the files without an IP address is no different than trying to find a person without their postal address."

Andrew knew that most killers make a mistake, leaving a trail that eventually leads back to their doorstep. So far this individual or group had either failed to follow the norm or they had simply failed to find the mistake.

Duke of Bridgewater Estate, Worsley, Lancashire, April 2010

The breakthrough everyone had been praying for finally arrived a week later. Jenny had decided to drive up to the Duke of Bridgewater's estate in Worsley where he lived for much of his life, more as a distraction than any expectation of discovery. The woman who ran Worsley Old Hall was at first reluctant to welcome the woman who had been pestering her for weeks, but a carefully worded phone call from Jenny had persuaded her to co-operate.

"All the records on the duke have been sent to the canal museum or returned to Ashridge, Miss Cross." The woman greeted Jenny as she had expected.

"Yes I'm aware of that Miss Nicholson," Jenny replied in her sweetest voice. "I was rather hoping I could look at some of the other documents I believe you have."

"You mean James Gilbert and the others who the duke employed?"

"Please." There were only three boxes containing a variety of ledgers which gave details of wages and other expenditures of the house before construction on the canal had begun and a company formed. She idly turned the pages which only confirmed what she already knew. The dates were all too early to contain any reference to William, let alone his son. After an hour she began to wonder why on earth she had made the trip. She might become an expert on early canal construction but was no nearer finding any references to Robert. But something was tugging at her thoughts and she continued her task. After another hour she picked up another ledger detailing the household accounts. Halfway through the book, she absent-mindedly turned yet another page. Neatly folded and stubbornly hanging onto the folds of the page was a letter. It was dated November 1760 from the duke to John Gilbert. In it he asked his land agent to *Use your best endeavours to secure employment for the Moore boy* at the Park Silk Mill in Stockport where Gilbert's brother was a foreman. *His father William was persuaded into my employ from his native north east and has given us great knowledge that will save lives and cost and I believe I bear a responsibility to help the son.* Robert would have been twenty five years old and if unemployed, unable to raise a family. This was sure to have caused William great anxiety and may have affected his work.

Jenny took a photocopy of the letter and drove directly to the Stockport Local Heritage Library. During the half-hour drive she called Lambert and broke the good news.

"That's fantastic Jenny, well done."

"I had a feeling if we were going to find anything it would be in an unlikely place."

"Do you want me to join you?"

"Not yet," Jenny replied, "we have the letter but as yet no evidence that Robert actually worked at the mill."

Lambert knew she was right and they agreed he should continue the work at Ashridge to its conclusion.

"Perhaps you can speak to Andrew Larkin and get someone to ring ahead so I can start work straight away?"

Lambert considered the request.

"Why don't we see how things turn out at Stockport before we tell more people what we are doing?"

The heritage section was contained within the Stockport Central Library building situated in the centre of the small town on the southern outskirts of Manchester. Thankfully the librarian in charge of the section was very helpful. Jenny recognised herself in many of the woman's mannerisms and guessed she was grateful to have a task to enliven what could be a series of dull days. The original Park Mill had been destroyed but had, in its day, been a major producer of silk in the area. Silk had been the forerunner of cotton production in the North West and had been one of the reasons the textile industry had settled in that part of the UK.

"The records that survived the fire were transferred here about ten years ago and I personally catalogued them," said the librarian as the pair began transferring the volumes from the five boxes stored in the building's vaults. "What period are we concentrating on?" she asked.

"From 1760 until around the turn of the century, I would say."

"That was the period when they would probably have switched from silk to cotton spinning," said the woman.

"I just need to locate if a Robert Moore was employed in the factory from 1760," said Jenny conscious of what she was there to find. The woman thought for a few moments before removing the top from one of the boxes and taking out several record books and placing them on the table.

"Here are the ledgers containing the employee records," she said placing one in front of Jenny and opening the cover of the one she had before her. "Here we are," she said a few minutes later.

"Sorry?" Jenny looked up from her book and took a double take.

The woman placed her ledger over Jenny's and pointed to an entry half way down the page. "Robert Moore, aged twenty five. Paid fifteen shillings for a week's work."

Jenny was staggered. Twenty five people had spent weeks trying to find a reference to Robert Moore and she had stumbled on two in a single day.

"There's a reference here to a deduction for rent so he must have lived in a cottage provided by the mill." She quickly found another volume and within a few minutes had located what she sought. "He lived in a cottage a mile from the factory with his wife and son."

"What parish is that situated in?" The woman thought for a moment.

"That would be Disley."

Jenny decided that to attempt a hat-trick in a single day was too much to hope for and booked herself into a local hotel for the night. She rang Lambert from her hotel room.

"Was there any mention of the boy's name?" Lambert asked.

"Sadly, not, but I'm sure I'll be able to locate a record of Robert at the county records office now I can be so much more specific."

"Let's hope so," said Lambert.

Cabinet Offices, Whitehall, London, April 2010

"We now have to assume that whoever is responsible for these atrocities has the capabilities and resources to target the queen."

Andrew was once again standing at the head of the large boardroom table that was squeezed into the Cabinet Office room that contained the COBRA group.

"And how do you suggest we protect Her Majesty?" The home secretary was chairing the meeting in the prime minister's absence at a summit in Brussels.

"To begin with, I think it very unwise for her to attend any public events until this is over."

"Impossible," said the head of SO14, the Royal Protection section of the Metropolitan Command. "She will never agree to that."

Andrew glanced across at Anthony Neild but found little support in his superior's expression.

"Can we assume that before targeting the queen that this merchant is next in line?" asked the chairman.

"I think that's a logical assumption at this stage," replied Andrew. "But of course Mathew Blackmore, the footballer, was murdered out of sequence. However, we're convinced that was more to do with the opportunity in Hawaii, than any other reason."

"When are we going to let the army take over this operation?" The head of the Joint Chiefs of Staff, attending for the first time tossed his briefing papers on the table. "You people," he said waving his arm at the MI5 and special operations team members, "have been chasing shadows for months. Are you going to wait until the Head of State is lying in Westminster Abbey before you stop your internal bickering and bring the professionals in?"

"If you believe you can track this person down Sir Geoffrey, then please feel free to share your plan with us?"

Andrew was relieved that it was Neild, his head of section, who had responded to the challenge.

"Do you think that parking a tank on every corner and lining the streets with heavily armed soldiers will make this person come out with their hands up?"

For the next forty minutes the group discussed various methods of protecting the monarch and senior politicians.

"We will deploy a protection team for members of the cabinet and throw a ring around every royal residence," said the home secretary. "Except for that awful man Ross, the Scottish First Minister, this killer could do us all a favour by seeing him off." He managed a weak smile but few people shared the humour. He quickly changed the subject. "But what about the next victim?"

"We've already issued a warning through the normal channels," said Andrew "and we have raised the threat level to *Severe*." Andrew noted a few people in the room looked slightly vague. "That means an attack is highly likely," he explained. "There's only one state above that which is *Critical* where an attack is imminent."

"But we can't provide personal protection to the thousands of people who could be classed as a merchant," Neild stated. "They will have to rely on private security if they feel sufficiently threatened."

It was agreed that a group be assembled from across the various services to work on contingency planning for protecting the queen at the public events she was due to attend over the coming months.

"If we can make it to the summer then we can turn Balmoral into a fortress and even keep her there for a while longer," said Sir Geoffrey.

"The last queen kept in a castle in Scotland ended up losing her head," a voice commented, referring to Mary Queen of Scots. A silence descended on the room.

"Who are we going to second to the queen's group?" said Andrew as they left the room.

"You leave that to me," said Neild. "You just concentrate on finding Williams."

Disley, Cheshire, April 2010

St Mary's Church in Disley was similar to a thousand other mediaeval examples dotted in every corner of Britain. Jenny had travelled there after spending two days at the Manchester County Records office where Robert's records should have been kept. But she had already spent several days there a few weeks before and even armed with more precise information, was unable to locate any references to the family. The parish of Disley was unusual in that it had produced duplicate records which were kept in the church and Jenny hoped they would somehow contain the missing clue. The church warden was a pleasant lady of around seventy who was happy to leave Jenny to hunt through the volumes in her own time. Although it was a warm April day outside, the heat had failed to permeate the thick stone walls and she was glad of her woollen cardigan to keep the chill at bay. Each book measured around twelve inches by eight, with eight events per page, and the small room contained dozens stacked neatly on shelves that lined three sides, the fourth holding a desk below a small window at which the archivist sat. The late eighteenth century was a time of huge population growth so the number of books Jenny faced daunted even her. All she knew for sure was that Robert had lived in the parish whilst he worked at the mill and that he had a son. She started by looking in the register of christenings for the year 1760 when Robert had moved into the area and taken up his position at the mill. When she had reached 1770 with no trace of a Moore, the warden brought her a warming cup of tea and a slice of her home-made cake which Jenny ate with guilty pleasure. She had just picked up a volume spanning 1774 when the lady popped her head around the door and reminded her it was 5.30pm and she needed to close up the church for the evening. Luckily it was fairly close to the hotel and she was able to drive there in just a few minutes.

She had arranged to continue her search early the next morning and so was at her impromptu office at 8.45am. At precisely 10am she turned a page and glanced at the top entry *1775, June 15th*. She knew it was the top of the hour as the church clock struck each one with what was becoming a hypnotic regularity. Each page was neatly printed with several columns, the third of which was headed 'Parents' Name'. There, in a clear elegant script, was the surname *Moore* with the adjacent Christian name *Robert* and the child's mother *Deborah*. Additional columns revealed that Robert was a mill worker and his wife a seamstress. The boy's name was George and the family was recorded as living in Offerton.

A few hours later a team of eight researchers had accompanied Lambert on the three hour journey from Ashridge and had removed every book from that date. He and Jenny supervised the search through each volume of christenings, marriages and burials at the Manchester headquarters of the regional counter-terrorist unit. After spending weeks on a fruitless search, the team was able to put together a brief history of the family within hours through a combination of the books and online records. Robert had three children with George being the eldest. Robert had passed away in 1798 at the age of sixty three with his wife joining him five years later. It transpired that the central records office had mislaid a number of volumes from Disley so hundreds of records were never transferred to computer.

"So where do we go from here?" Lambert and Jenny were sat in front of a large wall-mounted monitor, looking at the features of Andrew Larkin who was connected via the video conferencing facilities at the CTU in Manchester.

"At this point, all we know is that George was born in 1775 in the same parish of Disley as we found his father's records," replied Lambert.

"So back to square one?"

"We warned you that this was going to be difficult Andrew."

"What's the news from Hughes at Kew?" said Andrew.

"The last time I called him he was stuck in the Welsh Valleys." It took the pair a moment to understand Larkin's feeble joke.

"I'm sure we would have heard had he discovered anything new," Jenny suggested. "Hopefully George lived until the first census in 1801."

"That would make him, what, twenty six?" ventured Larkin.

"If we're fortunate he stayed in the Stockport area throughout his life," said Lambert.

Andrew saw a figure emerge behind the two genealogists and the three immediately began an earnest conversation. After a minute Lambert turned to face the screen once again, but this time with a huge grin on his face.

"Something interesting?"

"It would seem George Moore was the vicar of St Mary's Church in Disley from 1805 until his death in 1865 at the grand old age of ninety." Lambert held up an ancient-looking book. "His name is listed on almost every entry in these record books of christenings, marriages and burials."

"This is a tremendous breakthrough Andrew," said Jenny. "We should easily be able to find information about his family and we'll undoubtedly be able to refer to census records which will speed things up."

For the first time in months Andrew felt the tide turning in his favour.

"And don't forget that this almost certainly proves there's no link between the Moore family and Paul Williams."

"How can you be so sure?" Andrew asked.

"We know George Moore died in 1865 with three recorded children," continued Jenny, "and we know Thomas Williams' father was David, not George. So we just need to establish that his eldest son was born prior to 1846 which is highly likely as he was eighty by then."

"It's just possible that there is a genetic link but even then the Williams' line would not have had any claim to the English throne," said Lambert.

"I don't want to get into any debates about claims," said Andrew, aware of how dangerous such talk would be viewed by the establishment. "How can we be absolutely sure?"

"Why not send a message through the *Monarchy* website?" suggested Jenny.

Disley Church, April 2010

Jenny and Tom stood in silence looking down at an ancient headstone located in the centre of the cemetery of Disley church. The stone was covered in lichen and the inscription faded and would have been almost impossible to read had they not already known the words.

George Henry Moore
March 1775- October 1865
Vicar to this Parish 1805-1865
Loving Husband and Father

"He was one of the most popular vicars the parish has ever had," said the church warden who had supplied Jenny with tea and cake during her previous visit. "They wanted to intern him in the church itself, but apparently he'd insisted he wanted to rest with his flock."

They both smiled at the elderly lady but made no comment and sensing her presence was no longer required; she turned and walked slowly towards the church.

"Let me know if you need anything else."

"I wonder how she will take the news that we'll be applying to have the body exhumed?" said Jenny, watching the old woman disappear from view behind the building.

"It's the first opportunity we've had to try and match the DNA from Elizabeth with a known member of the Moore family," replied Lambert. He waited until they were sitting in Jenny's car before he dialled Larkin's number.

"No Tom, you did exactly the right thing in contacting me first. We can't afford a moment's unnecessary delay."

"We have the equipment at Cardiff to carry out the tests," said Lambert. "We just need permission to start on the hair samples from the queen's corset in Westminster Abbey."

"OK, where is the sample?"

"It's still at the Abbey, they wouldn't let me remove it."

Andrew realised he was going to have to start at the very top if he were to make things happen at the speed needed.

"I suggest you head back to Cardiff and hopefully I'll have organised the necessary arrangements for both before you arrive."

Central London, April 2010

"Ok, I'll co-ordinate our response straight away." Andrew terminated the call and dialled Neild's number.

"We've just received a call from SO15, looks like a package has been discovered at the London offices of ASTO."

"That's Albert Spice's company isn't it?" Neild walked over to his office window as he replied.

"Yes that's right, it stands for Albert Spice Trading Organisation, I think. The onsite security team have already x-rayed the package and it has all the signs of an explosive device and large enough to cause some real damage."

"Get yourself over to the scene now and I'll brief the DG. I expect they'll call a COBRA meeting whatever the outcome."

Andrew was greeted by a colleague of Bill Frost when he arrived at the cordon a few hundred yards from the Bank of England in the city of London.

"Bill's on his way from Cheltenham and will catch up when he arrives," said the man, showing Andrew into a mobile command centre that had been set up to co-ordinate the operation. "We're in the process of evacuating all the buildings within a half-mile radius."

My God, thought Andrew that must be thousands of people.

"We calculate more than a hundred buildings and 10,000 people," said the special branch man sensing Andrew's thoughts.

"Do we have access to any of the x-ray images?" said Andrew.

The man turned and spoke to one of several uniformed officers sat at computer screens and seconds later the screen directly in front of Andrew displayed an image similar to those seen at airports throughout the world.

"Luckily they have just installed one of the new generation of mail room scanners that can create much more detail."

Andrew scrolled through several images taken by the scanner from various angles and highlighted different densities using colours which made identifying suspect materials much easier and more accurate. He paused on one.

"How do I zoom in?" he knew what he was looking at long before the rectangle filled the screen.

"It even has the correct number written on it." Bill Frost stood beside Andrew looking at the same image, having arrived an hour later. "Seems our man has made his first real mistake," said Frost.

University of Cardiff, April 2010

Lambert stood in front of a large monitor, studying two sets of images.

"It looks pretty conclusive to me," said the lab technician standing beside him.

The hair from Elizabeth's corset had arrived at Cardiff before Lambert, delivered with a police escort after being flown from London. A bone sample from the skull of the Reverend George Moore arrived twenty four hours later after a specialist team from Manchester police forensics department had carried out an exhumation of the body in record-breaking time.

"How can you sure?" Jenny was standing on the other side of the professor.

"We've been able to get a close enough match across eight or nine markers which gives us a ninety per cent probability that the two samples are from related individuals," answered the technician pointing out the similarities in the two images, that looked to the untrained eyes like an old fashioned piano roll. He pointed to various points on one image which were replicated on its neighbour. As he spoke the image changed to a graphic representation of the results which simplified the process of identification to the uninitiated.

"That should make it easier to understand" said Lambert, who had changed the image from an adjacent computer workstation. "This is close enough for us to tell Larkin that the Moore family is directly related to the Tudor monarchy."

"If we can obtain a sample from a male relative then we can carry out a Y chromosome test which will be even more conclusive," said the technician.

"Let's not get carried away," said Lambert, "I doubt we'll get permission to exhume the body of Elizabeth I's father and even then we would need a large sample to extract enough DNA."

"This will enable us to continue the hunt for the relatives of the Moores," said Jenny.

"Now we'll be able to use the early census information, it should enable us to accelerate the whole process," Lambert said, dialling Larkin's number.

Farnborough Airfield, Southern England, April 2010

Fred Bradstock was very pleased with himself. That in itself was not an unusual event as he had been used to feeling pleased with himself for over thirty years, ever since his first successful business venture. After that, everything he had touched seemed to quickly develop a golden colour. But he had known failure as well. His first business idea was underfunded and he did not have the experience to overcome the inevitable hurdles when they arose. But that was understandable when you are twelve years of age and are trying to establish a nationwide chain of coffee shops.

He had cursed the narrow-minded people at the bank who had laughed at him when he turned up for a meeting to discuss the venture. They had assumed from the detailed business plan they had received, that they were due to meet a seasoned professional, even though the actual idea seemed fanciful. When the schoolboy had presented himself at the reception of the headquarters in Leadenhall Street in the heart of the city of London their first question was,

"Where is your father, young man?"

"I have no idea," had been the young Frederick's response, since his father had deserted the family when he was five.

They had listened to his presentation mainly out of curiosity, but constantly interrupted with inane questions about details of the operational side of the proposal.

"So where are you going to source the coffee from young Mr. Bradstock, the local corner shop?"

They had all thought that rather amusing until he had referred them to page thirty five of the documents.

"As you can see, I have already reached an agreement in principal to import beans from a new source in Colombia. As experts in the field, I'm sure you'll note that the price is around twenty percent less than that paid by the major importers." The astonished looks were quickly replaced with one he had seen before. "I've carried out all the negotiations by telephone and letter."

What had annoyed him most was the fact that not a single one of them had enough raw business acumen to spot the potential of the idea. He had set up a stall in a local market and had been quite successful until the sample bags of beans he had been sent from South America had run out. The grower had wanted him to place a minimum order and pay fifty percent in advance by way of a letter of credit. He did not even have a bank account and no way of raising the £5,000 required. But the lessons he had learned had served him well in the years to come. He now owned the two largest coffee shop chains in Europe, only exceeded in size by the American giant. Together they generated over a billion pounds of revenue each year. He never failed to smile when he recalled the approach from the chairman of that bank trying to persuade him to work with them on a particular project. He had accepted his invitation for a meeting at the bank's headquarters, but did not attend himself. Instead he sent a twelve-year-old, the son of an employee, with a letter explaining that Bradstock Enterprises would not be taking up the bank's kind offer of funding at this time, or indeed at any time in the future. It suggested they might like to look up the details of a meeting held some thirty five years before regarding a proposition for upmarket coffee shops. It also pointed out that the chairman himself had attended that meeting and had remarked that nobody in their right mind would pay £2.50 for a cup of coffee, however much cream had been squirted on the top.

Bradstock looked out from the rear seat of his white Rolls Royce Silver Shadow. It was one of three he owned, the others being red and blue. He was proud to be British and the chairman of an organisation that employed more than 15,000 people in the UK alone, with a turnover exceeding £5billion and with a £500million profit. The fact he had paid only £20,000 of personal tax last year to the British Government did not cause him the slightest concern. It was his duty to exploit every legal opportunity to maximise his return. Without him, those 15,000 would be numbers added to the welfare bill at a cost far exceeding the tax he had saved.

The car slid to a silent halt at the gates of Farnborough airfield in Hampshire. Once home to the Royal Aircraft Establishment which had produced many inventions used by the Royal Air Force during both World Wars, including the bomb site used to ensure Barnes Wallis's bouncing bomb was released at precisely the right moment. It had also been the location of the first manned flight in Britain when Samuel Cody flew 1,400 feet on October 16th 1908. In the last few years its military capabilities had been run down, although it was still home to the air accident investigation branch. The large hanger it called home was situated at the southern edge of the site and had witnessed amongst many others, the reconstruction of the Pan American Boeing 747 brought down by a terrorist bomb over the Scottish town of Lockerbie. It was now most widely known for the bi-annual international air show, attended by every major military and commercial aviation manufacture on the planet. Many multibillion dollar deals had been signed at the show over the years and the daily spectacle of the latest fighter blended with spitfires and the Red Arrows aerobatic team ensured a memorable day for professionals and public alike. One of the reasons the airfield could host such an event was the length of its runway. At 8,000 feet long it was capable of handling any aircraft, even the giant Russian Antonov AN-22 cargo transporter.

It was for this reason that Bradstock found himself staring out of his Rolls Royce. It had been his dream since he was a boy to fly. He had never found the time to learn himself, having been too busy making himself a billionaire to indulge in any other passion. But he had made sure that he had created an aviation company as part of his empire at the first opportunity. Now, Bradstock Aviation was a leading supplier of advanced aeronautical systems to military and commercial customers worldwide. One of the reasons why Bradstock was a billionaire ten times over at the age of forty seven was his uncanny ability to spot a trend before most even realised it existed. He was not unique in having that gift. What made Frederick George Bradstock different was his ability to take that gut feeling and turn it into a product that could sell and make a good profit. One was useless without the other as far as he was concerned.

"That's great news Tom. Can you and Jenny get back to Manchester as soon as possible and pick up the trail again." Andrew punched the air as the implication of Lambert's discovery sank in. If they could find the living relative of George Moore then they would find the killer. He was standing in the street outside the mobile command centre at ASTO's London headquarters and noticed he was being studied by several of the officers who were manning the barriers a few yards away.

"I don't think Manchester is the best place for us now Andrew," replied Lambert. "I'd prefer to take Jenny and myself to Kew and work with Peter Hughes."

"Oh, ok if that's what you think best."

"We'll have access to everything we need in a single place."

"Ok, be ready to leave in an hour and I'll arrange for you to fly into Northolt. It's only twenty minutes to Kew from the airport."

Andrew made a call to the control room at Thames House to organise the transport and then dialled Neild's private number. He was going to enjoy this call.

"Good work Andrew," said the section head. "So how long will it be before your professor chap locates our man?"

Andrew could picture Neild gazing out of his office window over the river and imagined throwing him into the dark waters.

"He's on his way to the National Archives at Kew as we speak," replied Andrew. "George Moore died in 1865 which means they can now use the census data which should speed things up."

"Good, I'll let the PM's office know straight away." There was a pause on the line before Neild spoke again. "What are we going to do with you when this is all over?"

The line went dead before Andrew had any chance to reply. As he turned back towards the control vehicle Frost burst through the door, the look on his face making any relief Andrew had been feeling instantly disappear.

Today, Bradstock was at Farnborough to witness an important milestone. Important not only for himself and Bradstock Aviation, but for the entire world of commercial aviation. For the last five years his engineers had been developing and perfecting what Bradstock knew would be the next big leap forward in the industry. Pilotless commercial aircraft. As soon as he had heard of the capabilities of the latest generation of military drones deployed by the Americans, he had realised that the technology existed to allow a plane to take off, fly to and from a specific location, return and land in one piece. Of course the availability of a reliable and secure GPS satellite navigation system, the advance of camera technology and the prodigious computer power now available in such small payloads had made the dream realistic. There was now no technical reason why a commercial aircraft could not perform in exactly the same way as a drone. There was however some, as yet, insurmountable issues that meant no country would issue an airworthiness certificate to such a plane. These were, on the surface, safety related. The most often cited was that a computer was fallible and not able to apply the same level of instinctive reaction to unforeseen events. The reality is that more aircraft accidents are caused by either pilot error or the inability of the crew to react to a situation they had only ever come across in a simulator. Computers now effectively controlled every aspect of commercial aviation from takeoff to landing, in fact without them no modern plane could stay airborne. The real reason was public perception. No one would set foot on a plane that had no pilot. Bradstock had foreseen this issue at the very outset of the project. He had organised two separate teams to make it happen. One technical and one PR. He headhunted the best technical director in the business, the man who had designed the latest generation of drone systems for the giant American defence contractor, McDonnell Douglas. He also did the same when setting up a team to plan and implement the task of persuading governments, airlines and the flying public that it was safe. Today was to be the first public demonstration of the *Winterberg Virtual Pilot* or WVP, on board a commercial airliner. He had named the system after the German-born physicist Friedwardt Winterberg who had first proposed using atomic clocks placed inside orbiting satellites to test general relativity theories, the scientific basis on which GPS is based.

Bradstock climbed from the car to be met by a barrage of flashing lights and TV cameras. The world's press was out in force. This was no surprise as his team had invested enough time and money in ensuring the flight would be beamed across the world. Despite the fact he had leased an Airbus 320 jet at enormous cost for R&D purposes, Bradstock still had to cover the entire $70million cost of the aircraft. No insurance company would as yet cover such a flight. The aircraft stood waiting outside the small terminal building at one corner of the airfield that housed the private commercial flights that now accounted for most of the aircraft movements on the airfield. To the untrained eye it was no different to any one of nearly 5,000 aircraft that had flown over a billion passengers over its twenty five year life.

Bradstock was guided to a small podium set in front of the aircraft. It already contained the heads of the main teams that had helped develop the system to the point it was today. A caravan-sized mobile command centre stood a hundred yards to one side. This was, in fact, a backup and also for the benefit of the press. The main centre from which the aircraft would be controlled was ninety miles away at the company's main research centre just outside Bristol. "Ladies and gentlemen, welcome to what we will all learn to remember as one of the great days of aviation history. A day to remember alongside the Wright brothers' first flight and Lindbergh's first solo crossing of the Atlantic."

Bradstock looked at the bank of media in front of him. It was moments like this that he lived for. Few things could compare with the power that came from being able to command the attention of the world's media with a few emails and calls.

"Today we are going to witness a worldwide first. The first totally unmanned flight of a commercial airliner. For years our transport systems have become increasingly automated and the need for human intervention gradually reduced until today we have, for example, whole urban train systems running totally unmanned."

Five hundred yards away on the opposite side of the airfield, a small lane ran alongside the southern perimeter fence. Laffans Road was reached via a steel bridge which straddled the Basingstoke Canal and had been constructed by the army some fifty years before. A lay-by sat beside a small entrance gate, one of dozens found around the two mile extremity of the field. It was rarely used so the sight of a small van parked outside would cause little concern, and even less chance of preventing a vehicle seeking entry or exit. The vantage point offered an uninterrupted view across the entire site with the runway no more than fifty yards away at its south western end. Sat in the rear of the van looking through a pair of binoculars across the field was someone who had more than a passing interest in the proceedings. Bradstock was hidden from view by the aircraft, but even from this distance it was obvious that something out of the ordinary was going on. Satellite vans and all the various paraphernalia associated with a TV outside broadcast could clearly be seen with the naked eye. There was therefore really no need to watch proceedings at all. But curiosity was a powerful thing and the real need for the magnified view was to check for the telltale receiver dish mounted on the underside of the right wing. This confirmed that the plane was fitted with the remote device as expected. After what seemed like an eternity people began to move, signalling something was about to happen. Through the binoculars a figure emerged into view at the base of the stairs leading to the aircraft's forward door. The figure climbed a couple of steps and turned to face the throng, waving both arms in salute, before ascending the rest of steps and disappearing behind the fuselage. But there was no doubt that Fred Bradstock was boarding the plane.

The gathered media had no idea that Bradstock intended to be the sole human on the test flight. Only a few selected members of his team had been told a few months before when planning for the event began. He informed them all during a video conference whilst he was in America and had sworn them all to the utmost secrecy. The plan had worked perfectly. At the end of his speech he had simply left the podium and continued walking towards the plane. After pausing a short distance up the steps, he carried on ascending. He lingered at the entrance to the plane for effect and waited. His head of PR was waiting on the podium and on cue, announced.

"Ladies and gentlemen. Mr. Bradstock is very aware that millions of people across the world will be watching today's demonstration. Many of those will harbour doubts as to whether they could ever fly in an aircraft with no onboard pilot. Mr. Bradstock would like to show how much faith he has in the safety of the WVP system, by being the only human on today's flight."

Silence followed to allow the assembled media to take in the statement. Bradstock waited until he could see the throng suddenly erupt into a frenzy of activity. He had guessed that many networks would now show the flight live and for the rest it would be the lead story on every news bulletin and front page headline in print. That was why he had timed the flight for 6pm. Early evening news across Europe and lunchtime on the east coast. After a few seconds, enough time for the cameras to focus on him, he stopped waving and made a dramatic turn before disappearing into the plane.

The reaction of the press could be seen even from 500 yards. A smile crossed the lips of the vans occupant. Nothing could stop the chain of events that the arrogant Bradstock had put into motion. A quick run through to check all the equipment was fully operational. If he wanted the world to watch his toy fly, that was fine. Let the show begin.

Bradstock quickly sat down in seat 1A. The bulkhead immediately in front of him contained a camera so the world could watch him as his dream took an important step forward. He knew it would be many years before this concept would be accepted, the first stage would be to reduce the crew to one. At an average salary of £60,000, the airlines would immediately save millions simply by halving the crew on the 20,000 commercial jets currently flying. With a ten per cent annual growth in air traffic predicted over the next twenty years, the numbers spoke for themselves. Add in the reduced costs of training and stand-by crews and the argument became overwhelming. His ground-based operators could comfortably handle twenty flights each and he would charge the airlines a fee for the service, or allow them to set up their own command centre. After that it would only take a short while to allow one of the cabin crew to double up as an emergency operator. Totally unnecessary, but a step. Bradstock predicted that every airliner built in the next fifty years would have the system fitted. As he held patents on all the elements that made the system seamless, his company would stand to make billions.

At the command centre in Bristol, the chief flight operations manager confirmed the message from the ground crew that all pre-flight preparations were complete. All visitors had been moved to a temporary site erected for the event. The atmosphere was thick with anticipation.

"Ok, let's go!" The flight operator glanced down at his control monitor and pushed a single screen prompt. On the fifty inch monitor mounted a few feet above and in front of him, he could see a pilot's view of the front of the aircraft. There were more than eighty cameras mounted on the aircraft, including thirty externally, enabling the operator to have a visual check from every angle and monitor all the flight surfaces. The two engines of the A320 started in sequence and settled at their idling speed. Another prompt from the operator ran a series of preflight checks ensuring the rudders, ailerons, flaps etc. responded correctly to the commands issued via satellite to the onboard systems, which in turn commanded the computers to mimic the same fly by wire the aircraft had fitted as standard.

"Why reinvent the wheel twice." Bradstock had said.

When all was confirmed as satisfactory, the operator took control of the plane via the same joystick control as would be found on many of today's jets. He increased the thrust just enough to enable the aircraft to start moving before gently maneuvering the 230 foot plane on to the taxiway. It took another five minutes before the A320 was in position at the eastern end of the runway, poised to claw its way into the sky. But there was still time for a final act of showboating by Bradstock

"Ladies and gentlemen, you are about to witness a moment of history."

The operator received his final clearance and initial instructions from the Farnborough tower. Immediately after takeoff, air traffic control would pass to National Air Traffic at Swanwick. After a final glance at each other and the 'ok' from the boss, the operator pressed an on screen prompt labelled 'TAKE OFF', and sat back. The two Rolls Royce V2500 engines could generate 33,000 pounds of thrust each and as their rotations increased to a high-pitched scream, the brakes were removed and the plane set free to begin its historic journey. Bradstock was nervous, although he would not admit that to a living soul. He maintained a steely grin as the plane picked up speed. Sensors on the plane ensured that it maintained a straight line as it careered down the tarmac.

"V1," called the operator as the A320 reached the first speed marker.

At the southern end of the runway, the plane grew in size as it approached. There was an urge to reach out and pluck the bird from the sky as it passed by; it would be less than three hundred feet away. But bringing the plane down with some form of rocket propelled grenade or missile would have been extremely risky and most likely discovered beforehand. It was obvious that the security services would be keeping an eye on things, although the item on the news just a few minutes earlier had confirmed that a package containing some form of explosive device had been intercepted at the London headquarters of the prominent businessman Albert Spice. That would keep them occupied for a while. The plane left the runway and gently rose into the sky, clearing the perimeter fence by some 200 feet as it passed overhead.

The plane climbed to 5,000 feet and after two miles, began a slow turn. All of these maneuvers had been preprogrammed into the TAKE OFF module and the operator merely kept an eye on the forward facing camera he had chosen. Down the right hand side of the large monitor, five other views were available, including one of Bradstock.

"All ok?" asked the chief.

"Fine sir," came the reply he already knew was coming.

For the next ten minutes the plane carried out a series of passes over the airfield. Bradstock peered out of the window at the runway below and felt an immense sense of pride at his achievement. The plane levelled out and as he knew it would be flying level for a few minutes he rose from his seat and taking a half dozen steps forward, opened the door to the flight deck. Even he was momentarily taken aback by the sight of the two empty chairs that confronted him. But he was comforted by the calm glow of the flickering monitors and the movement of the joystick controllers.

Eight thousand feet below him a laptop was opened and brought back to life. Buttons were pressed and systems connected via an online satellite transmitter set into the roof of the van. It took less than three minutes to establish a link with the upload/download station of the Winterberg systems GPS ground station. All remote flying systems rely on the dozens of GPS satellites that orbit the earth in geostationary orbit. Military drones do not rely on the commercially used GPS systems launched by the Americans in 1994 and given access to the world by President Reagan, that would be too risky. They had their own satellites, secure, safe and resilient to hacking. Bradstock, however was not able to access these systems as his was a commercial application and far from being approved by the FAA. This was fine when you were controlling toy planes for a research and development programme. If something failed and the toy plane veered off course it could, at worse, be destroyed in flight. Bradstock's need to demonstrate the Airbus in action had caused him to overrule the warnings of his team, and this had opened up a window of opportunity that would now be exploited to maximum effect. There was no need to build a duplicate of the flight control system currently flying the aircraft. Just a few simple commands would suffice. A hand moved over the touchpad on the laptop and clicked on an onscreen prompt.

Bradstock was on his way back to his seat when he was suddenly launched forward by the sudden increase in the plane's speed. He just managed to reach out his hand and prevent himself sprawling into his seat in full view of the world's eyes. In Bristol the operator frowned at the red light that appeared on his monitor. The chief appeared over his shoulder in an instance.
"What the hell was that?"
"That signals that the aircraft has departed from the pre-programmed sequence."
Both men stared at the screens waiting to see what would happen next. After ten seconds they both let out a long breath, which was just as well for it was the last opportunity either would get to breathe easily for some time.

In the van, confirmation that control of the aircraft had been interrupted had caused an unforeseen and sudden increase in the plane's engine speed. This was quickly corrected with one of the available commands. A quick glance at an inlaid map showed the plane was around three miles west of the airfield. A GPS co-ordinate was entered into a prompt box and sent. Altitude and speed commands followed. This was easier than playing a video game.

If the computer onboard the aircraft had had any human qualities it too would have frowned. For a full two seconds all communication with the GPS satellites was broken, the equivalent of taking a parachute from a skydiver. But then the link was re-established. It was not to know that the next set of instructions it received would have made any human drop their jaw in amazement. Fred Bradstock was not happy. He just hoped that the blip would not have been noticed by the media, but that was doubtful from 10,000 feet. He waved weakly at the camera, hoping it would show the world he was relaxed and happy.

In Bristol, pandemonium had broken out.
"For God's sake what do you mean you've lost control?" The chief stared wide-eyed at his operator whist he tried everything he knew to re-establish the connection.
"Whatever I do, I can't get it to respond."
They watched in horror as the plane began to climb and bank to the right. It climbed to 15,000 feet before pausing as the life-giving thrust disappeared and fell gracefully into a vertical dive. The new GPS coordinates were perfectly set and a testament to the engineering teams responsible, the system was working perfectly. How easy it had been to infiltrate Bradstock Aviation IT systems and download the information necessary to write a simple programme to block the programme command signals and give the plane a new set of simple commands. *Climb to fifteen thousand feet, navigate to co-ordinates 51° 16' 31" N 00° 46' 39"W, shut down engines.*

On board Bradstock was gripped by a combination of fear and confusion. He dare not cry out as the camera would pick up his every move. The plane had suddenly banked and begun to rise quickly. He was pushed back into his seat, unable to move, although where he would have gone was unclear. But once he felt the power ebb away and a silence descend in the cabin, he could no longer control the rising panic. Looking out of the window, he could see the airfield rush by as the plane, now devoid of any lift, began to fall back to earth. In the confusion no-one had thought to cut the live feed from the plane. So the world watched every reaction of the billionaire during the forty seconds it took to plough into the centre of the runway at more than 500 miles per hour. The laptop had been closed well before the impact and the small van was already half a mile along the A323 Fleet Road when a giant explosion, followed by a rising fireball of flame and smoke, rose above the trees. Several cars stopped to take in the spectacle, but the van carried on. While the world watched in horror, it joined the M3 motorway at junction 4a.

At the lavish funeral ten days later, no one was quite sure who had sent the small wreath with the strange card with a bear and ragged staff motif on one side and a handwritten number fourteen on the other.

Thames House, Central London, April 2010

The package delivered to Albert Spice and the way its discovery had been dealt with started a firestorm at the highest levels. It had all the characteristics of a genuine explosive device and bore all the hallmarks of Middle Eastern origin in its materials and construction. It even had the tell-tale card fixed to the outside. From the moment it had arrived at ASTO's head office it was treated with suspicion and when scanned readily revealed its contents. It had taken the bomb disposal team four hours to disarm it without a controlled explosion which, as well as being highly undesirable in central London, risked destroying vital evidence. During this time a fatal mistake had been made and the team handling Bradstock's close protection had been moved from black to amber by a junior staff member at the control centre at Thames House. It was unlikely that this simple clerical error had contributed in any way to Bradstock's death as it appeared the killer had managed to infiltrate the computer systems at WVP and alter the software programming and thus allow the aircraft control to be hijacked remotely with disastrous results. But the paranoia surrounding the case within the government and security services meant a scapegoat must be found and Andrew knew that Neild would not hesitate to put his name forward should the opportunity arise.

"Are you near a computer?"

"I'm surrounded by dozens of them," answered Andrew, who was standing in the Thames House control room.

"Log on to the *English Monarchy* site. Our friend has responded to the blog entry," said David Scott.

Andrew tapped Jackie on the shoulder and whispered for her to go to the site. It took a few seconds for her to find the reply. *Did you enjoy your Welsh excursion? Take a trip to 53° 21' 14.4" N, 2° 23' 13.2" W to discover what you seek.*

"It's been updated with Bradstock's details too," said Jackie pointing to the table on her monitor.

"The co-ordinates are for a lake called Rostherne Mere," said Scott.

"Just a few miles from Altrincham station," said Andrew pointing at the satellite images on his computer

Sale, Greater Manchester, England, December 2009

Paul Williams peered down the street from his hiding place in an alley at the end of a block of terraced houses in a Manchester suburb. The slightly-built NCIS operative was dressed in a dark coloured raincoat and scarf to protect him from the autumn weather and shield him from any prying eyes. He was cold and hungry, having been prowling the area for over three hours waiting to see if his hunch was correct. He glanced over to the opposite side of the street, alerted by a brief glimpse of light from the window as the occupant peeked through a crack in the curtain for the third time in as many minutes. He pulled his phone from his pocket as he took a step backwards into the shadows and again decided against turning on the device. He knew he should share his discoveries with Jackie Crowther and the other members of the ELG at GCHQ, but as a new recruit he was not confident that he would be proved correct. He had spent what seemed like every waking minute of the last five years studying to ensure he received a first class degree, the golden ticket into the career he had dreamed of since childhood. Even in these supposedly enlightened times, his working-class background made it difficult for him to be taken seriously for entry into MI6, his chosen organisation. He had accepted the position in the NCIS purely as a stepping stone to greater things and he was determined he was going to maximise the career potential of his discovery. He just needed to confirm his information before presenting his evidence to the right people. He had quickly understood the systems at GCHQ and took every opportunity to learn from the best analysts such as Mary Ward, picking up a few passwords on the way which had enabled him to interrogate many of the data sets produced by Echelon. He had also learnt the footprint of the *English Monarchy* killer and the programme he had created to scan the incoming signals for tell-tale signs and had picked up a clue missed by everyone else. That clue, an uncharacteristic oversight from someone who was one of the best he had seen, had enabled him to trace the origin of the files. He had also been able to gain access to the suspect's personal computer which proved an Aladdin's Cave of information once he had broken through the impressively encrypted security. That information had led him to this nondescript part of the North West and his moment of destiny.

Williams caught site of the curtain twitching across the street again and cursed the occupant for their curiosity, but he was confident they would not be able to identify him from that distance in a shadowy alley on a dark evening. His eyes, well-adjusted to the artificial sodium street lighting, caught another movement further down the street and his heart began to pound. A hundred yards away there was a break in the terraced houses, identical to the one he was concealed in. From the shadow cast by a street light, a figure leant forward to look at a car that had pulled up outside a house fifty yards further down the street. The figure quickly disappeared back into the shadows, but Williams had seen enough to know his assumption was correct. A young man emerged from the car and headed for one of the houses before returning to retrieve something. At this distance it was difficult to make out details, but it appeared he had gone into a house with a *For Sale* notice outside. In the still air the sound of the door closing was unmistakable and it prompted the figure to emerge once again from the shadows, this time with more confidence. Williams ducked back behind the wall to avoid any chance of detection should the figure look his way, but after a few minutes he could not contain his curiosity and peered around the corner again. To his horror, the figure was no more than thirty yards away and walking quickly in his direction and he retreated as far back as he dared before watching as it walked across his field of vision and disappeared behind the next block of houses. He was contemplating his next move when the world around him was transformed into the sound and vision of hell. The night sky became day accompanied by an ear shattering noise and he looked up to see a cascade of debris flying in every direction and instinctively crouched down with his hands over his head. After a few seconds the light faded into a glow visible above and around the wall, and the sounds of falling debris stopped. He ran into the street and stood in horror at the scene that met his eyes before forcing himself to ignore the carnage and turn to see where the figure had gone. He saw a glimpse of the figure walking quickly away before darting into an adjacent street. He gave chase, determined not to lose the chance and turned the corner just in time to see a flash of raincoat turn right and so dropped into a fast walk whilst forcing himself to stay calm. He was inexperienced at following people but was sure he had not been spotted. The road was straight and he could now easily keep his quarry in view. Sirens wailed in the distance and a police car sped past, lights flashing. After a hundred yards Williams could see the sign for the Metro station of Brooklands and the figure turned into the entrance. As he approached a train arrived and Williams had to run to ensure he could board if necessary. As he ran onto the platform he saw the person look in his direction before disappearing into a carriage close to the front. He darted through the nearest opening just as the doors slid shut and the train moved off. After a few minutes it slid to a halt at the next station and Williams gingerly half-stepped out to peer down the platform. He waited until the last moment before retreating to avoid the doors, but there was no sign of an exit. The routine was repeated at every station before the train arrived at the terminus of Altrincham. Williams waited until the suspect passed his carriage before alighting and following at what he supposed was a safe distance. His mind raced as he tried to decide on the best way to get close enough without arousing suspicion. When he emerged from the station along with thirty or so others, he looked around until he saw the familiar raincoat heading into the car park. Quickening his pace, he felt in his pocket for the reassuring coldness of the pistol he had managed to acquire from the small firearms store at NCIS headquarters. At this time of the evening there were still enough cars for Williams to be able to close the gap between them without causing alarm. The figure opened the door of a small car having unlocked the door a few paces away with a remote key. Williams was just a few yards behind and his decision was made when the engine burst into life as he passed the front of the vehicle. In a flash he sprang alongside the passenger's side, opened the door, sat down, pointed the weapon at the driver and smiled.

"Hello," said the fugitive, "I've been expecting you."

Rostherne Mere Lake, Manchester, May 2010

Andrew could see the expanse of the lake as the helicopter approached from the south. It was pear-shaped being around 900 yards long and 600 at its widest point, narrowing to less than a hundred at its northern tip. The area surrounding the water was filled with dense forest and paths and the pilot hovered looking for a suitable landing spot.

"That's the M56," said Jackie pointing at the motorway that ran east to west just a few hundred yards north.

"How far is it from Altrincham station?"

"About two miles," Jackie replied.

Eventually the helicopter touched down in an adjacent field and the pair trudged across the muddy terrain to the mobile command centre to be greeted by the local special branch commander.

"Do you want to see the body?" he said glancing down at Jackie's mud covered heels.

"Yes please," said Andrew "and a couple of pairs of boots would be nice too if you have any spare."

"I'm sure we can find you something."

After a five minute walk they came into a clearing filled with a dozen or more people, including a police diving team packing up their equipment and several bio-suited officers. Lying on a large sheet in the centre was a plastic body bag with what presumably contained the NCIS man's remains. They looked down at the face that had been uncovered. Williams' unmistakable features were frozen in a moment of terror and pain, the source of which was clear to see. Andrew turned to the commander who, guessing his next question, called over a white-suited member of the team.

"Initial conclusion on the cause of death is a puncture wound to the brain from a long thin object thrust in through the left eye socket."

"How long has he been dead?" asked Jackie, turning away from the gruesome scene.

"Difficult to say," he replied. "The state of decomposition points to around five months, but it's too early to be accurate. We should have some more details after the post mortem."

"Anything else that will help us?" Andrew enquired of the commander.

"The body was discovered in ten feet of water just a few yards offshore and there appears to have been little effort made to conceal it."

"What makes you say that?" said Jackie having found her composure again.

"We found a few stones packed inside the bag, but not enough to weigh it down sufficiently."

"A rush job?" said Andrew.

"Nothing to really suggest that," answered the special branch man. "Certainly a well-executed one."

Andrew's puzzled look prompted the man to continue.

"By piercing the brain through the eye there would have been minimal blood loss."

The trio turned and began to walk back toward the command centre as the wind picked up sending a rush of freezing air across the lake into their faces.

"We found tyre tracks right down to the edge of the water so it's probable the murder took place elsewhere and the body was brought here for disposal."

"Any other clues so far?" The commander stopped and produced a small bag from his coat pocket. Andrew and Jackie recognised the small card and the explanation of how it had been found on the body proved unnecessary.

Rostherne Mere Lake, Manchester, December 2009

The figure watched as the bubbles disturbing the surface of the water finally petered out and all traces of the body had disappeared. It did not matter that it was only a few feet beneath the surface and only yards from the edge of the lake, as long as it remained undiscovered long enough for the plan to serve its purpose. What could have been a disaster had turned into a beautiful opportunity to keep the police and security services chasing shadows until the time was right to lead them to this spot, and if the body was discovered beforehand it would have no effect on the long-term plan. It was no surprise when the man had jumped into the car at the station. He had first been noticed hiding behind the wall a few yards along the street. The fool thought he had been clever enough to discover where the web files were uploaded but had only succeeded in raising the alarm. It took just over an hour to trace the source and learn the identity of the would-be hero and the discovery that he had kept the information to himself had proved highly advantageous. So when the gun was produced in the car it simply started a chain of events that had been meticulously planned.

"Head for the motorway. We're going to the Manchester counter-terrorist unit offices and you can explain everything there," said Williams.

After following the directions for a few minutes the car left the motorway.

"Where are you going? I didn't tell you to exit here."

At the top of the ramp the car took the third exit into a quiet road that the driver knew lead nowhere. Williams was becoming more agitated and waved the gun in the driver's face.

"Stop and turn around you bastard, before I use this," he shouted.

But he did not have the courage to shoot anyone at such close range and they both knew it. A hand reached down into the door and gripped a thin bladed knife. In a flash, the left hand swept across and deflected the gun down whilst the right hand buried the blade in Williams' left eye socket, penetrating his brain and killing him instantly. There was surprisingly little blood, but no detail had been left unplanned and if Williams had been more astute he would have noticed the plastic seat cover. A bag was produced from the back of the seat, placed over his head and tied around his neck to prevent any leaking blood, whilst a quick look around the car interior showed no signs of any splatter. Walking around to the passenger's door Williams' body was slid down so it was invisible to the casual observer and the driver set off for the final destination. There was no fear of the car being identified as the Metro station cameras had been disabled remotely and the licence plates altered to ensure any number plate recognition systems positioned on the motorway bridges would register an error. It was just a short drive to the lake that had been chosen and at this time of year, the entire area was deserted. Within twenty five minutes of his death Williams was lying in ten feet of water in a weighted bag and his killer was heading south on the M6.

National Archives, Kew, May 2010

"So it looks as if the letter was genuine after all." Lambert sat in Peter Hughes's office in Kew having arrived a few minutes ago following a sixty minute journey from Cardiff via two airports, two sets of police cars and a military helicopter flown by a pilot who had recently returned from active service in Afghanistan. By the look on Jenny's face throughout the twenty minute flight, she was convinced he believed he was under enemy ground attack. Lambert had sent her to recuperate at a hotel that had been hastily arranged for them.

"Certainly the content," Lambert replied, still slightly dizzy from being thrown around. "That reminds me, I must call that old dealer in Wales."

"I would be careful what you say Tom," said Hughes, you know what the MI5 man said. Lambert nodded before pulling his cell phone from his jacket. Hughes burst out laughing. "Tom Lambert with a smart phone, whatever next."

Lambert ignored the joke and looked up the dealer's contact details. Although he would never admit it, the instrument had quickly become indispensable to him, taking over many functions of both his laptop and diary. He dialled the number and waited for what seemed like an age before the line was answered.

"Hello," said the old man slightly out of breath.

"It's Professor Lambert, Mr Carter, I'm sorry I haven't been in touch for a while but things have been a little hectic."

"I was wondering when you would call," said the old man. "I have some interesting facts about the trunk."

Lambert took a moment to remember the source of the letter. His trip to the old man's workshop seemed like another lifetime, so much had happened in the intervening ten months. The old man took his silence as the cue for him begin his story.

"I went to see the solicitor of the lady whose house clearance produced the trunk," he began. "At first I couldn't find any clues as to its history, but a few months later I was contacted by a relative from Manchester." There was a pause on the line.

"Are you all right Mr Carter?"

"Just getting a chair so I can sit down young man."

Lambert glanced at Hughes who gave him a stern look and put his finger to his lips by way of a reminder about staying silent about the letter.

"You take your time."

"Anyway where was I?" the old man continued.

"The relative from Manchester," said Lambert helpfully.

"Ah yes. It turns out that the trunk had been in the family for centuries. No one could remember how it had come into their possession but the lad who called made some enquiries and discovered an old aunt who remembered hearing a story about an ancestor who had been a servant to a queen."

Lambert sat upright in his chair waiting for the story to unfold.

"Well, as things were quiet in the shop I thought I would see if I could find out more about this ancestor."

Lambert fought the temptation to tell the man to *get on with it* and listened as patiently as he could.

"So with the help of the young man and the solicitor we managed to trace her back to the fifteen hundreds."

"What was her name Mr Carter," said Lambert finally letting his desire to know overcome his manners.

"Mary Sidney."

Lambert recognised the name immediately. Sidney was her married name, having wed the poet Sir Henry Sidney, but her maiden name was Dudley. Mary Dudley was the eldest daughter of John Dudley, Duke of Northumberland, and one of Queen Elizabeth's most intimate confidantes during the early years of her reign. Her duties included nursing the queen through smallpox and acting as her mouthpiece to diplomats. A sister of Robert Dudley, Earl of Leicester, she always remained loyal to her family. She retired from court life in 1579 to her husband's castle in Ludlow, from where he carried out his duties as President of the Welsh Marshes after serving the queen in Ireland for many years. Who better to have at the queen's side during her pregnancy and confinement in Alnwick. But how could the letter have come into her possession? Surely Dudley would not have given it to her for fear it would fall into the wrong hands, sealing his fate and that of the queen.

"What about my letter Professor Lambert?"

The old man's question startled Lambert back into the present.

"Is it genuine? That Lady Sidney was a lady in waiting to the queen so it would make sense for her to have a letter written by the queen."

"I'm sorry Mr Carter, the letter turned out to be a forgery, albeit a very good one. I've only just got the final results back from the various tests we have carried out."

"That's a shame," said the old man. "I would have sworn that was the genuine thing."

"From what you've just said, I would say that somebody forged the letter to hurt the queen. Perhaps Mary intercepted it and hid it to avoid any trouble."

As Lambert said his goodbyes to the dealer promising to return the letter as soon as he could, a promise he knew he could never fulfil, an idea began to form in his mind.

"Well that certainly adds weight to the conclusion that it was genuine," said Hughes after hearing Lambert recount the story.

"But why would she hide the letter?" Hughes continued. "She would have known its contents would cost her brother his head and her mistress the throne."

"What if Dudley never received the letter," Lambert replied. "He was more than 300 miles away. It would have taken a few days to arrive and needed to pass through several hands. The risk of someone opening it would have been too great given its contents."

"So why not burn it?" said Hughes.

The man from Kew had retrieved the letter from a filing cabinet and the two men stared at the parchment in silence trying to put themselves into the mind of the woman who held the life of her brother and the throne of her mistress in her hands.

"I guess we'll never know," said Lambert finally. "But its importance has not diminished during the 400 years it lay hidden in that trunk."

Glendower Estate, Scottish Highlands, May 2010

"Look, I can understand the need for extra security after what has happened, but why would a madman want *me* dead?"

The head of the team assigned to protect the Scottish First Minister had to use all his twenty five years' experience in close protection and security to keep his thoughts to himself. Instead he uttered, through a steady gaze and imperceptibly gritted teeth, the words that would ensure he received his pension.

"Mr Ross, sir. I understand you received a full briefing this morning on the situation and the background?"

"Yes, yes. You can bring as many of your trigger happy gunslingers with you as you want, but I am not cancelling my holiday. It's one of the rare occasions I get to really relax. If you had told me the English Government was out to kill me then I really would be worried."

Paul Ross rose from his chair and looked out of the window at the magnificent view of the Highland estate of Glendower as it swept down to the banks of the loch. It was a beautiful, still day and the distant mountains reflected off the water like a mirror. He would never get used to the way it made him feel.

"How on earth have these people managed to gain access to the sort of information and equipment to carry out these crimes? Aren't you meant to know what's going on before it happens?"

Clearly Ross was not someone who had national security high on his agenda and why should it be, for as head of the devolved Scottish Parliament that was all taken care of down at the vipers nest he called Westminster.

Ross had been elected as the leader of the Scottish Devolution Party five years before, and First Minister after the nation's parliamentary election two years later. He was the first Scottish leader to have a working majority in the Scottish Parliament, which meant his party could pass any law it chose without having to make any concessions to those halfwits in the Labour Party. Or worse still, have them block legislation which he felt was the wish of the majority of Scottish people. He had fought his way to his present position through a combination of hard work, determination and when necessary, the odd bloody nose. No one who had been raised and survived in the tenement buildings of the Govern area of Glasgow, could have done so without learning quickly how to look after themselves in a fight. But he was blessed with one thing that many of his contemporaries were not; intelligence. He had earned a scholarship at the local grammar school under a programme for disadvantaged gifted children and from there progressed to Edinburgh University and a first class degree in political science and economics, the first Govern boy to achieve that accolade. After spending five years in London as a research assistant and secretary to the then leader of the Scottish group of Labour MPs in the English Parliament in

Westminster, he secured a job as a trade union representative in a Glasgow shipyard. This was the early eighties and the Thatcher Tory Government was hell-bent on destroying the power of the unions. He led numerous walk-outs and manned many picket lines during those early years and vowed he would see the day when he was in a position to reverse the laws put in place at that time which he firmly believed denied Scottish working men and women the right to withdraw their labour. That was the only true weapon they had against the rich and powerful who would be happy to see a return to the mid-nineteenth century before trade unions existed. Ross was a hard man who had learned to curb many of the natural instincts that dominated the first fifteen years of his life, including the instinct reaction to punch anyone who tapped him on the shoulder from behind. He had spent his life fighting against one thing or another. From thugs on his estate as a boy, people constantly telling him he could never make it out of the life assigned for his sort, to the political elite who had tried everything to undermine the rise to his present position. During those years he had found little time for the pleasures of life. He had married a Govern girl and raised two healthy children and he had remained faithful over the years despite numerous opportunities. But that was not the passion which made his soul sing. There were only two things that made Paul Ross truly happy. From an early age he had formed a connection with the magnificent land that was Scotland. He would walk miles over the hills and mountains and as he grew older, he had learned the skills that enabled him to enjoy every inch of his homeland. As his influence grew he was invited to visit many of the great estates and fish in some of the most famous salmon streams in the world. For the last few years the opportunity to indulge his passion had been restricted by the demands of his job. But he had always managed to find an excuse to spend some time in the glens and mountains and these MI5 Sassenachs with their wild story about a madman with a desire to take on the English throne, had provided a perfect excuse.

"Listen sonny," he turned from the window, "I'm not going anywhere and that's a fact. If you think I'll be spending the next few weeks in a bunker somewhere forget it."

The MI5 man sighed.

"With your permission, I'll continue the work on securing the estate as quickly as possible."

Ross looked the Englishman straight in the eye as he rose.

"That's fine, so long as I don't keep tripping over your people every time I wander into some long grass."

The agent gave a weak smile and excused himself. Ross waited until the door had closed and then a little longer to ensure no one was likely to enter. His secretary had flown to Greece the day before so she would not be disturbing him. He crossed the room and unlocked a door which revealed a small storage area within, lined with shelving. It contained various stationary and office equipment including a copier, and a small safe. Ross looked around until his eyes rested on his goal. He was suddenly aware that someone had entered the room. He froze and waited for a head to appear. Nothing. Gingerly taking a pace toward the door, he carefully peered around. Across the room a waitress was laying out the contents of a small tray on his desk, which included a water container and glass.

"Hello sir, I hope this is what you wanted?" said the girl, not looking up from her work.

"Yes, that's fine. Thank you very much," he replied, emerging into the room.

"Is there anything else I can fetch you sir?"

"No, thanks, that will be all."

Ross ushered the girl out before returning to his original spot. The room was at least ten degrees cooler than the outer office, but that was fine and made the location even more appealing. He lifted a small package, one of two present, off the shelf where it had been placed behind a set of toner cartridge boxes and away from prying eyes. He would return for the other soon. The package was around twelve by six inches and eight inches deep and was made from white polystyrene which made an unpleasant squeaking noise when handled. Removing the tape that was securing the two halves of the box, he lifted the lid with an air of anticipation. He had not had the time for this for at least two weeks and he needed it as soon as possible. Four items were set into moulded sections of the box. Ross lifted each in turn and studied them with pleasure, carefully returning each to its proper place, then carried the box to his desk in the main room. He again removed each of the four items and placed them on the tray that had been left moments earlier. A spoon, a glass, a bottle and a small jar. He discarded the glass as being too large for his purpose and retrieved one from his case. He removed the screw-top off the jar and gazed at its contents, tempted to partake immediately. But he resisted as, for him, the ritual was as important as the result. He set the jar down and carried out the same routine on the bottle, except that he poured some of its clear liquid into the glass. He picked up the tiny spoon and teased a spoonful of the jar into its tiny bowl. He could wait no longer and felt his arm rise and deposit the contents on his tongue, letting it sit there for what seemed an age whilst the impact burst all around his mouth. After thirty seconds he picked up the glass and drank the liquid in one hit.

"Wonderful," he whispered to himself. He repeated the ritual twice more before quickly replacing the items in the box and secreting it behind the boxes, locking the door and striding out of the office to get changed. What was called for now was a long walk by the river. Very few people knew about the one vice in Paul Ross's life. If it became known it would destroy his reputation as a hardnosed Scottish politician who had dragged himself out of the ghetto to be the hero of the working classes. It would also make him seem unpatriotic and one of the rich elite he despised.

"He's being as stubborn as we feared, Andrew."

James Kennedy, the MI5 liaison heading the special SO12 team assigned to protect Ross was clearly exasperated.

"Don't worry James, as long as you can erect a screen around and over the estate we should be fine."

"I guess, but he doesn't seem to realise just how vulnerable he could be. After what happened to Bradstock, we really have to treat this like a wartime threat."

"Just keep everyone on high alert and call me if anything unusual happens."

Andrew terminated the call and sat back in his chair in the operations room at Thames House. He was all too aware of the facts. The killer or killers had been able to avoid every security resource they had at their disposal. Every lead they had discovered had led them up a blind alley, eating up precious time and resources. Whoever had sent the package to Albert Spice must have been directly involved with bringing down that plane. The card on the dummy device had no handwritten number, the most obvious evidence that it was a red herring. They had correctly predicted that it would deflect attention from Bradstock's demonstration and cause them to lower their guard, but there was to be no repeat of that. The team covering Ross was one of a dozen that had been hastily assembled to prevent anyone harming the highest profile figures in the UK. As well as the prime minister, the leaders of all the major parties and their deputies had been covered. Most had readily agreed to the suggestion to keep a low profile and thereby make it easier to create an effective protective screen. The PM's team had been briefed to limit his time in open areas and others had reduced their public appearances. But Andrew knew that however comprehensive the shield around these figures, they were all terribly vulnerable.

On a craggy hillside some hundred feet above the river valley a lone gunman watched the tartan-clad figure striding along the river bank through a high-powered telescopic sight. It would be so easy to put a bullet through his skull from this distance. The fool was making things even easier by stopping every fifty yards to gaze into the river. There are more than a hundred armed security personnel on the estate trying to protect him and he doesn't do a thing to help himself. The cross hairs of the sight moved on to the targets right ear, no need to compensate for the wind at this distance. The Glendower estate covered more than 7,000 acres and was one of the largest in the Highlands. Within its boundaries were rivers, streams, hills and valleys on open and concealed ground and was like a training camp for the special services teams. The nearest public roads were ten miles away in either direction. To reach this point undetected would take a trained soldier, avoiding the aerial and ground surveillance net and travelling mostly at night, over sixteen hours. The owner of the Accuracy L115A3 sniper's rifle, capable of killing a man at nearly two miles, had reached this position in seventeen.

"You up there yet, Taffy?"

The SAS corporal's earpiece sprang into life and roused him from his relative slumber.

"Yes sarge, arrived about ten minutes ago, it was easier than I thought," he replied smiling to himself.

"Eleven actually. We picked you up on the surface radar about a mile out. You crossed a small piece of open flat ground and bingo it pinged right back. After that it took Jimmy and Pete about five minutes to get a visual on you, but a decent try."

Two dirty faces appeared as if by magic from behind rocks a hundred feet away, both grinning like monkeys. The corporal had been dropped off at the outer perimeter and tasked with testing the capabilities of the team to detect and apprehend an infiltrator. After the events at Farnborough, they were taking no chances.

"Lucky bastards," he cursed to himself.

The sergeant turned to his superior who was standing over him in the mobile command centre set up in the grounds of the estate. The captain was not grinning, in fact he was not smiling at all.

"Not good enough Jackson, not nearly good enough."

"No sir. I'll arrange to have the radar units repositioned so they can pick someone up nearer the road."

The captain gave a curt nod and negotiated the three small steps from the command vehicle. Waiting for him was the MI5 liaison. Bloody civvies, he thought to himself as he crossed the gravel covered ground between them. Kennedy raised both eyebrows to ask the question. "Everything working perfectly Mr Kennedy. We picked him up before he could have caused any problems. MI5 can relax, our Scottish cousin is in safe hands."

Paul Ross had a passion for caviar and vodka, but not just any caviar. Only the finest Beluga harvested from sturgeon caught in the Volga River in southern Russia where it enters the Caspian Sea, would suffice, washed down with the world's best vodka. His passion had only been aroused a few years before whilst on an exchange visit to Moscow. A government official, keen to see what information concerning the submarine base at Faslane on the Clyde he could prise from a Scottish Minister who obviously hated the English, had taken him to dinner at one the best restaurants in the city. Ross had known from the start what the official was planning, but if he wanted to wine and dine him on his expense account, that was fine by him. The Russian may not have been an expert at espionage, but he had certainly awakened something in Ross which had lain dormant for all of his previous fifty-odd years. The Cafe Pushkin was famous for serving the world's best caviar and Ross had spent the evening being introduced and tutored in the finer details of its delights. If you eat caviar than there is only one drink that can accompany it, or so he was told at the time. So as well as the caviar Ross had sampled a dozen or more vodkas including Stolichnaya and Kauffman. The official had become a friend since then and if Ross was honest with himself, been the beneficiary of the odd slip of the tongue on how he felt about the presence of nuclear missiles on Scottish soil. But none of that was top secret and he was not in a position to do anything about it... yet.

National Archives, Kew, London, May 2010

"George had three children, the oldest of which was Andrew born in 1805," said Jenny, looking up at a bank of several computer screens as Lambert entered the research room at Kew. "We know he joined the navy at fifteen as his father kept a journal which he left to the parish on his death."

"That's a stroke of good fortune," said Lambert handing her a coffee.

"I've got a couple of archivists looking at the Royal Naval Officer Service records now to see what they can find."

"That's assuming he wasn't just an ordinary seaman," replied Lambert sitting next to her and casting his eye over the information displayed on the monitors.

"George mentioned that he had received his commission as a Lieutenant in 1830, so we know he should be included in the records," said Jenny.

"So we have yet another link with the list on the *English Monarchy* website," Lambert grimaced as he remembered why he seldom drunk the coffee at

Kew. A man entered the room and handed Jenny a file which she quickly read.

"Seems like Andrew had a colourful career, rising up the ranks to captain his own ship. He was on board *HMS Nemesis* when it was involved in sinking a number of Chinese Junks during the Opium wars."

"That's great Jenny, but I've had Andrew Larkin on the phone and he's not going to be interested in what battles his namesake was involved in. I think we need to concentrate on getting the family tree completed so we can identify this terrible person as soon as possible." It was the nicest rebuke she had ever received, but it still hurt coming from him and it clearly showed on her face. "I'm sorry darling," he said taking her in his arms. "Am I being a grumpy old man?" she raised her head from his chest and smiled.

"Yes, so you can bloody well stay in here and help me."

They spent the next few days working their way through the records, both digital and physical, available to them under the one roof. Andrew had three children, the oldest of which was Joseph. His occupation was listed as 'Land Agent' in the 1871 census, one of the first to capture this data. The same document listed his son Henry as being eleven and all were living in the London Borough of Richmond-on-Thames. It transpired that his oldest son John, born in 1890, had been a minor celebrity. Having failed in his attempt to find a career in commerce, he found his vocation playing football for London team Clapton Orient, up until the outbreak of the war in 1914. Peter Hughes at Kew correctly guessed that he would have probably volunteered as did so many young men at the time. He located his service records through the online system and discovered he had enlisted with the First Battalion of the London Regiment soon after Britain had declared war with Germany in August 1914. After seeing action in the Battles of Aubers and Bois Grenier, he was killed on the morning of 1st July 1916, the first day of the great Battle of the Somme in a diversionary attack on the German stronghold of Gommecourt. Hughes showed Tom and Jenny a picture of his headstone in the British Cemetery No.2.

"One of more than 900,000 young British men killed in four years of carnage."

"I guess John's time playing football is what led to the killer targeting Matthew Black," Jenny noted solemnly.

"The fickle finger of fate," said Tom.

Glendower Estate, Scotland, May 2010

Ross spent the next two days wandering the estate, taking in the hills and valleys and salmon fishing in the streams. His family would be joining him in a couple of days, which he did not mind. But it was during these times of solitude, out in the air of his beloved land, that he felt truly at peace. On the third evening he was walking the last mile back to the main house as the spring sun began to lose its power as it began the last part of its daylight journey. In this part of Scotland the days lasted nearly seventeen hours at this time of year, but now the shadows were beginning to lengthen and the light had softened from the brightness of the mid-afternoon. He glanced at his watch as the house came into view; an hour before dinner would be served. He was famished and was looking forward to tasting some of yesterday's catch. He had not had a chance to visit the white boxes since nearly bumping into the staff girl and was beginning to feel a little twitchy. Over the years his love of the fish eggs and white spirit had grown into an obsession bordering on addiction. He was not an alcoholic and knew it was not the seventy per cent proof spirit alone that he craved, nor did he ever take more than three glasses at once. It was the combination of the delicate taste of the eggs as they hit his tongue, with the fiery liquid exploding in his mouth. It was the ritual of the spoon and shot glass. And above all it was the fact that it was his secret.

He had received the second box at his office in Holyrood by special delivery, literally as he had been leaving for the break. He was surprised and more than a little embarrassed to be confronted with the motorcycle courier holding the package in the crowded reception area of the parliament building. His supplies normally came directly to his constituency home in Gifnock from a specialist dealer in London. He had stopped taking gifts from Vasily years ago, but always took his advice on what to buy and he was never wrong. He knew straight away what the white polystyrene box contained and also knew it would be given to the security team on site for scanning and checking. But he was in a hurry and the last thing he wanted was a dozen prying eyes gawping at a bottle of expensive vodka, and a jar of caviar, not to mention a small silver spoon. The press would have a field day with that and he shuddered as he imagined the headlines. He had been able to get hold of the box and exit the building quickly explaining as he went that he was expecting the books and had to rush to miss the traffic. It had seemed like an eternity until he was alone at home and could reveal the surprise package. He was half-way through opening it when the thought struck him that it might not hold the expected contents.

"Too late now," he said out loud as he quickly removed the lid like a bowl covering a spider. There was a letter from Vasily. The box contained what the Russian described as the greatest find in a century. A species of Sturgeon thought extinct for more than 200 years had been discovered in a lake in the Sevan National Park in Georgia. This fish was thought to produce the finest caviar ever tasted and had only been given to czars and visiting royalty. In the box was a small sample from an early batch. Knowing how much he would appreciate it, Vasily wanted his good friend to be one of the first to try it. The Scot had tried to call to thank him although the letter had said that he would be at his Dacha by the time the package arrived and he had promised his family he would not take any calls and emails for at least a month. But his mobile was not working properly and he gave up after a couple of attempts. By the time Ross entered the main house he had decided that he could wait no longer to have this new taste on his tongue. He bounded up the stairs to his bedroom, dismissing the dozen staff and security in the hall with an airy wave.

"See you at dinner." As soon as he closed the door he threw off his outer coat and jacket and headed for the small walk-in closet. He had moved the box the same day he had arrived, guessing correctly that he would never be left alone in his office long enough to carry out his ritual. But he could still find the solitude he needed in his bedroom. He carried the box to the small desk with the reverence of a religious relic, and placed it in the centre. He had everything he needed and removed each piece before casting the packaging on to the adjacent bed. Ten minutes later he stood gazing out of the first floor window over the countryside feeling a contented man. This had indeed been the best caviar he had ever tasted.

National Archives, Kew, London, May 2010

"Here we are," said Hughes laying the music hall poster on the desk, "Archie Moore, comedian."

Tom picked up the poster for the Palace Theatre in London and located the reference towards the bottom of the list of performers headed by the singer Randolph Scott.

"Wasn't he famous for the song *On Mother Kelly's Doorstep?*" asked Lambert.

"I have no idea Tom, how on earth do you know that? I didn't know you were a fan?"

Lambert laughed. "I seem to remember tracing the history of a family that had a music hall background some years ago and his name must have come up at some point. But how did you manage to find this?"

"You'd be surprised what we hold here now," replied Hughes.

"Archibald lived in London, but I can't seem to locate any children for him and there is no census data I can search," said Jenny. She hoped the innocent question would prompt Hughes to explain the hundred year disclosure rule that prohibits the publishing of detailed information from the 1921 census onwards, and more importantly what he could do to get around the problem.

"I'm afraid you will have to wait until 2021 before you can search those records," he replied predictably.

"Given the situation, can't we make a case for being given access to the original data?" asked Lambert.

"Well I suppose we could," answered Hughes thoughtfully. "But nothing has been digitalised yet so we would be searching through thousands of hand written returns. It would take too long. "But we know they lived in London so that narrows it down," said Jenny hopefully.

Hughes, who had taken a seat at one of the computers in the research room, did not answer. Jenny and Tom looked at each other but said nothing, aware that he was engrossed in an idea. After a few minutes he suddenly sat back on the chair.

"There!"

The two rushed to see the contents of the screen.

"Archibald Moore and his wife Daisy, living in Edmonton North London."

"The electoral roll," said Tom.

"But I'm surprised his wife was listed, when did women get the vote?"

"1927," said Hughes smiling. "This was the first one to include every woman over twenty one so we've struck lucky."

Jenny had already returned to her own terminal and begun a search of births deaths and marriages in that part of London.

"There can't be too many Archibald Moore's in Edmonton," said Lambert, joining her.

Twenty minutes later they had printed several certificates and convened in Hughes's office.

"Married at twenty to Daisy Applegate," said Jenny laying a marriage certificate dated November 1910 on the desk. "And more importantly," she produced copies of two birth certificates, "Frederick in 1914 and Mary in November 1916."

"Fantastic work Jenny." Lambert picked up the copies and studied them. "We can link Archie to the killers list by virtue of his profession as an entertainer," he said pointing to Hughes's computer that showed the latest table from the *English Monarchy* site. "Bryan Stewart was the thirteenth victim, which means Archie's son must have been involved in business in some way as we know that poor Mr Bradstock could certainly be classed as a *Merchant.*"

"We need to act quickly to bring the family tree up to date as we are only two generations from the killer," said Jenny heading back to the research room. Before she could reach the door she paused and stopped as a strange sound emitted from Hughes's computer. Leaning over the desk she gasped at the blood-stained image of the queen moving slowly across the screen accompanied by a trumpet fanfare. Hughes hurried from the office and she sat at the keyboard. "Nothing is working," she said clicking the mouse and pressing various keys. The image faded to the home page of the National Archives where a message in the same style as the rest of the site immediately caught everyone's eye.

*Due to a technical error this site is unavailable until
further notice.*

"What's happened?" said Lambert. At that moment his cell phone rang as Hughes burst through the door looking ashen-faced.

"The whole site has been taken down by some sort of cyber-attack."

Glendower Estate, Scotland, May 2010

"Poison. Bloody poisoned." Larkin watched as Anthony Neild burst into the library of the estate. "You lot have made us the laughing stock of the world, although what there is to snigger about I for one am at a loss to understand."

Gathered around Andrew were the various heads of the units assigned to protect the now deceased First Minister.

"Larkin, fill me in on the facts known so far." He rose and Neild took the vacated chair. Andrew had arrived by helicopter four hours earlier and had been fully briefed by Kennedy, who sat in a corner, trying his best to disappear into the chair. Andrew stood with his back to the fireplace and explained the events as they were known, some ten hours after Ross's body had been discovered. Dinner had been arranged for 8pm and the First Minister was always very punctual. The house maid had tried to get a response at 7.30pm when he failed to show for drinks.

"Just before 9pm we got one of the army lads to force the door." Andrew drew breath to begin describing the scene.

"Why did it take more than an hour to find someone to knock the bloody door down," barked the head.

"It didn't sir," replied Andrew. "The housemaid didn't want to cause a fuss and assumed he had fallen asleep. It wasn't until the call for dinner that one of the other guests mentioned his absence."

"So he might have been saved had we reached him earlier?" said the captain heading up the SAS contingent.

"I doubt that," said Andrew "We've had a preliminary report back on the substance. It's a very old type of poison, often used in medieval times. Apparently it acts very quickly, paralysing within a couple of minutes. Heart stops within three or four, all over in five, maximum. If we didn't know better it would look like a heart attack."

"That's why he had no chance to raise the alarm." The section head rose and attempted to pace the room. This proved impossible and he shuffled to the fireplace and signalled Andrew to sit. "What's this I hear about caviar and bloody vodka?"

Everyone in the room seemed to shift uneasily in their chairs for a moment, each glad he was not the one tasked with explaining the discovery of the contents of the polystyrene packaging.

"Seems Mr Ross had a thing for caviar, but not just any caviar. We found another package in a locked storeroom in his office downstairs. We've not had a chance to get that off for tests yet." Andrew went on to describe the other items found in both packages and gave a one minute overview of caviar and vodka consumption amongst the rich and famous.

"Could he honestly be described as rich or famous?" asked the section head.

"It gets worse," said Andrew gingerly as Neild's head snapped up and looked him straight in the eye. "The package that killed him contained a letter. It was from Vasily Rominsky. He's a well known agent of the SRV. Ex-KGB. Seems he'd been linked with Ross since a visit to Moscow about five years ago. We're getting Moscow office to dig up some more details." Neild moved to a window overlooking the vast estate and stood motionless for what seemed like an eternity, weighing up the potential ramifications of what he had just heard. The First Minister of Scotland was a Russian informer who liked secretly eating the most expensive caviar money could buy off a silver spoon.

"I want this whole thing locked down with immediate effect."

May 2010

The killer tapped quickly on the keys of the laptop, bringing the *English Monarchy* website fully up to date with details of the death of the Scottish traitor. Caviar? Who would have thought a boy from the wrong side of Glasgow would abandon his roots so completely. A quick, anonymous email to a few newspapers should decide tomorrow's headlines. Things were coming together better than could have been hoped for. All the necessary planning for the final, glorious event was almost concluded with just one or two items to be placed in their correct locations prior to the big day, only two weeks away. It had been even easier than anticipated to obtain the passes and clearances to gain access to even the most sensitive locations. How the British establishment liked to pride itself on how clever it was at keeping its secrets in, and unwanted visitors out. This blind arrogance made it all the easier. A screen appeared on the laptop for the issue of passes for a forthcoming event. The page belonged to the intranet of the Metropolitan Police Special Branch and access was only available to a handful of people. It had taken the killer less than ten minutes to break into the main site and armed with the passwords taken from a convenient word file that a secretary kept on her desktop to remember the dozens she needed, had issued an access all areas pass. A few keystrokes later and that same name appeared on the rota for officers required to attend that same event. No one would know of this deception as to even the most expert IT technician, the requests appeared to emanate from an internal workstation. A few more enabled a check of the GCHQ Echelon database files. It made sense to keep an eye on what they were up to as they had almost stumbled on the source IP of one location. Given they were using some of the most powerful computers on the planet a few close shaves were inevitable, but keeping one step ahead and being vigilant had paid dividends.

"Let's see what our friend Mr Larkin has been up to."

Andrew's Outlook page appeared on the screen and the killer noted the meeting scheduled the next day. A frown crossed the face as two instantly recognizable names were amongst the attendees. Those troublesome genealogists were the one area that had not been foreseen. That damn letter had been discovered at the worst possible time. They were getting closer and now they had established a direct link through the DNA sampling of George Moore and the queen, it was only a matter of time before they discovered the truth. Something had to be done to slow them down.

MI5 Headquarters, London, May 2010

The conference room at Thames House fell silent as the director general entered the room, followed by Anthony Neild. A few of the twenty people in attendance who were still filling coffee cups, quickly took their places as the DG moved to the head of the large oval mahogany table and scanned the faces until his gaze locked on two that were unfamiliar. Sensing the unspoken question Andrew rose.

"Sir, this is Professor Lambert and his assistant Ms Cross. He is the genealogist who discovered the letter and has been tracking down the descendants of the queen's child."

The DG nodded in Lambert's direction and sat giving the signal for the meeting to commence. Neild stood and beckoned for Larkin to join him.

"The DG and I have come directly from a meeting of COBRA," he began. "After the latest murder they are, to put it mildly, in a state of shock and fear."

Neild produced a copy of *The Daily Mail* which he tossed into the centre of the table.

"Is this your idea of a lock down Larkin?" he asked as every eye in the room spotted the headline *McCaviar Politician Slain at Highland Retreat*.

"That's the least of our worries," the DG continued. "The fact that this killer was able to penetrate such a comprehensive security operation is of true concern." The DG fell silent but his eyes were firmly locked on Andrew. "Perhaps you would be kind enough to bring us up to date Mr Larkin." Neild motioned for Andrew to take the stage.

"Let's start with the leak," he said as he walked around the table and another headline flashed on the large monitor that almost filled one wall. "An email giving just enough information to appear credible was received last night by the editors of the major news organisations, and all at exactly the same time."

"Suggesting?" said Neild.

"That whoever sent it had a reasonable level of technical aptitude. These particular addresses are not in the public domain and are used for private communications," replied Andrew scrolling through several screen shots of equally embarrassing headlines. "We've been unable to locate any, but the indications are each mail had a separate source.

"Our friend?" the DG suggested.

"It has all the signs, sir."

"We ran a check on all the people who have access to those email addresses and don't believe any of those could have been responsible." Jackie Crowther chipped in, glancing in Andrew's direction.

"Move on," the DG ordered.

The screen filled with footage of a building reception area.

"We know the caviar that killed Ross was delivered to him by a courier as he left the Scottish Parliament in Edinburgh, as it was captured on these CCTV images, but it appears he was able to avoid having the package scanned and searched as would normally be the case for any incoming mail."

"I doubt he would have wanted anyone delving too much into the contents," said the DG. Andrew went on to explain how, although the likelihood was small because of the *English Monarch's* calling card, MI6 had made discreet enquiries with the Russians and had been assured that it had not been sent by Vasily Rominsky. The package had been booked in at a walk-in depot in Manchester a week before it was delivered with very specific instructions on when and how it was to be passed to Ross.

"However tight the security ring we had at the estate, we were relying on his cooperation. The killer knew this was his weakness and using the poison meant he never needed to come within a hundred miles of the place."

"Very clever," said Neild. "But how are we going to stop him getting to the queen?" Larkin looked across at Lambert and he stood.

"Professor Lambert is going to give us an update on the search for the descendant of Angus Moore. I still believe this is our best chance of identifying the killer."

Lambert walked to the large monitor which now showed the Moore family tree.

"As you can see we've been able to trace the lineage from Angus's birth in 1576. It took a great deal of effort and some good fortune to find him as you can imagine his existence had remained secret for more than 400 years."

The DG shuffled in his chair as Lambert began to tell the story of how he and Jenny had worked through the various clues to find Angus's son Richard.

"Thank you professor," interrupted Neild "I'm sure this is a fascinating story, but sadly one we don't have time for today." Andrew gestured for him to continue with a discrete *speed it up* motion of his right hand.

"We've located a descendant, Archibald, who was born in London 1914. His oldest son was Frederick." Lambert paused and Neild looked at him and then Andrew. "That's when the National Archives site was taken down."

"For how long?" asked Neild.

"The attack not only caused the site to crash but once inside the hacker loaded a programme that systematically wiped the data from every server and there was nothing that could stop it." Neild looked over at a young man dressed in jeans who was sat next to Jackie.

"Have you had a look at this?"

"Yep, its top quality work, I would have been proud of it myself."

"I assume it's too much to hope they left any traces we can follow up."

The man shook his head. "We're helping the IT guys to reload the backups but it's a big job that will take a few days."

"In the meantime we're searching through the paper documents and hope to get the help of some of the commercial sites who have their own databases," said Lambert.

"No one we can't control gets to hear anything about this," said Neild firmly.

The professor looked uneasily across at Andrew who gently shook his head.

"This could well be the work of the killer which means he knows we are hot on his heels," Lambert continued. "Frederick is the fourteenth descendant, so it shouldn't take us long to find number sixteen."

"Get yourself over there as soon as we're finished and call on whatever resources you need to get this information back online," Neild ordered the young IT man as he turned his attention back to Lambert. "Are you positive that this search will lead to the killer?" The genealogist paused before giving his reply.

"Mr Neild, I can't answer your question as I'm not in the law enforcement business, I'm an academic. But what I can tell you is that we're close to concluding our search for the descendant of someone who, as the DNA evidence shows, is almost certainly related to Queen Elizabeth I." Lambert put his hand on Jenny's shoulder as he spoke.

"The evidence is so strong that I think we can be sure of this," said Andrew.

"You're the one who's sure Larkin." Neild pointed out, distancing himself from any potential disaster.

Andrew ran through the security arrangements that had been put in place for the whole royal family, and especially the queen who was refusing to remain out of the public eye. Resources being utilised included elements from MI5, special branch and sections of the armed forces including the SBS and SAS, who were checking every venue and the routes to and from as never before. Armed guards were being stationed inside a two-mile *ring of steel* at least two days before any event with constant monitoring for explosives and any attempt to interfere with the communications infrastructure. All royal vehicles were being kept under twenty-four-hour guard and searched every twelve hours. All personnel that would come within half a mile of Her Majesty had been carefully vetted and personally approved by their commanding officer.

"She has agreed to some minor changes to her travel arrangements and allowed some extra physical protection such as bullet proof screens, but it's a logistical nightmare."

"That sounds very impressive," said the DG, rising. "I seem to remember similar assurances being given before." The DG rose, thanked everyone present and headed for the door.

"Larkin, the DG wants a more detailed run down of our arrangements for the 15th," said Neild beckoning several other attendees to follow them.

Parliament Square, May 15th 2010, , 10.30am

The State Opening of Parliament is the main ceremonial event and start of the British Parliamentary year. The queen's speech sets out the government's agenda and business for the year ahead, and gives an outline of the policies and legislation they propose. It is the only time where The Sovereign, in whose name Parliament exists, and the two chambers, the Houses of Lords and Commons, meet. It is a glittering state occasion with all the pomp and ceremony for which Britain is famous.

The route for the queen's journey from Buckingham Palace to the Palace of Westminster was well known. In fact the parliamentary website provided a downloadable file which included a useful map showing every detail and a timetable of events. For a country well-known for its obsessive secrecy, the details of the whereabouts of the monarchy were very public knowledge. The special team set up to organise the massive security operation designed to protect their ultimate employer, knew this and made their plans accordingly. The route of the procession would take the queen's horse-drawn carriage from the gates of Buckingham Palace and down Pall Mall. Just before Admiralty Arch, the procession turns right into Horse Guards Road. It then leaves the public highway opposite the Guards Division Memorial and heads across Horse Guards Parade, site of the 2012 Olympic beach volleyball, and emerges into the courtyard of the Household Calvary Museum on Whitehall. It then passes through a narrow set of iron gates set in between the famous arches, home to the two mounted members of the household calvary, where thousands of visitors flock each day to admire the young men with statuesque stances, pristine uniforms and highly polished brass helmets complete with brightly coloured plumes. A tight right turn takes Her Majesty on to Whitehall itself, home to many of the great departments of the British State. The Ministry of Defence, the Cabinet office, Downing Street, The Foreign and Commonwealth office and finally on the corner of Parliament Square, the Treasury. Looking up to her left, she would see the 316 foot tower of the great bell, otherwise known as Big Ben. At the furthest point of the Palace of Westminster lies Victoria Tower, containing a large gated arch known as the Sovereign's Entrance. The queen's carriage enters at this point marking her arrival and the end of her journey. The authorities knew that the total distance measured one point two miles and that it would take around fifteen minutes to complete the journey in the horse-drawn transport, as it had been walked and ridden numerous times to determine several important criteria. Now a uniformed officer stood every ten yards, on each side of the route. Every building had been searched for explosives, secreted weapons and hiding places. On the top of each, and at many other vantage points, police and army marksman covered every inch of the route. As an added precaution two officers were stationed on each floor, one at the lift exit, and one on the stairs. Plain-clothed security staff, many armed, mingled with the crowd, searching for anything suspicious. Fortunately many of the buildings were state-owned and so made restricting access far simpler. Two police helicopters hovered above, gaining an overall picture of the scene. A third was stationed at Wandsworth heliport, located on the south side of the river, less than a mile upstream from Westminster Bridge. This contained a section from the Special Air Service, especially trained in hostage and terrorist attacks. Several unmarked vans were parked in the side streets along the route, some containing officers from the Metropolitan Police's SO14 armed response unit. Others were packed with the latest electronic surveillance equipment to enable the listening and possible jamming of communication devices that any threat might deploy. In total 2,300 men and woman were directly involved on the ground, with several hundred more behind the scenes. The

British taxpayer would be asked to find around £10million to finance the operation.

Andrew watched a bank of television screens showing images from various security cameras, plus the BBC coverage of the event. In the next room was the Gold Command Centre, the central operations room at New Scotland Yard, only a few hundred yards from Parliament Square. He could not think of a single thing that had been overlooked. He knew that the best minds in the country had been drafted in to oversee what was the biggest operation of its kind. But with the previous success of whoever was behind this twisted plan, nothing could be taken for granted. At least there is only *one* British queen to worry about, he thought.

"What do you think, Bill?" asked Andrew.

"Looks sound to me," replied Bill Frost, the special branch liaison officer from GCHQ. "My only worry is the pure logistics of finding so many uniformed officers. If I were a burglar, I'd have a busy day. Bound to leave things light elsewhere."

"I agree," said Andrew thoughtfully, "but there's not much can be done about that. The queen would not hear of cancelling or changing anything, so all we can do is cover every angle. At least she agreed to travel in a covered carriage."

They continued to monitor the screens and listen to the various units carrying out final checks. Andrew quickly became restless.

"I think I'll take a walk outside," he said.

"Don't be long, she leaves in twenty minutes," cautioned the special branch man.

"Actually I might mingle with the crowd, I've got my comms set on," replied Andrew, opening his coat to reveal the small radio receiver.

"You might need this," said Frost, pulling back his own jacket to reveal a gun holster under his arm.

"I'm still barred from carrying Bill, but thanks for the thought." As Andrew walked across the square he placed the small speaker in his ear. It required no wire so was invisible to all but the most observant. In his pocket he carried a small control that enabled him to switch across the various frequencies used by the different elements of the operation such as the SAS, special branch, and MI5. Each was fully encrypted preventing any prying ears from eavesdropping. However, not every radio could decode every channel, but Andrew's clearance gave him access to everything, whilst all anyone else would hear would be a series of high-pitched bleeps. He walked the half mile in a few minutes, crossed the grassed covered square to the far side, turned down the volume, and gazed up at the imposing statue of Sir Winston Churchill, the great wartime prime minister, perched atop a marble plinth. He was looking toward the Houses of Parliament. Such visions never failed to stir something deep inside Andrew. He knew that they could protect the queen from whatever threat lay in store, it was when things were at their worst that the British really came into their own.

He crossed the road and gazed up at the imposing site of St Stephen's Tower, better known as Big Ben. Andrew instinctively looked at his watch, not because he necessarily needed to know the time, but because he wondered if the great bell would sound whilst he was so close.

"Ten fifty five," he muttered to himself.

No bells for a while, but the queen would leave the palace in around fifteen minutes. She was scheduled to reach The Palace of Westminster at 11.20am. With an anticipated journey time of fifteen minutes, that left five minutes spare.

From where he stood, he could look down Whitehall. The Cenotaph, that iconic stone tribute to the dead of two World Wars and countless other more recent conflicts, was clearly visible in the centre of the road. But he could move no further. A sea of bodies, ten deep, were pressed against the steel barriers that lined the entire route. Facing him was a policewoman, her eyes searching the crowd for anything suspicious. The crowd was in good spirits, many waving Union Jacks and enjoying the early spring sunshine. Turning back, Andrew could see the brightly coloured stall where many of the flags and other tacky souvenirs could be bought. He made his way along the rear of the throng until he reached a specially prepared walkway. It was guarded by a uniformed constable. Andrew flashed his identity card and the man moved aside. He climbed a small flight of stairs that led to a raised platform that ran behind the pavement. He could see down onto the square and turning to his left, Whitehall. However the platform was crowded. Andrew found himself a small space at the rear and feeling in his pocket, raised the volume on his radio, and switched to the main police frequency. This gave the best overall picture of what was happening.

"General warning." The voice took on a sudden urgency. "Subject leaving point A in ten minutes, repeat ten minutes. All personnel to Yellow."

Andrew noticed the uniformed officers along the route suddenly jerk to attention. They had obviously heard the same message. He switched to the SAS channel, but heard nothing for several seconds. They were probably listening to the same frequency. The clever little radios would automatically override if a message came through for an individual on their particular frequency. Suddenly a voice broke into the silence.

"Team two move to red. Suspect seen on riverboat zone red alpha, Standby."

Andrew switched back to the police frequency, only to hear the chief constable's voice, giving his people a last minute speech. He held his hand near his mouth and glanced down at the tiny wireless microphone attached to his watch and switched to the special branch frequency.

"Base, this is Larkin. Patch me through to Bill Frost." After a few seconds the familiar voice filled his ear.

"No panic, Andrew. One of the marksmen thought he saw a boatman acting suspiciously. Poor bloke got a visit from a couple of SBS lads stationed in a fast inflatable. Nearly died of a heart attack."

"Serves him bloody right," said a relieved Andrew.

But it just showed how, despite the most meticulous planning, that it was simply impossible to provide a one hundred per cent cover for anyone.

"You coming back?" asked Frost.

"No, I think I'll stay out here now."

"Ok. If you need to get in touch quick, go to channel ninety. I'll get it set up as a direct link."

"Thanks Bill," said Andrew, "I've got my mobile as well."

Andrew decided he could not stand on the packed platform a moment longer. He descended the steps and after negotiating the crowd and a couple of checkpoints, found himself in the middle of the road. After just a few steps an officer broke from barrier duty and approached him. Andrew produced his ID card, and the officer retreated. He clipped the badge on his coat to avoid this happening every few paces, but he was glad to see everyone on their toes. The assassin could be disguised as anyone, and was hardly going to walk around looking like... well an assassin. But that was just the point, what did an assassin look like? As he paced along the road, studying the faces in the crowd, hoping something might strike a chord in his memory, a few of the more vocal called out.

"You famous, mate?"

"Show us yer legs."

Despite the seriousness of his task, Andrew could not help but smile and just stopped himself giving the crowd a royal wave. As he looked to his left he could see the modern windows of Portcullis House, the home to more than 200 MPs and the location of many committee hearings, somehow out of place with the other historic buildings. A voice cut into his ear.

"Subject leaving point A, repeat, subject leaving point A. All personnel to green."

He looked around him and could sense the atmosphere change. Quickening his pace, he noticed a police control van parked on a small piece of green, set back from the crowd at the corner of Birdcage Walk and the west side of the square. He found a gap in the barrier and forcing his way through, managed to make his way to the van. Inside, he was able to watch the royal procession as it passed through the outer-gate of the palace. He glanced at his watch, knowing it would take them around ten minutes to reach his location. He watched as the coaches made their way around the Queen Victoria Memorial and into the wide avenue of Pall Mall. A camera behind the party clearly showed Admiralty Arch in the distance, and beyond the tall, thin column of Nelson in Trafalgar Square. Although this route was not the most direct from the palace that was via Birdcage Walk and St George's Street, it allowed a far larger crowd to see the entourage. Andrew switched his radio to the frequency used by the police marksman. He heard a commentary given by the man closest to the procession. Each handing on to the next as they passed in and out of sight. So far so good. Perhaps the target was some other *queen*. How could you read into the mind of someone who could plan such crimes? But he knew that, unlike the prime minister, there was only one monarch who could possibly fit the profile.

"Andrew are you there, man?" The voice of Bill Frost, sounding unnerved.

"I'm here Bill, what's up?"

"That genealogist professor, what's his name, from the university has been trying to get you on your mobile."

"Tom Lambert," said Andrew, reaching into in his pocket and retrieving the phone. "Looks OK to me."

"He says he keeps getting a busy tone," said Frost.

"No problem I'll give him a call," said Andrew, beginning to dial.

"Andrew," said Bill quietly.

But Andrew could not hear for the bleep, bleep of the busy tone in his ear.

"Andrew, listen," the special branch man cut in. "He says he's found the last descendant.... Andrew, it's a woman."

11.00am

The killer stood, looking down Whitehall, her vantage point affording an uninterrupted view past the Cenotaph in one direction, and Parliament Square behind and to her left. To the right Westminster Bridge was less than a hundred yards distant. She could see the marksman on the top of the Treasury opposite and by following the lines of the Foreign Office, could make out another two. She had picked this spot very carefully, the buildings denying those gunmen nearest her a clear line of site. Those on the rooftops and windows surrounding the square would prove no problem as the distance was too great to risk a shot and the crowd would provide her with cover, whilst directly in front and to the right was an entrance to Westminster underground station, a possible escape route. Had she been standing in this spot on a normal day she would have been hit by a car or trampled by pedestrians within seconds as she was in the middle of the road next to a crossing point. She felt in her pocket for the small, simple mobile. It was identical to the one she had used on the pop singer in Hyde Park, and had proved itself most reliable. It had been remarkably easy to obtain the uniform and pass and arrange to be stationed in this position, much better than taking a chance by mingling with the crowd that would have meant getting over the barrier, and immediately alerting the security forces. This way she would gain those vital seconds needed to carry out the first stage of her plan. She looked to her right, at a policeman standing a few yards away, and smiled. If only the young fool knew he was looking at the future queen and avenger of her ancestors. He would soon be swearing a new oath of loyalty to her. Once the deed was done, she would announce she was the rightful heir. They could hardly try a member of the royal family for murder and anyway the foreigners, who had ruled this land since Elizabeth I, had murdered tens of thousands between them.

"Subject leaving point A, repeat, subject leaving point A, all personnel to green," the voice echoed in her earpiece and she smiled to herself.

"Excuse me officer, can you tell me how long before the queen arrives, only I've been here since last night," a middle-aged lady called out.

"Yes madam. She's just left the palace, so about fifteen minutes."

11.05 am

Andrew froze. A woman? But why not, it was just something that had never seriously crossed his mind.

"Bill, I can't get out on this blasted cell phone, can you patch me through to him?" Thirty seconds later the professor's voice came over Andrew's earpiece.

"Her name is Elizabeth Moore, Andrew. She would be twenty five years old. Father is, or was Peter Moore, a retired civil servant and local councillor who died last year."

"Address?"

"Not my department, I'm afraid but I've given the details to one of your colleagues."

"Thanks for all your help Tom, I hope it won't be in vain."

Andrew switched to the general channel. The carriages were still in the Mall, but would be here in just a few minutes. But what could he do? He switched to channel ninety.

"Bill, are you there?"

"Ahead of you," came the reply, "A team is on their way to an address in Croydon now. It's the parent's house, so she must still be living at home and Andrew, don't bother trying to use your cell, there's a problem with the system. Looks like someone may have overloaded the local cells."

Andrew felt helpless. Who could have access to the necessary information and equipment to jam the phone network? He knew it could be done, but only a few agencies had access to that level of expertise. He could never cross the fifteen or so miles before the queen reached her destination and even if he could, what could he do, even if the killer was there? He was just one of thousands, most of whom were in a better position to protect the queen and catch the killer than he. But she must be around here, now. Andrew spun around, searching the thousands of female faces. But she could be disguised as a man. This was hopeless. He stopped and leant on a set of railings that bordered one of the many grand buildings in the famous landmark area, head in hands. They were all powerless to do anything unless the killer made a move and all the odds were in her favour. What could he do? He didn't even have a gun. He cursed at the foolish actions that had put him in this position. The only good thing that had come from this whole affair had been meeting Jackie. He could hear the cheers of the crowd becoming louder as the procession emerged on to Whitehall from Horse Guards Parade. So far nothing unusual had happened but that only meant that each step along the route made the moment more likely. Andrew began to jog along the street, towards the procession. After a hundred yards, he stopped, seeing the queen's coach come into view. He could just make out the resplendent gold and red carriage pulled by four magnificent grey horses, one carrying a royal attendant. He turned and ran on, bumping into bystanders every few steps. He stopped and glanced around just as the lead horses passed.

"In a hurry, sir?"

A uniformed officer blocked Andrew's path. Andrew tried to ignore the remark and started to move away.

"No you don't, my lad." The policeman grabbed at Andrew's coat.

"Look you bloody idiot, I'm with MI5. If you don't let me go NOW I'll make sure you're on traffic duty until the day you get your pension."

Andrew backed off and reached for his pass. It was not on his coat where he had placed it a few minutes before.

"Where's your pass then Mr 'MI bloody five'?"

Andrew looked around, and to his relief saw the badge just a few yards behind him, lying on the ground.

"There it is."

He ran back and retrieved the pass and pushed it into the officer's face as he passed.

"Good work, constable."

The delay had enabled the carriages to gain a fifty-yard start on him.

"Andrew, it's Bill. No surprises. The house is empty and according to the neighbours, has been for a while. They're searching it now. I'll keep you up to date."

"Ok, thanks, Bill," Andrew replied.

That was to be expected. This killer was far too smart to leave anything worthwhile somewhere as easy to locate. She must have known we would trace the family tree eventually, why else leave the calling cards. He began to run again, for no particular reason, he realised, except that he knew that the killer was getting closer, the nearer the queen got to her destination. He could see the carriage in the distance. It took him a few seconds to notice that his earpiece had fallen silent. Bloody thing, he cursed to himself.

"Bill, are you there?" he looked up and noticed several of the police shaking their heads, pulling at their ears and looking at their colleagues. "Something's happened to the comms network," he said out loud. He reached into his pocket for his mobile, but remembered that, it too, had been out of action but in desperation punched a number and was again greeted with the busy tone. Over the next ten seconds Andrew experienced a growing realisation that something terrible was about to happen. He stood, rooted to the spot, not knowing what to do. Just then an explosion rang out.

Andrew froze, and together with every face in the crowd including police officers, security service personnel, sharpshooters on rooftops and thousands lining the route, turned to see one face of the giant clock of Big Ben shatter, creating a rainstorm of flying glass and metal.

11.08am

She watched the first police horses appear in the distance. It was no surprise as the voice in her ear had kept up a constant commentary, calling off predefined points. But even without this advantage, the cheers of the crowd would have warned her of the imminent arrival of the monarch. *Bloody German bitch*, she thought. As the group progressed, three mounted police officers, followed by six rows of four horseman of the Household Calvary appeared, trotting along at a sedate pace. The caravan stretched as far as she could see with several carriages, interspersed with horsemen from the Blues and Royals. Towards the rear she knew were the Range Rovers full of armed personal. She also knew that the calvary were not armed, apart from their ceremonial swords, but those in the cars would be on a high state of alert. Any sign of trouble even if they could not see it, would be communicated to them in an instant through the network of encrypted radios. Being forced to look over her shoulder was becoming tiresome, but her disguise required her to scan the crowd for would be assassins, not watch the pageantry. Soon it would begin and all the meticulous preparation would come to a glorious finale.

The lead horse was a hundred yards away. Soon they would slow as they crossed the junction into the Square. The hours of studying past royal processions had shown this happened every time. No amount of security would change that, the British were known for their traditions. She moved her hand into her pocket and feeling the cell phone, gently pressed one of the buttons. That would take out the network. Just a small device in the right location was all it would take. Half a mile away deep in the basement of New Scotland Yard, two tiny incendiary devices, responding to the specific frequency sent by the transmitter, blew the main processor unit of the central server that controlled the Tetra-based radio network encryption. Every message had to be routed through this one location to enable the total cross-communication that had been demanded, before it could be securely transmitted. With this unit destroyed, every radio message would be blocked for at least thirty seconds until the backup device was able to take over.

Redundancy was built into every computer system, particularly one as important as this. The second device blew this unit. The slim chance of both malfunctioning simultaneously, together with funding restrictions in the force had prevented a third device being installed.

Around her, colleagues began to notice the sudden termination of their commentary. An air of confusion began, each looking at each other. The young constable looked over and mouthed

"What's happened to the radio?"

She shrugged her shoulders in mock confusion. The lead horseman paused and looked behind, seeking reassurance from his colleagues that all was well. This slight delay was enough for those following to have to slow more noticeably to avoid a possible collision. By the time all six rows of Guards had slowed, the queen's carriage had to stop abruptly in a scene reminiscent of a motorway traffic jam. The killer looked directly at the queen's carriage which was alongside her now. She felt and pushed the second button.

The noise was deafening and the sight spectacular. Everyone stopped to gaze in shock and wonder as the centre of the famous clock erupted and cascaded to the ground in what seemed like slow motion. Everyone except for the killer who calmly walked forward two paces, opened the unlocked door of the queen's carriage and quickly placing one leg on the edge, pulled herself inside, closing the door behind. The young constable who had been just ten yards away did not even notice she had gone.

The queen and Prince Phillip sat alongside each other facing forward. The killer simply filled one of the seats opposite.

"Don't worry Ma'am," she said, "looks like something's happened to Big Ben. I'll accompany you for the rest of the journey as an extra precaution."

She drew a small pistol from her tunic.

"Bloody hell," said Phillip, rising "What in God's name is going on?"

The killer gently pressed him back into his seat and was barely able to suppress a smile.

"Best stay put sir, you never know what danger may be out there."

Now in his nineties, he was not in a position to argue. She could not resist a glance up at the tower to see the spectacular results of her handiwork. She had realised that it was too risky to place a large amount of explosives in the famous clock, they would have been discovered during the numerous and thorough searches carried out by the security services at Westminster. Instead she had arranged a visit to the palace, as any member of the public could do, and was able to strategically place a surprisingly small device in front of the clock face, set to emit a powerful sonic blast at the exact frequency that would cause the glass to vibrate and shatter. For good measure she had also programmed the unit with the sound effect of an explosion using the amplifying effect of the glass as a speaker milliseconds before hitting it with the sonic blast. The overall effect gave the impression that an explosion had destroyed the great clock face. So far everything had gone exactly to plan.

The front riders, realising the holdup they had caused, quickly spurred on their mounts to allow the procession to begin moving again. They knew that stopping en route was something to be avoided at all costs. The Household Cavalry followed suit and the carriage suddenly jolted forward almost throwing the royal passengers from their seats. As the carriage passed in front of the tower it was plain to see the damage the explosion had caused. The entire face of the west side of the great clock had been replaced by a void that exposed the inner workings. However, the two giant hands were still intact, seemingly hovering in mid-air. The majority of the glass had fallen within the grounds of the palace, thus avoiding mass causalities. The shards that had drifted over the railings and onto the street had struck a dozen people, causing terrible injuries to two people and minor cuts to the rest, but the fear and panic it caused was far greater. Hundreds of people close to the area just wanted to get as far away as possible, fearing further explosions. Most headed across Westminster Bridge or down the Embankment opposite, both more lightly fenced and patrolled.

11.13am

Andrew stood rooted to the spot, watching the face of Big Ben disappear. He caught a movement in his periphery vision and focused his full attention on the golden coach just in time to see someone enter and close the door behind them. He took a step forward needing a double take to convince himself he had not imagined what he had just witnessed. He was sixty yards from the queen and began to run, desperately trying to close the gap. The next thing he was struggling on the ground having been rugby tackled by an overzealous officer panicking at the sight of a lone figure sprinting toward the carriage. Andrew shouted at the man as several others surrounded him.
"I'm MI5 for God's sake."
"Let him go you lot." The officer Andrew had argued with moments before pulled him to his feet and brushed him down. "Are you ok, sir?"

He looked over his shoulder to see the procession had moved off and was now half way across the square and gaining speed. He knew the security plan, meticulously worked out, called for the team to head for the nearest safe-haven and guessed it would be the final destination in the palace which was only 300 yards further away. He looked around and called two armed special branch officers to his side.

"Stay with me," he said holding his badge firmly up for them to see. As the small group began to run towards the distant sight of the carriage, Andrew noticed it suddenly pull up.

A surreal atmosphere descended upon the square. Security personnel from all the various groups police, army and security services, were frantically searching on the airwaves, on the river, in the air, on every roof top and building trying to locate the direction of the threat. Their training included procedures if such an event occurred and they began to close off roads and block entrances to underground and rail stations in the area. Radio communication was beginning to be restored among the individual armed forces as they slowly began to realise where the problem lay and redirected their signals, abandoning the centralised encryption service. Their communications were still encoded, but they could no longer automatically contact other groups.

11.15am

As Andrew stood watching the scene unfold, his cell phone rang.

"Andrew, are you ok?" asked Frost.

"Yes, yes, what happened and what's happening?" he blurted out the two questions at once, immediately realising he was showing signs of panic. He stopped and took a deep breath.

"They've managed to get the cell network back. It was purely localised affecting the half dozen cells located in the immediate vicinity of the square."

Between them the cell infrastructure, small towers located on the rooftops of the buildings, could handle hundreds of simultaneous calls.

"Every cell had been occupied, hence the busy signals. The data centre controlling the area had seen the explosion on TV and had already begun to action the emergency procedures."

These procedures forcibly dropped all calls and instigated a priority override that exists on the mobile network, allowing appropriately equipped phones to continue working even if the public network becomes overloaded.

"How did they manage to communicate?" asked Andrew, momentarily distracted.

"By landline! Old technology has its place."

It was something that had not occurred to Andrew as he now rarely used the fixed telephone system.

"They think there is some sort of sophisticated system transmitting multiple signals. Andrew I can't see how this can be the work of a lone madman, or woman for that matter. Explosions in Big Ben, taking out the Tetra and cell phone network, it's impossible for one person. It must be a terrorist cell of some sort."

He could not disagree with his colleague's conclusion. Had he been wrong about the plot? Was it an elaborate plan by terrorists to confuse them and divert resources and effort from the real perpetrators?

"What's happening, why has the carriage stopped again?" said Larkin, pulling his attention back to the scene in front of his eyes.

"Has it? The plan says they head directly to the palace entrance."

Andrew started walking again and watched in amazement as a police officer holding the queen very close stepped down and guided her towards the crowd.

On a vantage point one hundred yards above the square, a marksman watched the small party emerge from behind the vehicle through the cross hairs of his telescopic sight. He had a clear view of the queen and her escort, a WPC, but had no thought of pulling the trigger. He had no radio contact with his controller and no idea whether the scene unfolding before him, although not part of the evacuation plan, was officially sanctioned. But in any case, who was going to issue the order to shoot when the queen was so close? However good a marksman he knew himself to be, the chances of a bullet striking the monarch was just too high. The WPC was also constantly moving around the lady altering the angle and preventing a consistent line of fire. A high velocity bullet could well pass straight through her body and enter the queen.

The killer guided the queen through a gap in the security barriers designed as an escape route.

"What are you waiting for?" she shouted. "Someone get in the carriage with Prince Phillip and get him out of here."

Armed police officers stepped forward to offer protection and move the crowd aside, one shutting the carriage door and shouting at the coachman to move off. The bemused crowd parted like a wave as the group proceeded through a small gate set in the railings and down a narrow path bordered by the church of St Margaret's on their right and the exterior of the Lady Chapel of the Abbey on the left. Most of those gathered were paralysed by the combination of being so unexpectedly close to the monarch, seeing her being manhandled by a group of armed police officers and trying to work out why she was there at all.

"Please everybody, make a path for Her Majesty," the killer called out as they emerged from the path into the area in front of the north entrance to the Abbey. "We have a security alert and need to evacuate her to a safe place as soon as possible."

The queen herself was as bemused as everyone else, but seemed content to follow the instructions of the young policewoman who had climbed into the carriage. She did not recall this being one of the emergency scenarios discussed during the security briefing the night before. But although she was the Queen of England she was also an elderly lady in her eighties so in no position to do much to prevent this unexpected diversion from the intended route, she just did whatever was asked of her. They entered the Abbey through the Great Gate into the north transept, sweeping past tourists, clergy and staff, yet even in the midst of such stress and panic they all paused for a moment to take in the spectacle. A thousand years of British history lay before them in one of the most magnificent churches in the world, its gothic-style fan vaulted ceiling stretching more than a hundred feet above them. They were in the widest part of the building and the queen could not help glance at the spot, directly in front of her, where she had been crowned sixty years before. Of course the great Coronation Chair she had sat upon was missing, it was presently in its normal home in St George's chapel. The Stone of Scone for which King Edward I had ordered the chair built, was absent, having been returned to its original home in Scotland. However, the killer was in no mood for site-seeing and taking the queen under her arm, propelled her forward. They passed to the left of the

Confessor's Chapel and down a small flight of stone steps, the two police officers bringing up the rear and provided cover in the event of a sudden attack. Neither had questioned the armed police woman who appeared from the carriage and demanded they provide support for her mission. As they hurried through the church sweeping their weapons back and forth, they caught each other's eyes and for the first time the true enormity of what was happening seemed to dawn on them both at once.

"What the bloody hell is going on?" said the older of the two.

"No idea, but we must protect the queen, and this is a good a place as I can think of."

"I wish these damn radios would come back on-line," said one, tapping the receiving unit in a vain attempt to repair whatever fault was causing the failure.

They were both brought back to the immediate task as they nearly lost their footing on the small steps, polished by a thousand years of use. They turned and seeing the other two pass through a narrow entrance and disappear to the right, instinctively lowered their heads, and followed them into a long narrow room. The queen and her protector were just a few yards ahead, the police woman shouting at the terrified visitors to leave immediately. They began a hasty retreat towards the front of the room, through an exit they as yet could not see. Pausing for a second one read a sign attached to the wall. *Tomb of Queen Elizabeth I and Queen Mary I.* This appeared to be their destination. The journey from the carriage had taken them under two minutes and they took in the scene around them.

11.18am

Andrew started to run again, followed by his two armed escorts. The vast majority of the officers lining the route had held their positions, having received no further instructions and they were too busy controlling the panicking crowds, preventing them spilling over the barriers, to have noticed anything else. A number of special branch and senior officers had gathered in the centre of the road and were debating the loss of communications. A group of three who had noticed the carriage had stopped, were walking towards the scene to find out why. He had lost sight of the queen and her new escort and frantically scanned the area. As he passed the trio he called out.

"Someone got into the coach when the explosion went off and has taken the queen from the carriage."

One of the group instinctively activated his radio before realising it was still dead. When Andrew's group was twenty yards away they started to follow at a run, calling colleagues as they went. By the time they reached the spot the carriage was almost at the entrance to the palace. The crowd were all facing away from the road straining to catch a glimpse of something more interesting. Andrew grabbed the first officer he could find.

"What's happened?"

"They've taken Her Majesty down there," he pointed at a small gate.

Andrew pushed his way through the crowd and stared down the path. He could see people gathered around an entrance and looking up to his left realised it was the Abbey. He looked over his shoulder and seeing the other two, started to walk.

"Do you have a sidearm?" he asked one.

"Yes, but," Andrew held out his hand until a pistol was placed there.

"Don't worry, I've got the necessary clearance," he lied.

They pushed their way through the crowd until they reached the entrance.

"They went in there," someone called out. They rushed through the door and were immediately confronted by a dozen officers barring their way. Andrew held up his ID and a police sergeant stepped forward.

"We're not sure what's going on, why has she been brought in here?"

11.21 am

The tomb of Queen Elizabeth I and her sister Queen Mary is situated in the north isle of the Lady Chapel in the north eastern corner of the Abbey, the part nearest the Palace of Westminster. The north isle runs to one side of the main chapel, with a similar sized duplicate on the opposite side that houses the tomb of Elizabeth's cousin Mary Queen of Scots, who she reluctantly consigned to the block in 1587. The walls of the north aisle are predominately of white marble, the dark floor, a mosaic of different coloured stone. The magnificent tomb is positioned at the far end of the narrow isle, being eight feet across and around forty in length. Set in the floor just in front of the tomb is an inscribed white marble tablet.

NEAR THE TOMB OF
MARY AND ELIZABETH
REMEMBER BEFORE GOD
ALL THOSE WHO
DIVIDED AT THE REFORMATION

BY DIFFERENT CONVICTIONS
LAID DOWN THEIR LIVES FOR
CHRIST AND CONSCIENCE SAKE.

The tomb is surrounded by a four-foot-high black metal guard rail, topped with more than a hundred gold painted heraldic symbols. Ten black marble pillars, each six feet in length, support a large structure that rises a further twelve feet, almost touching the ceiling. The white marble effigy of the queen lies sleeping in full regal outfit including her trademark ruffle. One hand holds a sceptre, the other a gold-topped orb. Her head, topped by a bejewelled golden crown, is cradled by two cushions.

"We need a chair or something for her to sit on."

The voice of what was, for the time being, their commanding officer, broke the silence. One ran around the front of the structure and emerged with a small high-back chair.

"Think it's used by the guides," he said placing the seat in front of the now exhausted elderly lady.

"Would you like to sit down ma'am?" The monarch nodded and lowered herself into the chair with as much royal bearing as she could manage.

The killer knew every inch of this part of the Abbey, especially the areas of vulnerability and entry and exit points. They had entered the north aisle through its one entrance and those present at the time had been evacuated through the other, a doorway into the broad expanse of the main chapel. She had chosen the spot for its historic significance, but had been delighted to discover it could be easily defended when she had considered its merits in a different light when planning this day of days.

"Ok," she said in a voice that gave no room for question. "One of you take each end, and don't let anybody near. I don't care who they say they are, we can't afford to take any chances. The terrorists could be disguised as security, tourists, anybody."

The two exchanged a glance

"Could even be the bloody Archbishop of Canterbury."

"You," she pushed one toward the front exit, "get that lot cleared out of the main chapel and then cover that area. It's the same layout across the way so watch out for anyone trying to enter from there."

She pulled two smalls devices from a pouch on her belt which had small rubber suckers attached. "Set these up so we can keep an eye on anybody trying to sneak in." The officer turned to go. "Hey, you idiot!" The killer took one hand and slapped a Smartphone into his palm. "You'll need this to see."

If the young man was surprised at a WPC carrying such equipment, it did not register on his face. He turned once again, disappeared through the door and could be heard ordering the assembled group from the chapel. The second policeman was given a similar task so they would also have eyes on the route they had taken to the chapel.

11.22am

Andrew gathered several officers and moved off. Groups of tourists were still wandering around and several pointed to where the group had headed.

"Get this place evacuated," he called to the sergeant as he approached the Confessor's Chapel.

"In there," a voice called out, pointing to an entrance ahead. Something stopped him marching straight down the steps he could see ahead and instead turned and waited for the area to be cleared. He pulled out his cell phone and dialled Frost's number.

"Bill, I'm in the Abbey."

"I know, we followed everything on CCTV from the moment she got out of the carriage. Did you get an ID on anybody?"

"Nothing conclusive," answered Frost, "but one of them is a WPC."

A shock went down Andrew's spine as a terrible realisation began to dawn.

"Let's get this place sealed off Bill, and get some back-up in here as soon as you can." He killed the call and started to move cautiously towards the stone entrance. Immediately a voice called out.

"Stop right there please, sir."

She knew that the time she had bought herself by disabling the radios and cell phones would end soon as the problem would be identified and a solution found. The army units would come back on line first as their systems were designed to be more resilient to attack and the personnel better trained in overcoming every possible problem. The systems used by the emergency services, although completely separate from any public communications infrastructure and with a high degree of security and reliability, were an easier target. That was one reason why she had chosen police officers to escort her when she had left the carriage. She would know the instant communications were restored, which she calculated would be in around ten minutes, that being the time it should take them to isolate the fault and by-pass the encryption hardware. The smell from the melting processors would have given a handy clue too, she thought. A voice, calling from the entrance snapped her attention back to the present.

"It's ok, I'm with the security services," Andrew called out taking a step closer.

"I have strict instructions not allow anyone to enter this area."

Andrew stood his ground and was joined by the sergeant who looked across as if asking what do we do?

"Who gave you the instructions?" asked Andrew somewhat puzzled.

"The lady who's in charge."

The sergeant took a pace forward and was met by an explosion of sound as a round was fired, crashing into a pillar a few feet behind him. Both dived for cover as the bullet ricocheted off another before embedding itself in a wooden panel.

She covered the distance from the tomb in a few seconds after the shot was fired and instinctively crouched as she approached the source. The young officer looked over at her and smiled.

"That should make them think twice before trying that again ma'am!"

The older officer appeared but was despatched back to the task of setting up the cameras. She peered as far around the door as she dared but was unable to see any movement.

"They've retreated back behind the third pillar on the right," he said, pointing into the distance.

"Let me know if anything happens, however small; and get that camera set up."

When she returned to the tomb she saw that the queen had risen from the chair and taken a step toward the exit.

"They will all be waiting for me. They can't do anything without one there you know, but thank you so much for your kind assistance, my dear."

The killer jumped up and grabbed the monarch before roughly pushing her back into the seat.

"German bitch. Do you know who I am, Mrs Saxe-Coburg-Gotha?" she glared, using the German name dropped by the royal family in 1917 during the First World War to be replaced by the now familiar Windsor. From within her tunic she produced a small collar which she attached around the queen's neck. The monarch was beginning to understand that the young policewoman, who had rescued her from danger in the carriage, may not be her protector after all. Throughout her sixty years on the throne, she had undergone many traumatic episodes, both personal and on behalf of the nation. From the very moment she discovered her destiny whilst on safari in

Keyna, the Falklands war, the death of *Uncle Dickie* Lord Mountbatten at the hands of the IRA, the breakup of the marriages of Anne, Charles and Andrew and the terrible tragedy of the untimely death of Diana that had shaken the foundations of the monarchy to the core. But even though there had been a close call at the oil terminal in Scotland in 1981, she had never been afraid, whether through confidence or ignorance. But she felt every one of her eighty-odd years at this moment and as vulnerable as any pensioner threatened by a mugger or abusive carer. She moved to feel the collar, which was loose around her neck but her hand was knocked, unceremoniously away by the woman. "Don't touch that dear," she said, "we don't want you setting if off by accident do we."

The queen had little knowledge of technology, only just managing to use a computer for simple tasks, but even the worst technophobe would know that this necklace was designed to do her harm. The killer could see the realisation and fear growing on her face and smiled grimly.

"So best to do as you are told and sit there quietly."

The bogus policewoman held up a cell phone and pressed a key. The queen felt a small vibration in her neck as the device, responding to the remote signal, came to life, which did little to reassure her that she would emerge from the ordeal unharmed. A few minutes later the older officer appeared and gave a thumbs up before returning to his post. She checked the images on the smartphones which gave a 110 degree-wide angle view that would show any attempt to catch her unawares. The tiny units had a built-in motion sensing ability which would cause the device to vibrate should movement be detected. This would give her valuable time should they try anything and meant she did not have to constantly monitor the screens. For the first time since they had entered the area, she was able to take a breather and properly take in her surroundings. She walked over and peered at the marble effigy of the sleeping Virgin Queen over the railings that separated them. For the first time she allowed her mind to wander and imagine the moment she had spent half her life preparing for. Nothing could get in her way now and soon 450 years of wrong would be swept away.

The two police officers were still positioned where she had ordered them to stay when she checked on them whilst the queen sat motionless in her seat, exhausted by the day's events and the fear of what lay ahead. The killer left the dozing old woman and entering the main chapel, was immediately drawn to the magnificent ceiling. The officer stationed at the entrance to the south aisle did not notice her approach until she roused him from his daydream with a sharp jab in the ribs.

"Imbecile!" She hissed at the startled man "Keep your wits about you. Do you want the death of the queen on your hands?"

The officer shook his head and stood to attention, grabbing his machine pistol with both hands in an effort to impress her. Shaking her head in disbelief, she continued down the south aisle, until she reached the entrance. She could make out the officer, kneeling on the steps that lead to the main chapel and to each of the north and south aisles that ran either side. Sensing her presence, he turned to face her and gave a thumbs up. She crept closer until, kneeling alongside him, she had a view of the area beyond. It was not possible to see clearly into the main transept as the view was blocked by the numerous pillars that supported the great structure and the tombs and monuments that had been added throughout the centuries. Directly in front she could see the Confessor's Chapel, where the body of Edward the Confessor lies, and beyond that through a screen, the high alter. The spot was almost unique in the Abbey as it was a large area that was accessible through a single, narrow entrance point and thus easily defended. Only the circular Chapterhouse equalled this spot but its small size made it as much a prison as a refuge and a well-aimed stun grenade could end her plans in an instant. The officer tensed and raised his weapon to the firing position.

"Second pillar from the end on the left ma'am."

As she strained to make out the cause of the alarm, a movement caught her eye. She smiled as she saw the end of a gun barrel protruding from behind a pillar on the other side, although it was no more than she had expected as her earpiece had sprung to life a few minutes before as the communications systems came back to life. The two officers however, could hear nothing as she had instructed them to use a frequency she knew would not be used. She adjusted the small microphone attached to the earpiece so she could speak and checked the correct frequency had been chosen. The time for secrecy was over.

"Can you hear me?" she said quietly.

11.30am

After scrambling for cover when the shot rang out, Andrew left the now reinforced team covering the entrance to the door and made his way to the north entrance where Bill Frost was waiting.

"All the comms are back on line now Andrew."

"Is everyone clear?"

At that moment a heavily armed team from SO13 approached, headed by Jack Scott who Andrew recognised from the terrorist raid in Cambridgeshire.

"We've been sent to take command and secure the building and set up a command post somewhere secure."

Half an hour later a group of ten people crowded into the Dean's office in the western area. Scott explained the events of the last ninety minutes from the moment the radio communications systems had been sabotaged.

"So do we know who's in there with her?"

"We're pretty sure, but we can't reach them by radio to confirm," said Scott. He opened a large scale plan of the Abbey and fixed it to the wall. "They're holed up here, in the Lady Chapel. There's only one entrance and they obviously have that covered.

"Well that's a stroke of luck her being forced into a dead end like that," said Frost brightly.

"I hope you're right Bill," said Andrew. "But given how carefully she has planned everything else, I wouldn't be too sure it was an error. Remember it's our only way in too."

Scott called on the Dean, who was sat next to Andrew, to explain the layout of the area.

"Can we get someone in the ceiling above them?"

"I'm afraid not, the Lady Chapel was an addition to the main building and there is no access except through that door."

"How about breaking a window and throwing in a few stun grenades?"

The Dean's face turned white and he spluttered uncontrollably as he tried to answer the SO13 man, before Andrew cut in.

"We can't be sure how many people are in there or where they will be."

"There's absolutely no way we can start bludgeoning our way in whilst Her Majesty is in there," said the head of SO14, the royal protection section.

"The problem is we are totally blind," said Scott "Is there anywhere we can get a cable through, as we have micro cameras that could give us audio and video?"

The Dean considered the suggestion for a moment.

"I suppose you could come in through the roof or drill a hole through a wall, God help us."

"It would be too noisy," said someone else. Andrew looked at Frost.

"So not such a mistake after all." A head popped around the door.

"Someone's made contact on the special branch frequency sir, and two shots have been heard."

11.37am

"Who is this?" Came the reply. "And how did you get on this frequency?"

The officer next to the killer thought the original question had been directed at him and so turned to answer. He then heard the earpiece of the woman activate, although could not make out what was being said. He was puzzled as to why his own set was silent and peered down to step through the channels in the hope of joining the conversation. Failing, he looked up to find himself staring down the barrel of a pistol. The bullet passed between his eyes, killing him instantly. He slumped down the steps as the echo of the gunshot reverberated off the walls of the great church, blood pumping from the wound and slowly cascading down each step, forming a pool at the base. She immediately set off down the south aisle and intercepted the other officer, alerted by the shot, coming in the opposite direction. She waited until he was within two feet before calmly raising the pistol and repeating the same shot. This time the bullet passed just above the left ear as the man showed a speed of movement she had not thought he possessed, and turned his head in an instinctive moment of self-preservation. Gathering his weapon, she ran, entering the north aisle just in time to see the queen rise from her chair, stirred from her slumber by the noise. She grabbed her arm and forced her back into the chair.

"Stay there or you know what will happen," she said, waving the cell phone in air. She walked quickly back down to the steps and fired three shots through the doorway.

"If I see anyone make a move, you'll have the blood of a queen on your hands."

She knew how they would react and moved swiftly to maintain control over the situation. "Before you take any action you'll regret, I suggest that someone has a look at this IP address." She gave a list of numbers that she knew, when entered would give the operator a view of a small CCTV camera positioned no more than ten feet from where she was standing, showing a frail old lady sitting in a chair. She had a collar around her neck and looked very frightened. Twenty seconds later a voice appeared in her ear.

"We can see. What do you want?"

"The necklace contains a small amount of plastic explosive, but more than enough to severe an artery. If I don't send a coded signal from the cell phone I have in my hand every thirty seconds, then the device will automatically detonate."

She paused to allow the full effect of her message to sink in, before removing an exact duplicate from a belt pouch, activating it and tossing it on the floor.

"I have a few more of those clever little cameras around the place, so don't think you can play any of your games and creep up on me." She turned and strode back down the steps and into the north aisle and pressed a key on the phone which detonated the spare collar. As it disintegrated with a sharp crack, none of those present were left in any doubt what would happen to anyone wearing such a device. The queen was in exactly the same position as when she had left, looking more tired and afraid than ever.

"Now, Your Majesty, it's nearly time for you to carry out a very important task." The monarch looked up in surprise. "No, no, not the opening of Parliament you silly woman. You're going to abdicate."

11.38am

The group burst from the office and hurried towards the northern end of the Abbey, just in time to hear three shots echo off the walls of the Confessor's Chapel. They all dived for cover, not knowing the path the bullets might take. As he crawled around a corner Andrew could hear a voice in the distance. He ducked as low as he could and made a dash between a large wooden statue and a pillar to get as close as he could. A few seconds later a sharp crack filled his ears. He looked over his shoulder to see Scott behind the same statue he had vacated moments before and gave him a 'what was that?' look. Scott shook his head and then rose, pointing in the distance. Andrew turned to see an army captain calmly walking towards them. All three gathered in a sheltered alcove and the man explained how the collar had been detonated.

"Any chance of finding out what frequency it's transmitting on?" asked Scott.

"It's possible," he answered, "but if you're thinking of intercepting the detonation signal then think again. This woman has already proven that she's very smart and anything we do is just as likely to set the thing off. It's just too risky."

"Agreed, but let's get a scanner up here so we can monitor the signal. We need to know what we're dealing with."

The captain nodded and left.

Andrew had returned to the Dean's office with the rest of the group and was studying a laptop that had been hastily set up showing the feed from the killer's camera. The queen sat on a small chair looking very frail with the collar clearly visible on her neck. He pressed a key and was able to step through the half dozen cameras that had been set up to monitor the area outside the chapel and immediately outside the building. He could see two men stationed outside. They had attached a listening device to one of the windows which should enable them to hear what was happening in the north aisle where the queen was being held.

"Get your people away from the window and get them to take the microphone with them," a voice burst in his ear.

He watched as the device was removed. Andrew switched the image back to the queen and turned to Scott and Frost.

"We have to be very careful not to push her until we have a better idea of her next move." Scott nodded and left the office.

"She's providing us with the only information we have," he said. "This whole thing has been meticulously planned down to the last detail."

11.55am

"I beg your pardon dear?"

The queen stared at the killer with a mixture of surprise and contempt. She had been on the throne for more than sixty years and was determined to exceed the sixty three years and seven months of her distant cousin Victoria. Throughout her reign there had been several calls for her to stand aside for Charles or more recently William, but she had remained steadfast in her duty to the country and had no intention of changing her mind at the behest of this madwoman. The killer could see by Elizabeth's expression that she was not warming to the idea. She calmly leant her back on the railings that surrounding the tomb and explained why she had no choice.

"I am the rightful heir to the throne of England" she began. "Unlike your ancestors who stole everything by marriage and murder, my family is directly descended from the first Elizabeth." She leant forward inches from the present queen's face. "That's right; she did have a child, a secret child. She had to have the baby taken away to keep it safe. If the choice had been hers she would have married Dudley, the child would have been crowned and it would have stopped all you foreigners ruling ever since."

The expression of the old lady had changed to that of someone listening to a child telling a fantasy story.

"One way or another your reign is at an end," she said producing a document from her tunic. "Sign this and you live, refuse and you'll lose your head quicker than Anne Boleyn." The queen took the proffered letter and read it.

"You want me to abdicate today, right now. Are you insane?" She stood up defiantly and threw the letter to the ground. The killer raised the cell phone in her hand.

"If I don't push this button in the next ten seconds, you will die. Do you understand?"

The queen had met many thousands of people throughout her reign, including some of the worst despots such as Idi Amin and Robert Mugabe. She had learned to recognise the look of someone who could kill without hesitation or remorse and she saw that look in the eyes that stood before her. Where were the royal protection officers? Why had they not prevented this woman from getting close enough to climb in the carriage? But they had failed and now she was sitting on an uncomfortable chair in a cold church with some hideous device around her neck which could kill her. Self-preservation took the place of duty and her shoulders dropped. The killer produced a pen and the monarch duly signed.

"Now we'll need to organise the coronation of a new queen." She tuned her radio to the frequency used by MI5. "I want to speak to the prime minister."

Andrew left the office and walked around the building, staring up at the magnificent vaulted ceiling. He could see the network of platforms that had been erected high above him to enable cleaning and other maintenance on the upper reaches and was glad he didn't have to negotiate them. After ten minutes he reached the western end of the nave, recognising the entrance through which the great and the good had passed for most of the ceremonial occasions such as royal weddings and coronations and was admiring the view when his cell phone rang.

"What's the latest?" It was Neild.

"Fine, apart from the fact that we have a serial killer in an impregnable position with the Queen of England held hostage and liable to have her head blown off at any moment."

He walked through the entrance into the daylight and was immediately aware of the cordon erected around the site, preventing prying eyes seeing inside. He looked up noticing the sound of a police helicopter patrolling the skies and stopping any media capturing the scene.

"Is there anything you need?"

"It's nice of you to offer, but I don't think so. I'm having trouble keeping control of what's happening here, there's a turf war going on for whose lead agency."

"I heard your professor finally tracked down the last ancestor, seems it's a woman. I'm not sure if anyone seriously considered that prospect," said Neild

"Only in passing to be honest, but I have Thames House working on finding anybody who might fit the profile."

"This has all the makings of a disaster and I want us as far away from the front line as possible. I'm happy to let the army or special branch have the spotlight on this for the moment. Keep your head down and me up to date so I can position us correctly."

Andrew shook his head, the queen was in danger of becoming another victim and all that concerned MI5 was political self-preservation. As he continued around the north side of the building, he noticed the growing media circus beyond the makeshift perimeter. Police were still erecting the screen along this section and he was aware of the interest his presence was causing. He turned his head away and hurried back into the Abbey via the same north transept entrance as the queen. As he did the chatter he could hear on his headset suddenly took on an urgent tone.

"Bill, what's happening?"

2.00pm

Larkin was shown into the COBRA meeting room which contained everyone who was present at his last attendance, plus one or two new faces all in police or army uniforms except for a man he recognised as the attorney general. Neild nodded for him to stand at the rear of the room as the home secretary rose and began by going over the events of the day, calling for comments from various people to confirm a point or fill in missing details.

"So in a nutshell this person was able to take down the entire communication system in the area paralysing the network, snatch the monarch in plain view of the world and under the noses of 2,000 security personnel, calmly walk into Westminster Abbey and has now barricaded them both in an unassailable area having placed an explosive collar on the queen?" An embarrassed silence filled the room which was finally broken by the PM.

"There'll be plenty of time for inquiries when this is all over. I called this meeting to discuss this woman's demands."

The home secretary gave a signal and the room was filled with a replay of the earlier conversation giving the details.

"Why is the sound quality so much better when I speak?" asked the PM?

"We're not sure sir, but we think she has limited the frequency to mask her voice, similar to an old-style telephone connection," a communications expert from the table answered.

"Whatever the quality, we can't seriously consider this, it's madness?"

He tossed the abdication letter, collected from the steps to the vault where the killer had left it, on the table and looked across at the attorney general.

"I've been consulting colleagues Prime Minister, and there is simply no precedent for this situation. When the queen's uncle abdicated in 1936 it was, of course, his own choice. I can't believe Her Majesty is a willing participant in this."

"But is it legal?"

"Again, we have nothing on which to base any judgment except Vi Coactus." Everyone in the room looked at each other hoping for some enlightenment.

"Under constraint Prime Minister. If a contract is signed with the letters VC added it is said to have been signed under duress."

"But it's not."

"But we could use a similar argument as it appears obvious in this situation."

A murmur of relief went around those present sensing a possible way out.

"And what about the chair and the Archbishop of Carlisle?" said the PM.

"She's insisted the coronation chair is placed in the sacrarium facing the high altar, which is its traditional position for a coronation," said a woman sitting in front of Andrew, who was obviously the expert on such matter. "As for the Archbishop of Carlisle, it appears he crowned Elizabeth I as the incumbent Archbishop of Canterbury had refused." Neild continued.

"These requests are being carried out now sir, to buy us some time. We sent a helicopter to Carlisle about twenty minutes ago."

The meeting spent the next few minutes discussing their options for rescuing the queen, which turned out to be extremely limited. Andrew was asked if he believed the killer was capable of carrying out her threat to kill the queen.

"Without a doubt sir. Unless we can find a way to neutralise the collar, I would not recommend taking any chances."

"We're working on that sir," Neild added.

"She holds all the cards Prime Minister," said the army chief of staff. "So I don't believe we have any choice but to proceed with her programme and plan for this phoney coronation tomorrow morning at ten."

"That's only a few hours away, can this get any worse?" said the PM banging his fist on the table in frustration.

"I'm afraid it can." All eyes turned again towards the attorney general. "If this woman is actually crowned and becomes the monarch, then she will technically have immunity from any prosecution for the crimes she has committed."

The room erupted in a frenzy of indignant disapproval before the PM raised his hand and called for quiet.

"The law of this land is ultimately delivered by the monarch," he went on. "Every case is brought by the monarch against one of his or her subjects, which means it's impossible for the queen to prosecute herself."

8.10pm

The killer watched the image on her smartphone as the chair was moved into its final position and smiling, showed the screen to her captive.

"It won't be long now and don't worry, I'll make sure you have a seat right next to me so you won't miss a thing."

She looked at her watch and calculated it had been nine hours since they had entered the abbey. The queen was exhausted and barely able to stay awake and therefore she had no worries there would be any attempt at an escape, not that it would do her any good. She retrieved the cell phone from her tunic and pressed the four digit sequence that sent the inhibiting signal to the collar. She had lied about having to do this every few seconds as she was, in fact, able to programme the device for any length of time she chose plus a warning bleep sounded thirty seconds before giving ample time to prevent her captive losing her head. She knew they would be monitoring everything she did so had programmed another phone to send a regular signal every ten seconds that would appear genuine. A voice calling from outside the chapel caught her attention.

"We have some more food and water."

She walked towards the entrance but kept far enough back in case some fool decided they would take a pot shot at her.

"One of you can bring it in," she called out. A young policewoman, fear in her eyes appeared, laden with bags and bottles of water and attempted to pass her.

"I'll just put them in here for you." She laid her arm across the officer's chest.

"I suggest you leave now before you end up like your colleagues."

The woman immediately dropped the packages and retreated. "And get someone in here to remove those bodies, it's beginning to smell."

9.05pm

Parked discretely in the grounds behind the abbey, the unmarked van was only distinguishable from the thousands that deliver goods all over the country by a small array of aerials and a satellite dish measuring three feet in diameter that adorned its roof. Inside two men sat silently monitoring an array of equipment designed to capture every electrical signal within a five hundred yard radius of where they sat. Any communication coming in or out would be interrogated and its source located. Even if a light was switched on or off they could pick up the change in the electromagnetic field. The unit was connected directly to GCHQ and from there to a little-known facility nestled in a remote area of the Utah Wastach mountain range blandly named the Utah Data Centre, adding the cryptic deciphering expertise and most powerful computers on earth to the task.

"There it is again." The technician pointed at the sudden burst of activity disturbing the otherwise flat green line on his screen. "It's longer than the others and is being sent at random times." His colleague span around and wheeled his chair the six feet to join him. "The others are at regular ten second intervals, but this is different." He adjusted his headset and relayed the information to his superior a hundred miles away in Cheltenham.

"Send the data over to me and we'll get working on the encryption. Our cousins in Utah will be interested to have a go at this too."

Five thousand miles away the fastest supercomputer in the world had been constructed from 18,000 computer processors, similar to those found in pairs in a standard computer server. It can handle more than seventeen thousand trillion operations per second. The site has been designed to handle enough data to store the entire sum of human knowledge a million times over. Yet even this massive computer power could take years to crack the algorithm by a brute force, pure number crunching attack. However, the experts on both sides of the Atlantic studying this cipher were some of the most experienced on the planet and added human intuition and skill to the race against time.

5.03am

Andrew watched the first rays of sunlight creep over the distant buildings and dance on the river from an office in Thames House. He had been able to sleep for an hour or so in between ensuring the MI5 responsibilities in the vicinity of the abbey were in place and working with David Scott at GCHQ on tracking down any further information on Elizabeth Moore.

"She's a ghost Andrew, no traces of her anywhere."

He turned and cast his eye on millions of pounds of the most technically advanced equipment available. Billions had been spent at GCHQ and probably trillions across the Atlantic. But despite all the equipment and the combined knowledge and experience of thousands of the top minds on the planet, a single person had been able to evade detection, murder fifteen people and outwit them all to kidnap the Queen of England. He had been left a virtual spectator of the events inside the abbey as the security operation to secure the area and work out how to rescue the queen was being coordinated by units from the army and the various special branch special operations units that all seemed to have a reason to attend. The only notable absentees were SO14, the royal protection branch, who were all providing additional cover for other members of the royal family. In all there were more than 200 members of the SAS, SO13 and the Met's own 'SWAT' unit CO19 ready to move on any incidents within the abbey or the buildings in the immediate vicinity of Parliament Square and Whitehall.

7.08 am

The coronation chair had been moved from its home in St George's chapel in the west end of the nave and placed in its ceremonial position and the Archbishop of Carlisle transported by helicopter and set up in residence within the abbey grounds. The dean had been tasked with helping the elderly bishop with the details of the coronation ceremony, not one with which many people were familiar. The killer had insisted that the outfit worn by the queen on her coronation day on June 5th, 1953, be brought for her to wear, together with the rod of mercy, the orb and sceptre and of course, St Edward's crown. At present these were under armed guard in an underground crypt at the abbey having been transported in secret from the Tower of London overnight for fear that a plot may exist to intercept the priceless articles. Despite the number of people in and around the buildings and the nature of the situation, a calm had descended upon the sacred and historic site and even though it was late spring, a chill hung in the air causing even the most hardened of the military special forces to shiver in the cold atmosphere.

The killer had managed to doze throughout the night, confident that the movement detectors on the cameras would alert her to any attempt to storm the chapel and set the mobile device to automatically send the inhibitor signal to the explosive collar around the sovereign's neck every five minutes. She looked at her watch; four hours to the ceremony and the culmination of a lifetime's work to put right 400 years of injustice. The queen, covered by a blanket, stirred in her chair. Deciding to leave the old woman, she walked to the edge of the chapel steps. She could see no signs of movement but within a few seconds heard stirring sounds from behind the pillars and walls that filled her view. Knowing they would have their own detection equipment and her movement had alerted those in the front line to her presence, she pressed the transmit button her on comms set.

"Is everything ready?"

After a few seconds a voice confirmed what she wanted to hear.

"I want to see it for myself," and calmly walked up the steps and around the left side of the Confessor's Chapel, heading towards Poets Corner and the South Transept. As she passed various pillars she could see the startled look on the faces of those hidden behind.

"Don't even think about coming anywhere near me or the German gets a pain in the neck," she said holding up the mobile in one hand and smart phone in the other. "I can see her with this and kill her in an instant with this."

It took her only twenty seconds to cover the distance walking around the sanctuary and she smiled at the site of the king's chair sat in its proper place. She looked around, seeking any signs of a trap, at the same time changing the setting on the smartphone to video and sweeping the unit around capturing anything unusual for study on returning to the chapel. A dozen armed men appeared from the darkness and stopped abruptly at the unexpected site.

"Don't make any move," came the instructions over their headsets.

She held up the devices and calmly turned her back on the group. In a little over a minute she had completed a full circle and returned, having confirmed her instructions had been carried out and checked the numbers of armed security in the area.

7.15 am

"Did you get any decent images on CCTV?"

Andrew had taken the call from Frost whilst shaving in the bathroom adjacent to the office and promptly cut himself.

"She managed to keep her head down and with the WPC hat and the poor light…"

Andrew tossed his razor into the sink in frustration.

"Not that I guess it will do us any good," he said, swapping the phone from one hand to the other as he wiped the soap from his bleeding face. "I'll be down there in half an hour."

He dialled Jackie's number but received her voicemail again and was about to ring Frost to ask if he had heard from her when a voice called through the door.

"The CCTV footage has come through sir."

An hour later Andrew stood with a group of fellow MI5 operatives outside the north entrance, flanked by Anthony Neild and Ken Greaves.

"So we have everything covered from our side?"

Andrew nodded and walked inside the building. It was just over two hours until the ceremony was due to start and as yet nothing had emerged that would enable them to prevent this woman being crowned. Whatever the legal arguments the news would send shockwaves around the country and the world when it emerged and he knew, with the number of people involved the chances of keeping it under wraps were slim. He watched as the queen's dress was carried towards the chapel by a nervous looking young woman and immediately recognised her as one the girls from the night he stayed at the Marriot hotel with Tim. He watched as she disappeared towards the steps and then spotted Scott in a small group of senior special forces officers and attempted to join them.

"I'll come over and see you when we've finished," said Scott, ushering Andrew away.

He walked further down the north aisle and called Bill Frost.

"I shouldn't worry Andrew, every group will have its own unique set of instructions and you know how secretive the SAS boys are."

He looked up as a sound caught his attention and noticed several snipers moving into their final positions in alcoves and balconies to ensure every potential angle of fire was covered. As he stood looking skyward Scott tapped him on the shoulder having approached noiselessly.

"Blimey, you made me jump, creeping around like that."

"Second nature."

Scott briefed Andrew on some last minute changes to the operational plan. "So apart from the archbishop and the dean all the clergy will be our people?" Scott nodded. "Are we sure this is going to run smoothly?" said Andrew as they walked towards the sanctuary which had now been cleared of all but the most essential personal.

"All I can do is carry out my immediate task, the rest is down to those with much bigger pensions than me."

9.08am

The young girl looked petrified as she helped the woman into the dress. She had been given a flurry of instructions on what to do, what information to gain and to note any points of weakness they could exploit. Most of those had been forgotten in the first minute of entering as she was forced to strip to her underwear and undergo the indignity of an intimate search for any recording devices or weapons. Her clothes now lay a few feet outside the steps to the chapel. The queen had not moved since her arrival and looked very frail although having never been this near, she was unable to verify if this was just how she normally looked. She had been told to keep a careful eye on the mobile devices, in particular the key sequence used to inhibit the collar, but each time she pressed the buttons she was careful to turn away. However, she did hear the distinct click as each key was depressed, a total of four. The woman instructed her to don the plain white cotton habit which she had brought with her.

"You will have the honour of attending your new queen." This had not been part of the plan and the girl betrayed her uncertainty like an open book.

"Sit down and shut up you snivelling girl." She looked in the small mirror that had been brought in by the servant girl and felt slightly nervous. Was this really about to happen? She opened the small makeup bag and started to apply the various items, she must be as presentable as possible for her new subjects.

Had the bell in the clock tower of the Palace of Westminster been working, it would have struck 9.45am. Andrew watched the workman scurry around the missing face, erecting scaffolding and beginning work on restoring the famous landmark even though the woman in whose name the building stands was in mortal danger just a few yards away. He turned and retraced the steps the killer had taken immediately after leaving the carriage and again marvelled at the audacity of the plan. As he approached the north transept a familiar face beckoned him inside as the great doors closed. Once sealed Scott radioed confirmation and moved off with a section of his men to secure the other entrances. Andrew was led towards a group of pews which had been laid out for the ceremony and told to stay put. Looking around there were only a few spectators to witness this occasion, unlike the previous event for which special grandstands were built in the abbey to house more than 8,000 people whilst millions around the world watched the first televised coronation. Andrew became lost in his thoughts until those around him began to stand. It had begun.

"This way your majesty." The girl helped the old woman to struggle from the chair.

"Not any more my dear, just plain Elizabeth Saxe-Coburg I'm afraid or Windsor if you prefer the deceit played out for the nation ninety years ago."

The girl looked at the woman without a flicker of understanding.

"Never mind, get her over here and help me."

They gathered up everything and the new queen ran her hands down her dress one last time. I suppose I'll have to put up with the army webbing she said to herself as she noted how it spoilt the line of the dress, but she couldn't trust those bastards out there to accept the German's abdication and honour her divine right. She checked the magazine of the pistol and placed it in the belt in the small of her back and viewed the smartphone cameras one last time. Armed with the mobile in one hand and a small chain attached to the old lady's collar, the small procession left the confines of Elizabeth's tomb a little more than 400 years after the great queen had made her own journey towards the king's chair.

As he got to his feet, Andrew knew the countdown for the day's events had started and nothing could now wind it back. He felt helpless just standing like a family member at a church wedding but he had no part in the plan that was now about to unfold. If everyone came out alive it would indeed be a miracle and he instinctively felt for a weapon until he remembered he was still unable to carry a firearm. As he strained to look down towards the chapel where the activity was developing, all he could see were groups of armed officers retreating from the small party as they moved forward. A light, being held aloft on a pole to illuminate the path, suddenly stopped.

"Move back," a voice called out, its sound bouncing off the stone walls and muffling the detail. After what seemed an eternity he saw the first glimpses of a white dress through the dark mass of uniforms and then his breath stopped as he recognised the queen leading the group, a chain leading from her neck.

"Andrew, I need to speak to you right now." He had forgotten to mute his comms set and the voice seemed to echo for a hundred yards in every direction. He bolted from the pew and retreated as far away from the scene, finally squatting behind a pillar half way down the north aisle; but was moved further back by those flanking the rows of seats. Eventually he fought his way to the exit to the nave and out into the sunlight. It took him several attempts to get through as many of the channels were inoperable or jammed. In frustration he pulled out his cell phone and dialled the number.

"What the hell is it Bill?"

"Andrew, they know who it is."

"Who knows who it is, what are you talking about?" At that moment the stopwatch arrived at its predetermined spot and Andrew's world changed forever.

After the throng of armed people retreated step-by-step, the procession finally emerged into the sanctuary. She had pulled on the German's chain several times to stop her wandering and remind her subjects who was in control. The mobile was safe in her hand and held by a wrist strap to avoid any nasty accidents. If anyone was going to kill the bitch it would be her.

She allowed herself a moment to take in the majestic scene before ordering the girl to the left of the coronation chair, walked up three small steps and lowered herself onto the wooden seat, forcing Elizabeth to sit to her right.

"Would it not be easier for her majesty to stand?" asked an attendant. She gave the man an icy look.

"When I am crowned her head will be below mine," she said, pressing the buttons on the mobile for effect. "And do not refer to her ex title again." She tugged at the chain forcing the woman's legs to buckle. "You may begin."

The Archbishop of Carlisle, attended by the Dean of Westminster who traditionally instructs the new sovereign, nervously approached the chair. The Archbishop bowed and turned to the odd congregation and called.

"God save the Queen."

A few voices responded automatically thinking they were blessing the old monarch. He turned again and commanded the woman to take the sovereign's oath which was placed before her by the dean.

"I promise I shall rule according to the laws of my kingdom, to exercise justice with mercy and maintain the Church of England."

As a murmur went around at how swiftly this woman was becoming their queen, the killer raised the mobile above her head as a reminder of where the true power lay. The archbishop anointed and blessed her and then called for the ceremonial garb including the sceptre, orb and crown. Two attendants made their way from the sides and ascended the steps, one with the crown placed on a large red cushion. As the dean removed it the cushion fell to the floor to reveal a pair of cutters around six inches long, held in the hand that had supported it. At the same moment half a dozen powerful lights, targeted at the throne, burst into life blinding everyone including the killer. The attendant, an SAS officer, moved quickly towards the queen and began using the cutters on the collar at the point where it was fastened. The two clergymen stumbled towards the stairs in panic and were saved from falling by two burly SAS sergeants on their way up. Smoke bombs were tossed into the area to confuse and disorientate but stun grenades had been ruled out for fear of injuring the queen and other civilians.

The killer was alerted the moment she saw the two attendants who, despite their best attempts at disguise, had the cold look of killers in their eyes that she recognised instantly. Whilst the archbishop was lifting the crown from its cushion, she reached behind her and retrieved the pistol whilst still holding the mobile aloft. As soon as she saw the cutters she lowered her arm, produced the gun and was hit with a shaft of blinding light. In the next few seconds smoke filled the scene limiting her view, but she felt a tug on her hand and could see the attendant was cutting the collar. She had to decide whether to kill him or the queen and making up her mind in a split second, shot the SAS man in the head killing him instantly. Are they mad? Do they think they can save her? She hesitated in the confusion knowing that to kill the queen removed her only protection from the dozens of guns pointed at her. But the smoke made identifying a target impossible and gave her a few seconds in which to act. Looking to her left the young girl was still sat beside the chair, paralysed with fear so she grabbed her by the hair, pulled her and the queen up and fired three shots into the air causing everyone to freeze.

"One more move and I'll blow her fucking head off," she screamed, leaving no one in doubt of her intentions. As the smoke cleared a dozen special forces personnel, all standing in various positions on the steps, had their guns pointed at her head.

"You," she bellowed at the archbishop, "put the crown on me, NOW!"

The startled man gathered the crown, hesitantly made his way over to the group and gingerly placed the crown on the killers head. She held the mobile in the air and pressed the four keys. "They all have a death wish for you Elizabeth," she said sinking down on the chair. "Why else would they ignore the fact that I can kill you any time I choose?" Looking up into the heights of the abbey, she could see several reflections from gun sites and pulled the girl to sit on her lap as protection. The gunmen had all taken a step closer and seemed to be looking for a kill shot.

"One more move and I'll kill these two, I swear." A second later they all listened to the same message and immediately retreated.

"I am now your queen," she said, pushing the girl away and almost losing the crown in the process of standing.

Twenty yards away Jack Scott cursed and slammed his fist on top of the nearest pew. The plan had been worked out to the split second and had only failed because the SAS sergeant took a fraction of a second too long to move for the collar. His delay had cost them the chance to remove it before the killer realised what was happening, and the sergeant his life. Scott walked along the south aisle and found a quiet spot before opening up a special communications channel to which only a handful of people had access. He spoke for thirty seconds and then listened for the same period before terminating the link.

Andrew heard the commotion as he turned to re-enter the building. At the same moment the inner and outer doors were closed on cue and he was left stranded in the centre. No one present would speak with him and his comms set emitted a sound like a screaming gull which he instantly knew was a form of jamming. He could just hear a shot in the distance, followed by a further three, he guessed from the same gun, twenty seconds later.

"What's happening?" he mouthed through the glass of the inner door to no effect. He felt so frustrated that, after so many months tracking down the killer, he was being denied the chance to witness the last act. Finally he sat down in his glass prison and waited.

Scott was half way back to the sanctuary when his earpiece gave him the message they'd dreaded.

"She's on the move, what shall we do?" This is going to be difficult enough, he thought, without any further complications. He spotted two of his senior officers and stopped to brief them on their next actions, before walking as fast as he could to the front of the pews. As he stepped into the glare of the lights he could see the three women were half way between the chair and a set of pillars in the north transept.

"Don't come any closer, I command you as your sovereign."

"I'm afraid it's all over Elizabeth Moore," he said and calmly walked towards the old lady, taking a small pair of cutters from a jacket pocket.

"If you shoot me then you'll die before I hit the floor." Scott took hold of the collar and began working the cutters into the metal clasp, breaking into a sweat as his instinct for survival fought against his training and the knowledge that if he failed, the queen would die. The killer stared at the officer with a mixture of fear and amazement as realising she had no option but to detonate the collar, lifted the mobile and punched in the five digit firing code, bracing herself for the bloody aftermath.

Andrew finally managed to re-enter the abbey when a senior officer ordered the door opened. He showed his pass again and half walked, half ran down the aisle towards the sanctuary, a distance of two hundred yards. He was stopped several times and it took him precious minutes to talk his way past them all. As he approached the floodlit area he was suddenly pinned to the ground by an SAS corporal who gestured for him to stay silent. Andrew crawled on his hands and knees around several rows of pews not daring to raise his head for fear of either losing it or catching the eye of the murderer. As he approached the front pew he could see the legs of the three women as they walked down the steps. Suddenly a pair of black khaki combat trousers brushed past his ear and emerged into the open, followed by the unmistakable voice of Jack Scott.

"Traitorous bastards!" she cried as she pressed the last button and immediately pushed the young girl in front of her towards the abbey walls. Scott was caught by surprise but could not leave the collar which was still attached. Everyone had dived for cover expecting the worse with Andrew thinking, even as he hit the floor, what had made Scott sacrifice himself and almost certainly the queen for the one in a million chance of getting the collar off before it was detonated. But there was no explosion, only the screams of the young girl as she was pushed away. Andrew popped his head over the pew and saw Scott still battling with the collar. He leapt over the obstacle and ran to the SO13 man.

"I've nearly got it off." A man arrived armed with a set of giant bolt cutters and split the collar in one movement and within a second it had been placed in a bomb proof container and whisked away. Andrew ran in the direction of the fleeing women just in time to see them disappear through a small door, then back to Scott who was helping the queen to her feet.

"What were you thinking of?"

Scott handed the old lady over to two medical orderlies and turned to Andrew.

"I'm not mad, son, let's just say I had some inside information. Now which way did they go?"

The two women had burst through a small access door and were now climbing a set of enclosed narrow circular concrete steps. She knew about the door but had only managed a cursory glance inside during her many visits and a brief explanation from a guide that it *led somewhere high*. After a few minutes they reached a small landing with a door.

"Hold on," she said pushing the now weakening girl to sit. She paused and took a small knife from her webbing causing the girl to whimper for mercy, before stabbing it into the dress just above the knee and tearing the material away. She opened a small flask and offered the girl a drink after taking one for herself, then sank down on a step and allowed herself a moment's rest.

What had happened to the collar? She knew the mobile device was functioning correctly or the thing would have exploded on its own, then remembered the sound in her ear cutting through the flashing lights and smoke. The bastards jammed the radios; they must have cracked the encryption on the collar or why else would two men take a chance on forcing it off with a pair of cutters? She thought that code was unbreakable. The sound of a door splintering several floors below brought her back to reality and she forced them both to continue climbing the stairs.

Andrew, determined not be side-lined again, persuaded Scott to loan him a pistol and was the last of the six strong party to squeeze up the narrow confines of the stairs. After a few minutes he heard someone call out they had found parts of the dress and shortly afterwards he passed an exit door and saw the white satin hanging from the handle. He decided not to follow the group and pushed against the door, emerging onto a walkway covered by a low oak-beamed ceiling which even he had to stoop to navigate. After twenty yards the ceiling disappeared and he looked into a void above and below. Thirty feet above him he could see another, similar walkway on which the two women were carefully moving, although the gloom prevented him seeing any detail. The young girl looked down and catching his eye, screamed for help. The killer looked over, fired two shots in Andrews's direction and pushed the girl further along the walkway until they disappeared into the roofed area. Looking down at the floor far below, he wondered how the workman carried out their tasks day after day. He noticed a metal platform alongside the walkway a little further up and looking at the series of cables and pulleys, realised it would enable him to raise himself to the next level. He ran to the spot and climbed over the rail and onto the platform which wobbled alarmingly when his feet hit the metal floor. There were more controls than he expected so he hesitated before pushing what he hoped was the UP switch. The platform jerked into motion and he hung onto the rail as it travelled to the next level which was over a hundred feet from ground level. As he climbed over the wooden rail he could hear raised female voices in the distance and suddenly ten yards away and heading directly for him, was the young woman, screaming for help. She rushed past Andrew almost knocking him off his feet and was followed by two shots that ricocheted off the wooden ceiling. He ducked as low as he could and a second later felt someone tumble straight over him and the guard rail.

After climbing the stairs for another five minutes they came to another similar door where the stairs ended. The woman pushed it open. As they bent to pass through they could hear voices below describing the dress they had discovered.

"Keep going," said the killer but the young girl, now with a look of anger to accompany the fear, refused to move.

"What you gonna do, kill me? In answer the killer laid the barrel of the pistol across her face and then pushed her across the walkway that lay ahead. As they staggered across the wooden slats the young girl glanced down at the drop and noticed a man on a similar platform twenty five feet below.

"Help me, this mad bitch wants to kill me." The killer looked down and fired two random shots in the man's direction before shoving the girl again. After a few yards they disappeared into a roofed area which looked to give them a hiding place and a chance for a short break; she needed time to think through her next move. How had it all come to this, trapped and hunted like a rat? She knew she would have to kill the girl soon as her new found petulance made a rash move increasingly likely. A whirring noise interrupted her thoughts and before she could react, the girl had darted out.

"He's coming up," she cried, turning back to see the knife glistening in the killer's hand. Rather than snivelling for mercy as the vicar had done, the girl scooped a handful of dust from the floor and tossed it into the killer's eyes shouting:

"Fuck you Queenie," at the same moment turning and careering down the walkway past the startled man. Half blinded by the dust, the killer could hear the girl on the wooden floor so followed as fast as she dared. Stumbling along the walkway she tripped and crashing through the barrier, felt herself in free-fall.

Andrew felt a sharp pain where whoever had tripped over him, had kicked him in the back. He gingerly peered over the rail to the floor far below and braced himself for the gruesome sight. He searched the area where the body would have landed, but could see nothing but several armed men pointing their weapons in his direction. He ducked back over the railing and was trying to work out what could have happened, when a noise caught his attention. He followed the sound and saw a pair of arms attached to a body face down on the platform, just a few feet below him. They were pulling themselves up, scrabbling for a foothold, using the ropes and pulleys that lay strewn around the crazily angled metal tray. Andrew realised the person had broken their fall by landing on the platform and instinctively wrapping their arms around enough debris to prevent themselves sliding off. He must have hit a lever as he left the platform which had released one set of cables. All that now held it aloft was one full set and a single strand from the other. His gaze followed both as they disappeared into the black void above, presumably fixed to a static point in the roof.

"Are you ok?" he called out and the body twisted her face to see him. It was a face he recognised instantly.

He dropped to his knees in shock and amazement and took several seconds to regain his composure before standing. He stared at the prone figure, still trying to connect a mass killer with the intelligent and attractive woman before him.

"Mary?"

She twisted her head again to face him and he now saw the eyes of a killer.

"Why?" said Andrew, in a state of shock,

"Why? If you need to ask why then you'll never understand." As she spoke her movement caused the platform to rock from side to side.

"Don't move Mary, we can get you out of there if you just try and stay still." She laughed.

"Andrew you always were so naive, what do you think awaits me down there?"

He could not help but look down at the floor below which was now crowded with dozens of people, all gazing up at the circus high above.

"A life. Mary you're sick and you need help." She looked over her shoulder once more but now with a look of fear in her eyes. Sensing he was getting through, he carried on.

"You'll never go to prison Mary, you know too much, they need you." Andrew tried to reach over the rail to hook one of the cables, but could not reach. He ducked under the wood and again tried to find some way of reaching her. Sensing what he was trying to do, she began to rock and as it swung it came ever-closer to Andrew's outstretched arm. Finally he was able to get a hand around a cable and pull it close. This manoeuvre twisted the cage around and Mary's head was now directly below Andrew's.

"You can climb up now Mary, come on." She looked up at him and seemingly making a decision to live, started to pull herself up.

The cables holding the far end of the cage came whipping down from the ceiling above, narrowly missing them both and trailing down towards the ground. The platform rocked crazily almost tossing Mary out and she cried in anguish, looking up at Andrew for help.

"It's ok, you can still climb up to me." As the cage began to settle Andrew glanced up into the ceiling above. The sun's angle had changed and light streaming through a nearby window now illuminated the scene. Sitting on a rafter twenty feet above him, Andrew could see a man in army fatigues with the special air service winged dagger on the shoulder of his tunic. For a moment Andrew thought he recognised his face; perhaps a mission in Afghanistan? He watched in awe as the man held a finger to his earpiece receiving a message from an unseen colleague. He glanced down at Mary, who had managed to force herself halfway out of the platform and back up at the SAS man. Their eyes met and the man gave a weak smile before releasing the second cable. In the millisecond it took Andrew to realise what was happening he glanced down at Mary who had looked up and beyond him and knew too that her life was over. Her eyes were defiant and she made no sound as the cable overtook the platform. It seemed to hover in the air for a brief moment before plunging to the ground. Andrew watched as the flagstones around Mary's twisted body turned crimson. He stared at her for what seemed an eternity and even from this height he recognised the look as the same one Nancy had in the morgue. He turned to look up at the soldier who had released the cage, he wanted some answers and quickly, but he was gone. On the floor below several members of the assault team were gathered around the scene. A body bag appeared into which Mary was placed and quickly removed out of Andrews's sight.

Thames House, London, May 2010

Five days later Andrew sat in a familiar seat in Thames House. When he had been shown in, Anthony Neild had been standing in the same position, looking out over the river, as he had eight months before and again waved for him to sit. Since the dramatic events in the abbey, Andrew had been kept in a safe house in south London for debriefing, a situation he knew was primarily designed to keep him out of the way. He had learned that four pedestrians had died and twenty six had sustained various cuts and abrasions as a result of injuries from falling glass, and that three officers had lost their lives in the abbey. The queen was shaken but unharmed after her ordeal, as was the young woman who had been taken hostage. The dean and several abbey attendants were still in a state of shock, but unharmed. It was only after refusing to go over the same questions for the fourth time and demanding to speak to Neild, that this meeting had been arranged. The head of K2 turned and offered Andrew a drink which he refused with a shake of his head. Neild poured himself a whisky, added a splash of water and studied the golden mix in a ritual that Andrew sensed the senior man was using to make a decision. He walked to his desk and placed the glass down, removed a thick brown folder from a drawer, placed it in front of them and sat down in the large leather chair which Larkin noticed with a mixture of amusement and contempt, allowed him to look down on his visitors.

"Andrew," he began. "Let me start by thanking you for the tremendous work you have done for us at GCHQ and this case in particular."

"When did you know it was her and why was she killed?"

Neild rose and again took up his favoured position.

"It came from the very top. Can you imagine the media frenzy at her trial, not to mention the embarrassment for the queen herself who is in no hurry to have the abdication letter she signed made public. And as for the classified information Ward may have divulged." Neild shivered at the thought of how the woman had been able to infiltrate and manipulate just about every element of the infrastructure of the service and several other public and commercial operations. He knew the DG had already been forced to promise the prime minister a complete review of all operational and vetting processes, an immense task that would almost certainly land on his desk.

"She was never going to leave that building alive, *whatever* the cost."

Andrew looked at the MI5 man seeking the implication of his words, but received none.

"In the end the chance to make it appear like an accident was a piece of good fortune."

"For you," Larkin retorted.

Neild's eyes followed the path of a river cruiser filled with tourists as it passed under Lambeth Bridge on its way toward the Houses of Parliament.

"GCHQ identified her by chance from her voice pattern, something even she couldn't hide. Seems with all the processing power available to us from across the pond they were able to check a thousand times more data than normal, so they just threw every database they had at it. Amazing what technology can achieve these days."

"But why wasn't I told?"

"David Scott rang me directly and I decided it was too sensitive for all but COBRA." He returned to his desk and removed a smaller folder which he held out for Andrew to take.

"The truth is just too inconvenient and as well as rewriting history would cause all sorts of constitutional issues. With an election next year and the royals finally managing to stop fighting amongst themselves, they just want the whole thing buried."

"What's that?" said Andrew, looking at the slim folder.

"Belize. It's quiet and warm and really not that bad I'm told. Just for a few months." Andrew rose and took Neild's whisky filled glass from the desk.

"You're not going to kick me into the long grass again, Tony," and emptied the drink, tossed his ID badge onto the desk and walked from the room without looking back. Neild dropped the folder on his desk and pressed a button on his phone. A few seconds later his secretary entered the room and waited for instructions. He nodded towards the folder.

"Can you get that over to the archives as soon as possible please Joan?" She lifted the badge from the folder and looked towards him. "And pass that on to personnel will you," he said, walking over to the window.

Pausing at the bottom of the steps to Thames House, Andrew looked back towards the large archway that formed the entrance. It was strange to think he would never pass through those doors again. He walked through the line of bollards that protected the entrance from vehicle attack and slowly crossed the road, looking over the railings at the wide expanse of the river to the South Bank beyond. Even though it was a bright and warm day, the water looked cold and grey. He covered the hundred yards to the bridge entrance in slow steps and continued until he was half way across the span before looking to his left and making out the tall pointed shape of the Shard in the distance. Turning, he could just make out the futuristic outline of the MI6 headquarters a little further upstream. He leant over the chest high wall and contemplated his next move as he idly watched the water lapping against the riverbank opposite. He wondered how many companies might want an ex-spy for an employee.

"Daddy, daddy!" A voice cried out from behind and he turned to see Charlotte on the opposite side of the bridge with Jackie holding one hand and her favourite teddy bear in the other. Andrew waved at his daughter and paused at the edge of the road as a car sped past. The little girl was so excited to see her father that she broke away from Jackie and took the shortest route to reach him. Jackie screamed after her but she ran into the road waving and calling his name. Andrew froze in terror as a white van screeched and skidded in front of the child coming to a halt sideways on, blocking his view. He could hear the screams of anguish and time stood still.

He ran around the vehicle in what seemed like slow motion, feeling the blood draining from his face and his legs beginning to fail. The driver leapt from the vehicle and ran in front of Andrew, breaking the spell. When he arrived his view was blocked by the man and Andrew roughly pushed him aside to view his daughter's body. She lay on her back, eyes staring blankly into space.

"She ran straight out in front me, there was nothing I could do."

He looked into the man's eyes and saw terror and concern. Time seemed to stand still and Andrew's head filled with a rushing sound and his wife's funeral casket appeared. He walked slowly towards it and peered over the edge of the bridge to see Charlotte's face in the water and knowing that his life was over, it suddenly seeming warm and inviting. But it was Nancy's face he could see now and she was smiling, just like she had on the beach that day. He could not understand why she was so happy and his lips moved to cry out to her. Suddenly the air was broken by a scream and everyone turned to see the little girl pointing at the van.

"Daddy, look what happened to Bertie Bear."

His eyes instinctively followed his daughter's outstretched arm to where the small toy lay under the wheel of the van. It took half a second to realise what had happened and then Andrew ran and scooped Charlotte off the ground before realising the foolishness of his actions, she must be injured. He placed her back on the floor and was amazed to see that apart from a graze on one check, she appeared fine and more concerned for the bear than herself. The small group that had gathered let out an audible sigh of relief. Andrew turned to see the driver looking more relieved than he, with the toy in his hand having retrieved it from under the wheel.

"Here you are little girl, he looks a bit dirty, but he'll be fine."

Charlotte took the small bear and hugged it tightly with one hand and buried her head in Andrews's legs.

"Thank God you weren't travelling any faster," said Andrew.

"I've got two of me own and I'm always on at them about running out in the road so I guess it makes me aware of things."

"Thank you," he repeated. Jackie appeared at his side, ashen faced.

"I'm so sorry Andrew; she was holding my hand one second and in the road the next. By a miracle, she ran straight into the side of the van." Andrew said nothing but took his daughter's hand in his and placed the other around Jackie's waist, kissed her gently on the lips and walked slowly across the bridge leaving the chaos and confusion behind. Now he knew exactly what he was going to do with the rest of his life.

University of Cardiff, June 2010

Tom Lambert sat at his desk in the history faculty putting the final touches to his report on the search for the descendant of Elizabeth I. In the ten months since he had received the phone call from John Giddens at Christie's, his life had changed more than in the previous ten years. Glancing down at his open wallet he smiled at the small passport sized photo of Jenny laughing back. She was still working at the records office in Northumberland and they only saw each other on the odd weekend, but it was a start. He roused himself from the daydream and re-read the final few chapters. Frederick, the fourteenth descendant and son of the music hall comedian, had been born in London in 1932 only six months after his parents had married. The young boy and his sister Sophie, born five years later, never saw much of their father as he was working the music hall circuit. The family stayed in London for much of the blitz except for a short spell when the children were evacuated to Devon, but Fred's mother brought them home in 1943 and the family were able to spend some time together as Archie was stationed in London manning the capital's anti-aircraft guns. Fred was thirteen when the war ended and having had much of his education disrupted, decided there were better ways to educate himself than in a schoolroom. By the time he was twenty he had his own transport company removing rubble from bomb sites, which later became Moore's Construction, a major international business of which he was chairman until his early death in 1985 from a heart attack, aged fifty three. His only son Paul worked in the company until 1997 when he entered parliament as one of Tony Blair's New Labour intake, but never made it off the back benches as he still maintained an active involvement with the company, which did not endear him to many within the party. His daughter Elizabeth was born in 1980 in Croydon University Hospital and went to school at Wallington County Grammar School from where she won a place at Durham University reading maths and computer science. After her graduation with a first-class degree, all traces disappeared. Despite extensive research Lambert and a team of ten researchers within MI5 were unable to locate any electronic footprint including national insurance, tax, electoral or national health records and no traces of a career. It had been concluded that she changed her name to Mary Ward a year before she applied for her role at GCHQ and had been able to break into several government networks to create an entirely false identity that had been robust enough to withstand positive vetting, a fact that Lambert knew was going to lead to some heads rolling with the security services. As Mary Ward she had excelled at every task and had become one of the brightest stars in SIGNIT. He knew there was a great deal of additional information on how she had managed to manipulate, deceive and control the investigation to hunt down her alter ego, but this had been classified and not for his eyes. However he did know that DNA tests on her blood had proven the same link as her relative George to Elizabeth proving, at least in theory, that she had a claim to the English throne however farfetched it would seem to the outside world. He knew that even a cursory look at the history of how various men and women came to wear the crown, or died trying, revealed countless tales of political manoeuvring, murder and deceit. Some simply disposed of their rivals, young or old, whilst many were reluctant claimants thrust into the role of figureheads for the causes of others. Some used more subtle means to draw lawmakers and advisors into manipulating wills and birth rites. As time progressed the pen replaced the dagger as the preferred weapon as parliament passed countless bills to ensure only those who supported England's protestant future would be borne to Westminster Abbey. It had taken Lambert just half an hour to show that Elizabeth I had indeed been the last true English monarch as Mary had claimed and he realised, as did every historian, that had the rightful royal descendant been crowned throughout the ages that Queen Elizabeth II would most certainly not have made it to the throne. However, had Elizabeth Moore been born 400 years earlier, men may have fought for her right to be crowned on the same spot and in the same chair as her ancestor who herself had to battle against many threats including several on her life and even her own father's express wish, to ascend to that title and become one of England's greatest monarchs.

As he finished the report the door to his office opened and the principal, James Matthews, entered followed by a man he had some recollection of seeing before.

"Tom, this is Mr Greaves, he's from the Department of Education."

Greaves sat down without invitation, looked at Lambert without a trace of warmth in his eyes, and beckoned for the principal to join them. He produced a slim file from a briefcase which he handed to the administrator.

"I'm delighted to confirm that you have been granted an additional £5million for the next five years to help fund the important work you have started here Mr Lambert." The principal's face lit up like a Christmas tree, but Lambert remained impassive as he feared the price for this bribe.

Greaves talked for a further five minutes about the great research work Cardiff was carrying out and how everyone, including the Secretary of State, had commented on the advances the university had made under the guidance of the principal. As he rose to leave Greaves asked if he might have a few moments alone with the professor.

"Nothing important enough for you to worry about James," he said. "You must have so many important issues to attend to." He did not bother seating himself again and instead, turning with an even colder look, he began. "I've been asked to pass on the thanks of Her Majesty's Government for the service you have given this country over the last few months professor."

"This document doesn't contain any classified information; it's all in the public domain now," said Lambert. Even as he spoke, Greaves's expression made him realise how significant the *now* was in his sentence.

"Professor, I hope I won't have to repeat myself or somehow fail to explain to you the importance of your cooperation." He sat before continuing. "This whole episode has been classified to the highest level of secrecy possible by the government. Every trace of Mary Ward's existence, what she did and any evidence, however much you may think it should be made public, will be erased." Lambert opened his mouth to speak but was stopped by Greaves' raised hand.

"You will inform the dealer and his friend from Christie's that the letter has been proven a fake and has been destroyed. Offer them £100 each from university funds, then forget any of this happened. You will provide me with a copy of your report and then arrange to delete every piece of information from your computer files, and that goes for your girlfriend too." He rose and placed a card on the desk. "We will be watching you Professor Lambert," he said as he reached the door. "Please don't do anything rash that would cause the principal to reconsider your position here at the university."

Lambert sat in silence, considering his next move. He thought about ringing Andrew Larkin or perhaps the press but guessed that his words would fall on deaf and even frightened ears. Two minutes later there was a knock and the vice principal's head appeared around the door.

"Your new senior researcher is here professor."

Lambert was shaken from his thoughts and was about to correct the error when the door swung open and a smartly dressed woman who he recognised from the records office in Ashington, filled the frame.

"Hello professor," said Jenny smiling, "aren't you going to welcome me to my new job at Cardiff University?"

Government storage unit, June 2010

The lift door slid open and the young woman emerged into the cool atmosphere. There were no windows or any other means of entry into the concrete-lined corridor and only the quiet whirring of a ventilation fan to break the silence. She walked quickly, her heels echoing noisily off the floor towards one of several large doors that lined both sides. Arriving at one, she stared for a second into a small oval unit mounted at shoulder height on one side, to allow the device to take hundreds of readings of the unique pattern of her iris and check the result against the central access database. A loud electronic buzz signalled that the electronic door lock had opened and she was able to turn the heavy handle to gain entry. Beyond was a small room around eight feet square, resembling the inside of a bank safety deposit vault, with thirty metal-fronted doors of various sizes lining the walls. She wrinkled her nose at the odour and consulted the memo in her hand. Locating the correct door, she selected a small key from a bunch hanging from her belt and slid it into the lock, entered a six digit code into a small keypad and when it gave her a green blinking light in acknowledgement, rotated it. She slid out a metal drawer labelled **Indefinite Retention** and turned to retrieve the brown folder that she had placed on a small table, spilling a clear plastic envelope onto the floor as she did so. She bent to retrieve it, noticing it contained what looked like an ancient, yellowing document written in a foreign language. Any thought she may have had of inspecting the contents further were rendered unwise by the presence of the small dome camera set into the ceiling. She returned it, making sure the package was correctly sealed and began to thumb through the identical looking folders in the drawer, reading the titles on the front covers. *Diana Princess of Wales; Death of, Dr. David Kelly: Death of.* She added the new folder *Elizabeth I/Earl of Leicester: Child of* in its correct alphabetical location in front of another marked *HRH Prince Harry: Paternity,* although she had no idea why it merited being placed there. It was not her job to make such decisions and she gave it no further thought. The archivist closed the large metal door to the vault and looked at her watch; it was almost lunchtime. She quickened her pace as she headed for the lift that would take her back to ground level and the date with her boyfriend.

Author's Notes

Although this book is fictional, many aspects from the work of the security services and the life of Elizabeth I are based on known facts. The Echelon system actually exists and is expanding rapidly as the demands for gathering information to keep one step ahead of criminals and terrorists increases. RAF Menworth in Yorkshire is a real base and as depicted in the book, is actually run by the U.S. The Americans do have access to all the data, unlike everyone else, and it is all routed via Fort Meade. I took some writers' liberties with aspects of the technology used, but through careful research, never strayed too far from what really happens. Truth is always stranger than fiction.

Most of the events described in the parts of the book that involve Elizabeth were as close to the truth as I could make them. Elizabeth's hold on the throne was as tenuous as suggested in the early years of her reign and many wished her removed, particularly those who wanted a Catholic monarch. She earned her title of The Virgin Queen for steadfastly refusing to marry and putting her love of the country before her own happiness. Robert Dudley was said to be exactly as I described him and he was a favourite of the queen for most of their lives. Many stories exist showing how close they were and it's quite possible that they were lovers, despite his marriage to Amy Robsart whose suspicious death in 1560 was widely thought to have been arranged so that he would be free to marry the queen. Unfortunately for him, the scandal effectively ruled this impossible. The party at Kenilworth Castle actually took place with Elizabeth in attendance and the fireplace with the bear & ragged staff symbol is there for any visitor to see. However, William Shakespeare would have been eleven years old at the time and *A Midsummers Night's Dream* was not written until about 1594, so apologies to the purists. Elizabeth was, in my opinion, the greatest English monarch of all time. She came to the throne at the age of twenty five after narrowly surviving attempts to declare her illegitimate (she was the daughter of Anne Boleyn, beheaded for adultery when Elizabeth was just three years old) or murder her. England was weak and almost bankrupt, but she reigned for forty five years and transformed the small island nation, setting it on a path to becoming the world's first global super power through dominance of the sea. She saw off many threats from European neighbours such as France and Spain, both richer and more powerful at the time. Her spirit was epitomised by the swash-buckling adventurer, Francis Drake, who was in reality a legalised pirate. Rumours abounded at the time and have persisted ever since, that Elizabeth did have a child by Dudley. The story that describes the assertions of the young man apprehended on his way to Spain is again historical fact, although his claims are open to scepticism. Elizabeth never visited Alnwick Castle but she was known for disappearing for 'summer progressions' when a secret pregnancy could have occurred. So what would have happened had Elizabeth given birth to a child by Dudley, or anybody else? Historians who are far better acquainted with the facts may disagree with my conclusions, but the timing would have been crucial. If the child had been born in the early years of her reign it would have prevented her marriage to a foreign suitor and forced Elizabeth into a match with either a protestant or catholic, something she worked so hard to avoid. If born later when her reign was stronger, it would have secured a successor. But whatever the speculation, if the child had been legitimised by whatever means were deemed necessary, then the course of English history would have been changed beyond recognition. The basis for Mary's claim is true, although if every offspring of a king had claim to the throne then the list would be long. Marriage was for duty, mistresses for fun, so many children were sired out of wedlock, but none would have a legitimate claim. The line of true English monarchy was broken when James Stuart, a Scot, took the throne after her death and every king or queen since has come from Scottish, Dutch or German descent. Our present queen comes from the House of Saxe-Coburg-Gotha and the surname Windsor was only adopted in 1917 after anti-German feeling during WWI.

ABOUT THE AUTHOR

John Ford is 57 years old and lives in the rural county of Hampshire in the south of England., with his wife Jackie. He has been involved in various sales roles throughout his career. The Royal Descendant is his first book and one that has taken nearly thirteen years to finish. He has two children, two step-children and three grandchildren. He hopes to continue writing with his next novel coming along a little quicker.

January 2014.

Printed in Great Britain
by Amazon.co.uk, Ltd.,
Marston Gate.